AIRAY

POWER FORGOTTEN

AIRAY

POWER FORGOTTEN

BOOK 1

COZ K.A.

Cozka Studio
USA
AIRAY: Power Forgotten
Copyright © Coz K.A. 2024
Cozka Studio
P.O. Box 4054
Clarksburg, WV 26301

First edition: November 2024

Text copyright by ©2024 Coz K.A.
Cover art and chapter illustrations by ©2024 Coz K.A.
Map illustration by - ©2024 Travis Hasenour/To the Moon and Back Design
Typeset/graphic design by ©2024 Travis Hasenour/To the Moon and Back Design
Printed and bound in the USA

ISBN 979-8-99-12334-2-2 (paperback)
Library of Congress Control Number: 2024916289

Visit www.CozkaStudio.com to learn more about the author, upcoming releases, and mailing list info.

For anyone who's dared to dream.

BRYNDEN KA
ABIERA
ANAIESS
ALINTH
PALYRA MOUNTAINS
CALIRUE
VENBURG
THE BASE
DARNAR
BENOVA MOUNTAINS
HYEVA MOUNTAINS
KEYLON
CORE
N
W
E
S

BRYNDEN KA
DASHTYN
VELKOST
MCARDTA
DANTE MOUNTAINS
ECTOR
ALDOR
CALIN
BENDALLI
CALKA
THE BASE
LIBRARY
CAFETERIA
MED BAY
SUNROOM
STUDENT WING
DOCKING ZONE
DEFENSIVE WING

BRYNDEN

News Today

Thursday, November 18, 2637

News for all of Brynden Ka || comm

1 No. 298

AVARI INTEGRATION
PROGRAM SHUT DOW

Elemental Investigation Forces Demand Answers

Wednesday, the 17th of November, Elemental Investigation Forces (EIF) attempted to seize control of the Avari Integration Program (AIP) after gaining alleged clearance from Anaiess Government Officials. News Today reporters were denied access to the facility until late that day, where EIF Officer Barron Coin reported that all Avari had retreated through the ARC, back to their home planet. Speculation of lack of cooperation on AIP staff and members over the last few months had ultimately led to growing problems.

Many citizens on Brynden Ka and other parts of the world have long expressed worry over the new species integrating with society. Questions quickly arose over their alleged powerful, unexplained abilities. With tension already on EIF to control local Elemental issues, the prospect of controlling an entire species that possesses similar power became a hot topic in recent years.

EIF scientist, Elarni Veyn, explains the growing problem:

"We have studied Elementals for years. Their abilities, while often mild, have already caused upsets in the past. This has been a problem from the start. How does a bustling account for citizens who ... atural abilities ... ability to

EIF's plans to take control of the program, to further investigate claims, and to determine the legitimacy of the program, have seemingly failed. Anaiess Government officials have come forward, claiming the AIP facility is under control of Governmental Forces, ensuring its proper shutdown.

It is unclear if there will be further ...munication between Anaiess ... and Avari Council ... growing tension

AIP staff ha ... thus far af ... escorted off ... Mentors, as ... the progr ... comment ... up to t ... rising ...

ve refus ...
ter repor ...
the prem ...
well as scie ...
m have be ...
for several we ...
EIF raid, su ...
oing problem.

ut at Elen ...

N INTEGRATION
RAM SHUT DOWN
Heavy rain
South: Rain showers
West: Rain showers
News for all of Brynden Ka || comm. # 2360
tion Forces Media attempting resolutions
ation Forces M
INSIDE
Farmers in the West preparing for long winter.
New air highway making travel across Brynden Ka faster than ever!
Bustling Southern towns express hope in expanding waterways across peninsula.
Core Sector being introduced to Albara technology!
BRYN
News
EL 11, Nyx 71 No. 298
Thursday, Novemb
AVARI IN
ROGRAM

CHAPTER 1

A KNOCK AT THE DOOR

NOVEMBER 18TH, 2637
(El 11 Nyx 71)

Early morning, as fog clung low in the air, fate lingered within it. For the town of Calin, in the small forgotten peninsula of Brynden Ka, quiet dreary days were nothing new. A woman in a hooded cloak rushed down the dewy neighborhood streets, void of life so early in the day. Even the sun had yet to wake. The only disturbance in the chilled air was her quick steps as she passed each house.

In her arms, she held a thick bundle of blankets with a satchel secured over her shoulder as she scanned her surroundings. It had been a while since she visited. She might not even remember which house it was—but she knew Seelia was always one to plant flowers. Her eyes glossed over the yards, bare of color and life, until she saw soft purple and white flowers neatly lining the yard of a small familiar house on the end of the street. Even with her memory as foggy as her surroundings, she knew it must be the right one.

Her pace quickened at the sight of it, looking over her shoulder once more in paranoia. An anxious hand pulled at her hood to conceal her red hair and uniform while she headed for the door of the flowery house. No one could see her. There could be no trace of her on these solemn streets.

Knocking quickly and quietly, as if the wrong person could hear, she turned back to the street and bit at her lip. No one. The damp street was empty. That unsettled her even more. Lost in glancing at every corner and house, she was shaken back to reality by the door creaking open. A gasp escaped her lips as she whipped around to face a woman in a morning robe, her mousy brown hair in a bun.

"Rose?" The woman squinted, rubbing the tire from her eyes.

"Seelia," Rose breathed, relieved.

"What's going on?" Seelia opened the door more, motioning her to come in. She eyed the thick bundle of cloth in Rose's arms. "Are you okay?"

Rose nodded as she pulled her hood down and let out a heavy sigh upon the door closing. The sharp scent of fresh coffee lingered in the air as warmth of the house stung her frozen hands. She fought for her breath to stabilize. She was safe, at least for a bit. Seelia repositioned herself carefully, watching Rose with creased brows as she clutched her sky-blue robe. "I didn't know who else to go to," Rose started in a low voice. A man appeared in the doorway to the kitchen. There was coffee in one hand as he ran his other hand through his messy brown hair. She gave him a half smile. "Hi, Jack."

"Is everything okay?" Jack asked, pulling his hand from his hairline to the shadow of a beard on his face. "We heard about the—uhm…" he stared at the floor, trying to find his wording. "The program."

As Rose fought for an explanation, Seelia beckoned her into the living room to the left, the confusion across her face melting into worry. "Sit down," she urged. "Tell us what happened." The couple followed Rose as she sat on the familiar sage green couch, adjusting the bundle in her arms.

"They tried to take over everything. There was nothing we could do." Rose started to peel back the layers of blankets in her arms as guilt built into her chest from bringing them into her mess. With a last pull of the blanket, there was relief, seeing the child peaceful in sleep. "He couldn't go with them."

Seelia's gaze widened as she watched Rose uncover the newborn hidden among the bundle of brown and gray blankets. "Oh . . ."

Jack spoke instead, his tone cautious. "He's one of them?" He raised his chin to try to see the child.

Rose nodded, her expression twisting in pain. "They told me to get him somewhere safe. I didn't know who else to—" she couldn't find the words.

Jack exchanged unsure glances with Seelia. "And they're all . . ." he inquired. "They left the planet?"

Rose gave another nod, fixing the thin dark hair of the child, who was stirring.

Seelia stood, swiping a hand through her hair as she approached Rose. Taking a seat beside her, there was the smallest tremble in her hands as she looked over the child nestled within the warmth of Rose's arms. Her mouth parted in a tiny gasp as he shifted in the blankets. "How old is he?" Seelia cooed, pulling the blankets aside to get a better look. His long, pointed ears curled slightly, sure to perk up to a point in a matter of days. The baby's eyes were beginning to open from his slumber. They were a striking deep gold, with the odd trait of his species' slit pupils, similar to a cat. Aside from the subtle differences, he looked human—for now.

"He was born yesterday morning. The seventeenth." Rose gave the child a sad grin, taking a careful breath to think over her next words. "I know you two have been talking about—adopting, uhm," her brows furrowed, "a child for a while. I figured he needs a safe place to stay while this all . . . blows over."

Jack adjusted in his seat, his thoughts clear on his brow before they even left his mouth. "Are they after him? After *you* now? How would we protect him?" His troubled brown eyes watched Seelia's interest in the child and the way she reached ever so gently for the babe's hand, who took hold of her right away.

Rose offered the bundle over to Seelia as she composed herself. Seelia hadn't removed her eyes from him since the moment he appeared from beneath the blankets.

Adjusting her cloak to dispel her energy, Rose pressed further, speaking softly. "They don't know who has him, but they know he's here. They're trying to find all the Mentors right now. I don't have a ton of time—I just know they didn't follow me. If he stays with you, he's safe—for now."

She let out a heavy breath, realizing the weight she had just handed them was far more than just the weight of the small newborn. With luck, he wouldn't be obvious as an Avari until later; years later, she would hope. With the mix of several different species on Anaiess, maybe he could hide away safely. "His markings won't come in for a while. I'm sorry, it's a lot to take in. You know I wouldn't ask this if I had any other choice." She spoke to Jack with an urgent tone until her gaze shifted to Seelia, who hadn't said much. She was simply holding the thick blankets, staring at the child.

Sorrow laced Jack's face as they both watched Seelia's enamored demeanor with the baby. For a long while, silence befell the room.

Seelia ran her hand over the small child's hair before her eyes finally lifted to meet Jack's. No words came between them. She turned to Rose, her eyes glossy. "We'll take him."

Rose checked Jack's somber face to confirm. His expression was hard to read, but from his silence, she knew he agreed. "Thank you," she whispered.

With the deal made, there was only another moment of stillness before Jack stood, rubbing his hands together as he faced Rose. "Can I get you anything? A drink?"

Rose stood as well, snapping out of her peaceful relief. "No, no. I need to go. I shouldn't be here long." Her arms felt empty without the child she had sworn to protect, but she pushed herself toward the door, stopping to take the satchel off her shoulder. She handed it to Jack, who had followed after her. "Here's some supplies. It's not much, but . . ." Jack took the bag.

Nearly forgetting, she pulled the folded paper from her pocket. "Take this." Rose held the paper out to them. Seelia had stood with a worry coating her face, joining Jack as he took it. "It's a backup plan. If something happens, if they start looking for him here, get him to Joel," Rose said. "He'll know how to help, but not now. Not anytime soon. Don't contact him until you absolutely have to. Give him that note. He'll know I sent you."

Seelia shuffled forward. "What about you?"

Rose shook her head with a scowl. It didn't matter. "I need to disappear for a while. The farther I am from you, the better." She toyed with her empty hands. "I'm sorry."

Seelia took a hand from the blanket and moved in to hug her. "Please be safe," she said, her voice shaking. "We'll take care of him."

Rose fought back tears as she embraced Seelia. Pulling back, she took one last look at the child, parting the blanket to bid farewell. She smiled, running her hand over his dark hair one last time. "His name is Konali."

The next few years were full of careful planning from Seelia and Jack as the child grew. He was easy enough to hide as a child, as he looked decently human, save for his eyes and pointed ears. Thankfully, in a bustling society of many varying species, he could pass as a mix of Rilinquin or Felinian—pointed ears and bright eyes were nothing rare. But they knew soon enough his dark markings would come in, and he'd get taller, something they couldn't hide; attributes that *would* draw an eye. They weren't entirely sure how much time they had, but from articles and books written on the Avari, they guessed his markings would start to show around age ten.

The boy, called "Kon" to avoid any suspicion his full name could bring, was fast to pick up on things. They prepared for the worst from a young age, mapping out the route to Calka, as Rose had suggested. It was a path through the woods to the green house and barn. They walked it several times a year, planting roses and different types of bright flowers that would appear yearlong across the path, ensuring it would never be lost. When Kon was old enough, they'd lead him down the path as well, telling him if anything were to happen, to "follow the roses and various flowers to the green house," in hopes it was a direction only he would know to follow.

Meanwhile, the Nation of Anaiess was enacting chaos over the new Elemental Laws in Brynden Ka, the peninsula they resided in. Kon caught a glimpse of the papers and books his parents would read—the anger the nation felt toward the unnatural power that a few citizens in Brynden Ka possessed. They had a similar Elemental power to Avari, some mutation taking place on the small peninsula in a few rare citizens. Now, the Avari were gone and answers became even harder to get. Elementals were deemed dangerous and in need of being removed from the public. Thus, the Elemental Military Enforcement, the EME, was created.

Even if Kon could pass as a Human or Rilinquin mix, his powers made him a target to the EME. Whether they knew he was or wasn't an Avari, they would pursue him the same as an Elemental. As time passed, Seelia and Jack watched the news of Elementals boil. Some fled the planet, others went into hiding, and some were fighting back. They worried of an EME sweep on the town. They knew that above Elementals, the EME was still looking for Avari—one Avari. Rose's words stuck in their anxious minds like glue: *They don't know who has him, but they know he's here.* They would only be safe for so long.

Seelia and Jack Jones didn't know how or why the EME decided to come through Calin. Maybe one of the kids outside had gotten too close and saw Kon's markings coming in, or maybe the EME had finally traced who had the child ten years before when the mentors fled the program. Maybe it was completely out of their control. Nonetheless, they did their best to minimize the problem of his markings. Seelia caught them early, the faint shaky lines coating up his arms, across his body, and onto his cheeks.

They had hoped this day would never come, but luck didn't work like that.

They pulled him from school as soon as the markings came in, trying to formulate the right plan to escape, but before they could, Calin announced the sweep. Whatever the cause, it was a long time coming, a long time preparing. They had to hope that the man at the green house with the barn would be there after all those years.

"Do you have everything?" Seelia asked, straightening Kon's jacket with fluttery hands before reaching to fluff his dark wavy hair.

His golden eyes watched her, lightened with age to a bright gold. "Are you sure we have to go?" He fiddled on the straps of his backpack as she continued fretting over covering every inch of skin that she could on him, adjusting his tousled hair over his pointed ears the best she could.

"Hey, we've got this," Jack piped in as he entered the room, zipping up his jacket. "We've been preparing since you were little, remember?"

Kon nodded and watched the ground. Things had happened so fast. Just that morning the alarm had gone off, putting the town into lockdown. That was the first sign the EME was about to sweep through, and likely their *only* warning sign to get out while they still could.

There was a small wall behind their house separating the town from the woods. All they had to do was get over it and into the woods to the trail. Seelia and Jack had explained this to Kon countless times. It had gotten bad the previous two weeks, ever since Seelia did her usual check on his arms, where she found the faint start of markings. He had discovered them himself in the mirror after she fled the room to call Jack, tears welling in her eyes. He didn't know what they were, but he knew they were something bad.

"Alright, we need to leave," Seelia huffed, checking out the front window one last time before they exited through the back door and toward the wall. Kon rushed along with them, trying to make the most of the trek. Maybe it would be fun. Seelia pulled up his hood, just to be safe. Their shed bordered the stone wall, coming right to the top of it. They had stacked boxes to get onto the shed and over the wall a week before when they noticed the markings forming on his arms. The climb over was easy enough, and they headed down the outside of the wall. All they had to do was find the roses that had sprouted just on the edge of the trees.

"So, who is it?" Kon asked, watching Seelia and Jack check in all directions as they made their way down the long grass bordering the woods. "Who's at the green house?"

"We're going to find out," Seelia said in a hopeful voice. They kept straight with the wall, looking for the subtle markings they had made.

"There," Kon pointed at a blossoming rose bush sprouting small white roses. Checking the trail for flowers was always something he enjoyed. He felt the eager beat in his chest to get into the woods—a glimmer of excitement in the turn of events. He looked back to smile at them. "Who is that?" His smile had barely formed before it faded as he stared directly behind them at the strangers in the distance. He could only make out dark masked uniforms. His parents checked over their shoulders. Though far away, it was the unmistakable outfits of the EME.

The three men didn't take long to notice the travelers, increasing their speed at the sight of them. "Hey! Stop!"

Seelia and Kon froze. They must have gotten the order to watch the wall for this very possibility. EME had gotten good at sweeping towns. Jack quickly gripped Seelia's shoulder, snapping her out of it. "Get him into the woods, now!"

"Calin is on lockdown! Stay where you are!" The voices were much closer.

Seelia's expression turned to stone as she grabbed Kon's hand and started to lead him toward the roses ahead.

He pulled against her, looking back at Jack in dismay. "What? We can't leave him!" Kon called, trying to squeeze from her grasp.

She kept her hand locked on his and knelt, placing her other hand on his shoulder. "Listen to me, they cannot catch you, okay?" She spoke in a hardened voice. "*Do not* let them."

"What—?" Kon started, but as he looked past her, the men had almost reached Jack. He was starting to realize Seelia was preparing to send him away, *alone*. "Please don't."

As the EME got closer to Jack, he was trying to talk to them, arms up to block their path, but they pushed past him. With no option left, he finally leaped at one, yanking the EME back and ensuing a fight. The two remaining officers headed straight for Seelia and Kon.

Seelia stood between them and Kon as she finally released her grasp on his hand. "Go into the woods, now. Run!"

Kon took a step back, but only one. As he saw them preparing to grab Seelia, hostility in their movements, he felt the rising energy around him. A familiar feeling. He rarely used his powers, always being told to keep them a secret, but strange energy fueled his anger.

The men were even scarier up close, dressed in black military uniforms, dark angular helmets covering their features, leaving only an emotionless black triangle in the place of a face, coupled with the long rifles strapped to their chests. Kon's heart was in his stomach. They had reached Seelia. One grabbed her arm and began to draw her away. They didn't get far before both men were slammed by an invisible force. The soldiers hit the grass with a *thud*, looking to Seelia, startled. Then their stare drifted past her to where Kon stood, fire flickering around the bending and warping energy surrounding him.

"Kon." Seelia's cold voice cut through the chilled air. "Go!"

The men scrambled to their feet, one grabbing something on his belt, the other calling on his radio.

Kon had never heard her shout like that. With one last look at her, Kon turned and bolted into the woods next to the blossoming white rose bush.

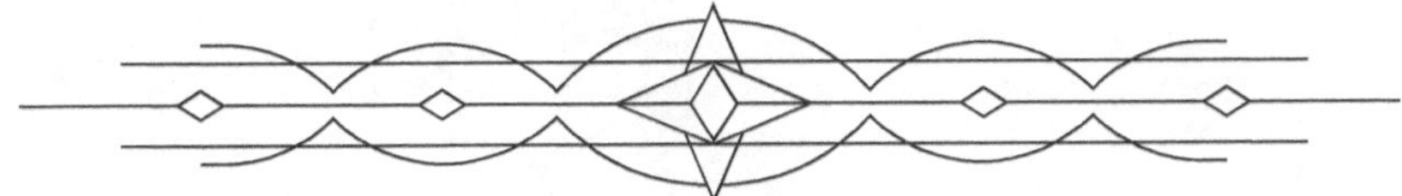

CHAPTER 2
FOLLOW THE ROSES

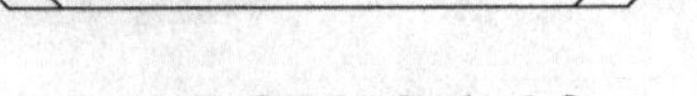

MARCH 2648
(Lyn 15 Nyx 71)

Ten years since Avari left.

Everything blurred as Kon darted through the trees, following the flashes of colorful flowers. He could still hear distant arguing, but it was turning faint. His stomach flipped as he replayed the moment in his mind. Using his powers had made the situation worse. Worse for him and his parents. He used them to *attack* people. He didn't mean to; he was trying to *protect* them.

His racing thoughts cut short as he tripped over a branch, tumbling straight off the side of a steep hill. In the mix of branches snapping and underbrush slicing him, he landed against a tree with a *thud*. The world spun. Trees danced over his head. Something in his arm burned as he slowly gained his thoughts back and staggered to his feet. The confusion melted into the pain in his upper arm, where he looked over the tear in his jacket. Red soaked into the fabric. Still stunned, he clamped his hand over the wound and checked his surroundings, now overcome with fear. The EME could still be chasing him.

He needed to move, but he was hit with a sudden realization—no flowers. He must have run too far. Seelia and Jack intentionally made sharp and wide turns in the trail so no one else would follow it, but he had veered off somewhere. His eyes panned up the sharp incline he had just fallen down. If the trail were anywhere, it was back at the top. Taking a deep breath, he scurried back up, slipping over branches and leaves. The trees swayed in the gentle wind. It wouldn't be long before nightfall would hit. The trail to the green house was still an hour or so walk. He didn't have much time.

Finally, he could peek his head over the top of the incline. Sure enough, in the distance, white roses. Before he could stand, rushing footsteps barreled down the trail. Ducking behind the log he had previously tripped over, he froze. Two sets of footsteps stomped closer. Kon wondered for a moment if it could be his parents, but he remained motionless just in case.

"See anything?" an unfamiliar voice asked.

Kon closed his eyes, pretending he didn't exist, and waited.

"No, let's follow this path." The footsteps veered off—to his relief, in the opposite direction of the rosebush. After a long wait, to where the footsteps were almost gone, Kon finally bolted back onto the path and toward the bush. He tried to push away his racing thoughts: that everything he knew was gone, that he was heading to the green house—alone. Maybe Seelia and Jack would meet him there. Maybe.

It all happened so fast, like at any moment he might simply wake up from the nightmare and pretend it never happened. The rising ache in his arm reminded him, however, that his nightmare wasn't one he would be waking up from. He checked his wound again, the red stain growing. Squeezing his hand over it once more, he looked onward.

The trees whispered in the setting sun, flowers of various kinds dotting the hardly traveled path. They were questionably the only sign that a trail lay there at all. That's how they wanted it. Some flowers were winter roses, others were smaller cold-weather wildflowers. He was going the right way. The soft spring air could have been seen as peaceful. Maybe in a way, he did feel peaceful, or maybe it was better to believe that. Maybe he was in shock. It didn't matter. All that mattered was finding the green house that the roses were leading him to. His pace had slowed to a brisk walk as the events that had unfolded began to wear on him. Night was setting in. No sounds had come from the forest behind him. It seemed he had gotten away, but danger still lingered in the air.

Deep in thought and exhaustion, he almost missed the light in the distance, but as he reached the end of the forest, he saw it. The green house. The color was hardly noticeable as green with the night so close, but his parents had taken him to the tree line a few times to show him the house. They didn't dare go toward it before, but it was time. He headed for the back door. Crossing the short field alone, past the old barn, he reached the door. A shaky hand grabbed his backpack to pull out the slip of paper his parents had given him. The paper was old, yellowing around the edges. It was for whoever was inside.

He folded it up and knocked on the door, checking behind him again. The woods were pitch black. This was the only path forward. The cold night air clung around him. Crickets and frogs sounded out in the forest. He looked back to the door. Nothing. Another knock, a bit louder. He waited. His breath was leaving him. Still nothing. He took a step back and peeked around the side of the house to the front. Houses sat through the trees, and kids laughed in play somewhere across the field. He ducked back, knowing he shouldn't be seen by anyone.

What if no one is home? Looking at the door once more, he grabbed the handle. To his awe, it opened. The old wooden door creaked as he let go and stepped back, unsure if he should enter. Darkness hung thick inside. The options were forward into the house or back into the woods, where the EME was surely still looking.

Dust was heavy in the air as he cautiously stepped inside. He could see slightly better at night than Humans, but it was still hard to make out where he was. Seelia had told him to use his eyesight to his advantage in one of the few times she acknowledged his differences, but both of his parents stayed vague on what he was. *Who* he was.

He seemed to be in a garage or storage room; boxes lined the walls and tools dotted the space. Across the room, light leaked from the bottom of a door. Maybe it led to the actual house. Focused on the door, he missed the toolbox on the floor, once again tripping. He winced as it made a painfully loud clang, and he caught himself with his injured arm, sending a ripple of pain through it. The room was quiet again, though the ringing of the noise lingered far into the silence.

With what was first relief that no one heard him, turned to horror as the door across the room opened, and the shadow of a man stood in the doorway. "Who's there?" the man called out. Heavy boots stepped down the stairs, where a switch clicked. Light flooded overhead. Kon could see the glint of the pistol in the Human's hand as light illuminated everything. "Don't move!" he spoke as he saw Kon in the corner, backed against the wall. Upon spotting him, the man's expression softened behind brown eyes as he moved the weapon away.

Trembling, Kon's legs stopped working. He shrunk down the wall and curled up on the floor.

"Hey—it's okay," the man said, showing the gun in a non-defensive posture before he laid it on a box. "Are you alright?"

Kon didn't respond. Pressure filled his head, his powers rising up, but that time, it happened out of fear. The air in front of him started to warp and distort as the light overhead flickered. He tried to fight for his breath, but no amount of air seemed enough.

The man inched closer and then crouched before him, pushing his short brown hair back. "Is that you?" He pointed up at the light, a look of gentle acceptance on his face. He looked similar in age to Kon's parents, subtle signs of gray starting in his hair.

"I can't control it," Kon croaked between breaths.

"That's fine. Just breathe. How did you get here?" he asked, pulling up the sleeves of his flannel.

Kon still held the paper in the hand of his injured arm, his other coated in blood. He held it up to the man carefully as it fluttered in his trembling hand. "They told me to follow the roses here if something happened."

The man took the slip of paper and unfolded it, reading it over. As he read the last line, a half grin spread across his face. "Roses, huh?" He folded the paper back up. "Smart." As he stood, he extended his hand out to Kon. "Well, you're at the right place." Joel smiled. "Let's take a look at that arm and get you warmed up."

Kon caught the small movement in the doorway. A girl, no older than he was, stood in a white nightgown, watching with wide eyes. His breathing got easier, slower, and the light ceased its flickering. He finally accepted the hand.

Joel looked back at the girl as Kon's eyes stayed on her cautiously. "Mallia, can you go get the med kit?" he asked in a soft tone as he directed Kon past the boxes toward the door.

She smiled for a moment before disappearing back inside.

"Sorry about the scare. I didn't know it was you," Joel said as they entered the door leading into a kitchen. "I thought it was . . . someone else." There was an island table in the center. Joel gestured for him to sit on the stool.

"*Me?* You know who I am?" Kon asked, carefully taking a seat as he continued to catch his breath. The house smelled gently of cinnamon. Cozy low lights illuminated the homey kitchen.

Joel stopped, looking him over for a long moment as if he was verifying his information. "Well, it's been a while, but yeah, I know you."

Kon began retracing his memory for the man. *Had* they met?

His confusion must have been clear on his face as Joel spoke again. "Well, your parents."

Kon stopped. As the words clicked in his head, he met Joel's gaze. "My birth parents?" Seelia and Jack never hid his adoption from him. They weren't clear on it, however. He knew he was different, that there were things about himself he had to keep secret that no one could know—and that his real parents left when he was a baby. He sat on the stool, wondering what vital information they had left out.

Joel smiled again and opened his mouth as if to say something, but Mallia returned with a large red box. Joel helped her place it on the table and opened it. It was full of bandages and medicine. "Let's take a look at that arm, huh?"

"I'll take your jacket!" Mallia offered, positioning herself beside him, hand extended. He recoiled only slightly as she ran a hand expectantly through her long brown hair. An excited grin covered her face, her brown eyes full of eagerness.

"You can put your bag on the table," Joel said as he set out several things from the box.

Kon took off his bag and laid it on the granite table. Then he carefully removed his jacket, becoming very aware of the sharp pain in his arm. He winced once more as the adrenaline wore off and the actual pain set in. He peeled the jacket away from his arm carefully.

Mallia grabbed the dirty jacket and inspected it. "I'll put it in the wash," she cooed, hurrying away without another word.

Joel took her place beside Kon and looked over the blood-covered short sleeve he had on. Kon lifted the sleeve to reveal the gash, which was sizable.

"What did this?" Joel asked as he wiped it with a damp towel, handing him another for his hand, still covered in blood.

"A tree, I think." The tumble down the hill seemed like forever ago, even though it was merely an hour or so.

"It got you good. Were you running from someone? You said something happened?" He finished wiping the blood, dabbing it as he reached for the ointment.

Kon hesitated. He didn't know what Seelia and Jack would've wanted to tell Joel—maybe everything. But everything he could tell him were also things they told him never to share. Now they weren't here, and he could only guess. "We were trying to get out of Calin, away from the EME. We were supposed to come here. They said you would help." His eyes found the tan tiles below. Maybe they weren't coming.

"They? Your parents in Calin?"

Kon nodded. "They were supposed to come with me, but the EME caught up to us before we could get in the—woods," he trailed off, as retelling the story began to set in the reality of the situation. His brows creased as the tiles below him blurred into each other. A sniffle drew from him as his eyes glossed over. All he could think to focus on was wiping his hand with the cloth.

"Hey, you're safe now. They got you here." Joel paused as he reached for the bandages. "Okay?"

"What's going to happen to them?" Kon asked, trying to compose himself.

Joel's expression folded in sympathy as he thought about his answer. "I don't know, but they'll be alright." He started wrapping the bandage around Kon's arm, gentle with each spin.

Mallia had crept back into the room, distancing herself across the table to give him space. Her hands held the granite countertop stiffly as her large eyes stayed locked on him. "Is he going to stay here?" she asked, taking it upon herself to make herself busy. She grabbed several cups to fill them up, somehow still keeping her eyes on him before sliding one across the table to Kon.

"I don't know." Joel fixed Kon's sleeve, stepping back. "Did your parents say what you'd do when you got here?"

Kon thought for a moment and shook his head. "No, they just said you could help us . . . figure something out." Once the blood was off his hand and arm, he could again see the faint markings across his skin. *What would Joel think of them? Would he be equally horrified?*

"Have you guys talked to Rose since the note?" he asked, moving back to the table to put away the medical supplies and to read the note again as if it would reveal more the second time over.

Kon blinked at him. "Rose?"

Joel opened his mouth, brows folding slightly in disappointment as he pursed his lips together at the note before looking back to Kon. "Never mind that. When did they come in?" He gestured to Kon's arms.

"What?"

"The markings." Joel traced a hand over his own arm before pointing to Kon's.

Kon's stomach lurched at the question. They *were* noticeable. "I don't—recently. What's wrong with me?"

Guilt flashed over Joel's face. "Nothing," he said. "I suppose you're at that age."

Kon's next thought was to scan Mallia's arm for markings as she sipped on her water. Nothing. "Does—everyone get them? What are they?"

"Oh, they didn't . . . tell you?" Joel was cautious with his words. Kon only scrunched his nose in thought. Joel quickly shook his head. "I can tell you all about it tomorrow. You look tired. I don't want to put too much more on your mind."

"He can stay in the spare room!" Mallia added, clacking her cup down on the table. The sound made Kon jump.

"You good with that?" Joel asked. "We can see what we can figure out in the morning; when you've rested up. See about your parents, too, yeah?"

Kon looked between the two of them and nodded slightly.

"What's your name?" Joel tilted his head.

"Kon."

A flash of a grin crossed his stubble as he nodded. "I'm Joel. That's Mallia. Are you hungry, Kon?" Joel pushed back from the table. "Mallia makes a mean cinnamon toast."

Kon stayed in the chair, partially frozen in thought. His mind whirled with everything that had happened. "Are they still looking for me?"

Joel gave a sympathetic tilt of the head while Mallia had already begun digging in the bread box. "They won't find you here, okay?" He glanced at the note. "I'll make sure of that."

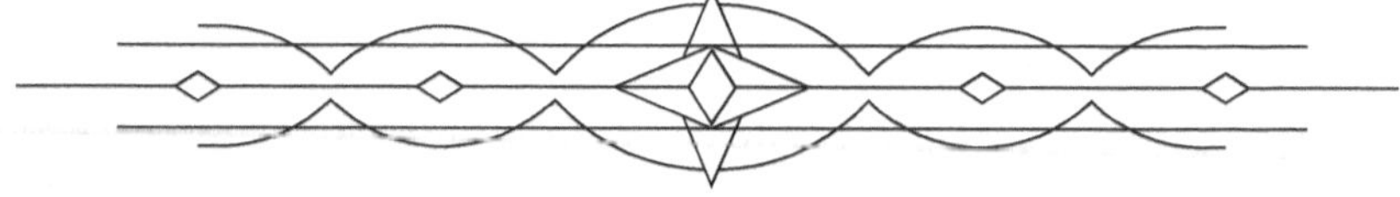

CHAPTER 3

THE BASE IN THE WOODS

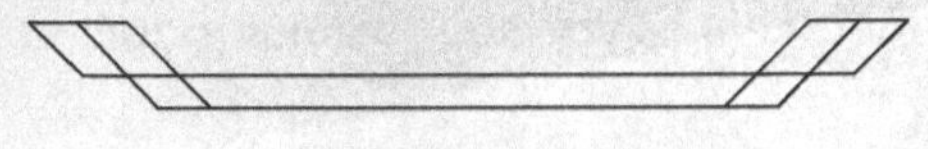

2657

(El9 Nyx72) Present Day

Nineteen years since Avari left.

Light rainfall descended from the sky, battering the sparse foliage of the woods. Footsteps disrupted the ferns scattered across the trail as Para hurried along the path in the mix of the woods. She held her arms close to her side in her long poncho, avoiding the drizzle as her boots splashed mud with each step. Her hood blocked the slight rain as she kept her head down, focused on the diamond-shaped tracking device. It pinged a signal coming from ahead.

"We can go tomorrow, you know," the voice on the comms radio spoke, only slightly fuzzy. "The storm's getting worse the longer you're out there."

"No, I'm almost there, anyway," she said, fidgeting with the loose blonde braid over her shoulder.

"Terrance is checking the radio signals. There's nothing coming in from it," the man explained. "This doesn't seem right."

"Well, we can't just leave someone out in the rain if it *is* right." Her eyes dipped from the screen to the trail in front of her, becoming familiar with her surroundings.

"You know these things get buggy sometimes, Para."

"You're not helping."

"Fine. You're about one hundred feet off. See anything?"

Para slowed, listening as she picked up the usual musical humming of the device she was tracking. Its musical trills rang out over the patter of rain around her. Maneuvering over some branches and thicket, she made her way closer until the small device in the ground was clear. She stopped just short of it, staring at the ground in confusion.

"Para?" Another voice picked up, a bit deeper. "What do you see?"

Para lifted the radio, eyes still scanning the ground. "There's footprints."

"Okay, so someone *did* kick the signal."

"A lot of footprints," she said as she stared down at the mud surrounding the small metal device in the ground. Heavy boot prints.

The radio was silent for a few seconds. "What?"

She lowered the comms and moved toward the device located in the center of the collection of muddy shoe prints.

"Para, be careful."

She hardly heard the response. Her face was frowned as her eyes panned over it. There had never been a group of people at those devices, no more than two or three at a time. She knelt to look at the device, a metal box, partly in the ground. On top, it had a dome and an electronic screen to relay words to whoever activated the signal, but it was cracked. The screen was malfunctioning with the words: "Help is on the way!"

Her eyes traced under the device where the control box had been torn out, wires hanging and conjoined together. Someone was trying to override its system. Realization hit her that it wasn't the work of Elementals in need of help like the device was supposed to be used for. It was something bad. She stood, raising her comms, but before she could talk, an icy chill went down her spine.

"I wouldn't do that," someone spoke from behind her. "Put it down."

She lowered her comms, subtly clicking it off. Her cold gray eyes locked onto the EME soldier before her, rifle in hand. The angular mask tilted as he examined her. Perhaps he expected a more frightened reaction as she faced him, a cold frown across her face. "This wasn't for you." She pointed at the broken machine, mounting anger growing in her tone.

"Enough." Another voice from her left. A second soldier. She assumed they were all around her. "Hands up."

Para raised her hands, still watching them closely as she spoke. "Think about this." There was a flicker of movement from the tree line on her other side. Three of them. "No one has to get hurt."

"*You're* threatening *us*?" the first man growled, lifting the rifle as Para kept her stare.

"Hey!" the second man called to both of them. He looked to Para, cocking his masked head. "Why'd your friends stop talking, huh?" He gestured to the radio. She met his masked face, watching her behind the black window. "You all on your own—?" His words cut short as the rifle in hand turned ever so slightly to something behind Para.

Before her eyes, the air between her and the man started to ever so slightly distort and crinkle like warping glass. Terrashock was subtle, usually, hardly noticeable until it erupted, but that power wasn't her own. The man didn't see it forming between them, still staring straight behind her. A second later, the terrashock detonated, sending the man flying backward. She didn't take another moment, turning to the man on her other side who was pointing his rifle behind her. From her extended hand, a bolt of electricity surged straight at the man, who convulsed, falling on the muddy ground. She turned, ready to strike at the other, but they were already on the ground as well. Quickly scanning the trees for anyone else, she only found foliage. Silence befalling the woods again, she turned to face the greater threat.

A tall figure stood amongst the brush. Wavy black hair partially covered his golden eyes that hovered on the men on the ground, then drifted to her. He was dressed in dark gray clothes with a thick black jacket, looking a good bit younger than she was, likely nearing his twenties. A backpack hung over his shoulder like he was passing through the area. Para's heart fluttered at the realization that there *was* an Elemental there as the terrashock had suggested. Perhaps the trip wasn't a waste.

They both stood in silence until he started to move, headed for the men on the wet ground. As he got closer, it became clear just how tall he was. She would hardly reach his shoulder. Para snapped out of her confusion as she watched him. "Uh, thank you—"

He glanced at her, and with a rough and quiet voice said, "You should get out of here before more come." His attention then set back on the ground, kicking the guns away from the men and examining their armor with a scowl. He didn't seem interested in talking.

Her gaze followed him, muted communicator buzzing in her hand. She stuffed it in her pocket and opened her mouth to say more, hesitating at his disinterest. "They're Core Sector." Looking over one of them, she continued, "I saw the badge. They shouldn't be here." She assumed he was thinking something similar. His eyes only panned up at her for another moment, the striking gold of them visible from where she stood, but no response came. As she watched him, she noticed the dark tattoo-like markings on his neck and face. They stood out across his tan skin—long, shaky stripes across his neck, straying onto his cheek. Not wanting to address her suspicions yet, she looked back at the destroyed device again, trying to start conversation once more. "Did you alert this, or did they?"

He had stopped checking their uniforms. "Wasn't me." Without anything more, he turned away.

Para fought for words at his sudden departure. "Wait!"

He looked over his shoulder, seemingly unamused.

"Us Elementals should stick together, right? I mean, Core Sector EME shouldn't be out this far. There might be more," she started slowly, trying to find the right words. "I have a safe house nearby. It would probably be the safest place for us until this blows over, you know?" She saw the smallest frown cross his face at the mention of a safe house.

"Those aren't safe."

"This one is."

He tilted his head to the side. "They all say that."

Para pursed her lips for a moment, her communicator buzzing again in her pocket. "You haven't seen this one—but I bet you've heard of it."

His gaze swept over her, then down to the device sticking from the ground before it set back on her. "You're the EPS?" he said dryly, still void of interest.

"Elemental Protection System, yes." She smiled. "We set these up along the woods. They're supposed to alert us when an Elemental comes within a vicinity. When they reach it, they can call for help, and we come." Hearing her own words, she looked down at the ruined device. "I don't know how EME found it . . ." She shook her head. "Anyways, we're the biggest safe house in Brynden Ka. You really won't find a safer place to stay."

He didn't waiver, just looked up at the clouds, the rain coming down at a steady pace.

Para made one last attempt. "Look, even if you can handle yourself, which I'm sure you can, it won't hurt to at least know where we are, in case you ever need us. Wait out the storm. If you want to leave when it passes, the door is open." She held out her hands, grinning.

He still didn't look bothered but let out a sigh as he pulled at his large backpack. "Fine."

She didn't give a moment to let him change his mind, immediately starting back down the path she had followed. "Great! Come on. More might be coming."

He hesitated, as if he might bolt after all, then cautiously followed behind her.

Para's communicator went for the final time as she finally answered it. "Indigo. I'm fine."

"Para? What's going on? What happened?" the man on the other end spoke in a panic.

"I'll explain when I get back. I'm bringing company." She looked back at the young man, who was watching her closely.

"Gods, Para. I have the hoverform launching—"

"I'm sorry, I'm sorry. I'm coming back. It's okay."

"I gotta go call off the craft." The man on the communicator faded from the mic. A moment passed as another voice got on.

"You're going to give him a heart attack, Para." Their tone was far more humorous.

She chuckled and glanced back to make sure she was still being followed. "I'll be back soon." She lowered the communicator. "I'm Para, by the way. You?"

His expression read like no answer would come as he watched the ground, but eventually, it came quietly. "Kon."

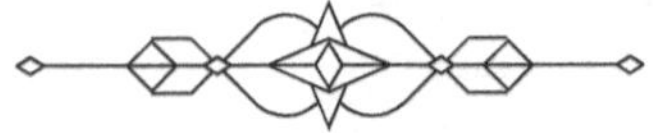

Kon had heard of the EPS—murmurs from around Brynden Ka about how they were the biggest defense against the EME. Giving it little thought, he had more assumed it was a myth or greatly exaggerated, though with talk of a *hoverform* in their arsenal, a military-grade aircraft, he couldn't deny being curious.

As he followed Para down the muddy path, his eyes scanned the woods. There were patches of ferns and tangles of weeds around the otherwise bare floor of the forest, where rocks lay at the start of one of the tall mountains around them. No more EME yet, but it wouldn't be long. He couldn't say for sure why he had intervened. Something about the situation felt familiar. *She* felt familiar. A Human, with her golden blonde braid and spitfire attitude toward the soldiers. The EME had likely been following his trail anyway. He planned to turn and face them if they hadn't backed off. Nearly twenty—the EME rarely scared him. Either way, she had a good point; staying together might be smart. The last month watching EME movements, he had noticed the erratic activity they were making, and it seemed Para did as well. Maybe she knew something.

"How long have you been traveling alone?" Her tone flashed concern, peering over a shoulder at him as they traveled up the soggy path. Her braid stuck out under her hood as freckles dotted her cheeks. She looked late twenties and held a warm disposition in her stormy gray eyes.

"A few years."

"Oh," Para picked at her braid lightly. "Have EME encounters amped up lately for you as well?"

"A bit." He pulled up his hood and stuffed his hands in his pockets as the air chilled with the increasing rain. He'd figured the EME activity was purely focused on him, but her comment made him wonder.

"We've been watching them on the radar. They seem like they're getting antsy over something. Their comms have been off the charts, too," she explained.

He didn't respond. Maybe she already saw the markings and the height and put two and two together. If she had, she wasn't addressing it. She was right, however. Fighting off strings of EME groups had become a regular thing. Maybe they were getting bothered that he wasn't just running and hiding. On top of rising Elemental numbers, they were dealing with him, an Avari they were desperately trying to get ahold of. The only Avari left on Anaiess. Making matters worse was the fact that he was no longer a scared child and their plans to find him at a young age had failed. He finally spoke up. If he was going to get roped in by the EPS, the biggest Elemental protection effort on the peninsula, he might as well ask questions. "Have they attacked those things before?"

"No. It worries me that they did, though." Her response sounded sincere as she shook her head. "We'll have to check the others. Maybe shut them down altogether." As they approached the field in the distance, Para slowed a bit. "Now, this safe house is a bit . . . nontraditional," she began. "It's not actually a . . . house."

Kon only gave her a blank look.

The tree line started to thin as the field lay ahead in the middle of the woods. The grass was tall, a mix of wildflowers and rocks decorating its flat stretch. He could make out a large, low structure placed across the field. Upon exiting the trees, he pulled down his hood to see it in full. A bunker of sorts. It had pillars on two sides of the wide door in the middle. The sides slacked down until they nearly dipped beneath the ground. The span of it took up a large portion of the field. Kon couldn't even guess the size of it inside. The long-tapered roofing was coated in a thick layer of grass. It had to be nearly invisible from above.

"What is it?" he asked.

"The Base," she smiled, pushing down her hood. "It's an old military bunker, actually. Decommissioned." She pointed up to the top as they approached where the grass was, hardly visible as it started to tower above them the closer they got. "The whole thing retracts into the ground. Virtually undetectable when hidden."

Kon looked up at it once more as they moved under it to the over-hanging entryway. He would give it to her. He *hadn't* seen an Elemental safe house like that. Her confidence in the "safe" house was starting to make sense.

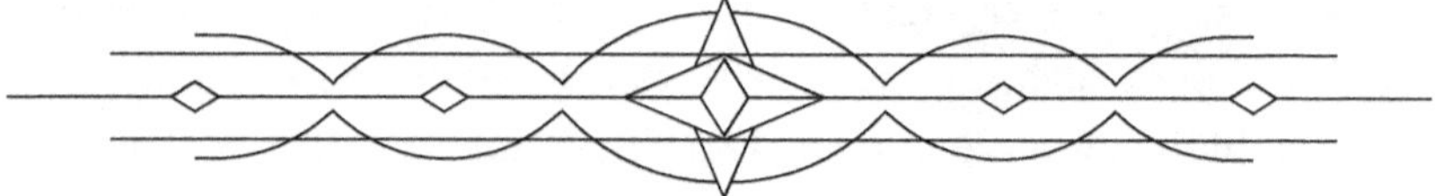

The heavy doors creaked as Para pushed them open, beckoning Kon in. He took a final breath of the cool outside air before ducking under the door.

The door shut behind her as she moved to the center of the large room. It was a circular entryway with tall ceilings and bright, warm lights. It was already far more than any safe house *he* had seen; usually, they were small houses or abandoned buildings housing worse for the wear Elementals doing their best to hold out. There was a long span of hallway on both sides of the tall room. Behind Para, on the far wall, a mural of colors and patterns stood out—after he had finished scanning every other wall for danger. Nothing was ever truly safe, even Elementals.

The mural took up the whole wall, a menagerie of painted shapes, species, and animals. It looked as if it had been worked on by countless people, seamlessly blending each tiny blot of artwork into a vast mural; a mark, maybe a show of how many people had been here. Along with art, handprints covered the wall in a rainbow of colors. In the center was a symbol he had seen a few times. The mark of the EPS. It was the same shield symbol as the EME, but instead, a crack spread across the shield where a handprint covered the center, fire sitting in the palm. A twist of the EME's symbol, maybe even a threat to them, as the gears in his head started whirling. *How?*

"Welcome to the Base." Para grinned, her voice echoing slightly as the mural framed behind her. "It's gearing down for nightlife. The lights will be dimming soon for our Luneduine residents, but I can still show you around—"

"Para!" The voice came from the left hallway, where two men headed toward them. Walking briskly, the man in front looked her over as he approached. His brows creased where a deep scar cut through his right brow from his cheek, curving up into his dark hairline. He and the second man were dressed in some sort of military garb, both having muscular builds and holsters that sat on heavy belts. Kon recoiled slightly as they approached, pushing his hands into his pockets. Military people—in an Elemental *safe house?*

"You okay?" the man asked as he stopped next to them, his tone hardly matching his stiff disposition as a hand tapped Para's arm. His short, fitted t-shirt exposed a tattoo across his tanned arm, something of a bird.

"Yes, I'm fine," Para fussed, giving him a small curl of the lip.

The other man was removing an earpiece as he pushed back his brown hair. Same fashion and build. Both of them were fairly tall, for humans, but nowhere near Kon's height. The brown-haired man tilted his freckled face at Kon, who stood as still as a deer. "Ran into company?"

"Yeah. This is Kon." Para held her hand out in his direction, where Kon had moved a step back toward the door. Maybe it was clear, his discomfort, though it was probably hard to tell. His expression wasn't one to show much emotion in general, but his overall stillness had cued her in. Para lowered her hand gently, careful to keep her distance for him as she continued. "Kon, this is Terrance, my husband." She gestured to the first man. He gave a nod to Kon, flashing a forced smile that faded quickly. "And our radio specialist, Deyin, who's also an old friend." Deyin gave a bigger smile, overall cheery as he rested a hand on his belt.

"What happened?" Terrance asked, crossing his arms as he stayed put beside Para, his eyes falling over Kon.

"Kon just had to rescue me back there a bit, nothing we couldn't handle." She chuckled, trying to share a grin with Kon. He didn't move.

"Rescue? Rescue you from what?" Terrance asked, eyes narrowing. There was an accent to his voice, but it was hard to place its origin.

"Yeah, we weren't getting any signal from the Key," Deyin said, stepping back to shadow Terrance as he eyed Kon. From the furrow in Deyin's brow, Kon could only guess his thoughts.

"EME. They're getting bold. We can try to access the footage tomorrow," Para explained with a frown, pulling out a bag from under her poncho to stash her communicator.

Terrance nodded, hesitating with his words for a moment. "Well, speaking of the EME, you should come look at the transmitters, probably has to do with . . . whatever happened out there." Terrance kept his voice low to avoid the echo the large room gave.

"Transmitters?" Para panned over his expression with a scowl, silence falling over the room.

"He's tall," Deyin commented, quickly cutting the silence as he looked over at Kon.

Para peered back at him, a more sympathetic look, as Kon hadn't warmed up to the idea of conversation yet. In fact, despite his height, Kon seemed to be shrinking, hands defensively bunched in his jacket pockets while his gaze stayed locked on their every movement. "Yeah, he's just going to wait out the storm, check out the base in the meantime. I was going to show him around . . ." She glanced back into the hall behind her where someone had appeared, trying to blend in as they watched the crowd. Her smile grew. "Ah! Peter."

Kon had already seen the boy appear a minute before, peeking a head into the hall as he crept closer. Peter, looking in his teens, a few years younger than Kon, seemed surprised he was caught—standing in plain sight or maybe surprised that she was now beckoning him. There was a large leather book clutched in his thin arms as he approached. He was short—shorter than Para. Taking careful steps, he scooted himself into the group. Dressed in pajamas instead of the strange military outfits the older men wore, he finally croaked out words. "You're back." There was a feigned excitement as he hugged the book in his arms tightly, tight enough to notice. "I was just . . . worried, you know. It was getting late." His glance at Kon was hardly subtle.

Para ignored his fidgety movement. "This is Kon. Do you think you can show him around? I have to go look at something." Her tone stayed warm, almost too warm.

Peter's eyes grew wide. "Yeah! I can do that."

Para turned to Kon, her expression careful, as he looked as if he might've moved even farther away from her. "So, that hall to the left is the Defensive Wing. Terrance handles that. We try to keep students out of there so staff can do their job and monitor things for us."

Students? She must have meant the Elementals who were forced into hiding. Maybe giving them the tender name of "students" softened the blow of it all as if they chose to come there. Most Elementals were young anyway, the largest percentage of them being teens Kon's age.

Para watched him closely, likely worried he was about to dart. "Don't let that scare you, though. They're here to scare the EME, not us," she said lightly. Terrance gave a tiny crack of a smile but stayed rather flat in expression as he toyed with the scanner in his hand, something impatient in his movement. Para continued, "And over here is the Student Wing, where most of our younger Elementals stay." She directed Peter between her and Kon. The boy was still fumbling in his movement, staring at Kon with large hazel eyes. Para put her hand firmly on his shoulder. "This is Peter. He's a long-time resident and student. He's more than capable of showing you around while that storm goes through."

Peter nodded with a sheepish grin to Para as she joined Terrance. Kon shifted in his weight finally, breaking free from his cautious freeze. His golden eyes followed after them, unsure of what to think as they headed into the supposed military hall. All he knew was the farther the armed "Defensive Wing" people got, the easier it was to breathe. He hardly noticed the nervous blob that was Peter, still staring, until he opened his mouth. "Uh—" Peter stuttered, fixing his glasses and swatting at dirty blonde hair to compose himself. "Sorry . . . I just can't believe you're here. I mean, I was about to go to bed, but I wanted to see if Para still needed my journal, and—wow."

Kon blinked, staring at him. "What?"

"You're—an Avari? You're *the* Avari. I told Para, I *told* her you were here," he said. "I mean, you are, right? You're super tall, you have the markings, your eyes—" He stood on the tips of his slippers, trying to get a closer look at Kon's eyes.

Kon shrunk a bit more, shoulders bunching to push his jacket hood into a position that might better cover the dark patterns over his skin. Some sort of fear stuck with his claim, as if his words would expose him, though he had the suspicion Para already knew of his origin. Either way, there was no one else in the stark gray halls to hear, hopefully. He paned back over Peter, keeping his voice low. "Is it that obvious?" A few years ago, he might've had little problem blending in with Elementals, as long as no one scrutinized too hard. Once his height had hit and his markings darkened, maybe there was no escaping the truth.

Peter's face flashed panic for a moment. "No. *No*—no, I mean . . . I know a lot about them. That's how I knew." His voice decreased to a whisper. "I'm just really excited to see a real one." He unwrapped his arms from around the book at Kon's puzzled expression, turning the cover to him; *AVARI: Everything Known*. "I have studied every non-classified document on Avari *and* some classified ones. I know like . . . everything there is to know." He took a few heavy breaths to calm down his excitement.

Kon narrowed his eyes. "Uh-huh." The ecstatic kid before him had nearly made Kon forget about the uncertainty in the "base." He finally moved forward to look down into the two hallways. The group had disappeared into the Defensive Wing, gone from sight as Kon scanned the ceilings, walls, and every inch of the place.

"C'mon. Para said I should show you around," Peter interrupted, pointing down the student hall.

Kon held reservations about exploring the large bunker. Part of him wanted to wait out the rain next to the door or leave entirely in that very moment—but with the grand magnitude of what he had happened across here, curiosity was striking deeper than his need to flee. *For now.* Kon hesitated another moment, taking a last look down the Defensive Wing with a frown before he turned to follow Peter.

The parts of the walls that weren't painted in a mural were a light gray; the warm, round lights overhead emitted a low glow. Para had mentioned they were on a night cycle. It meant that the shifting orange lights followed the outdoor day cycle, dimming to a low red glow at night to accommodate the nocturnal Luneduine, something he didn't often see on Brynden Ka. A thin line of black connected every light to the next. Black vents lined the paneled top corners of the walls, humming just slightly as they blew cool air through the halls. Everything about the base was far beyond the normal technological advancements he had seen in the peninsula.

Slow to pick up on the newest tech in the capital, most of Brynden Ka only had the basics. Hardly anyone owned a hovercraft, and the peninsula lacked the sophisticated air highways to travel in them. There were only a few across the small span of land. Hoverforms were likely the newest advancement, and Para had already mentioned that they had one here, somewhere. The thought was ridiculous. The Core Sector was the only place where there might be signs of newer technology. Robotics and cyber tech were present in Brynden Ka's only true city, Valdor, which were things the giant Anaiess skyscrapers relied on in their towering electronic cities—something he had only read about in magazines.

"How did they get this . . . *base*?" Kon asked slowly, still tracing every detail of the halls. Into the Student Wing, the gray walls were coated in posters of just about every color and matter; clubs, events, classes, motivational quotes. They stuck over nearly every inch of wall students could reach, forming a different, more temporary mural cascading down the hall.

Peter had a permanent beam on his face. "Uh, I don't know. I think the donors maybe."

"Who?"

"They're kind of anonymous, I'm pretty sure . . . But there are people in Abeira who support the cause or something."

Abeira. The Capital of Anaiess. It was hard to believe anyone there cared about Brynden Ka. Most people outside of the region would hardly even know the name of it.

"You should just ask Para later. She'll want to talk to you anyway. Her office is right past the Med Bay," Peter explained as they passed the first room labeled as such. *Med Bay.* Then the second, an office with Para's name, which was equally decorated with posters.

Supposed Elemental "students" came into view as they moved farther down the hallway where more halls connected. The first intersection led to a short set of stairs, leading down into another hall. The base was even bigger than it showed above ground. There were various species meandering about the halls, since any of the several species on Anaiess could possess Elemental powers. Several Luneduine were coming out now that the lights were dimmed. They were the nocturnal humanoid species with pale pink translucent skin and large black eyes, sensitive to any amount of light.

A Felinian girl was taping a poster to a wall in a small gap. Felinians resembled cats a bit, with more hair than humans and long tails, ranging in a wide array of patterns and colors. Her round eyes lifted from the poster for a moment to stare, pointed ears rotating forward. Next to her, a horned Kalimyrin handed her another poster. A close relative to humans, they grew horns from their heads and held bright, colorful eyes.

Kon avoided towns and pretty much everything to do with people. Being in the biggest Elemental safe house wasn't something he'd planned on, and eyes were already beginning to fall on him. Something Peter hadn't noticed.

"So, there's classrooms down this way." Peter pointed down the hall to the stairs. "Up here is the cafeteria; it only closes for an hour or so between meals. Did Para give you a room yet?"

"No, I'm not—"

"Peter!" A Rilinquin called as she exited the cafeteria. Rilinquin were a digitigrade species, slightly taller than humans with purple hues of skin and long pointed tails. She looked similar in age to Peter, late teens or so. Her burgundy, almost-red hair stuck under a beanie as she flashed a smile at them.

A pink Takti stuck on her shoulder, another sentient being that resided on Anaiess and the smallest of the multiple species. They stood only two or so feet tall and ranged from shades of pink to yellow. Three large tails, called *tagune*, hung on their head in place of hair, coupled with a round face with big eyes. They were known for adopting a "taxi," an average-sized person of another species, who was willing to let them ride on their shoulders to get around faster. Though excellent climbers, it was hard for them to get anywhere fast without a taxi. Same with Luneduine, there usually weren't many Takti in the area. With advancements slow, Brynden Ka didn't have the same massive overhauls in economic structure to incorporate the different needs of the two species. Towns did what they could to assist the small and nocturnal species, but it paled in comparison to the bigger cities.

"Peter!" The Takti mimicked as they approached, her voice a bit higher as she perched on the Rilinquin's shoulder wearing a drape over her head and tagune, full of beads and stitching. It was a common cultural outfit for Takti.

"Oh," Peter said, looking back to Kon. "This is Stormy and Jyune. My, uh . . . friends."

"Why'd you say it like that?" Stormy, the Rilinquin, retorted, scrunching up her pinkish-purple nose. Her arms were full with a plate of fresh cookies, and she was dressed casually, similar to Peter. At least the Elementals of the base didn't wear the same uniforms as those he had met at the door. It was a small relief in mounting discomfort.

"Who's that?" Jyune asked, running a hand down her tagune as her circular yellow eyes traced Kon from her perch, reaching her other tiny hand toward the plate.

"He's new. This is Kon." Peter faced Kon, who had frozen again.

"Cookie?" Jyune held one out. When Kon responded with a shake of the head, she offered it to Peter, her grin only sinking slightly.

"Did the recipe work?" he asked.

"See for yourself." Stormy shifted her weight onto a hip as her pointed tail swung low. "This is a game changer."

"Yeah, that's pretty good," Peter commented through bites. "Anyways, Para wanted me to show him around."

"Oh! We know the *best* spots!" Stormy boasted, a smile curling across her lilac cheeks.

"I can get you any food from the cafeteria in three minutes flat," Jyune said, head held high before taking a giant bite of her cookie.

"What do you want to see?" Peter asked, pushing his glasses back up his nose. "Or should we get you a room—"

"No," Kon finally spoke. "I'm just waiting out the storm."

They all paused, their movements drooping as they stared.

"You're not staying?" Peter croaked, his smile fading for the first time as his demeanor deflated.

Jyune swallowed the rest of her cookie before perking up. "Wait! We can show you the sunroom!"

"Oh, yeah!" Stormy joined in. "If you're really waiting out the storm, that's the place to do it. There are no other windows in here," she explained. "No one ever goes in there. C'mon." She hardly waited as she turned with a flick of her tail.

Peter looked to Kon, tilting his head. His voice had gone quiet. "They're right. You can see outside."

A sigh escaped Kon's lips as he surveyed his surroundings again. Elementals still lingered, or what he assumed were Elementals. They were all young, ranging from tweens to his age. Some pretended not to look, while others outright stared. It was hard to read how they felt by their faces, and Kon didn't want to stare long enough to find out. Maybe their sunroom *would* be quieter.

With a shrug from Kon, Peter made no hesitation as he beckoned him down the hall, a bit of his pep returning. They passed the busiest part of the base, the cafeteria—a large white room lined with long tables. There were a few Elementals inside, most reading or eating. Even with the low traffic, it felt like entirely too many people to Kon, who was quick to move on.

Posters still lined the walls past the cafeteria. A majority looked handmade, drawn, or painted. His eyes scanned for anything of notice. Anything to spark danger in his mind. When nothing came to note, he tried to read some of the passing posters. They were about various subjects, book clubs, lunch menus, study groups, and clothing sales. Stormy and Jyune were explaining their baking breakthrough to Peter up ahead, though he kept a close eye on Kon.

They passed a hall of dorms, then the common area, before they took a left turn down a long empty hallway. Kon was careful to plot his exact path to the door, watching for any other exits. There was a mounting pressure in his chest the deeper they went, though thankfully, the hall was quiet, void of life. There weren't as many posters down that far. At the end of the hall on the right, a set of steps led to a small door. Stormy cracked the door open and peeked in. "Okay, we're good." A mischievous grin spread over her face. "Not that many people even know this is here."

Jyune hopped from her shoulder into the room as Stormy held the door. Kon ducked through the lower entryway, entering the dark room. It was set up like a small round theater. Several long steps led down to the bottom where a single floor-to-ceiling window sat, looking out the back of the base. From the view, it seemed they were around the top of the structure. There were hardly any lights on inside, only small floor lights lining each step. Outside, the faint glow of sunset was dipping behind the two large peaks in the distance, though the darkened clouds nearly covered them. Rain came in a downpour, streaking down the glass. Occasional lightning struck in the distance.

Though Kon was used to the hazy weather of Brynden Ka, he couldn't help feeling somewhat relieved he wasn't seeking cover outside right then, while also likely dodging more waves of EME sweeps. It had been almost constant the last few days.

Stormy joined Jyune on one of the dark steps, laying her plate of cookies between them. "I love it here," she said, her tail wrapping around her.

Peter was on the other side of the step, beckoning for Kon to sit next to him with a smile. Kon took a deep breath and joined him, setting his backpack behind him. It had been a while since he'd watched the rain from inside. It was much more peaceful than being in it.

"What's your power?" Jyune spoke again, looking to Kon with a beam across her round face.

"He's an Avari, Jyune—he has multiple," Peter said. "You do have multiple, right?"

Kon looked off-put at his use of the word "Avari," wincing slightly. If they hadn't noticed, they did then. "A few."

Their reaction was nothing more than a tilt of the head, indifferent to Peter's remark.

"Mine is light," Jyune announced, flashing a bright glow of energy around her hand to the annoyance of Stormy, who nudged her to put it out. Jyune gave a curl of her tail, gesturing to Stormy. "She's fire, but she doesn't ever use it."

"I don't have a reason to," Stormy said. "There's plenty of overconfident fire blasters around here. I don't need to be one of them." She half chuckled, scowling. "Plus, I'd rather focus my time on learning a skill I can actually exist in society with one day." She gestured to the plate of cookies beside her.

"We're going to open a bakery," Jyune stated, plopping down to dangle her legs from the step.

Kon didn't have much to say on the matter. Maybe an Elemental *could* one day exist in society unnoticed. But not him. It was a dream he gave up long before.

Peter hesitated in the silence, fiddling with a hand as rain battered the window. "So, you're leaving when it stops?"

"For the record," Stormy began, glancing over at them as she leaned back. "I think you should give it a few days. It always takes new people time to warm up around here."

Jyune picked at the fur on the end of her tail. "Sometimes, people forget that everyone here is just like them." Her yellow, expectant eyes landed on Kon. "We're all the same at the end of the day."

Peter peered around Kon to Jyune, somewhat shocked at her sudden seriousness, before he straightened out. "Yeah, we've all been out there. Terrance says it's getting worse."

"It *feels* worse." Jyune curled up slightly, gaze set out the window.

"There's been more attacks. More Elementals coming in scared out of their minds," Stormy huffed.

"But Para says the best chance we hold is together." Peter grinned as he laid his book down between them. "It couldn't hurt to stay a few days."

Lightning ignited in the distant clouds. A slow breath escaped Kon. "It could if the EME knows I'm here. You'd all be in danger."

Stormy sat up slightly. "We already are. We're part of the EME's biggest threat."

"*One* of their biggest threats," Peter corrected. "What if their *two* biggest threats became one?"

The book beside Kon caught his eye. Thick dark leather, the words on the front sewn in intricately. The word "Avari" stung to stare at too long, as if it were an insult jumping off the page. "What's in that?" he asked, changing the subject. He hadn't seen many people with an interest in Avari. Most had some sort of aversion to them if they inevitably recognized his attributes. It was something that usually unnerved them.

Peter jumped at the opportunity to talk about the book. "It's one of the original books written by Andren Day, the lead scientist of the Avari Integration Program. He wrote down everything he could, even after it shut down twenty years ago."

Kon couldn't deny his curiosity. "Can I see?"

Peters' face lit up. "Yeah! Go ahead. Ignore the notes and extra pages. I've been editing it."

Kon lifted the old book gently, cracking open the worn cover. A picture flopped out from the front page; an old one, by the looks of it, a bit wrinkled and frayed around the edges. It was of several Avari posing with three scientists. The Avari were a good foot taller than the tallest of them. It was rare to see images of them. It was an odd sight. They all smiled at the camera; dark inky markings striped across their body. There was no hiding their markings back then, dressing in short sleeves and low collars. Instead, he was always sure to cover as many as he could. He was more troubled by them than anyone else was.

"That was from the program, before . . . you know." Peter toyed with his hands.

There was a deep pang of something in Kon. A feeling he couldn't place. It could've been any mix of anger, sadness, or betrayal that Avari never returned. He hardly noticed Jyune next to him, peering at the picture. Stormy was scooting closer as well, peeking over the Takti at the image.

"*You really do look like them,*" Stormy commented.

Kon flipped the page, bothered by the comparison for a reason he didn't know. The book started with how the program began, detailing the relations and meetings with Avari. As he flipped through more pages, skimming, he thought about the benefits of staying. If they had knowledge on the EME and Avari, maybe it wouldn't hurt to stick around for a bit. Only for a day or two. He was fairly confident the EME didn't have a solid lead on his location at the moment or what direction he was headed. The soldiers in the woods hadn't gotten the chance to call in his appearance. It surely couldn't make *his* situation worse, after all. Only theirs.

"So, are Avari back?" Jyune asked, looking from him to the pictures.

Kon stared at another image before him as the Avari on the page stared back. They weren't back. All that remained of them were these old, forgotten images. "I've always been here."

"Alone?" Jyune sat back on her haunches.

He shrugged.

"I knew he was here, somewhere," Peter said, a beam of pride in his smile.

Kon didn't see anything prideful about it; being alone on a planet with no answer as to why. Avari were gone. He could hardly even call himself one. Yet, there he was.

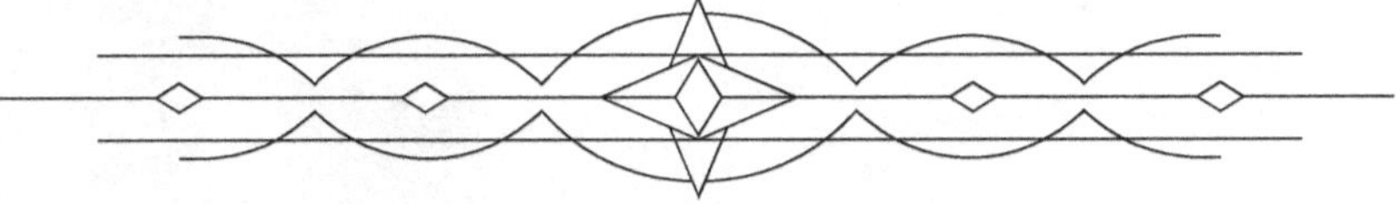

CHAPTER 5
A REASON TO STAY

The early morning was still and cold once the heavy storms the night before had drifted past. Light sprinkles fell from the gray sky, threatening to turn to snowfall with the dropping temperatures. It was no surprise for snow to begin that early into fall. Kon opened the door to the room Peter had convinced him to get. Though it wasn't much of a "convince"—more like Peter dragging Kon to the room key station and signing him up for one, saying he'd signed new people in plenty of times. It wasn't a horrible idea for Kon to have a place where he could hide his belongings while he learned more about the base.

As he stepped out, leaving his bag inside, there was a familiar form seated across the hall. Peter sat on the floor, reading. His sweatshirt bunched around him as he looked up from his book with a smile. "Calleah!"

Kon froze, only blinking at him.

Peter started to close his book. "Oh. You don't know any Felavari?"

"What?"

"Feilar Avari. The Avari that contacted us. Their native language. Yours?"

Kon shook his head.

Peter looked stumped, staring down at the tiles in thought. "I was hoping someone taught you it." His hand ran over the leather cover of his book. "I was worried you left."

"How long—" Kon looked down the empty hallway.

"I get up early."

"Earlier than this?"

"Yeah! Best time to read." Peter scrambled to his feet. "Usually, I go to the library or cafeteria or something, but I didn't want to . . . miss you."

Kon lowered his brows slightly.

Peter shuffled to his feet, closing the book in his hand. "I figured you might still need help finding things."

"Where's Para?" Kon asked with a frown.

"See? I can help with that! She's probably in her office, or—" he pulled his sleeve back to look at his watch, "should be soon." Peter beckoned him down the hall, a bit too much pep in his step for early morning.

A few Luneduine wrapped up their nightlife before the lights adjusted for day time. Their large eyes lingered on the two as they passed. One smiled a greeting to Peter, their pale pink arms full of books. It was fairly common for most businesses and schools to stay running day and night for the citizens that preferred, or needed, to do their daily lives away from the sun. Though in bigger cities outside of Brynden Ka, nightlife was much more integral for the bustling society. Here, it seemed mainly an accommodation for the small Luneduine population.

"Where are the other two?" Kon asked casually, feeling slightly more comfortable. The feeling unsettled him. Nothing was *ever* safely comfortable. There was the pressing feeling that every moment not on the move was a risk. A learned habit probably, but one that kept him safe.

"Stormy and Jyune? They said they were going to go make their next batches of cookies. The cook only lets them use the ovens late at night." Peter chuckled a bit.

As they turned the corner, Para was exiting her office in the distance, a paper in her hand. Her braid had been redone in the same position over her shoulder, though she was dressed in more casual indoor wear.

A smile spread across her face at the sight of them, waving them over as she lingered closer. Students were still slow to move around, only a few in the halls.

"Told you she'd be here," Peter whispered as they approached.

Kon had partially expected to see her again the previous night in his slight exploration around the base, but she never reappeared.

"I hope I didn't rush off too fast last night. Transmitter emergency." Her eyes traced over the papers in her hand before setting back on Kon. "I was worried you ran off. I guess Peter's been doing a good job."

Kon looked between the two of them. Peter was beaming up at Kon, waiting eagerly for his response. "Yeah," Kon murmured, pushing his hands into his pockets again as his eyes found the pale tiles below.

Peter gave Para a wide grin. "I got him a room, showed him around, and talked with Stormy and Jyune for a bit."

"Cookies?" Para asked flatly.

"Yup."

Para pursed her lips with a nod. "Well, I guess I put the right guy on the job. But . . . if you have a moment, Kon? I need to do your entry interview. Standard procedure. We do it with everyone who comes in." The confidence in her posture held steady.

Kon hesitated. From her demeanor, she didn't seem to be expecting a "no," though that was the answer he wanted to give her. But there was a chance the interview could answer more questions for him in turn. He took a breath. "Okay."

"Right this way." Para turned down the hall, casting a last glance over her shoulder. "Peter, go eat something." They headed past her office and toward the main hall.

"Isn't that your office?" he asked, the colorful door falling behind them.

"Yeah. We do these in Terrance's office, though," she explained, then promptly changed the subject. "You know, I haven't seen Peter smile that much—probably ever."

They crossed back past the tall mural and into the next hall; the "Defensive Wing" as Para had called it the day before. Kon paid close attention to the doors and signs. If anything were hiding here, it would be down that hall. The Student Wing only seemed to house teen Elementals, likely nothing of true importance. However, Terrance's office was the first door in the corridor. A sign toward the first intersection of the hallway read "No unauthorized student entry." He stared for a moment longer before Para beckoned him into the room.

Terrance sat behind the desk across the small office reading a paper. The room was fairly bland with dark gray walls, a black desk, a few shelves behind him holding books, and other light decor. The right wall was filled with monitors and boards with notes and maps. Terrance flickered his gaze to them and gave a stiff grin, as if hospitality wasn't his strong suit. Kon glanced over his shoulder, watching Para close the door as the small room started to feel *too* small. She slowed her movements, seeing his mood shift to something more cautious. "Don't worry. We just like to know if new people have seen anything that can help us. EME movement, other safe houses, stuff like that." She stepped lightly across the room, still careful in her actions. "And of course, we want to know if there's anything you need while here." She gestured to the empty chair as she took a seat.

Kon eyed the chair, dreading it, but cueing them into his caution seemed like a worse idea. He sat down slowly, his gaze locking on Terrance.

"Just answer with what you know. Easy," Terrance explained, his slight accent a bit clearer.

"Is that okay?" Para asked, watching him.

Kon shrugged, staring at his worn pants, quickly becoming aware of his differences to the others at the base. All of the staff dressed more . . . formal.

"Alright." Terrance's green eyes watched him a moment longer before they drifted to the paper, rolling his pen in his hand. "Where are you from?"

Kon frowned at the paper in his hand, guessing it was some sort of entry form. "From?"

"The town you came from?" Terrance inquired.

Kon shook his head. "I move around." There were reservations in mentioning any town he had been in, even Calin. He watched Terrance write his answer down, an edge of annoyance already present in his scribbled writing.

"Is anyone else in your family an Elemen—oh," he scowled. "Never mind that one. We might have to stray off the list . . ."

So, they do know. Kon had suspected as much.

"Have you stayed at any safe houses in the past?"

Kon hesitated. "One. A while ago." He had his fair share of passing through safe houses. Most he avoided entirely.

"Do you know who ran it? Where it was?"

The questions felt eerily familiar to a darkened memory of his past. Kon shoved the thought from his mind, lifting his chin a bit. "I don't know. North somewhere."

"What happened to it?"

"I left."

Terrance narrowed his eyes but wrote the answer down before looking back to the list, panning over the questions as if he were skipping over some. "Uh, how old are you?"

"Nineteen." Another question that chipped away at some deep suppressed memory.

"Any medical issues we should be aware of?"

"No." Kon sighed slightly, finding the floor a more comforting place to look in an attempt to hide his rising discomfort.

Terrance adjusted, his pen tapping the desk. "Have you ever seen any other Avari?"

Kon lifted his head at the question, where Terrance's blank gaze waited for him. His questions were more straightforward than he expected them to be. Almost amused at his confidence, Kon leaned back. "Have you?"

Terrance paused, giving him a tiny frown. "No."

"Me neither," Kon said, his annoyance starting to show through.

From the looks of it, Terrance was still trying to mask his own disdain. "Who did you grow up with?"

"Humans."

Terrance waited for any further information. Names, locations, nothing of which Kon dared to share. When it didn't come, he jotted down the dry response. "Hmm, how long were you with them?"

"A few years."

"Who did you stay with after that?"

Something in the question struck a nerve in Kon, though he couldn't say why. It all felt like pointless information to him. Probing. "I'm not telling you that." All he knew was he wouldn't tell anyone about Joel and Mallia—even the *Elemental Protection System*.

"Why not?"

Kon crossed his arms. "For their safety."

Terrance glanced at Para with a look that was hard to read.

Para took a deep breath before she spoke. "That's fair. How long have you been on your own?"

Kon tried to lighten his mood again, looking away. "A while."

Terrance tapped his pen, squinting at the next question before he started again. "Had any run ins with the EME? Aside from . . . last night."

"Plenty." Kon tilted his head to the side.

"Do you know a number? Estimate?"

"Never thought to count."

"What's the worst one?"

Kon's gaze immediately set on Terrance again. That time, no answer came. He pursed his lips together, feeling his breath becoming harder to manage, but he kept a solid glower on his face.

After a long few seconds of silence, the air thick, Para spoke. "Okay, you don't have to answer that."

Kon's glare broke, setting back on his lap as he pulled at his sleeve, trying to settle a bouncing knee.

"It just lets us know what we're dealing with," Terrance said. "Helps us keep people safe."

Para shifted in her chair. "We've heard a lot of stories that have helped us track things. The EME are usually pretty methodical about their path, but they've been acting up lately. It's good to know what people out there have seen so we can map their new behavior."

Terrance shuffled a few papers before pushing them to the side.

"We've been trying to piece together a timeline. Three or so years ago is when things boiled over. They swarmed up north and swept probably fifty miles—raided one of our partnered safe houses. A lot of Elementals fled south. We were just starting up, saved as many as we could. EME movement has been increasingly unstable ever since. Harder to predict."

Kon froze. That was it. The memories flooded back in. He could feel a rising heat in his body. Did they know he was up there? Maybe they wanted to confirm it, or maybe there were rumors. *They had to know, but how?* Something he often pushed to forget was front and center again in his mind. It must have been at least partially clear something was wrong as Terrance laid an elbow on the desk. "Do you know anything about that?"

"Terrance," Para mouthed quietly, leaning in slightly as Kon kept a hazy stare at the floor.

"No." Kon's voice was empty.

Para took a quick inhale, attempting to save the unsteady mood in the room. "Is there anything you need us to provide here for you?"

"No." After another pause of silence, he murmured, "Can I go now?"

"Of course . . ." Para hesitated, standing to grab the door, but Kon was already out of his seat, leaving the door ajar as he escaped into the hall.

The hallway was a blur as Kon rushed back to his room. More students were moving about, not that he noticed any of them. He was locked internally, trying to fight off the flow of memories. He couldn't get into the room fast enough as he slammed the door shut, pushing against it for good measure. His head fell back on the cold gray door as his eyes found the ceiling. *Deep breaths.* He couldn't figure out the emotion he was feeling. Overwhelmed? Frustrated? It didn't matter. Being here was a mistake. They knew what he was; that was a clear enough sign to run. Things had always been safer on his own anyway. He grabbed his backpack from the dark room, throwing it over a shoulder as he whipped the door open—almost jumping as Peter stood on the other side, hand raised in preparation to knock.

"Oh . . ." Peter's fist lowered, still clutching the old book.

Kon let out a huff as he closed the door around Peter and started walking.

"Hey, wait!" Peter was quick to tail after him, struggling to keep up as Kon headed out of the dorms and past the cafeteria, toward the entrance. Toward his escape. "Where are you going?" Peter blurted out, jogging to keep up.

"Doesn't matter," Kon growled, eyes locked ahead as everything in him pushed to get back to the safety of the woods.

"It does if you're leaving!" Peter reached for his sleeve. "Wait!"

Kon jerked his arm back as he turned to face Peter, who stumbled at the yank. Peter must've realized his mistake from the hardened scowl across Kon's face.

"I'm sorry—" Peter recovered from his stumble, distancing himself.

Kon held his glare, alarms in his head warning him to pick one: run or fight. Though, as he looked upon the "threat," his head cleared enough to finally see what stood before him—a boy with fear in his eyes. Kon's stance broke, fists unclenching as he backed away. Whatever emotion he felt, it had melted into a thick guilt. They stood in the nearly empty hall. Silence fell heavy as Peter kept his distance, no words coming.

"I don't belong here," Kon finally said, gaze set on the floor.

Peter fidgeted with his book, mouth open as he toyed with his next words. "I know you *feel* that way, but if there's anywhere on Anaiess you belong, it's here."

Kon let out a sigh, still scanning the tiles below him as he shifted his weight, trying to expel the trouble from his body.

"And if there's anywhere you're going to get answers, it's here."

Kon turned back to him. "Answers?"

A voice sounded from down the corridor. "Hey! There you guys are!" Jyune yelled as she and Stormy rounded a corner from an intersecting hall and bounced up the steps. She sat atop Stormy's shoulder, as always.

Peter and Kon turned at the same time, both setting their stare on the two with frowns.

Stormy stopped in her tracks at the top of the stairs. "Whoa—bad time?" She slowed her approach, hands full of posters.

"Didn't you guys go to bed like four hours ago?" Peter snapped.

"Business never stops, Peter," Stormy said with a confident sigh. She was dressed in a black cardigan and sweatpants with slight bags under her eyes. Jyune yawned as she shook her head at him, dressed in similar leisurewear. "Also, Jackson offered to help put up the posters. Jyune thinks we need someone taller."

"Isn't Jackson like—tall?" Peter pressed.

"Yeah, but Kon," she gestured at Kon and shrugged, "is taller."

Jyune stood up on Stormy's shoulder, looking over Kon with narrow eyes. "May I?" she asked.

Kon shook his head, a scowl still clear on his face. "What?"

"She wants a taxi. We've been working on *asking* before we jump," Stormy clarified.

"Where?" he asked.

Jyune must have taken that for an agreement, as she leapt from Stormy's shoulder to his. "*I'm* glad you asked!" She pointed down a hall. When Kon didn't move, her hand drooped, looking back to Stormy with defeat.

"Jyune, c'mon. Get down," Stormy said.

Peter's face was close to horrified after he had just seen how Kon didn't favor being touched. Though, Kon was staying rather composed, staring at the ground.

"Stormy, this is perfect. We can put our posters *miles* above the competition!"

"What competition?" Peter sneered.

"Down," Stormy said again, pointing to her own shoulder. Jyune jumped back to Stormy, muttering under her breath. "We would love if you guys could help, though," Stormy finished, looking between the two of them.

Peter glanced up at Kon, "Uh—"

Kon cut him off. "Peter was going to show me the library. Maybe later."

Peter blinked in surprise, following along. "Yes. That."

"Well, we'll be putting up posters." Stormy shrugged.

"With Jackson," Jyune grinned, giving Stormy a sly smirk. She scoffed as they turned away to leave.

"They're just helping with the posters!" Stormy defended as they left.

Kon watched them with a bored expression before looking back at Peter. "Library." Peter turned without another word, glancing up at Kon with a confused brow. He seemed cautious to speak again as Kon's expression remained. Back in the safety of an empty hall, Kon spoke. "What answers?"

Fumbling with his book, Peter fought for words, "As . . . the EPS, Para and Terrance don't just run a safe house. They're playing games with the EME."

"What does that mean?"

"This is what I'm trying to tell you. Unlike other safe houses, when the EME strikes, we strike back. We have the power to. We've been working our way into their database for a while. Files, plans, documents. Stuff from the Avari Integration Program—" Peter stopped to face him. "Kon, we have almost everything."

"Almost?"

"Well, the deep files on the AIP, we're guessing, are back at their original facility. It's too risky to go down there right now, though."

"And here?"

"Everything's in the database . . ."

Kon found his eyes trailing over the posters again, brows creased in thought.

Peter shifted on his weight. "We could ask Para."

"No." Kon checked that his sleeves covered the markings straying onto his hand. "Meet me at the sunroom after the lights dim." He turned down the hall once more.

"So, you're staying?" Peter said with a grin, staying put as he hugged the leather book.

Kon looked over his shoulder, unamused. "I'll be back."

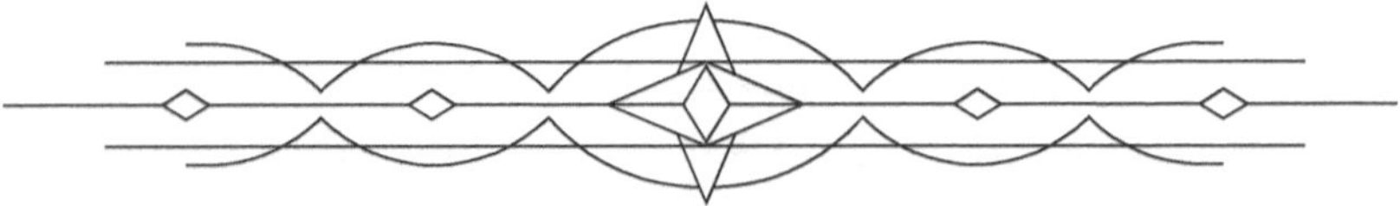

CHAPTER 6

A PLACE TO CALL HOME

MARCH 2648

Ten years since Avari left.

It had only been a day since Kon fled Calin. The sun leaked an orange-golden glow across the sky as he sat on the steps of the green house. The clothes he wore were loose, borrowed. It was all Joel could find for him. His hand pulled at the baggy sleeve as he stared at the trees in the distance, a fog over his mind. A gray cat purred nearby, keeping him company. Mallia had named the cat Nuffles, explaining that he showed up one day, similar to Kon, and stayed ever since. The cat lay beside him on the step as he watched the sky. He hardly heard the door open, followed by the careful steps behind him.

Joel sat with a sigh. "Okay, kid," he said, a sensitive edge in his voice.

Kon's gaze fell from somewhere in the trees to the side as Joel fiddled with a paper. No response came as he waited for the news.

With a heavy breath, Joel began, "I couldn't find out much." He struggled with the right words. "I heard a bit on the radio . . . I don't think we're getting them back."

Kon's breath stuttered as he composed himself. "The EME has them?"

Joel nodded a small, defeated nod. "Yeah. Even if they end up back home, the EME will be watching them, waiting for you." He shook his head. "You can't go back."

Birds sang in the distance, filling the silence. *Can't go back?* "Ever?" Kon folded his arms together.

"It would only put them—and you—in danger."

Kon sniffled as the news he waited all day to hear finally sank in. He'd known the truth before Joel told him. But with reality present, his eyes welled with tears. "But they need to know I'm okay."

"They're just gonna have to trust you."

"What am I supposed to do?" The cold spring air was getting dewy with night as Kon turned to Joel. "We were supposed to come here together—and then what? What do I do?" His hazy gaze rested on his empty hands and the faint markings forming on his wrists. He pulled the sleeves back over them.

"Did they have a plan after this?"

"They said . . . you would."

"Well . . ." Joel's eyes tracked the birds overhead as they flew in patterns over the trees. He looked back to Kon. "What do *you* want?"

"What do I want?" Kon knew the answer. He wanted to be back home. For things to be how they had been—something he couldn't have. That was gone, maybe forever.

"Do you want to learn—about who you are, *what* you are? Do you just want things to feel normal for a while? What is it *you* want here?"

Kon sat in thought. The blur of events that happened the day before hardly felt over. The day had been spent listening to the radio and watching the woods. No EME showed up. In the quiet, green house, there was a sense of peace. Safety. "I want to learn." If this was how things had become, he wanted to know why. His parents never told him much about why they had to plan for Kon's journey. There had to be a reason.

The door creaked behind them. Mallia poked her head out with a beam. "The cookies are done."

Joel glanced back at her, then to Kon with a sympathetic grin. "C'mon."

With plates of cookies and glasses of milk, the three of them gathered by the fireplace. Mallia had collected blankets around the floor for everyone as they placed themselves around the warmth.

"So," Joel began, "what do you want to learn?" He had held back telling Kon information the night he arrived to avoid dumping too much on him at such a sensitive time, but with Kon asking, it was time.

"What am I?" Kon started, looking down at his plate as he curled up in the large blanket.

"Did they never tell you?" Joel tilted his head in confusion.

Kon shook his head. "They said I was 'different.' That my parents left when I was a baby."

Joel nodded, watching the fire. "You're an Avari. Heard of them?"

The word sounded familiar: glimpses of newspaper articles he would see Jack reading, library books Seelia brought home; a word that was sprinkled throughout the things they read.

"I—think so? My parents read about them a lot."

"They were probably trying to learn about you." Joel chuckled, before the smile faded. "Avari tried to integrate into Anaiess years ago. It didn't . . . go well."

"Why?" Kon's voice was tiny by the crackling fire.

Joel took a deep breath, scrunching his nose as he fought for the right words. "You know those powers you have?"

Kon nodded, glancing at Mallia, who seemed unfazed as she listened intently.

"Well, all Avari have them. It's part of you. Unlike Elementals—whose powers are a mutation—yours are built into you. Also, unlike Elementals, your powers can't be removed." Joel shifted, careful with how he worded each answer. "These powers, that can't be removed, can't be controlled, are a lot more powerful than Elementals'. When word of that spread, people got nervous. There were already problems with Elementals and their powers. Now, Anaiess wanted to integrate an entire species with these powers. It didn't help that people had theories that Avari created the Elemental mutation in people."

"Did they?" Mallia asked, clutching her glass of milk as she looked at Kon. "Can he give me powers?"

Joel shook his head. "I don't think so. There's a connection, maybe—but I think Avari came here *because* of the connection. Whatever it is, it connects them to Anaiess. It's the reason they came here to begin with."

"Like with space crafts? Where did they land?" Mallia took another bite of her cookie while Kon soaked in the information.

"No, that's another thing that scared people. They found a way to . . . teleport here. Without ships or electronics. With just . . . power. They left that way, too."

"Teleport?" Kon said slowly. "Why did they leave?"

Joel seemed bothered by the question but not by Kon. He was bothered by the reality of it. "EME, they pushed and pushed until Anaiess government gave them control of the Integration Program. It wasn't going to end well. It wasn't going to be for integration. So, they left."

The next question ate away at Kon, possibly his whole life. "Why didn't they take me?"

The fire crackled as Joel pursed his lips. "I guess it gets more complicated there. I wish I had a real answer for you but . . . I don't." There was a hesitation like he held more words on his tongue, but they never came.

"You said you knew my parents?"

Joel nodded. "Yeah. I was your dad's mentor in the Integration Program."

Kon's voice was small, hesitant to ask at all. The answers might only hurt. "What were they like?"

"A lot like you," Joel said lightly. "Your mom, Padlin, she was sweet. Had these big golden eyes, just like yours."

There was the smallest lift in Kon's expression as he listened.

"Your dad, Jarauk, he was a bit quieter. It took him a while to come around, but we became good friends."

It felt weird having names for his biological parents. The new information maybe even stung. Names made them feel more real as if they were something he could lose. *Had* lost.

Mallia pulled her blanket around her shoulders more. "Are Avari going to come back?"

"Maybe," Joel shrugged. "But until then, Kon has to find his place here."

Kon shifted under his blanket, setting down his plate of cookies. They remained untouched as he stared at the ground. "The EME is looking for me." It was a realization, not a question.

"I figure they have been for a while," Joel admitted.

Kon's parents had also kept a careful eye on the EME over the years—another word he noticed in their newspapers. He knew the EME didn't like Elementals. He *thought* he was one of them. The truth of him being an Avari didn't change much as far as the EME went. They were still after him. The news just meant they'd be trying much harder to find *him* amongst the Elementals. How long did he have? How ready did he need to be? "What do I do?"

Joel watched the fire. "The best thing we can do is prepare you. For whatever might come." His expression twisted a bit. "You're safe here, but one day, you might need to fight them. I say we prepare for that, yeah?"

Kon nodded. "Yeah."

The spare room suited him well. Mallia had offered to renovate it before he was even settled in, filling it with blankets and toys of her own in an attempt to make him feel better. After the shock of that day wore off, it gave way to pain and confusion. Over the next few days, his swing of emotions stayed broad. At times, he was open to explore. Other days, he spent entirely hidden in his room, sometimes upset, sometimes angry. Many nights he couldn't sleep, hoping if he tried hard enough, he could wake up back in his own bed. He never did.

When sleep didn't find him, he'd depart from his room, to find some other comfort or even just familiarize himself with the house; his new home. The first few nights he found Joel awake, sitting at the kitchen table by the window, watching the woods from where Kon had come from. An old radio sat in front of him, low volume spewing the occasional chatter of what Kon could guess was the EME. He was scouting for them. Joel never admitted his worry, but it was obvious. Mallia's questions of why he was packing backpacks and stuffing them in the closets were only met with a, "Just in case."

Kon didn't step off the porch for a month, maybe more. The days blurred together. Once Joel was certain the EME had lost his trail, he started encouraging Kon to venture out. First into the yard, then small walks by their house. Sometimes he and Mallia would sit in the tall field, crafting grass bracelets out of the long straw. The next few houses were in sight but blurred by trees. Mallia often declined the neighborhood kids' offers to play after Kon arrived. She had no interest in it when Kon couldn't join. Kids always asked more questions anyway. It was probably how his markings were discovered in the first place.

But the isolation got to Kon, wearing him down further. Mallia's pleas to get him out of the house were answered eventually. Even Joel admitted Kon needed it. They had talked him into going to town with them, just to the market. Though his markings would take years to darken, to be safe, they dressed him in enough clothing to cover the majority of the faint wavering lines forming on his skin. He remembered his parents' warnings: avoid looking people in the eye, in case they noticed the slit pupil and his odd golden color, and conceal his pointed ears in his mess of fluffy hair—though ears could be easily explained as distant Rilinquin decent. It was still another question to answer, so most of the time, they avoided going out altogether.

The outing had gone decently, despite the panic he had encountered entering town. No one noticed. No one batted an eye. Joel told him there were other Elemental families there. It was an accepting community—one that strived to keep the EME far away, should they ever come looking.

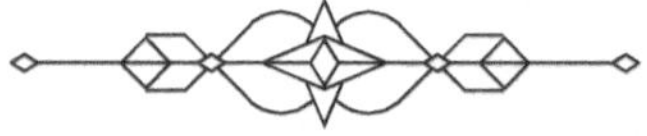

"Yeah. I understand. Did they leave?" Joel paced the kitchen, his communicator to his ear. His brows were furrowed in frustration as his voice strained. "How long does that stand for?"

Kon and Mallia stood in the hall outside the kitchen, listening just out of sight. They gave each other careful glances as Joel argued further.

"A month? That wasn't the agreement—" His voice raised. "They can't just force a search on us. The treaty was never broken."

Mallia peeked around the corner, hands stuffed in her worn dress pockets, watching as he walked back and forth. Kon hugged the wall, eyes darting to the floor. It was about him. The EME. He could feel it. Joel had warned him that EME activity would increase when they had realized the child in Calin that had escaped them a month before was the Avari they sought. Whether the soldiers had seen his faint markings that day by the wall or evidence had been found with Seelia and Jack, they knew. With the town of Calka being so close to Calin, it was clear they would get caught in the crossfire of searching.

"I'll be down there in a bit. Don't sign anything," Joel warned as he caught a glimpse of Mallia, who ducked behind the wall again, looking at Kon with a frown. The communicator clicked off. "You can come out."

The two appeared around the corner, slowly at first. They eyed him with troubled expressions. "They're trying to get in?" Kon asked, his voice wavering slightly as a shiver washed over him.

"Yeah." Joel sighed, rubbing his slightly graying brown hair. "But they can't get in without cause. That's what our agreement has always been. They're trying to override it. They have no cause." He headed for the door, grabbing his large dark jacket from the rack. "I've got to run into town and get it sorted. Don't go outside."

"Are they going to check houses?" Mallia asked as she played with her purple bracelet.

"No, they won't get that far," Joel said as the door slammed behind him, silence following.

Kon stared at the old wooden floor. He had only recently started to adjust. Would he have to leave again?

"It's okay," Mallia said. "I don't think they've ever swept Calka. Dad's good at scaring them off." She headed for the kitchen.

With a crease in his brow, Kon lingered, less convinced. "They're looking for me," he whispered.

Mallia glanced at him as she unwrapped the fresh bread from the market. "Let them look. We're too sneaky for them." She grinned.

"What if they find me?" Anxiety wracked his stomach, spreading as it tightened around his chest.

"They won't," Mallia said, casual in her tone as she sliced the bread. "Dad doesn't break promises."

Joel had promised Kon he'd be safe here, and if things became unsafe, he'd get him somewhere else. Kon didn't know why Joel cared. He had made the promise a month ago when they were strangers. But Joel treated him like family from the beginning. They spent the rest of the day watching out the window, switching from Mallia's bedroom to the living room. Mallia tried to suppress Kon's anxiety with games until, at last, they saw Joel returning, hands in his oversized jacket, a frown on his face.

Even as he came through the door, his tone was tired and curt. "We chased them off. Took a lot of—" He shook his head, rubbing his hair with a hand. "They can't come in."

And they didn't. Not in the following months. That stretched into a year, and then another. The EME had lost Kon. His parents' path in the woods, ever so winding and confusing, had properly led the EME astray. Joel's cunning plans had worked. It just had to last until Kon could learn to defend himself. To fight them.

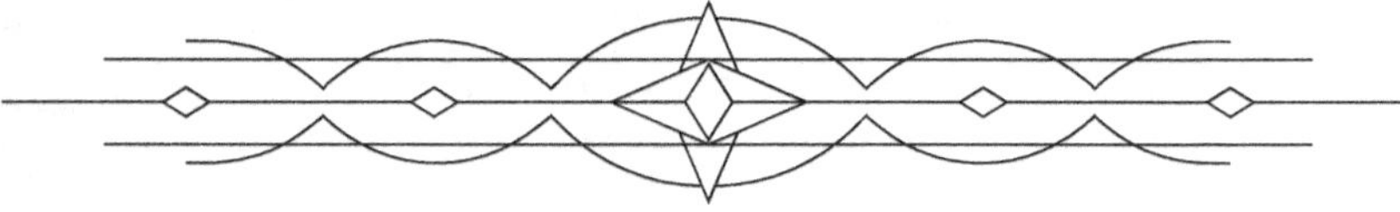

CHAPTER

7

THE GIRL IN THE SNOW

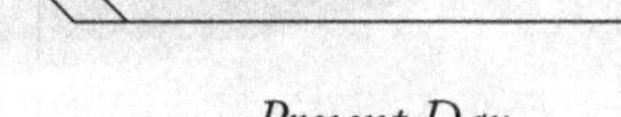

Present Day

The base was buzzing to life as the morning progressed. Kon hadn't seen how many students were actually there, but in the progressing morning, waves of Elementals filed into the cafeteria. A few glanced at him, probably because of his height. Some had looks of confusion, some of nervousness. The bustle of the hall slowed past the cafeteria. He tried to ignore the number of people as he headed for Para's office. It was his turn to ask questions.

The door hung open as he approached, still off-put by the earlier questioning. Para sat at her desk, reading something on the *digipad* screen. Her eyes caught a glimpse of him as they flickered to the door. "Kon, come in, please." Her expression faded as she surely noticed the backpack over his shoulder. It was only an instant of worry before she pushed a smile onto her face. "I was going to come find you. I figured I'd give you a bit."

He ducked in, a steady scowl as he prepared for her to address the heavy questions from her and Terrance. The expectation was cut short by the movement next to her desk. Two kids played on the rug, busy with their drawings and toys. They looked no older than six. The older girl, sharing a braid like Para's, looked up at him for a long second before she pulled her straw toy back into motion. Kon looked from them to Para, confused enough to forget the irritation in him.

Para squinted, following his gaze to the two children. "Oh, my kids. They hang out in here a lot." She pointed to the shaggy, dark-haired boy first, then the girl with the brown braid. "That's Ency and Kydah."

Kon stared for a moment longer before the color of the room drew his attention away. The room was a bit more comforting and livelier than the other office. Child drawings hung over the walls mixed with cards from students as well. Children's books and toys scattered the shelves and floors, decorated in soft shades of purples and pinks, and on her desk, in a small vase, roses.

"Come. Sit," she offered, but his scowl gave her his answer. "I'm sorry about the questions. Terrance isn't the best at—comforting the students. We shouldn't have jumped that far ahead to EME encounters."

Kydah stopped playing and moved behind the desk with Para, peeking over it at him. She picked at her brown braid as a hand slunk onto the desk to grab a pencil before she sunk back down and appeared once again on the soft purple carpet.

He searched for words to say that wouldn't sound like a fight as his anger started to dissipate. Maybe Peter was right. "I don't know what you guys want from me."

Para flashed sympathy in the scrunch of her freckled nose. "Nothing. Really. I think he just thought you knew something we could get a jump-start with. EME taking out our Help Keys really scrambled things last night."

"I just know to avoid them."

Her expression saddened. "Don't we all." Her mouth opened to speak again, but her communicator cut her off with a beep. She picked it up. "Yeah?"

"Hey, getting a signal on the radio." From the sounds of it, Deyin, the radio tech, spoke.

"What kind?" Para asked, glancing at Kon with a wary look.

"EME transcripts. They're looking for someone. Elemental."

Slight relief washed over Kon. An Elemental, not him.

The young boy was taking his drawing to Para as she talked, pushing it into her empty hand. "Where?" she then mouthed a *wow* to Ency and took the drawing, pretending to inspect it closely.

"She's from Alinth. Last seen up near Palyra," Deyin responded.

Para glanced up from the drawing to look at Kon and shook her head in confusion. He responded with a silent shake of his head as well, frowning at the words. Even he knew an Elemental in Alinth was odd. "Alinth? That's EME territory? Half their entry workers live there." She turned in her chair to help Ency pin his new drawing on her board.

"Yeah. Weird. What are we thinking? Trap?"

Para thought on it for a moment, rubbing her temple as she turned back to Kon, once again peering over the bag on his shoulder. "We can go look around. What's the description?"

"Are you sure? We don't need another encounter on our hands."

"I'll take a team. First sign of trouble, we turn back."

Deyin breath let out over the comm. "Human female, eighteen. Light blonde hair. Wearing a gray parka and backpack. Last seen heading up Palyra Mountain. They're closing in on her, though."

"Okay." Para deactivated the call and sighed, swiping a hand over her face before looking back up at Kon. "You up for it?"

"Me?" Kon scrunched his nose.

"Yeah. Otherwise, I'd have to form a team or go alone, and Terrance made me swear off that last night." She smirked, gesturing to his backpack. "You look like you were heading out there anyway. Personally, I think we made a pretty good team last night."

Kon rubbed his neck, eyes still darting the details of the room. "You want to fight them again?"

"I never aim to fight EME when I go out there. But you're good company if that's what it comes to."

"What if it's a trap like he said?" Kon never liked knowingly heading toward the EME. Her plan was risky but maybe showed a side of the EPS Kon was curious of—their interest to go on the offense.

"Like last night?" she smiled confidently. "I think we can manage."

Maybe it would help to get out of the base for a bit. Kon figured he could even part ways on the way back if he changed his mind. A way to slip out. Shifting his weight, he finally met her eye. "Fine."

Para stood, motioning Ency back to the carpet as she folded away the papers on her desk. "Let me grab my coat. I'll drop them off with Jasamie." She gestured to the kids. "Good chance for you to see our med bay, too."

Kon waited outside the door while Para grabbed a jacket, bag, and radio. The kids trotted out as she ushered them, closing the door behind her. Ency clutched his crayons as Kydah flew her straw doll through the air. "Okay, come on," she motioned for everyone to move toward the entrance, away from the busy cafeteria.

Approaching the med bay, it led into a waiting room of sorts and then through another door straight ahead into the small white medical room. Kon didn't go farther than the waiting room. A girl sat on the far counter reading a book while another woman sat at a desk, jotting something down alongside a stack of papers. Both of them paused to examine the visitors.

"Hey, kids!" The girl sat down her book, dark, coily hair bouncing as she hopped from her seat. She wore the same grayish style of clothing that most in Brynden Ka wore—baggy layered clothing, except she fashioned a bright yellow scarf, an odd pop of color in the usual style of outfit.

"Can you watch them? I'm running out for a bit." Para's hand slipped through Ency's wavy hair as he trotted in.

The woman at the desk leaned an elbow over the chair, dressed in a lab coat. "Is this about the radio?" she asked in a calm tone, brushing her long brown hair away from her freckled face.

"Yeah," Para started, glancing back. "Oh, this is Kon. He hasn't gotten to stop by." She gestured out the door where he waited. "This is Jasamie, our med student, and Alaura, my sister—one of our medics."

The resemblance between them was clear, though Alaura looked a bit older and much less expressive as she tilted a head around Para to watch Kon with an unreadable draw over her face.

"We'll keep the med bay open, just in case," Alaura's voice stayed monotoned as she turned back to her papers. "Be careful."

The other girl, Jasamie, looking roughly Kon's age, peeked around the door and waved at him before addressing the kids. "You guys want to share a coloring book or something?"

Free from the children, Para and Kon headed back up the hall and out the doors. The field was waving in a gentle breeze as they headed around the back of the base into the woods. The small rainfall was turning into light snow. Regardless, Kon was relieved to be back outside. Even after traveling for so long, he still found it . . . safe, in a way, though it was anything but, especially then. He just couldn't shake the comfort the woods brought him.

"So, you do this often?" Kon asked as they started into the bristly pines and toward the large mountain.

"Look for Elementals?" Para cast a look over her shoulder. "Yeah. It's been getting slower lately."

"And going toward Alinth isn't a bad idea to you?"

"Of course, it's a bad idea." She tinkered with her map. "But someone needs help. It's just us. We aren't going in with the hoverform or anything."

He slowed down a bit, pursing his lips. "You know if they spot me anywhere in this area—they'll send every ship they have down here. Last night was close."

"They won't. I meant what I said. First sign of trouble, we'll turn back. I'm not aiming to put either one of us or the base at risk." She met him with sincerity before focusing back on the digital map.

"The base is at risk the longer I'm there. You know that."

"We've been at risk. You're not making this any worse for us, Kon." She kept her pace in the snow as she navigated the map on a circular device with a clear screen. "And for the record, I've been dealing with people who want to take advantage of Elementals my whole life. I'm not afraid of them."

Kon didn't respond. He just looked to the side with a sigh, watching his breath flow into the cold air and dissipate. "So, what's the plan?" He shoved his hands in his pockets, flecks of snow falling around them.

"Well, if she was going up Palyra mountain, she could be trying to get over the pass to Calirue."

"What's in Calirue?"

"It's the closest town. She probably doesn't know, but it's an Elemental safe town. I hope that's where she's trying to go—if she can make it."

"What makes it 'Elemental safe'?" Kon had known for a while some towns were safer than others, but it was hard to tell by just walking right into one.

"Towns can reject EME supervision. The mayor can deny them as a private militia. *But* they have to be careful. If there's enough evidence that they're directly letting in Elementals or *someone else*," she gave him a sarcastic smile, "the EME can overrule the claim, and the town loses the right to deny a search. We see it happen a lot. We try to keep track of which towns hold what standings."

"Doesn't Calirue see a lot of Elementals so close to your base? How do they keep the EME out?"

"We have an agreement with them. They know we're . . . nearby. Somewhere. They let our students come down and shop. It's a small town. In exchange, we keep the EME out of their town. A lot of families there want it that way."

Kon almost scoffed. "How?"

"It's a lot more boring than it sounds, trust me. We can override their sanctuary claim if we catch it in time. They've been requesting a sweep of the town for a while. Not that they know we're here, but probably because of the number of Elementals they see around the town. But each time they try, we shut it down, internally."

"Huh," Kon let out a breath. "How do you guys . . . get all of this? The base, the paperwork?"

"A lot of allies," she said. "Allies the EME doesn't want Elementals to know about."

Kon frowned. He knew nothing of the war. Maybe he had let the EME control his vision of the world, keeping him from everything helpful, or maybe he did it to himself. There was also still a good chance that nothing was safe. The EPS still had to prove to him that they *truly* had the power they said they did.

The walk there took them a while as day settled in. They had gone far enough to be headed uphill into Palyra, through rocky forest. Para activated her radio, snow coming down in a steady flurry. "What's the situation, Deyin?"

A few seconds passed before the radio buzzed. "They haven't found her. A sighting at the pass though: south trail."

Para stopped, wincing as she shared looks with Kon. "That's right by us."

Kon scanned the landscape, trying to familiarize himself. He didn't know the area like Para. Usually, he stayed away from Alinth, purely due to its large amount of EME activity.

"Be careful. There's an EME squad out looking for her."

"Got it. Let me know what else comes in." She turned the dial on the radio and gestured to Kon, veering off the path. "Let's hope they find either no one—or us." Para headed through the woodsy mountain terrain. "The path should be this way. Keep an eye out."

They stepped light as they approached the trail ahead. Large rocks dotted the hillside amongst the tall evergreens. Kon slowed as they came upon a sparsely traveled trail. From Para's pause, it must have been the south trail. He scanned the ground, faint with snow. There was a light layer of white across the forest floor, void of any disturbances. "No one's been through here yet."

Para peered up the trail as her radio came on again.

"They just saw her again. Pursuing down south," Deyin said.

Para met Kon's expression, clutching her radio as she spoke through it. "Coming our way?"

Kon stopped, listening to the faint stomps in the distance. "Up ahead."

"I don't hear anything—" she shook her head.

"Shh," he whispered, turning his head to pinpoint the footsteps. At first, it was just one set. Then several. He backed off the trail. "They're coming this way."

"Stop!" someone shouted in the distance. Para clicked off her radio as they moved behind the cover of trees on both sides of the path, peering out at the scene.

A girl ran down the snowy trail, backpack bobbing over her shoulders, wearing a thick winter parka and boots. Her pale hair flowed behind her in a ponytail, almost white in the cold light. Following her were four EME soldiers, chasing close behind.

"Stop running before we shoot," one yelled, but she didn't stop.

Para locked eyes with Kon again, a look of concern across her face. He held up a hand for her to stay put as she nodded to him. It was time. Maybe a fight *would* happen after all.

The girl approached quickly as the EME gained on her. Kon listened for her steps only, gauging where she was on the trail. There would only be one chance to get it right. The fast steps drew ever closer down the trail as they nearly passed him before she abruptly tripped, falling to the ground on the frozen path.

She had made it far enough. If there were a fight, it would be best to make it fast and give them no time to call backup. Kon stepped out between her and the soldiers. There was little time for them to react as the air in front of the soldiers exploded in a ball of energy, knocking them backward as the blast sent the dusting of snow into the air like smoke.

Para recoiled at the puff of energy, the men flying back. Kon stood on the trail, fire starting to lap up his sleeves. The girl had spun around, sitting on the ground with wide eyes, watching the glow of heat rise in front of her.

A moment later, Para was at her side. "Are you okay?" she asked, kneeling.

The girl looked at her, startled. "I—huh?"

The heat from ahead drew Para's gaze back to Kon. The men were getting up, all attention on him where fire was still etching up his arms. As flames grew, turning the surroundings a warm orange, Para grabbed the girl. It was clear what was about to happen. The terrashock must've been an introduction. "Come on, hurry!" Para helped the girl up, turning away just as the entire area began glowing red with fire. They ducked behind a rock as the heat from the flames reached them, erasing the chill from the air. Para didn't dare move from her hold on the girl, whose eyes were closed tight. There was commotion from the soldiers shouting, another flash of fire, and then nothing. Finally, Para peeked around the rock as the fire faded, ready to help on the off chance he needed it. There was one final soldier kneeling on the ground, pistol drawn from his belt. He fired off a shot, aimed straight at Kon, but it impacted with something as soon as it left the barrel, never reaching its destination. It went up in a poof of fire as it detonated the terrashock, ricocheting back as the blast engulfed the man. He fell to the ground with the rest.

The moment had passed in mere seconds. Para turned back, a bit stunned as she processed how fast he had just dispatched them. There had been no time for them to process what had happened; that it could have been the Avari they seek. Despite seeing his powers in action, the night before, somehow, everything happened even faster, with ease. Next to her, the girl was breathing heavily, trying to catch her breath as a hand held her chest. "It's okay. You're okay," Para said, before standing to face Kon.

He stayed in the middle of the path, watching the men on the ground, unmoving. Fire slowly retracted down his sleeves. After another moment, he turned to Para with a look that seemed unfazed, maybe even bored.

The hazy feeling of the fight wore off as Kon watched Para. Her brows creased as if she felt some sort of remorse while staring at him as he stood in the wake of his recent destruction. The stunned silence lasted a bit longer before her attention turned back to the girl who was still somewhere behind the rock. "Come on. They're gone." Para held her hand out to help the girl to her feet. "Are you okay?"

Kon lingered to the side, watching for movement in the brush. He glanced over again, admittedly curious of the girl's wellbeing.

She had leveled herself, addressing the mud and snow over her clothes. Light bangs sat over her forehead as the rest of her pale hair fell over her backpack. "I think so." Her tone was soft as she opened the palm of her hand, revealing a decent cut. It seeped red before she cupped her hand over it, looking back up the trail. Her gaze hovered where the men lay before it drifted to Kon as he shook out the last bit of fire around his hands. Her obvious confusion kept him from moving, in case any of the fear in her eyes were toward him. Her blue eyes darted over the trail as if trying to make sense of the destruction.

Kon set his attention back on the brush. None of the soldiers had time to call. Though radical, his plan of attack had worked. It was the same way he kept ahead of the EME on his own. If any squad were to get too close, a quick dispatch was best. Holding back anything only gave them time to call for more.

When words came from the girl, they remained quiet. "Thank you . . . I thought they had me."

"We should go," Para breathed, reaching around to grab a bandage from her bag. "Keep pressure on that. We'll look at it soon."

"Where are we going?" the girl asked as she started pulling the bandage around her hand.

Kon kept his distance. Whether it was the situation she had just escaped or him, she was still afraid of something. It was better to stay put.

"Well," Para began, "we're from the Elemental Protection System. We picked up the radio transmissions from the EME. We have a base nearby."

Kon scowled at the use of "we," but remained quiet.

The pale-haired girl stared at the ground, thoughts mixing on her cold pink cheeks. "Oh."

"I'm Para." Para gestured to Kon. "This is Kon. What's your name?"

"Icelyn." She pursed her lips together as her arms folded over her torso, giving a forced grin.

Kon slowly moved closer to them, scanning the trees. More would come soon. The squad's lack of response would surely give away that something had happened. While better than the latter of them calling in help, it was still best to flee as soon as possible.

Para's communicator was buzzing on her side as she plucked it from her belt, turning it back on. "We're okay."

"Para, you need to get out of there." It was Terrance that time.

"What's wrong?"

"They know something happened. They caught part of it on the comms. You need to move."

Para turned to Kon, then Icelyn, her brows bending in for a moment. "Come on." They moved off the path, back down toward the base. "We're coming back," she said into the radio.

"Para," Kon said. Para and Icelyn both paused to look at him, surprised by his sudden words. "They could track us."

Para's worrisome expression panned down to the ground, sighing as she looked over their bootprints. The mix of mud would leave tracks. "We can lose them in the stream up ahead."

Icelyn clutched the straps of her backpack, watching between them with worry. They headed downhill away from the main paths for a bit before the water ahead caught their ears. It was a fairly shallow stream, dotted with rocks and ledges perfect for traversing.

"This way." Para directed them up the hill. "We'll go up, then circle back to the base."

Kon had stopped, however, staring through the trees.

"What is it?" Para asked, standing on a large rock.

There was a faint buzzing in the distant air. He figured they couldn't hear it yet; a familiar low growl in the sky. "Hoverform," he said. "Sounds far off, but it's coming."

They listened a moment longer before Para ushered them up the stream. "They'll stop on the path first. We should have time." She took careful steps.

The snow was picking up as temperatures continued to decline. It would start to pile up soon, hopefully covering their tracks. Para kept her radio close, updating the base as they walked. Icelyn was quiet, following Para's steps as Kon stayed in the back, checking the woods. He figured if worse came to worst, he could head north and lead the EME's attention away from the base. He felt a strange need to protect them, despite his dislike of the base so far. If they got raided, it would be his fault—that, once again, his arriving at a safe house marked it for doom. After years of avoiding everyone, being there felt riskier than the nomadic life of playing cat and mouse with the EME.

The air had chilled by the time they stopped. They were getting high up the mountain as Para surveyed the rocky incline. It was a sheer cliff from there. The stream expanded and veered in the opposite direction they needed to go. "Okay, let's head across and back through the woods."

Kon moved to the other side, stepping through the shallow water with ease.

Para took the careful path across the jutting rocks while Icelyn followed, clutching her backpack. On the last slippery rock, her boots slid, almost landing her in the frigid water had Kon not reached for her arm. Her wide gaze at the rushing water below lifted to Kon, who held her in place before he carefully pulled her up onto the rocky bank. She regained her balance, pushing her hair out of her face with a sigh of relief. "Thank you," she stammered.

"Are you okay?" he said in a low voice, stepping back.

She seemed surprised he had talked at all, meeting his blank expression with her icy-blue eyes. They widened only slightly at his golden eyes peering back. "Yeah," she said, dusting herself off as they turned to Para, who was checking the map again. She squinted at it before setting off back into the woods.

"So, Icelyn, right?" Para started as they followed behind her. Icelyn had fallen in step beside Kon. "Where are you coming from?"

Icelyn's expression creased for a moment before answering. "Alinth."

"Huh. What's your Element?" Para seemed confused that an Elemental was *living* there, as was Kon.

There was a long draw of silence as Icelyn held her injured hand. "I don't know the name of it."

Para looked back at her. "What does it do?"

"It doesn't happen a lot. When it does, I just get . . . cold? I don't know," she said, defeated.

"It's okay. You'd be surprised how many come to us not knowing their ability. They triggered a scanner before they even knew they were an Elemental. You may just have a low level." Para shrugged it off.

Icelyn watched the ground as she walked, questions clear in her expression. Her gray jacket hood was rimmed with light-colored fur, her long ponytail bunching over the hood, spilling onto her backpack. "How many other Elementals are at this . . . base?" she asked, fidgeting with her cold pink hands.

"We're getting close to two hundred and fifty, I believe," Para said. "We've got plenty of room for you."

Kon had turned his focus on the sky through the trees. He couldn't hear the buzzing of a hoverform anymore. It had faded off a while before at the stream. They were getting close to the base as the snow steadily fell at its same subtle pace.

It was nearing midday by the time they had reached the field. Terrance met them at the door, holding it open as they shuffled in. "Snow. Of course," he muttered as he got a glance of the field, grimacing as he shut the door. "Nothing on the radar. You must've lost them back at the mountain." He held one of the round digital maps in his hand.

"Yeah. I don't think they caught any signs of us." Para shook herself off. "We should lay low though, to be safe." She gestured a hand to Icelyn, who was looking over the mural in awe. "Let's get you to the med bay."

Kon lingered to the side, glad the attention wasn't on him. Part of him felt close enough to the door to bolt, but something else kept him planted.

"I'll get us online." Terrance headed for the Defensive Wing.

Kon narrowed his eyes at him, unsure of his meaning before reluctantly following the other way to the beckon of Para, who was still adamant about keeping him around. The med bay doors were propped open. Kydah ran past them and into the waiting room, a cape made of a paper towel on her straw toy as she zipped it through the air. Ency, on the other hand, ran to Para upon seeing her and clung close.

Jasamie waved them in. "Welcome back." She smiled at Icelyn, who gave a nervous greeting.

Alaura was coming from an office to the right of the waiting room, clipboard in hand. "Any injuries?"

Kon set himself at the door in his best attempt to stay out of the way.

"Just a small one," Para said, gesturing to Icelyn. "I need to go check on the system with Terrance, we should be—" As she spoke, the room shuddered slightly and the lights above flickered. "Yeah."

"What is that?" Kon asked in a low tone, watching the walls as the sound of mechanical metal churned somewhere above them. The room was shaking, ever so slightly.

Para plucked Ency into her arms and started to exit. "We're lying low, like I said. Retracting the top of the base into the ground." She grinned. "The door still works, don't worry."

"I'll join you," Alaura added, following Para to the door. "Jasamie, can you handle this?" She gestured to Icelyn.

"I've got it," Jasamie nodded, washing her hands.

As Para passed Kon, still lingering at the door, she lowered her voice. "Stick around with her for a bit, will you? Get her to Peter, maybe." She flashed a smirk before exiting into the hallway.

Kon scrunched his nose as she departed, staring until she dipped from sight. With a small huff, his attention turned back to Icelyn, who had hopped onto the examination table, peeking over her shoulder at him with a smile. One that was slightly more real than before.

"Let's see the damage, shall we?" Jasamie motioned for her hand. Icelyn focused back on her wrapped hand, pulling the layers off. He felt a strange obligation to stay nearby, and her look of comfort at him wasn't helping the feeling. Para had given him the job anyway, whether it was sincere or another ploy to get him to stick around longer. He moved inside a bit more and leaned against the door as Jasamie pulled out supplies in preparation.

"It's not that bad," Icelyn said, taking off the last few layers of bandages that were soaked in a fair amount of blood. Her tone sounded more like she was trying to convince herself as her brows furrowed at the reveal of the cut. She pulled up her jacket sleeve to keep it away.

"Ouch," Jasamie joked as she took Icelyn's hand to inspect it. "Well, the bleeding stopped, that's good. We should disinfect, though." She turned back to the countertops behind her and opened a cabinet above them, grabbing a bottle and a rag. "Alaura told me there were three EME yesterday. How many today?" she asked over a shoulder to Kon as she opened the bottle.

"Four." He pulled his arms over his torso.

"They don't learn, do they?" She shook her head before asking for Icelyn's hand again. "This should only sting a little." She applied the rag, lightly dabbing it into the cut.

Icelyn hardly flinched, watching her. "Are you a student medic?"

"Yeah. I can handle the smaller stuff while Alaura and Ryv are busy."

"Oh." Icelyn gazed across the room, taking in the details. "I was studying to go into medicine before . . . this. Do you guys have openings for more students?"

Kon turned back into the waiting room, checking his sleeves again as his actions crept into his mind. Two run-ins with EME. Surely a mistake on his part. Even if neither of them had alerted as Avari, it was rare for Elementals to do the damage he could do. To dispatch even two EME alone. Two attacks back-to-back would be suspicious to EME.

Inside, Jasamie was wrapping up. "I'll let her know. Take it easy, okay?"

Icelyn examined her new bandage. "Thank you." She joined Kon in the waiting room, who exited into the hallway without much word. Upon his swift exit, he was once again met by Peter, who was standing far too close, waiting for him. With a sigh, Kon backed up. "You need to stop doing that."

"Sorry." Peter grinned. "You guys found someone? Nice." He gave a friendly but far less eager greeting. "I'm Peter."

"Icelyn." She shifted on her weight, examining the long halls around her.

"Para left?" Peter had already turned his focus back to Kon.

Movement down the halls drew Kon's attention, students still buzzing around. "She said to find you."

"Ah, yeah. Kon just got here too," he said to Icelyn. "He doesn't know this place either." Peter put a confident hand on his hip. "Are you guys hungry? It's lunchtime. We can get you a room after."

"Uh . . . sure." Icelyn's gaze drifted over Kon for some hint of approval. He merely shrugged.

Walking toward the cafeteria, Icelyn fell in beside Kon, hardly reaching his shoulders as she craned her neck to meet his eyes. "You're new here too?" Her tone stayed hopeful.

"Yeah." He was at least glad that the fear in her eyes had turned to curiosity. Though, the caution of being in the base was coming back as they headed down the hall. The commotion inside, bustling with students, still felt harder to face than the threat of the EME outside the doors.

"Oh," she said lightly, a small smile forming. "I'm glad I'm not alone."

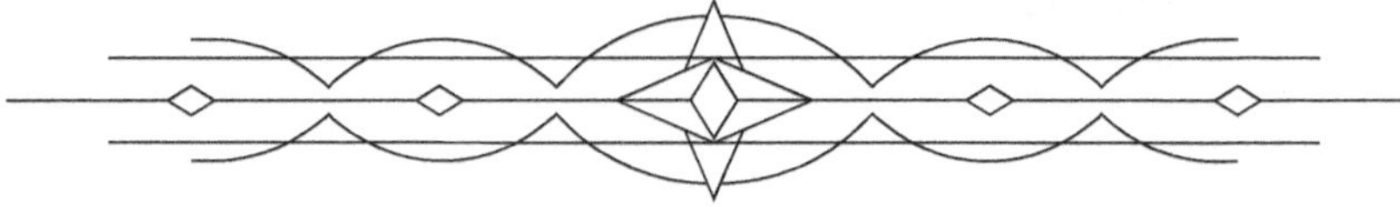

CHAPTER 8
QUESTIONS

"It's like the biggest mystery of the millennia," Peter said between bites. "I mean, scientists know Elemental power is linked to Avari, but the *how* is unknown. It's crazy to think—*still*—Avari, themselves, are behind it, right?"

Icelyn blinked at Peter before looking back at his book, open in front of them. "Yeah . . ." She flipped a page with an image of another Avari, as she glanced up at Kon across the table, whose frown held steady. Peter had gotten started again. Kon guessed she was comparing his markings, three stripes on each cheek, stopping around the middle of each eye. There was a tiny smile before she looked back down at the book.

"The crater theory is the only one with solid scientific evidence," Peter continued as he tore off more bread from his plate.

"What's the crater theory?" Icelyn asked, having hardly touched her own food.

"The meteorite that hit Brynden Ka thousands of years ago . . . we think it's from the Avari's home planet, Albara. Scientists already partially confirmed this with *Vinralinite*. The Avari at the AIP confirmed Vinralin was present on *their* planet, not ours."

Kon perked up slightly at the mention of Vinralin. He was all too familiar.

Peter jabbed a finger at the book. "We know it wards off the energy that gives Elementals and Avari powers. And it's only ever been found deep in that crater."

Icelyn squinted at the book. "So, *Vinralin* is making people Elementals? I thought it turned powers *off?*"

"It does. But it confirms the meteorite is from *their* planet." He pointed at Kon, who looked at him in question. The planet Kon had never been to, Peter meant. Kon rested his cheek on a fist as the explanation continued. He wasn't even sure why he was still listening. Peter hadn't taken a breath. "So, that means, whatever is *on* their planet—whatever gives Avari their powers—is here on Brynden Ka now, hence why *only* people on *this* peninsula ever start to possess powers."

"Huh," Icelyn's expression was a bit lost as her eyes traced the busy scribbled pages. She had only asked him about his book.

"It's just my own personal theory, really. Aren't you going to eat something?" Peter gestured to Kon, who was missing a plate altogether. He shook his head.

The cafeteria was as busy as Kon feared it would be. A good number of students were moving about, grabbing their lunches. Icelyn pulled up the gray sleeves of her shirt toward her hands before she grabbed another bite from her plate. Kon had been watching her loosely. She acted cold but made no motion to put on her jacket. The base's temperature seemed to stay fairly consistent. It wasn't cold.

"So, you said I could get a room?" Icelyn asked, looking down at her scarce belongings that sat beside her.

"Oh, yeah." Peter finished off his drink. "Are you guys ready?"

Icelyn gathered her belongings as Kon threw his over his shoulder. Back in the hall, Para was waiting, a paper in hand. With her expectant smile, Kon knew she had come for something once again. "Icelyn," she called with a smile. "How's your hand?"

"It's better now." Icelyn toyed with the wrap, still watching every face that passed.

"I'm glad. If you have a minute, we need to sign you in. Entry interview," Para explained. "We do it with every new person."

Kon winced at the memory of his interview earlier and watched Para carefully.

Icelyn stepped forward. "Oh, okay." She looked back at Peter and Kon, her hands pulled to her chest.

"Want us to wait for you?" Peter asked. "Then we can get your room."

"You don't have to." Her balance wavered as she watched them, afraid to lose track of familiar faces.

"We'll wait," Kon said in a low voice, kicking at the tiles below.

Para waved Icelyn to follow as they trailed behind. She started light conversation with her up ahead, but students busy in the halls drowned them out.

Peter slowly peered up at Kon in an attempt to be nonchalant. "So, did you still want to meet when the lights dim for, uh . . . library stuff?" he whispered.

"Yes."

Peter nodded, looking away casually. As they approached the Defensive Wing, Kon slowed, stopping inside the hallway to wait. Icelyn glanced back at them for a moment before she disappeared into the office. Arms crossed as he leaned against the wall, Kon watched down the hall. Occasionally, a person dressed in the same style as Terrance would walk by. It was hard to tell how many were there. Were they Elementals? He had the suspicion that Terrance wasn't. There were people who still wanted to help Elementals, despite their own lack of power—like Joel.

"Ever been down there?" Kon asked after a long few minutes of Peter talking about nothing that he could make sense of.

Peter peeked around him. "Down there? Maybe a few times, I dunno."

"How many floors is it?"

"Both wings have four floors."

"Connected?"

"Err—yeah, most."

"Cameras?" He had seen the subtle cameras at the end of the halls.

Some were small, round disks. Others, more obvious metal devices attached to a swivel.

"Yeah . . ." Peter's face scrunched. "Wait, what are you planning on doing?"

Kon glanced over him. "Nothing. How do you know so much about this place?" He gestured to the door.

Peter shrugged. "I don't know. I've been here a while. Sometimes, I help Para with the file detecting stuff. I'm really good with system navigations."

"Like the EME files?"

Peter smiled, a look of pride filling his face. "Yeah, I helped with some of those. I didn't really see them, though."

"Do students normally know this much?"

"No, they try to keep it low, so it doesn't freak people out."

"What would freak them out?"

Peter flashed confusion—or maybe guilt—as he fought with his words, kicking at the floor. "Oh, I don't know. Just, you know . . . EME movements . . . stuff like that."

Kon stared at him for a moment longer before his focus set back down the long hallway, where more military garb passed. Peter didn't have to tell him anything. He could find out on his own. At times, people from the Defensive Wing would walk by carrying crates of supplies or food toward the student section. They were importing stuff from somewhere. Another question to answer.

"What age did your markings come in?" Peter asked after another pause of silence, having gone back to reading his book.

Kon whipped his head around at the unexpected question. "What?"

He pointed at a spot in the book. "It says they come in ages seven to ten? I just figured I'd confirm . . ." He backed off as he saw the frown on Kon's face.

Kon peered back down the hall with a scowl, but he finally answered, "Ten."

Peter opened his mouth to say more, but the door creaked at the same moment. Icelyn crept out. Para gave her a smile before waving at the two of them across the hall and shutting the door. There was relief on Icelyn's face to be back in the hall. Her movement seemed a bit stiffer than before.

Kon straightened up. "Are you okay?"

"Yeah, questions just, tired me out. I don't know," she huffed, shoulders drooping as she pulled at her shirt collar. He watched her carefully, a pit in his stomach for her similar discomfort toward the questions.

"We can go get your room now," Peter suggested.

"Sure." Her shoulders sagged, watching the tiles below their feet.

The room key station sat in the main hall of the dorms. It was a small device on the wall with an interactive screen. Even seeing it the second time, Kon still didn't understand the buttons Peter was pressing. By the looks of it, Icelyn didn't either. After a few swipes and types, the window at the bottom opened and a key card slid out with a number on it. "See? Easy," he held the key out to her, a poof in his chest.

Icelyn nodded with a halfhearted smile. "Thanks." She grabbed the key, reading the number. "Where's ninety-five?"

"I put you in the same hall as us," he said, pointing to the specific hall at the end of the stretch on the right. "Did you want any classes or anything? I can sign you up for those too."

"That's okay. Maybe later." She took in the posters dotting the walls. On both sides, down the length of the main dorm divide, separate halls sat, full of doors.

As they stepped back from the key station, the familiar faces of Stormy and Jyune rounded the corner. "There you guys are!" Stormy called while Jyune yawned on her shoulder.

"Did you guys finish the posters?" Peter asked as they approached.

"Most of them." Stormy shrugged.

"We didn't get the ceiling ones up. We need Kon for those," Jyune said with a grin as Kon gave her a dry look.

"Ceiling—?" Peter blinked, before Stormy interjected.

"Another new person?" She looked at Icelyn with a toothy smile. "We're getting everyone this week, huh?"

"Yeah, I guess so. We're getting her a room." Peter had a sway in his body as he hugged his book.

Icelyn gave a shy smile at them as she spoke. "Hi."

"Is that all you have with you?" Stormy asked, gesturing to her backpack.

"Yeah, I just grabbed what I could." Icelyn surveyed her own clothes, her pants still muddy from the fall.

"We gotta change that!" Stormy declared. "I have, like, a hundred outfits, or you can go to The Closet. It's like a thrift store, but people take all the good stuff usually. What were you guys doing?"

"We were just gonna show her the room," Peter said.

"Allow the girls to take over from here. She needs some pampering now."

Icelyn held her shy smile. "You really don't have to. I can just go to that Closet thing tomorrow."

"Nonsense," Stormy smirked, wrapping her arm over Icelyn's shoulder. "We'll meet back up with the boys later." She gave Peter and Kon a lopsided grin as she whisked Icelyn away. "What size are you? I think we're pretty similar—"

Peter turned to Kon with pursed lips. "They'll probably do a better job than we will."

Kon's gaze lingered on them until they dipped around the corner. "I'll be back later." He headed for the main hall. There hadn't been time to truly investigate the other floors.

"Oh, okay . . . Yeah, I should go work on my studies." Peter lingered in the empty hall, watching him leave.

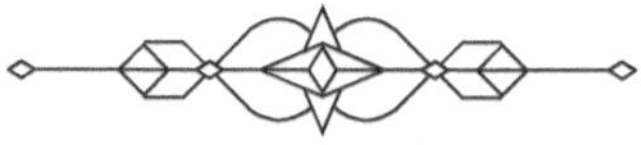

Down the hall, Stormy and Jyune led Icelyn to her room. They pointed out Peter's room, the first door in the hall. Room one hundred—decorated vaguely with his name and a few posters for the math club. Then Kon's, room eighty-seven—a few doors from hers and void of any identifiers.

"The rooms are super nice, trust me." Stormy grinned as Icelyn clicked the card against her own blank door, and it unlocked with a *click*. She wasn't sure what to expect from the base. She had only just learned that Elementals had safe houses. It was something she had rarely heard of, though she *had* heard of the Elemental Protection System.

Inside, the room was set in what was likely the default. Bed against the middle of the right wall, which was a lighter gray than the rest of the gray walls. It curved toward the top, where the long cool light illuminated the rest of the room in the shape of a "T."

Stormy paced the room. "I almost forgot what a blank room looks like."

"You have all this shelf space!" Jyune hopped to the dark bookcase by the bathroom door on their left. She sat atop it as she pulled her pink tagune over her shoulder, watching them.

"You can unpack all your clothes here." Stormy opened the dresser in the corner, examining the emptiness of the room. "Well . . . when you get more clothes, I guess."

Icelyn scanned the room from the dark floors to the control panel on the wall for the lights. The bathroom door was open, showing the quaint tiled floor inside and pale sink. "This is—pretty nice." She numbly sat her bag on the bed as she pushed away the anxious energy in her. She was safe. The base was safe.

"Just wait 'til you decorate it." Jyune climbed from the shelf, examining the rest of the room with a keen eye.

"You want to see our rooms? Get you some clothes too." Stormy had slowed from her excitement as she stood a fair distance from Icelyn, giving her a sympathetic grin. A slouched beanie covered most of her burgundy hair as she pulled at a strand of her short hair.

"Uhm. Yeah, okay." Icelyn looked herself over as she peeled off her winter coat, unsure of what to do with her bag or her jacket or anything.

Stormy's tail swished lowly and slowly as she spoke calmly. "You can just leave your stuff here. Only your key works for your room. It's safe." Perhaps she could sense Icelyn's nerves. Or maybe it was entirely clear on her face as she placed her jacket on the bed with her bag. She dusted her pants slightly. The dried mud stains remained.

"Come, we're nearby!" Jyune grinned, hopping to grab the door handle as she led them into the hall.

"Rooms one hundred and six and one hundred and seven are us," Stormy explained, as Jyune climbed back to her shoulder. Their rooms were in the same hall, across the center divider. Students had decorated their doors throughout the halls. Some used art, stickers, and photography, though the most decorated rooms lay before them: Stormy and Jyune's.

"Our rooms are kinda hard to miss," Jyune said with a grin as Stormy opened her door with a swing. It was a rainbow of colors inside as she pushed a makeshift doorstop against the door. A large rainbow macrame hung from the far wall, woven in colorful dyed yarn. Around it, posters and paintings lined the walls. The lights overhead had been shifted to a soft pink. Icelyn joined them inside, hardly believing this room started out like her own. The bed had been moved to the right corner where tassels hung from the ceiling around it. Every inch of the room was decorated in colorful, intricate décor; from the rug to the bedsheets to the set of bean bags set up across from the bed, making a small seating area.

"Wow," Icelyn breathed. "How . . ." she hesitated. "How long have you been here?"

"A few years," Stormy shrugged, no signs of discomfort as she moved toward the dresser. It was overflowing with clothes as she riffled through them. Jyune had climbed down again, fixing herself in the center of one of the smaller beanbags while Icelyn peered back into the hall.

"We like to leave the doors open. Let people filter in," Jyune said as she lounged. Icelyn's eyes crept over all the details of the room. She could likely sit in there for hours and still find things she hadn't seen before. Shelves had been put in by the bathroom, where several plants sat along with printed pictures, most of Stormy and Jyune, along with some other students.

"Okay." Stormy had gathered an armful of clothes at this point, which did little to lessen the mounds of outfits still in the dresser. "What's your style?" she asked as she plopped the heap on the bed.

Icelyn looked herself over. "Oh, uh . . ."

Stormy pulled out a flowy gray shirt with long sleeves and tiny designs along the low-cut collar. "Maybe like this?"

Brynden Ka wasn't known for its fashion trends. Most in the peninsula wore shades of grays in layers to protect them from the cold. There wasn't often color. Nothing like the stark colorful fashion of Abeira, the capital. People in Brynden Ka mostly focused on warmth and functionality.

"Yeah, that's fine." Icelyn clutched her hands together, still in the center of the room.

Stormy held up a few more, narrowing her eyes as she tried to gather a cohesive wardrobe: a long black cardigan, some more flowy lighter gray shirts, some zipper halter tops, and an array of soft pants.

"I really don't need much. I'm sure I can find stuff at that, Closet thing," Icelyn tried as Stormy continued to gather a pile of clothes.

She snorted, flicking her tail. "Nonsense, The Closet doesn't have anything good, unless you get there on donation day." She looked back to her open dresser with a click of her tongue. "Do you want to pick out anything? I swap outfits with people all the time. I like to keep my closet . . . *refreshed*."

"I like the stuff you picked," Icelyn said. It would be nice to get into clothes that weren't still damp with snow and mud. Maybe it would help her feel better in the mounting realization that she had really, truly left home. Escaped her fate. The questions asked in her entry interview still lined her thoughts, where a pit of guilt sat.

As they helped her stock her closet, Icelyn slowly became more comfortable. Afterward, dressed in dry, clean clothes, they gave her a tour of their favorite spots around the base. The sunroom at the end of a hall, the library, and common room. If Icelyn didn't think too hard on what she had just escaped, she could almost imagine she was moving into college. Chasing her interest in the medical field. Starting over. Somewhere fresh and new. She figured it was fine to have this little fantasy. Maybe it wasn't all fantasy. Jasamie had given her hope that she could work in the med bay; a hope of starting over in the wake of the truth—her dashed dreams—the life she had worked for, all ruined because of a power she could scarcely even conjure.

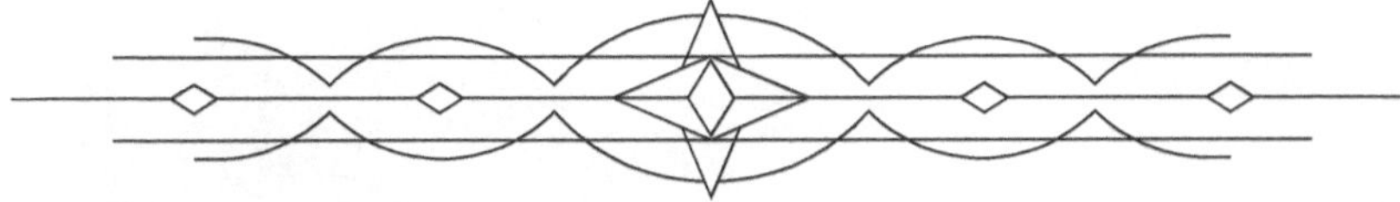

CHAPTER

9

FATE

DECEMBER 2650

Thirteen years since Avari left.

"Again," Joel called.

Kon caught his breath before he shot another wave of terra-shock at the row of boxes. One wavered before toppling over into the snow with a *thud*. He scowled and dropped his arms, sighing as his breath floated into the cold air. The yard around them was barren, coated in a layer of snow. The tall fence in the backyard hid them from the outside world. Joel had put it up soon after Kon arrived.

"You give up already?" Joel crossed his arms, looking over the five targets. "I'm sure the boxes are terrified."

"You filled them with stuff this time," Kon growled. "They weigh more than I do!"

"As much as an EME soldier. You're just lucky I didn't give the boxes guns."

Kon tilted his head at him in defeat. They had been out there almost every day practicing for a few weeks. The whole time he had spent there, he hadn't trained. After spending his childhood suppressing them, his powers were weak, something Joel intended to fix, despite his own lack of power.

Joel threw up his hands. "You said you wanted to train, *really* train. You've got to do more than that to take down a group of these guys." He fixed the box on the ground, placing the smaller box back on top, a face drawn on it like the rest—Mallia's doing, her way of helping. The path in the snow was worn as Joel stepped back and gestured for him to continue. "I said I wouldn't hold back if we trained. I don't want you to, either."

Kon pulled up his long sleeves, readying himself again. His eyes traced over the darkening markings on his skin. They had gotten more prominent since he arrived here. Checking his stance, he raised his arms, shaking the thought from his head. The terrashock began forming between him and the boxes, building onto itself in the warping air. Twists of purple bent in, distorting the view of the targets.

"Faster!" Joel called, causing the energy to detonate early. It flared out toward the boxes, which merely rocked a bit.

"Really?" Kon spat. "You did that on purpose!"

"They're not going to wait on you to create the perfect attack. You take that long, you lose." Joel shook his head. "Are you even trying? I know you can do more than this."

Kon readied himself one more time. In his growing anger, he stared at the boxes. Memories of Calin crept into his mind: the EME rushing toward him and Seelia, the first attack he had ever done on someone. It was enough to knock two of them backward. But now, he couldn't even knock back a box.

"You have to find it in yourself to fight them, Kon. They're not going to hesitate. Neither can you."

Kon pulled the energy back as the air bent. He held it with one hand until he twisted his body, detonating it with the other. It sundered the air and knocked into the boxes as four of them toppled backward, bending in on themselves from the blast. Only one on the end remained. Kon turned to Joel, pleased with himself, only to be met with a blank face.

Joel slowly walked to the last one, nudging it. "And then he takes the shot." He pointed at Kon, whose smile faded. "You still lose." His methods of teaching had been getting harsher over time. Joel had been gentle at first, but the approach hadn't brought good results. It merely made Kon afraid to use the full force of his abilities. Kon knew it was setting in for Joel and himself that if he couldn't fight them, his fate was sealed.

Kon stared at him with a look of defeat before he headed for the door.

"What, you're just gonna run?" Joel called. "That's not gonna save you forever."

The door slammed behind him. Mallia peered over from the couch as Kon entered from the garage to the kitchen, the frown clear on his face.

"What happened?" she asked, pausing the screen over the fireplace.

Joel entered the room behind him before he could disappear into the hall. "Why are you holding back?" he asked. "You can't tell me that's all you have. I've seen what Avari can do."

Kon stopped short of the living room. Something had ignited in him as he whipped around to face Joel. "Maybe that's why they left me here," he snapped, voice raised. "Maybe I just wasn't enough. I never am. I wasn't enough to save my parents, I wasn't enough for my real ones to stay, and I'm not enough for *you*." He headed for the front door, leaving little time for a response as Mallia looked between them in confusion.

"Kon." Joel's tone had shifted, back to his usual calm. "Wait. I didn't—"

"What did you do?" Mallia started to Joel, just as the door slammed.

Kon stormed off the porch and toward the woods. He and Mallia often took walks in the woods around the house. It had been safe for years. Calka made an effort as a town to keep the EME a good distance away. Joel had a bit to do with it, being a well-known and respected member of the town. He had been fighting the EME long before Kon even got to them, keeping them at bay from sweeping Calka whenever they felt like it.

He needed to clear his head. It wasn't the first time it all became too much, nor would it be the last. When he thought too hard about his situation, on what he had to learn and become, it was a short fuse. *Was Joel right?* Were his powers less than an Avari? Of course, the adult Avari Joel knew in the program had more power than Kon, who was barely thirteen—but it still stung. Maybe he *wasn't* like them.

In the festering problem of the EME, things had gotten worse outside Calka. Both Kon and Joel had grown tense. Between Joel's careful watch on their movements and Kon's adapting realization of his situation, they were clashing more and more. But in the end, they always found solace in being against the problems together. They were a family.

Kon just needed to get away for a bit. Think. In the open woods, pattered snow about the ground, he was already feeling better. Of course, Joel was right. He needed to learn this stuff. However, it was hard for Kon to understand why he couldn't easily trigger the power he had summoned years before.

The snow was crunchy underfoot. The sun high in the sky warmed the air as the thick snow stuck on the ground from the storms the night before. Birds called above him somewhere as the cold air met him with comfort. The woods were peaceful. It took all the years he had been there for Joel to get him to that level. He was at first terrified at the thought. But Joel was right; he needed to understand the forest. Avoiding towns and people would be the best route, as his markings came in darker each year. They had started taking small careful camping trips, always somewhere the EME would never be—in the deep woods.

Joel knew a few spots: one of which, an old cabin, in the dead of the forest. It was their escape should Calka ever lose its guard against the EME. It was a good place to camp, where Joel could teach Kon about surviving on his own, with only the forest around him. It was out in that wilderness that he realized how peaceful it was. Times like those, he wished he was at the cabin, where he could freely meander the woods and clear his head, but time had to be split. Mallia was still in school, and Joel never wanted to leave Calka for too long. Without his presence, the EME could sneak in and work their way past the other town members who weren't so versed in their warped agreements. So, Joel split his time.

At the cabin, they would focus on survival and bigger Elemental training. Fire mostly. At home, Kon would continue his homeschooling and work more casually on his powers. Terrashock was less destructive to practice in their tiny backyard, but Joel was getting frustrated with him. Kon could feel it. He knew it was based on the fear of knowing Kon needed to be able to properly defend himself. The EME dealt with Elementals every day. Kon had to be more than that. Better than that, or they'd use the same tactics to diffuse Elementals and get him too. His powers never completely understood him. Maybe it was normal for a young Avari. How would he know? The thought of it once again working against him made his blood boil. Enough that as he walked, he hardly noticed something wrong. The birds had stopped. The only sound was the slight sway of trees as he paused to look at them. *Why was it so quiet?* The hair on the back of his neck stood up.

"Lost?"

Kon spun to the sound of the deep voice behind him. His breathing caught in his throat. Four EME soldiers. He recognized the dark uniforms, heavy vests, and thick boots. The angular masks that covered their faces and the guns strapped to their backs. His eyes darted around his surroundings. How far had he walked? Why were they so close? The one in front tilted his head as he waited for an answer to his question.

"No," Kon stuttered, balling his sleeves over his hands as he attempted to hide all the markings he could. Did they know? They would soon if they had long to look.

"It's dangerous out here," the man said through the mask as it distorted his voice ever so slightly. "We've got lots of reports of Elementals. You should go home."

His voice sent a shiver through Kon. But he had an out. They didn't recognize him . . . yet. He nodded slightly and turned to leave.

"Where are you coming from?" the man asked, stepping a bit closer.

Kon hesitated, every muscle in his body tense, the feeling of energy seeping around him. *No. Just hold it in. They don't know.* "Bendalli," he blurted, the nearest town aside from Calka. He couldn't let them know he's from Calka. Their masked faces burned into him as he avoided looking straight at them. If they were close enough to see his eyes—they could also see his markings. Though his hair was wavy over his brows, sides fluffing over his cheeks, it was hardly a mask to cover the markings on his face and neck. He turned to leave again, trying desperately to pull in the loose energy around him. If it ended up sparking in a poof of fire or terrashock, he was done for.

"Wait."

Kon froze. He knew he shouldn't have his back to them, but turning to face them much longer would surely out him.

"Let us help you find your way," the man said, but that time, there was a deeper edge to his voice. "Like I said, it's dangerous."

He knew something.

Kon couldn't get his body to move. His fists still clenched around his sleeve, trembling as his blood ran cold. It felt like the cool breeze brought no air as he turned to face them at the sounds of footsteps. As they drew closer, Kon saw the device in hand. It was too late. It started beeping the second they approached. A silvery metal device, rigged with a scale of colors from green to red. Joel had warned him of these devices. They could detect Elementals. They could also tell them the potential power level of said Elemental.

The man lifted his hand to look at it, feigned surprise in his movements. "Huh. Look at that." A mocking tone, as he held the device up to Kon. The light below the scale was flashing red. Elemental.

Kon met his gaze as the others started to spread around him. "I'm . . . not." A pointless effort.

"You're not?" The man cocked his head, observing Kon. He couldn't see his expression. A smirk under that mask, no doubt. But as he stared longer at the device, the scale started to climb. It surpassed yellow, into orange, then stopped at the last tick. The darkest red. Danger. His movement slowed until the man had gone rigid. "You're not."

Kon didn't give them another second to surround him, though they already almost had. He stepped back, fire sparking around him in poofs of flickering energy. Recalling Joel's words of advice: *Fire scares people. Start with that. If they still want a fight, they won't see the terrashock coming.*

The men backed off only slightly as they pulled their weapons from their backs. "Easy," one of them said. "Settle down."

Kon stumbled back more until they were all in front of him again, fire raised in one hand as a warning. To his dismay, it wasn't scaring them.

Another pushed a button on their vest. "Code Alpha. We got him. Outside Bendalli."

The original man approached again, holding up one of his hands while the other gripped the rifle. "You don't have to get hurt in this. Put that out, get down."

Through Kon's shaky breaths, he knew he had to act fast. Something big. Knock them down, maybe out, and then run. Not toward the house. Somewhere else.

"Come on, kid," another said.

"You push that fire at us, we shoot." A bluff, no doubt. Joel had once told him their goal wasn't to kill him. They wanted him alive, but that didn't mean they wouldn't take a shot anyway and deal with the injury later.

He took another step back, getting into position, and raised his hands. The fire started to dissipate. Their guns lowered, but only slightly, accepting his alleged surrender—until terrashock took its place. They realized too late it was a second ability. "Terrash—" one tried to warn as the warping became visible before them, but the energy sundered out as Kon swung, giving it all the energy he could muster in his anxious body. *"Don't give them time to react,"* Joel had said. The wave split and tore in jagged colors as it knocked them back onto the ground.

It wasn't like the boxes or tree stumps he used for practice. It felt different, the energy connecting with bodies. He hadn't realized he'd *feel* the energy hit them, softer than the heavy boxes he had just knocked over. Something in him squirmed at the realization, but there was also a beam of . . . confidence. He had done it. Just like he had shown Joel he could.

Then he saw the one remaining. One soldier still standing. *"And then he takes the shot."* Joel's words rang in his head as the sound of the shots drowned out the forest. He landed on the ground with a *thud*. It had happened in an instant. The trees above him spun as something in his ribs and shoulder burned. His hand found the injury on his shoulder—it was going numb.

"Stun shots fired. He's down," someone spoke above him as he fought to catch his breath. The others were getting up, hazy imagery of them approaching, or maybe he was seeing double. *How many were there?* Fire sparked from his arms, out of his control as the numbing spread. With his good arm, he pushed himself to his side, then into a kneel. He had to get up. *Now.* Whatever it was that hit him was setting in fast. He couldn't tell what kind of damage was done. It didn't matter. Bouts of terrashock erupted around him in strange patterns.

His vision cleared only slightly, enough to see the drops of blood from his nose as his head felt as though it was swelling. The metallic taste in his mouth stung as he tried to pull his powers back, but they were firing off. The men surrounded him again, waiting for the effects of the shots to kick in.

"Put that energy away. You're just making this harder." Their voices were warped and muted in the ringing.

Even if he wanted to, he couldn't. He brought himself to his knees as he looked up again, met with the uniform standing before him. If they were talking to him, it wasn't registering. A hand grabbed him from behind, just as the terrashock went off, enraged all around him. Rays of light gleamed from it before it all detonated with a flash.

Then everything went still.

When he could see again, it was the trees above him. As his hearing came back, slowly, there were birds somewhere, content in their singing. He couldn't move his arm. Couldn't even tell if he was bleeding, what damage had been done. To him or by him. Nothing would move. If he was being honest, he didn't want to move. Panic had melted into a deep sinking exhaustion. Maybe he was dying.

It could've been minutes or hours before he heard heavy footsteps and a distant voice.

"Kon?"

Was he dreaming?

"Kon!" the voice called again. Familiar.

"Joel." A plead, but it didn't come out as one. He could hardly manage a sniffled cry as his head fell to the side where the blurry familiar form met him.

"Are you okay? What happened?" Joel knelt over him, pulling his shirt to the side to find the source of the blood seeping into the cloth. He felt around the wound, examining it as he wiped it clean. There was a sigh of something. Relief?

Kon wanted to warn him of the EME, but his mouth couldn't form the words. Where had they gone? Joel made no mention of them as he pulled Kon up slightly. "You're okay," he breathed. "Okay? It's just a tranq shot." Joel worked Kon into his arms as he stood. His limbs didn't feel like his own. The dizziness in his head only swirled more as Joel held him in his arms. "You're okay," he said again as Kon tried to focus on anything. His vision was fading. He could scarcely make out the form of a body—and another, lying still on the ground. Dark uniform. Vest. Then everything went black.

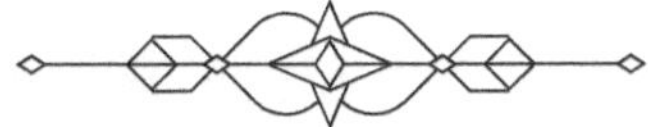

When he came to, it was with a gasp of air and panic. The last memories were of the EME. Those uniforms.

"He's awake!" Mallia cried, laying him back on the pillow. "Kon. You're home."

His vision was still making its way back, but he could see her dark, worried eyes. The deep ache in his shoulder was more apparent. Any small movement gave way to the sharp pain in his ribs as well.

Joel was at the door in a moment, looking him over. He stepped in as Kon grabbed at the pain in his side.

"What happened?"

"I got you home. You're okay."

"Did they . . .?" He attempted to look at his shoulder, but it was patched with a thick bandage.

"It was a stun round. They've got a nasty punch." Joel sat toward the end of the bed, careful with his movements. "Probably feels like you got shot. It's just a lot of bruising."

Memories flooded back of what happened. How stupid he had been—to be out there alone. How wrong it could've gone—*did* go. "I'm sorry." Kon's eyes glossed over, folding his arms over his torso. "You were right. I wasn't—enough." His words didn't yet make sense to him as they poured out.

"No, no. They shouldn't have been there." Joel shook his head, guilt in his expression. "You did better than they were prepared for. You did good."

"They're going to find us." Kon pulled back, grasping his ribs again as he winced at the thought. "We have to leave—"

"No, I'm listening to the radio. They're scanning around Bendalli right now. We won't let them come closer."

Kon opened his mouth to say more as a burning in his head brought something warm and wet from his nose.

"Again?" Mallia said, handing him a tissue. "It's been doing that off and on since he got back. Are you sure there are no internal injuries?"

Kon wiped the blood, staring at it. He only slightly remembered it starting back in the woods.

"I checked everything, Mal. We'll keep an eye on it." Joel shrugged and turned to Kon. "Maybe it's from your powers. Just take it easy."

Kon was still staring at the blot of crimson blood—the first time his powers had caused the reaction, but far from the last. And far from the last time he'd see the EME.

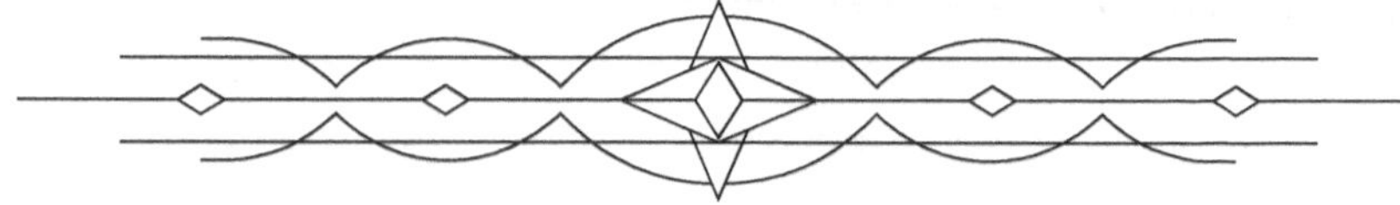

CHAPTER 10
SECRETS

Dusk hit as the base lights started to shift orange with it, part of the smooth nightlife transition. Students wrapped up their usual evening activities, heading back to their rooms while Luneduine peaked out of theirs, eager for dark. Kon was quick to avoid the mess of students as he headed for the sunroom, more familiar with the halls as he spent a good bit of the day exploring. Most of the students hovered around the main area of the cafeteria, leaving him to examine the other floors and halls without much interruption.

On the first floor, he found mostly classrooms and various dorm hallways. The stairs into the next hall had vanished entirely, to his surprise, as the base had retracted into the ground, leaving the two levels of halls as one even level. Past them was a large gym at the far end of the halls as well as a reinforced room that seemed rigged to more accurately calculate Elemental power. The finding disturbed him at first, the sight of the heavy door and thick metal walls, but students filed through it all day long, excited to watch their friends give it a try. The strong glass window looking into the room provided students with a decent window to watch. After an Elemental would dish out their fire or terrashock or other powers, the monitor on the wall would spit out a power number. It seemed some students spent all day trying to beat their friends' records or their own. Kon finally deduced it was nothing of worry and moved on.

The other floors had various things: storage rooms and extra kitchens. He even found a decent-sized greenhouse, carefully being tended to by the gardening club. His exploration hadn't brought up anything alarming so far, but the student section wasn't where he truly wanted to look. Nothing of importance would be hidden there. It was time to explore the rest of the base. He needed to get to the other side: the Defensive Wing.

Passing by the cafeteria, buzzing with students, familiar pale hair caught his eye. Icelyn was looking down at a map in her hand, occasionally glancing up to orient herself. Her gaze finally locked with his as her anxious brow softened on him. She stood by the wall, a bit lost in the crowd of students getting night snacks. He almost kept his pace, but that twist in his stomach pulled him to a stop as she stood alone, looking at him as the only familiar face. Students moved quickly out of his way as she stayed stuck at the wall.

"Hey." She tilted her head as her bangs drifted to the side. Her demeanor held stiff, hands clenched on her map.

"Where's Stormy and Jyune?" he asked as he paused beside her, looking back at the eyes of students.

"Selling uh . . . cookies? In the cafeteria." She gestured back to the cafeteria door where people were leaving with bags of cookies in hand. It explained the frenzy.

"Are you good?" he asked, looking over her troubled expression.

She hesitated. "Yeah, they offered me a spot at the table. I just felt too . . . restless." Her arms crossed over each other. "New place I guess." She wore a different outfit; a long black cardigan pulled over her hands, suggesting she made it to Stormy's closet. "What are you up to?" She traced the length of her ponytail with a hand, arms still crossed. The wrinkled map balled in her other hand—the same one Para had offered to him earlier for his exploration.

He contemplated mentioning anything. He only needed Peter to point him in the right direction, and not even that, but as she stood alone in the hall, he folded. It was her first day there anyway. "Looking for Peter," he murmured as several students eyed him.

"Need company? I was trying to figure out this map, but . . ." She shook her head in defeat as the map in her hand sagged.

He shrugged, gesturing for her to come along.

She let out a sigh of relief as they departed from the bustle. The sunroom lay up ahead, past the common area. When the halls started to quiet, she spoke up, still carrying herself as though she was cold. "I never got to thank you—for back in the woods."

"It's nothing." He pushed his hands in his pockets as students laughed in the common area beside them.

"It all happened so fast. I'm just glad you guys were there," she trailed off. "I should've left way before that."

"Alinth is pretty dangerous for Elementals," he commented in a low voice as a Rilinquin student passed by with books and a bag of cookies, tail swinging happily.

"I guess I thought I was safe *in* town." She shook her head. "I don't know why I thought that."

He glanced at her as they took the turn into the unvisited hall. "At least you're out now." He shrugged. "What was your plan, when you left?"

Her expression twisted a bit. "I don't know. I was stupid about it. I guess I hoped if I got to Calirue, I could catch a hoverbus somewhere south? I heard it's safer down there."

"That's more of a myth. The EME still go down there." He knew he was the reason they stayed up north usually. It was more familiar to him. Easier to hide than in the flatter southern sectors. The bigger cities in the south were also harder to traverse. He had only gone that far once, and it was a bad experience.

As the hallway came to its end, they rounded the last turn where Peter sat on the steps to the sunroom in a large gray hoodie and sweatpants. His book was open, and he was scribbling away at something with a pencil. Energetic eyes flickered to them as he shut his book and quickly stood, examining the lights. "They'll be dimming any minute. What is it we're doing?" Peter gave Icelyn a tilt of his head but didn't mention the prospect of her joining.

"Where is the database you mentioned?" Kon asked in a hushed tone.

"It's in the Defensive Wing—off limits to students," Peter tried, a silent warning to Kon; one Kon didn't bother to entertain.

"What floor?"

"The . . . third. Kon, you can't get in there," Peter protested, but Kon had already turned back down the hall. Icelyn stayed silent at their words but followed along as Peter trotted to catch up. "Hey, wait!"

Kon paused at the end of the hall, checking both directions, trying to plot the best way down. Trying to sneak past Terrance's office on the first floor would surely fail.

Icelyn rattled open her map and looked it over. "There's a staircase to our left."

Kon hesitated, eyeing the map, before heading left.

"Guys! Really?" Peter huffed behind them, checking over a shoulder to see if anyone had noticed them. "We can't be going out of the student section."

Kon ignored him as Icelyn pointed out the door to the stairs. He scanned the ceiling for cameras. He had done it earlier as well, plotting each camera's position on the first floor. One faced the stairs. As slight power channeled around him as he walked, a small boost of terrashock bumped the camera's view away from the door, farther down the hall. The door to the stairway swung open as Peter rushed in after them.

"Guys—stop!" He almost collided with Kon, already stopped, staring at him.

"Go back."

"What?" Peter composed himself, straightening his glasses.

"If you don't want to come along, go back," Kon said. "I need to know what I'm dealing with here."

Icelyn looked from Kon to Peter, who had gone rigid. "He has a point, Peter. Maybe we'd feel safer if we did some exploring and saw what this place has."

"Neither of you need to go. I can do it myself," Kon said.

"I'll go," Icelyn said with a confident nod.

"*Really?*" Peter argued.

"He's right. As a new person here, I want to see what they don't want us to," she explained, rubbing her arms as her face softened a bit. "I mean, my own town just betrayed me. How do I know I can trust this place?"

Peter glared at them both with guilt. "I . . . Fine, but you're not going to get past the doors."

Kon didn't wait another moment before he started down the steps. Icelyn and Peter tailed behind as they rushed down the flight of stairs. He only stopped when they reached the door labeled "3," pausing as he held his hand on the door.

Icelyn eyed the door, slightly out of breath. "What's wrong?"

"Cameras. Hold on," he muttered, looking down in concentration.

Peter was panting, climbing down the last few steps as he cleared his throat. "We *really* shouldn't mess with the cameras," he urged, as his shoulders drooped in exhaust.

"Well, what if they see us?" Icelyn asked, still clutching her map.

"It's temporary," Kon said after a moment. "Come on." He opened the door, a bit more cautiously. "What's down here?" They all slunk into the hall.

"Just student rooms mostly. A pool." Peter looked up at the small silver camera above the door. The power light was off.

"Pool?" Icelyn said.

"This connects to the third-floor defensive side?" Kon asked.

"Yeah, but . . ." Peter gave up as they headed down the hall. The lights seemed dimmer on that level. The halls were smaller too. Their usual light gray—but far less—posters decorated the walls. The smell of pool water clung in the air as they passed the double doors. Icelyn peeked in at the pool as they walked.

"So, what are we looking for?" Icelyn asked.

"I don't know yet," Kon kept his cautious pace. The hall took two turns, left, then right, before straightening out again. This time, there was a heavy door at the end of the hall. Kon slowed as he entered the hall. A camera watched the door. As he got closer, the light on it went out.

"If I wasn't *freaking* out, I'd love to know how you're doing that," Peter whispered, eyes locked on the camera.

They reached the door. Glass showed through to the other side, a long continuation of the hallway. The sign next to the door read, "Authorized Personnel only." Kon tried the handle. The same power that was interrupting the cameras wasn't taking the doors offline completely, likely a safety procedure, since it was an Elemental base with students that could possess Terrashock Type A; the type that takes out electronics.

"I told you we can't get past the doors," Peter said. "We should go back now."

Icelyn inspected the ID scanner on the wall. "Where could we get one of these?"

"It's only for the staff that work in the Defensive Wing."

"How do they become staff?" Icelyn said, tapping the glitching screen of the scanner as it malfunctioned with the camera. Kon had his back to them, taking his hand off the handle, frowning in concentration.

"Some were students, some family of students, some just support Elementals—I don't know," Peter muttered. "We can't get any farther than—"

The door opened with a beep. Both of them whipped back to Kon as he pushed it open.

"*What?*" Peter cried out before Kon shushed him.

"You can still go back," Kon said.

Peter shook his head, face entirely scrunched. A wide grin had spread across Icelyn's face. The rest of the hallway beyond the door was rather short before a four-way intersection appeared up ahead. The hall straight turned after the intersection, having only a few doors, none of which were marked as, "Database." They moved slowly, careful with each step. Kon listened for any signs of personnel, but the halls were still. Only their own steps and a buzzing light somewhere could be heard.

The lights had reached their full dim, casting the hall into faint red light. Kon stopped at the turn, carefully peeking around the corner. On the right was a short hall and then an elevator. On the left was a fairly long hallway with several doors. Each one had the name of the room over the door sticking out. "Storage." "Armory C1." "Database." That was it;

second door on the right. Kon turned to face the other two to realize they were beside him, peeking out as well, though much farther into the hall. They both gave him nervous grins. He sighed slightly and straightened out. "Come on. Stay close." If he really thought there was danger in what he was doing, he wouldn't have let them come.

They traversed through the hallway, Icelyn and Peter struggling to keep up with Kon's silent steps. When they reached the door, Kon held out a hand for them to wait as he listened, making sure there was no one inside before he tried the handle. *Locked.*

A quick glance down the rest of the hall confirmed they were alone. *For now.* There were no posters or signs of students here. Just the stark gray walls and dim lights. Kon turned his attention back to the door where Peter was pointing at the ID scanner. Kon glared at him as he held his hand over the handle again. Peter switched his weight between his legs as he hugged his book with white knuckles. The seconds ticked by. It was taking longer this time.

It wasn't a perfect art scrambling electronic signals with terrashock. Joel had helped him try to hone some of his powers in the few years he stayed there. Of course, it wasn't easy with neither Joel nor Mallia as Elementals, but they made do with what they could. Joel pushed for him to use the powers in resourceful ways: lighting a fire, blocking projectiles, scrambling cameras and other power sources, and opening locked doors. Fraying camera signals required a relatively low dose of Terrashock A, the subclass known for its electromagnetic disturbances on electronics, though he couldn't keep it up forever. They would need to be fast.

"Is it not working? We should go back—" Peter whispered.

Kon shushed him and concentrated harder. Icelyn and Peter's attention was drawn to the lights overhead as they started to flicker. Then the next set and the next. The field of energy grew with his increasing effort.

"Kon—" Peter started, just as the door clicked. They were in.

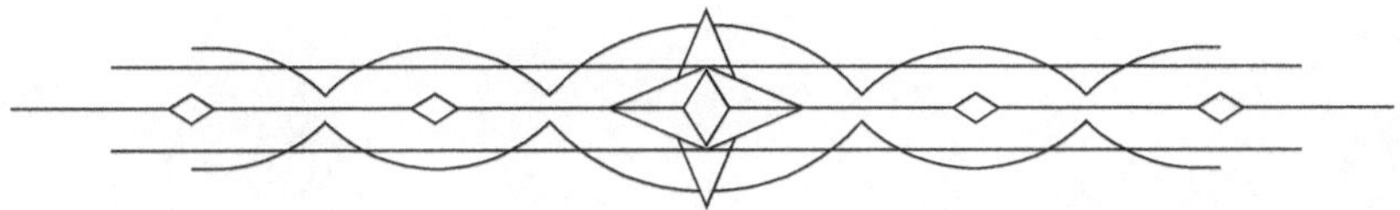

Entry Form

Name: Kon

* **Age:** 19

* **Species:** A—

* **Town/Origin:** NA

* **Anyone else in family an Elemental?:** X

* **Family:** Humans?

* **Elemental Power:** Terrastrck

* **Power level:** low / moderate / (high)

* **Job opportunities:**

* **Relocation possibility:** yes/no

* **Extra:**

* **Previous safehouses:** North?

* **Medical:** No

* **EME encounters:**

✶ **Notes:**

Combative

Standoffish

talk with Alaura regarding
Therapy

The lights overhead ceased their flicker as Kon quickly let himself in, assessing the room. It was dark inside, with rows of shelves. Glowing wires ran up the wall, connecting to a screen. He gestured to Icelyn and Peter quickly as he took one last glance down the hall before closing the door. As it shut, they let out sighs of relief as if they had been holding their breath in the murky hall.

Kon scanned the wall for a light switch as the faint wires didn't give off enough light to focus. Harsh cold light filled the room at the flip of the switch while they glanced around. It was a decent-sized room, with shelves running down both sides. There was a hall between them for walking.

"What exactly are you looking for?" Peter asked again.

Kon didn't respond as he started to scan the shelves, each one containing folders with alphabetic tabs. He went straight to the first shelf: "A." It didn't take long to find "Avari" in the mix. Kon grabbed the thin folder and opened it, seeing an article about Avari, dated a few years before, an EME transcript reading what seemed to be radio chatter, mentioning Avari sightings, likely him, a few more transcripts, and a map of alleged sightings. Then a letter from someone. He read over it:

*It is probable one Avari remains hidden on Brynden Ka.
Likely young as this would be the child born recently that
could not withstand the AIP Teleporter. Whereabouts of
the child were lost quickly after seizing the AIP. Indicators
show the rising tension amongst the AIP and EIF, having
something to do with the new birth as well as Avari power
levels in society.*

*Finding the child before international attention is
alerted would be ideal.*

Best regards, Dr. Zeyn

Kon's brow lowered as he read before flipping to the last page. His heart sank. It was a picture of him, taken by the EME. His eyes scanned over the info as his breath caught in his throat. Minimal information—description, age, and then a word he had only heard muttered from the mouths of EME scientists: "Airay." From the circle of pen around it, and the scribbled question mark, it was clear the base didn't know its meaning, and neither did Kon. All he knew was it had to do with him, in a way that punched deep into his stomach.

A flash of a hot memory struck his mind like lightning before he snapped the folder shut and placed it back on the shelf. They *did* know. Para knew what he was, who he was. His heart quickened in memories as he stood frozen. At least there was one solace in finding the files. Peter was right. They did have information: about the EME, their movements, and himself.

As he simmered in his mix of emotions, he noticed another folder marked "AIP." He pulled it out, a bit thicker than the other. The first few pages were numerous newspaper articles from around Brynden Ka, dated November, the year he was born. They all held various titles; "Avari Program Failed," "New Species Flees Planet," and, "AIP Raided by Elemental Investigation Forces." The next few pages were copies of old photos: Avari standing with their Anaiess mentors. They wore slightly altered Brynden Ka clothing, their markings showing in most pictures.

Kon had only seen a few pictures of Avari before. It was an odd feeling. They all looked happy, smiling or laughing in each picture. It was hard to imagine how it all went wrong.

"Hey, what's this?" Icelyn said from the next shelf over. She began reading, "Interplanetary mail, Jakteel. Regarding: Safe housing." Peter crept over as she continued. "It's not in my best interest to send 'gifted' students back to a dangerous situation. I suggest you consider an emergency evac for future students to send them off planet where they can better exist in society. I know you have experience fighting wars, but this isn't one you'll win. — Ghost." She looked at Peter. "Do you guys send Elementals off planet? Can you do that?"

"I've never heard Para mention it. I don't think we can." Peter's face twisted as he hugged his book. "Space travel is too regulated."

"It sounds like they wanted this person to bring Elementals *back* to Anaiess. Isn't it safer off planet?" Icelyn skimmed the rest of the page before flipping to the next.

Peter gave a shrug, still casual about it all. "I've heard bits and pieces from Para. She was apparently an Elemental that got off planet before security got bad. She said everyone out there wanted to get their hands on Elementals even more than the EME. That it's no safe haven—just a trap."

"This person doesn't seem to think so." Icelyn hovered on the page for a moment longer before closing the folder. "Do you know anyone named Ghost?"

Peter shook his head. "Never heard of them."

Kon was still reading, partially listening to them. Leaving the planet, or even the Peninsula, was something he gave up on a while before. The EME set up regulations and barriers at every way out, fearing Elementals would try fleeing to other corners of the world. The pages he had turned to contained some basic information—stuff Peter would talk about all day: Avari diet, medicine intolerances, biologic makeup. He finally flipped to a map. It had a marked location: "AIP facility." He recognized the area, south of the base. He pulled out the paper and skimmed the rest of it, seeing generic information and theories. Placing the folder back on the shelf, he folded up the map and shoved it into his pocket. Joel never told him much about the AIP facility. Kon figured the EME had guard over it, but it wouldn't hurt to know where it was.

He continued to scan the shelves. There was a large section titled, "Entry Forms," with folders in alphabetic order. He flipped through them until he found his own from earlier. The paper was only partially filled out from the messy interview—dots of empty unanswered questions, some marked out completely. He read the answers Terrance had written down. At the bottom was a "notes" section. Under it, Terrance had written a few words: Combative. Standoffish. Kon smirked slightly and shut the folder. In the same column, another large section read, "EME," with numerous thick folders, one reading, "Personnel."

He grabbed it as Peter started pacing nearby, walking up and down the shelves with deep breaths. The realization must have been kicking in.

"Para is going to be *so* upset with me."

"Only if she finds out," Icelyn said from her spot across the room, reading some more letters. "What do you think will happen if we get caught?"

Peter shook his head, squeezing his eyes shut at the thought. "Para and Terrance would just be . . . really disappointed—I don't know. They'd probably stop letting me on their digipads."

"Well, that's not too bad."

"I already told you they don't really have anything to hide from *us*. This is to make sure the EME and others can't get to it."

"Then they won't mind if we take a look, right?" Icelyn joked.

Kon flipped through various bios of EME members. He'd pause ever so often on one that looked vaguely familiar, but they rarely took their masks off. One in particular made him stop. He read the name. Ike Kernan. The man in charge of the EME movements. The highest up before it moved into Anaiess Military. He knew this face—a face that made his stomach churn. The dark eyes, slicked back graying hair, and sharp features. He could almost hear him introducing himself again. He shut the folder and sighed. Maybe this wasn't the good idea he thought it was.

Icelyn had moved back to the cabinet by Kon, skimming some of the files under the "A" section. She flipped pages as she examined the AIP folder. "Wait—is that?" Icelyn began, pulling the folder closer to look. Kon met her at the shelf, wanting to be away from the previous folder anyway. She read the words beside the picture. "Andren Alberos Day, lead scientist of the Avari Integration Program." Kon and Icelyn both leaned to look at the blurry picture. The man's face was smudged out, holding a book in his arm, the other arm around a young boy. Though the man couldn't be made out, the boy posed beside him with a smile, a bit clearer in the picture. Though young, it was a much more familiar face; glasses and messy blond hair.

"Peter?" she said, looking up.

Peter stood a few feet from them, face twisted in anxiety. "Err—what?"

Icelyn read on. "Day appeared at a rally conference concerning Elemental laws alongside his son, Peter Day . . ." They both watched him. Peter's eyes went wide before they started to soften.

"Your *dad* was the lead scientist of the AIP?" Kon asked. "He wrote that book?" He gestured to the book Peter clutched in his arms at all times.

"I . . . yeah. Yeah."

Icelyn skimmed the next page. "Andren Day went missing in 2654. Day's wife and son also went missing several months later." She met his gaze again.

"Fine, yeah, he disappeared—I'm not an Elemental. My mom brought me here because the EME was looking for us. They thought we had info about him, okay?" He slumped, staring at the floor. "I told you guys this was a bad idea."

Icelyn lowered the folder. "It sounds like he did all he could for the sake of the Avari—and you."

"I just wish I knew where he went." Peter's shoulders sagged as he stood at the end of the shelf, staring at the floor. "Everything was . . . weird when he left. I think the EME was after him for something."

"Sometimes people have to leave to protect others." Kon took a last look at the photo.

Peter sighed and turned away, unwrapping the book from his arms to look at it. "He gave me this before he left. His life's work. I feel like there's something in it that I'm missing."

"Maybe it's important?" Icelyn tried as Peter shrugged, lurking behind one of the shelves, clearly wanting out of the conversation. She hesitated another second before she flipped to the next page. It was another scientist. Icelyn shared a glance with Kon, lips pursed in her frown. Her mouth opened to speak again, but nothing came. Her hand skimmed over the page before she finally spoke. "This guy is near here, in Darnar. Garik Tally. Another scientist." She read the text. "Recruited by the EME after AIP failure . . ." She met Kon's golden eyes again. "Maybe he knows something?"

Kon peered at his portrait and then at the picture of him with some Avari. "Maybe," he murmured as Icelyn flipped to the next page. Another scientist, then a Mentor, then a name Kon had only heard a few times: Rose.

"Wait." He reached for the folder.

Icelyn handed it over. "Do you know her?"

Kon silently read the words next to the picture: *Rose Deeitro, location unknown. Former Avari Mentor for the AIP. Never contacted by the EPS. Missing since 2637.* He took in the picture of her, posed beside a female Avari, arms around each other smiling. Joel had talked about Rose more than his parents. It was the only way he had discovered who had escaped with him the night he was born. His heart sank, reading over the word "missing." His hope that they would have info on her had faded as he flipped to the next page, surprised by an even more familiar face. *Joel Gavins, Calka. Former Avari Mentor for the AIP. Last in contact 2654.* Kon reread the page several times to make sure he took it all in. *In contact? With the EPS?*

He flipped to the next page. It was just another mentor. He closed the folder, frowning. He never knew Joel to reach out to Elemental safe houses. It was a risk he wouldn't take lightly with the EME so closely watching. Why would he reach out to that one, a mere two years before, long after Kon had left? A pang of worry hit him square in the chest.

Icelyn had moved back to the other shelf, weeding through the transcript files again. Peter was still moping off to the side. Kon browsed for a moment longer before he put the folder back, just as Icelyn spoke up.

"Guys? Come look at this," she began. Kon moved to the next aisle, where she held the folder open. Peter joined beside him, flat-faced. "I looked up Garik Tally in the transcripts. Just to see if he's said anything about this place. Listen to this," she started, intrigued. Messages from 2654, from Tally: I suggest you investigate my claims. I am almost certain the boy is not the only one of his kind here. If what I saw is correct, there is another. He remains on Anaiess, as does the boy. I believe they both need immediate help. Getting involved in this may be in your best interest." She met their questioning brows with one of her own, clutching the folder with bunched shoulders.

"'The boy.' Like . . . he means Kon?" Peter asked leaning in slightly to peer at the folder, increasingly interested.

"The EPS responded," Icelyn began. "We appreciate you notifying us. As of now, we have no information or evidence that another resides on Anaiess. We will keep an eye out, however, to aid how we can."

"He thinks there's another Avari here?" Kon asked, scrunching his nose.

"Seems like it. The messages stop there." Icelyn shook her head, closing the folder.

"Another Avari?" Peter said in awe. "And you've never seen them?"

Kon shook his head.

"Do you think the EPS ever found them?" Icelyn asked, just as Kon held out a hand for her to stop. He was looking at the door, listening to the subtle footsteps of someone coming down the hall. Kon quickly gestured for them to stay as he clicked off the light. The steps continued at an even pace as they slowly passed them. He gestured to Icelyn and Peter as they stood in the dark, the room only illuminated by the glow of the walls.

"What do we do?" Peter whispered.

"Wait," Kon growled, listening for the steps. He figured it was someone doing rounds, or maybe they noticed the cameras go out. After a long few seconds, the steps faded down the hall completely. "Come on." He cracked the door open, allowing enough light for them to follow. He checked both ways before exiting, holding the door for them. Carefully, he closed it before they headed back the way they came. The intersection was close. They just had to get back through the door.

As Peter and Icelyn followed, they almost collided with Kon who'd stopped, hand reaching out. He was listening.

"What?" Peter whispered.

Up ahead, coming down the hall, straight in front of the divider, another set of footsteps could be heard.

"Storage. Now," Kon said in a low voice.

Icelyn immediately turned for the closest door on the left. She yanked it open. To everyone's relief, it was unlocked. "Come on," she whispered.

The three of them stuffed themselves into the closet. It had a small bit of floor room but was fairly tight. There was only a dim hazy light on. Kon closed the door and leaned against the back of it as he kept listening. The footsteps were at the intersection, turning their way.

Peter shifted slightly in the cramped room. As he did, a broom dislodged itself from the wall between him and Icelyn. Icelyn reached to catch it, wincing as she grabbed it with her injured hand. Kon's hand fell over hers. Her hand was ice cold. They didn't dare move as the steps passed by. He released his hold on her hand as the steps became more distant. She laid the broom back, to the exhale of everyone.

"Sorry," Peter whispered.

Icelyn stifled a nervous chuckle while Kon gave a knitted brow.

Confident they had left, Kon opened the door, peeking out before they exited again.

"Let's hurry." Back at the intersection, Kon checked down the adjacent section, almost missing the sign above the single door. "Elemental Emergency Equipment." Something about it struck him as odd. Without a second thought, and with no one else coming, he quickly headed down the opposite hall.

"What are you doing?" Peter whispered as they followed, watching over a shoulder at their escape route.

Kon reached the door and tried it. Unlocked. As it slid open, he motioned them in before following. Upon closing the door, both of them were stopped in front of Kon, scowling as they took in the strange setup.

"What is all this?" Icelyn held her hand.

The room was small with steel shelves lining the walls. There were several kits labeled on the wall; some appeared to be medical equipment. Others, devices and scanners. Kon instantly felt a sickly familiar feeling, a rising pressure in his head. He scanned the shelves as he spotted it; a small bag labeled "Vinralinite." The protective wrap around the stone was concealing some of its effects, but not enough; the energy already pushing his own away.

As his head spun, Icelyn followed his gaze to the bag on the otherwise empty shelf. "Peter?"

"Yeah?" Peter joined them in their stare at the shelf.

"Why does an Elemental base have *Vinralin*?"

Peter glanced at the bag, then at Kon, with a look of horror. "He shouldn't be near that."

"Why do they have it?" Kon repeated in a cold tone, the heavy feeling in his head rising as he reached for the door.

"I don't know. Probably Elementals?"

"Come on, let's get out of here." Icelyn's voice had shifted an octave, as she watched Kon. Back out in the hall, his head spun, no longer aware of his surroundings. "Are you okay?" she said in a whisper, as she surveyed both halls.

He tried to shake the feeling from his head as the effects lessened. "I'm fine. Come on," he grumbled, a pit in his stomach. *They had Vinralin here. Why?*

Peter rushed for the heavy door, pausing in his tracks ahead of them. "The camera is back on," he breathed as the light blinked. Kon rubbed a drop of red from his nose as Peter faced them. "Are you okay?" He became frantic. "If I knew Vinralin was in there, I would've told you . . . I didn't even think about it—" he stuttered.

Kon stared at the smear of blood on his hand with a frown before looking up at the camera. After a few moments, it went out again. "Hurry," he said as they approached it, swiftly filing through the heavy door before Kon closed it. It locked upon closing. Safe.

No one spoke as they walked back until they were nearing the pool. Icelyn was still watching Kon, hands pulled to her chest. His usual frown was a bit deeper as he rubbed his temple.

"Oh my god," Peter breathed. "I can't believe we did that."

Icelyn let out a nervous chuckle. "Yeah. You think anyone noticed?"

"I hope not," Peter huffed, before looking back at Kon. "Are you sure you're okay?"

"Yes." The headache lingered. It would pass after a while, but the feeling of unease would be harder to get rid of.

As they got up the stairs and back into the main level, Peter's energy was coming back. "Why do I feel so amped up? I've got so much adrenaline right now."

Ahead of them, coming from the cafeteria, Stormy and Jyune were carrying a clipboard and a plate full of bagged cookies.

"I'd say that was our most successful evening," Stormy boasted as she saw the three headed her way. "Oh, hey! You guys missed our cookie reveal!"

Jyune checked over the clipboard. "Almost doubled our sales!"

"We saved you guys bags," Stormy said as they slowed. "Where even *were* you?"

"Uh . . . just showing Icelyn around," Peter said, stone-faced.

Icelyn nodded in agreement. "It's a big base."

Stormy started tossing each of them their bag of cookies. Peter dug into his immediately, still riled up with adrenaline. Icelyn caught hers in her injured palm, wincing a bit.

"Anyone want to help us deliver the rest of these? We got some room orders."

"Sure, I've got some energy to burn. Are we done?" Peter checked Kon and Icelyn for signs as he bit into a cookie. When he received a nod from both, he broke off from the group. "You two stay out of trouble, okay? Don't like . . . go to the pool without me," he hinted.

Kon raised a brow but stayed silent.

Icelyn nodded. "No problem. Thanks for the help."

"Okay, the room number is on each bag. Can you take the one hundreds?" Stormy began as they started to depart. "See ya' guys."

Jyune waved to them as they passed.

Kon and Icelyn lingered in the newly emptied hall. Luneduine had started to come out, much quieter than other students in their rush for the cafeteria. Icelyn held her bag of cookies, one hand still pulled to her chest.

"How is it?" Kon finally said.

"What?"

"Your hand."

Icelyn opened her palm where the bandage held a red stain. "Oh."

Kon moved his hand under hers gently to inspect it. "Let's see if the med bay is open."

"It's probably fine," she argued lightly. "I just need to stop moving it."

"C'mon." He started down the hall.

Icelyn's words came carefully, still keeping an eye on him. "So—did you find what you wanted? In the . . . database?"

He shrugged, trying to dispel any show of discomfort. "Enough for now."

"Do you think it's safe? I mean with the Vinralin and stuff too?"

"I don't know. I'll see what Para has to say," he said in a low tone, checking over his shoulder to ensure no one was around. There was silence in the halls as they walked. Only Luneduine moved about, safe to come out in the dim, red light.

Icelyn's eyes widened. "You're going to tell her you found it—?"

"Maybe," he shook his head, unsure yet if it was wise to bring it up.

Icelyn clutched her injured hand, staring at the ground. "I can't believe this morning I woke up in my bed back home. Now, I'm here."

Kon looked over her as the pain in his head subsided. "You should take it easy."

"I mean, stuff like that kinda helped me forget. It was kinda—fun. I feel like now, when things are quiet again, is when I start to kinda . . . realize."

"Realize?"

She chewed on her lip. "That everything is different."

He stayed quiet as a Luneduine passed them with books in their arms. "I think everyone here has a similar story."

She didn't respond at first, looking down at the ground as her light bangs flopped over her forehead. "So, how long have you been here? Everyone says you're new."

"Yesterday."

"Really? Para doesn't make *all* new students go out and save people, does she?" she joked.

"I don't think so," he reassured her. "I think she's trying to get me to stay."

"Do you think you will?" she asked, her icy eyes meeting his.

"I don't know."

"Well, I'm glad you stayed today. I don't know if I'd even be here otherwise."

The pit in his stomach grew.

As they passed Para's office, it was closed, though the med bay door was open in the distance. They slowly entered to see Jasamie reading a book at the desk. She looked up at them with slight surprise. "Hey, guys."

"We weren't sure if this was still open." Icelyn took a step in.

"Yeah, I'm just waiting for Nem to come pick up the night shift. Is everything okay?"

Icelyn held her hand. "Yeah, I just think I need another bandage. I might've opened it again."

Jasamie stood, giving her a tilt of the head.

Kon stepped back into the waiting room. He never liked medical places. He could hear their conversation going on as he ran a hand over his face, still trying to make sense of the Vinralin. He had never heard of safe houses carrying it. Why would they?

"Be careful with this for the next few days, okay?" Jasamie explained as she dabbed some ointment on Icelyn's hand before looking back at Kon. "What about you? Are you settling in too? No injuries from the encounters lately?"

"I'm fine." He glanced toward the exit at the sound of distant footsteps.

Jasamie applied a clean bandage, tossing out the old one. "Check in sometime tomorrow. Maybe lunch?" She stepped back. "And Alaura said you can start here when you're settled in."

A smile spread over Icelyn. "Really?"

Jasamie nodded. "Welcome aboard."

The gleam in Icelyn's expression stayed even as she headed for the door.

"Be careful with it," Jasamie called as a Luneduine girl with short pink hair walked in with a bag. "Hey, Nem."

Kon paused once they were back in the hallway, looking toward the exit. Icelyn lingered, watching him as her smile faded. Maybe it was obvious what he wanted to do. "You should go rest," he suggested, pushing his hands into his pockets.

"Are you leaving?" she asked in a small voice, one that made him feel a pang deep in his chest as she watched him.

"I'll be back," he said.

"Okay." She took a step back, her expression unconvinced. "I'll see you tomorrow?"

"Yeah."

"Thanks again." She gave him a last grin before she headed back down the hall.

He waited for another moment, his brows furrowed as he watched her, before turning toward the exit.

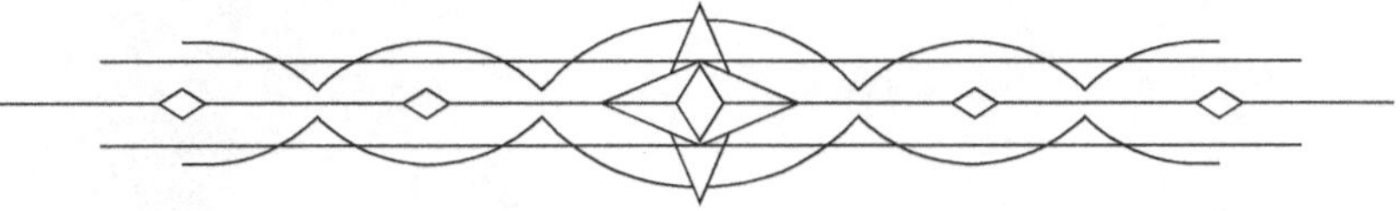

GARDEN CLUB
Find yourself
GAME NIGHT
Stop and Smell the Roses
COOKIE SALE
Stray Cats Club

CHAPTER 12
FINDING THE FLOW

The base lights were shifting to a cool daylight as the sun rose above the trees. Outside, the snow from the day before had melted, leaving only a cold dewy morning. The tall mountains around them still shined with snowy peaks. Kon approached the metal door on the floor of the field. It was weird seeing the base fully underground. At first, he didn't believe it could do what Para claimed, but coming back into the light, it was truly just a field. No sign of the base.

He also didn't believe that the door worked underground, but sure enough, the night before, he found that the base entrance led to a staircase that opened with a hatch in the ground, out into the field. Walking back, he searched for the subtle hidden hatch.

A quiet *coo* came from the grass. He turned to the stray cat lingering behind him. Para had mentioned that cats wandered around the field. Students often left food and treats for them. He had met a few of them in the woods around the base in his time outside. In his exploration of the surroundings, he had also found the woods around the base dotted with rose bushes. The sight of them only furthered the deep feeling that he had to go back. *At least, for now.* He gave the cat a last pet before pulling the hatch open.

As he entered down the stairs, he hoped it was still early enough to miss the bulk of people. The plump calico cat followed him down the dark steps as he adjusted the duffel bag over his shoulder. Carefully pushing the door open into the main hall, he glanced around. No sign of anyone. He made sure the door closed quietly as the cat joined him, seating itself in the open mural room in a casual sense. It seemed normal that the cat entered. Students likely let them inside from time to time.

Kon headed back down the hall, slowing slightly as he spotted it: Para's office door was open. With a tightened grip on his bag, he tried quickly to pass by, keen on avoiding questions.

"Kon?"

He stopped just past her office, sighing, before taking a step back to look in. Para sat at the desk, Ency on her lap, watching something on her monitor.

"Everything okay?" she asked as he stood still in the doorway.

"Yeah?" He narrowed a brow at her.

"We got the alert that someone left last night. I figured it was you," she explained, seeming to notice the bag on his shoulder. It was different from the one with which he arrived.

"I had to get more of my stuff," he pulled at the bag again, scanning the floor as he stayed put.

A smile grew across her face. "Of course. I'm glad you're back. No EME stalking around?"

"No, I checked." He carried on down the hall, leaving any remaining questions. There was some benefit to running into her. It seemed she knew nothing about their exploration the night before. A relief for Peter no doubt, but Kon still planned to bring up the Vinralin at some point—confront Para, or maybe Terrance, but not then. Peter was right; it had no negative effects on Elementals besides deactivating their powers, so having it around Elementals in itself wasn't a bad sign. However, how they got it was the looming question. Being one of the rarest materials on the planet, he had only ever seen the EME possess it.

Despite the alarming find, he still felt the database information gave him enough to stick around a bit longer. He had gotten into the habit over the years of leaving supplies around in the woods in case he ever lost his current bag. One specific supply was relatively nearby. He figured there was no harm in bringing it here if he planned to stay longer. Though leaving to get it late at night might've seemed like he was trying to sneak away, it was easier than trying to convince everyone he would return.

As he approached his room, the halls quiet with morning, he saw the familiar form waiting by his door. A breath escaped his lips at the sight of Peter. He paced back and forth outside the door, the book in his hand like usual. After a few more paces, he finally looked up, his expression filling with relief. "You're back!" Peter exclaimed, stopping in his tracks.

Kon slowed as he approached, giving Peter a dry tilt of the head as he reached the door.

"Where did you go? Icelyn said you left last night—"

"I said I'd be back," he murmured, pushing the door open.

"Well, she said that too, but I had to make sure." Peter stepped in as Kon went about his business, swinging his bag onto the bed. "You seemed mad last night after we found the . . . Vinralin."

"Wasn't mad." Kon placed his original bag beside the new one, opening it.

"I was just worried you . . . left." Peter shifted his feet, looking around the untouched room as Kon moved things around in his bag. "Do you think Para knows we went down there?"

"No." Kon zipped up his backpack and laid it aside before he turned to Peter finally, whose expression was riddled with guilt. "She doesn't."

"Are you feeling better? Vinralin effects usually wear off fairly fast."

"I'm fine."

"Are you sure?"

"Did you know they had it?" Kon asked plainly, watching him.

"I . . . I mean, yeah? I knew we had some somewhere." Peter rubbed his neck. "Like I said, it was just for Elementals who maybe come in upset and can't—control their powers . . ." He faded off.

Kon lingered a second longer before he headed for the door. "I'll see what Para says." The halls were cool and orange, still shifting color.

"What?" Peter tailed behind him, his expression turning to panic. "She'll know you went down there!"

"So?"

"We could get in trouble!"

"She doesn't have to know you were there." They rounded a turn, students heading for the cafeteria.

Peter struggled to keep pace with him. "Well, *someone* pointed you down there," he argued.

"I didn't need you to. I could've found it on my own. She knows that," Kon said in a low voice as they exited the dorms.

"Still—Terrance would be pissed."

"Okay." Kon paused outside the cafeteria. "Is there a reason I should be afraid of Terrance?"

Peter's face flashed confusion. "Uh . . . no? But—"

"Then just stay out of it. It's not your problem."

Peter's expression hovered on Kon with a frown before it drifted on someone behind him.

"You're back." Icelyn stood in the doorway. She held a mug in her hand, grinning cautiously. "Is everything okay?"

"Yeah," Kon mumbled.

"Are you guys getting breakfast? I've just gotten coffee so far," she explained, looking down into her mug.

"Yeah." Peter swiped a hand over messy hair.

Icelyn gestured for them to come in as she headed back to the table where Peter, Stormy, and Jyune usually sat in the far-right corner. Kon lingered, eyeing Para's office in the distance before he reluctantly followed them in.

"Wait, today is pancakes!" Peter exclaimed, a spring coming back in his step as he broke off to get in line.

Icelyn watched him before she sat down across from Kon. "Is he okay?"

"Something about last night. I don't know." Kon shrugged before he looked up at her. She had a cropped sweater on over a fitted shirt and her hair down, which was falling over her shoulders. He hadn't realized how long it was. "How's your hand?"

"Better. The medicine helped," she said as she rubbed the bandage on her hand before looking up to meet his gaze. "Did you just get back?" Steam rose from the mug in her hand.

"Yeah."

"You should get some sleep. You look tired." She pulled a strand of her hair over an ear.

"I did."

"Out there?"

Kon shrugged. "More used to it than here."

"Oh." Her eyes hovered over her sleeved hands, a minuscule crease in her blonde brow.

"What about you?" he asked. Her movements were a bit more cautious like the reality of her situation was finally setting in.

"Yeah, I got a little. More than I thought I would."

Peter finally returned with a plate of pancakes, eggs, a drink, and a grin on his face once again. "Are you guys getting in line? They make the best pancakes."

Kon shook his head while Icelyn stared into her cup again, giving a tiny nod. "Maybe in a bit."

"So, what's the plan now?" Peter asked, taking a swig of orange juice.

"What do you mean?" Kon asked in a bored tone, cheek resting on his fist.

"Since you found what you wanted in the database . . . what now?"

Icelyn watched Kon as well. He hesitated, not sure if he wanted to involve them further, but as they both waited, it seemed they were already involved. With a sigh, he sat up and reached into his pocket, pulling out the folded page. He unraveled it and placed it on the table. "Here," he growled.

Icelyn perked up and looked down at the map while Peter took a bite of his pancake. "The AIP base," Peter confirmed after a moment.

"Yes."

"You want to . . . go to it?" Peter asked.

"You said there was still stuff there."

"Yeah, I mean, Para thinks so, but we haven't been able to justify trying to get in. Even with it abandoned, the EME probably lurk around it a lot."

"Has anyone gotten in?" Kon asked.

"Not that we know of. It's locked down. I don't know how you'd—" Peter stopped, staring at Kon. "You could probably get in."

Icelyn nodded along with him. "Do you think there's something useful there?"

"I don't know," Kon admitted, looking down at the map. "Answers maybe."

"You don't think they've cleaned it out already?" Icelyn asked.

Peter shook his head. "The AIP Facility was probably more secure than any of the EME facilities. For in-person documents, the safest place to keep it away from everyone else was likely there." He poked at his pancake. "I mean, EME got the ruling to shut down the building after the Avari left. Anaiess government wanted everyone away from there."

"How do you know?" Kon argued. "They could've just gotten rid of everything."

"Well, I read up on it." Peter shrugged. "Shortly after the initial fight broke out, the government ordered EME and AIP staff to lock down the building and not return. They weren't allowed to take anything out either."

Kon frowned while Icelyn tapped her cup in thought. Behind him, Stormy and Jyune approached, their usual talk of cookies being loud. They stopped at the end of the table, stretching a bit. "Did you guys already eat?" Stormy asked as she looked between Icelyn and Kon.

Kon nodded while Icelyn shook her head.

"No, I should probably grab something." Icelyn rose from her seat and pushed her pale hair aside.

"Jyune, the usual?" Stormy asked as the Takti hopped down onto the table.

"Yeah." She yawned as she wobbled across the table. Jyune turned on her heel as her large eyes found the paper. Sinking into a sitting position, she inspected it, her small pink hand extending to touch it. "What's this?"

Kon started folding it up. "Nothing."

"A map? You going on a trip?"

"No."

"You're not leaving, are you?" she pressed.

"Jyune, leave him alone," Peter said through his food. "It's too early in the morning."

She looked over her shoulder at Peter, giving him a cold squint before she ran her tiny hands across one of her tagune. She had another beaded headpiece on, covering the start of the three soft tagunes on her head in place of hair. "Well, *I'm* a great navigator. I get myself and Stormy to Calirue all the time."

"How is that even comparable? Calirue is a straight path from here," Peter argued as Kon looked over toward Icelyn and Stormy getting their trays.

He tuned out the bulk of the fighting as he scanned the cafeteria. Most students were busy with a book or conversation. A few glanced at him from time to time. It probably *was* concerning to see an Avari here. It confirmed the legends that were whispered over the years, and it confirmed he was the EME's top priority—the thing they searched for above any Elemental. Now, he was here. Their fear wasn't unfounded.

He snapped back to his own table as Icelyn and Stormy sat their trays down. Icelyn pushed her hair over a shoulder, content with her tray. Her expression only folded when she met his, which must've shown trouble. "What?" she sat down cautiously, glancing at the other students.

"Nothing." He adjusted the collar of his jacket in some attempt to hide himself more.

Jyune was still going. "Well, I've navigated us to Darnar for baking ingredients, so how do you explain *that*?" she spat.

"You didn't say that. You said Calirue!" Peter clanked his cup down.

Icelyn examined her plate before her gaze darted back up to Kon with a look of surprise. He narrowed his eyes as she turned to Jyune. "Wait, Darnar?"

"Yep!" Jyune boasted.

"It's near here, right?" Icelyn inquired.

"Yeah, a ways south," Stormy said from beside Kon as she handed

Jyune an orange from her plate. "We get our chocolate chips down there sometimes. They have a great bakery."

Icelyn frowned at her plate again, lost in thought.

"I've never heard you say that you guys go down there," Peter argued.

"Well, we don't go that often." Stormy rolled her eyes, pulling at her pancake.

Their bickering continued. Jyune turned away from Kon and Icelyn as she peeled her orange on the middle of the table. Peter was still questioning the legitimacy of her claims as Kon stopped listening.

Icelyn was staring at her untouched pancake, frozen in thought. Finally, her eyes lifted to meet his, and she leaned in. "Darnar is where Garik Tally is," she whispered. "The guy that wrote the letter about—" she pursed her lips in place of the final words, careful to be discreet.

Kon understood enough, however, and nodded. "Maybe he's still there," he said in a low voice.

"You know," Stormy chirped, "this is the first time we've all sat down here together." She looked around the table, grinning.

"Yeah. Usually, it's just us three. Now, we got a real group going." Peter took another swig of his drink, pride in his smile.

"Everyone's all jealous we got the new people!" Jyune remarked in a smug tone. "They've been staring all morning."

They turned careful eyes to the rest of the cafeteria, where, sure enough, eyes watched back.

"I don't think that's why, Jyune." Peter glanced at Kon.

Kon pulled his undershirt farther over his hand, covering the few dark markings that strayed onto the top of it, rubbing his other hand over them as if he could simply wipe the markings away. When his eyes finally lifted from his fidgeting hands, Icelyn was peering at him with creased brows.

Stormy took another few bites of her pancakes before speaking. "Don't mind them," she said. "It's not every day new people come in."

"Also, we all kinda didn't think you existed too," Jyune admitted to Kon as she tore another section from her orange.

"Jyune!" Peter scolded.

Kon stayed quiet, focused back down at the table—the only place he could think to look where eyes wouldn't follow him. He could feel Icelyn watching him still, along with the eyes of who knew how many students from behind him. She only ate a few more bites of her pancake before she stood to dispose of her plate. When she approached again, she didn't sit but stood at the end of the table, fiddling with her own sleeve. "You want to help me find The Closet?" she asked Kon. "I don't want to keep stealing all of Stormy's clothes."

He didn't pass up the opportunity to get out of the cafeteria. The eyes of other students were getting to him. Spending the night back out in the woods had only heightened his discomfort for the commotion of the base, thus elevating the urge to simply flee back into the forest.

Back in the hall, Icelyn fluffed out her sweater, taking a breath of the cooler halls. "You seemed like you wanted out of there."

"Yeah, too busy," he said, shoving his hands in his pockets as he looked back at the doorway. Elemental eyes still lingered on him.

Icelyn combed through her hair as they walked. "Are you usually on your own? Out there?"

"Yeah."

"Seems . . . scary."

He glanced at her, remembering her recent experience in the woods was one being tailed by the EME. She had a right to be scared. "It's not so bad. Feels safer than this sometimes."

"Really?" she asked. "I'm not sure I'd have it in me." She chuckled, though her expression still held a tinge of trouble.

"You might."

Icelyn gave him a glimmer of a smile before looking away. Her hair sat in waves down her back before she perked up. "Oh, The Closet." She pulled out her map as they paused at the intersection between the cafeteria and Para's office. She held it out for them to look at. "I think it's . . . down this hall."

Kon leaned in to look, trying to make sense of the map in the quiet halls before a voice sounded out.

"Icelyn." They nearly jumped at the source of the deep voice. Terrance.

He was holding a clipboard, his usual stern look on his face. "I need to speak with you for a moment." His eyes drifted to Kon, whose gaze was defensively locked on him as they shared glares of disdain.

"Oh," Icelyn said, an edge to her quiet voice. "Sure." Kon watched her fold up her map and wrap her arms at her torso, her demeanor shifting. He switched between them, half expecting an answer of why, but she simply gave him a forced grin. "We can go to The Closet later, I guess."

She made her way to Terrance while Kon kept his scowl on him. Terrance gave Kon a last look over his shoulder before they departed. He found himself standing alone in the hall, feeling some mix of confusion and irritation. There wasn't much of an answer within his own mind about why he felt so defensive toward Terrance. Maybe the same authoritative demeanor he held was too often found on EME soldiers. Demanding of order and control. At least that's what it felt like. Maybe it was time for some answers of his own as he looked toward Para's office, the door open.

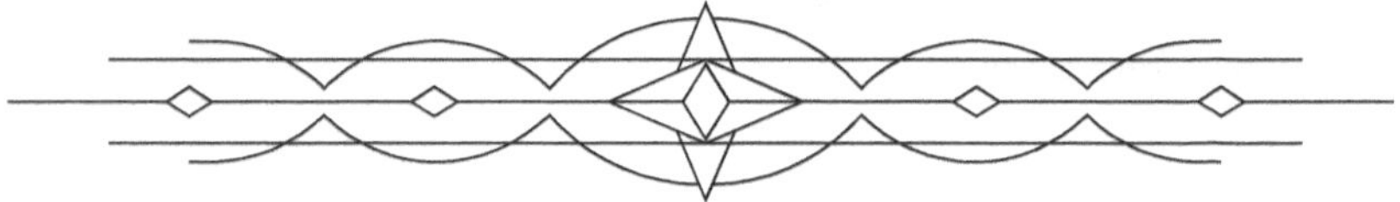

CHAPTER
13
DEPARTURE

MARCH 2653

Fifteen years since Avari left.

The green house with the barn was quiet. Mallia had hardly spoken at all—a stark contrast from the days before when she had fought hard to change Kon's mind. She and Joel knew he wouldn't stay forever, and Kon knew he *couldn't* stay forever, but it still stung.

"Got everything?" Joel asked, his voice much softer than usual. There was a hoarseness to his tone as he followed Kon out of the hallway. Mallia lingered in the kitchen, watching silently. Her eyes had been puffy for days leading up to that. She had thrown every solution at him, even begging him to wait a year, until he was sixteen. Anything to prolong it. It hadn't worked.

"Yeah." Kon pulled his backpack over his shoulder, packed with items he'd need, though he kept it light.

"Here." Joel held his large jacket, extending it to him. "It'll keep you warm."

Kon blinked at it before meeting his gaze. "Are you sure?" It was one of Joel's favorites. One he wore often.

"Yeah." He grinned. "It was my brother's. Was always too big for me anyway. You'll grow into it."

Kon dropped his bag next to him and took it carefully. "Thanks."

Mallia grew antsy as he put the jacket on and reached for his bag again. "Are you sure about this?" Her voice was hardly a croak. "It's *safe* here."

Kon gave her a pained look, wishing she would accept it. "They've been trying to sweep Calka for months. I need to be gone when they get in." EME in the area had only gotten worse. Ever since his run-in with them a little over two years before, things had been getting scarier. It was a matter of *when*, not *if* they'd finally get through.

"We could leave town…together. I'll go pack now. We can move towns—"

"No," Kon said, as gently as he could. "They're already watching you guys. I'll be okay." Joel had propositioned a similar idea to him: that they leave for his brother's old cabin. The one they camped at. Hide out for as long as they could. Kon was always quick to decline it. The EME was after *him*. If Joel disappeared from Calka, they would know it was for good reason. After that, it wouldn't take long for them to be after him, connecting the dots that an old Avari mentor fled town right before an EME search. Once they started, Joel and Mallia would never live a normal life again. They'd be on the run with him. He couldn't do that to them. Not even if they begged him. Her eyes were glossing over again as he gave her a smile and headed for the door.

"Alright, remember—you have the communicator if you ever . . . need us," Joel began as they stepped onto the porch. "Get to the cabin, stay there for a while if you can. Call us when you get in. And if things get scary—if there are too many EME—please, just come back."

"I will," Kon nodded.

Mallia followed them out, still distant.

Joel held back, looking down as he composed himself. "Be careful." Joel pulled Kon in for an embrace, his height finally matching Joel's.

"Thank you for everything," Kon whispered before he drew back and headed down the steps, turning to give them another smile. Joel held Mallia, who pushed tears from her cheek as she waved weakly.

He headed for the woods. He had plans: go south and get to the cabin. Avoid the Core Sector, it was too busy. Too many EME. Look for some of the safe houses set up in the east. Maybe they would have information, something to help him. Joel had named off a few other mentors he wanted him to find as well, hoping they would know something about the Avari, about him. Kon tried to sound more confident about his plan than he was. In reality, his biggest fear was losing them the same way he lost Seelia and Jack. It wasn't going to happen like that again. That was why he had to go.

"Kon!" Mallia called as she rushed down the stairs and across the field. She caught him in an embrace. "Please come back one day." Her muffled sobs fell into his shirt.

"I'll try," he wrapped his arms around her as he looked back at Joel, who had turned away, hand on his head. "Take care of him, okay?"

"I will." She drew back finally, looking up at him. "Here." She untethered her bracelet from her wrist and put it onto his—a delicate purple bracelet with tiny beads shaped in flowers and silver details. "Dad's jacket and my bracelet. A piece from both of us."

"Are you sure?"

"Yeah," she said, taking a big sniffle to hold herself together. Her mouth curled to form her best attempt at a smile.

"I'll see you guys soon. I promise." He grinned, making an effort to keep his own emotions at bay. There was no use letting them get the better of him. This was the only way to keep them safe. He was ready.

His powers had developed in the last few years. Confident with his control over them, Joel agreed he was capable of defending himself. He hadn't had any run-ins with the EME since he was thirteen. Part of him worried that maybe he wouldn't be prepared. No matter the amount of practice, nothing was like the real situation. They had worked on every scenario. Everything that could cause him to falter. Joel pushed him to work on his fear of the EME, to ensure even that wouldn't hold him back. That he could override the fear and turn it into something useful. Energy. Controlled power.

Joel had also taught him everything he possibly could about surviving on his own while traveling through the wilderness. Kon was usually eager to pick the information up, knowing it was something that would be vitally important to him. He was coming to terms with the fact he would have to live outside of society if he wanted to stay safe and unseen.

Getting to the cabin by himself was a nerve-racking trek in itself. He and Joel usually took a hoverbus to a closer town and walked from there. But with his markings dark enough to notice from a distance, towns and transportation were out of the question. Joel had suggested he climb to a nearby ridge overlooking the small town. It might help to see the path ahead, so he did. From the tall ridge, he could see for miles. Calin was just behind the distant mountain. The cabin was in the opposite direction, south of there. It had to be one of the best views he had seen. It even beat the cabin's view of the mountain. Mallia would've been starstruck up there. Maybe one day he could show her when it was safer. But for now, the view was all his, and he took in the sun casting across every tree in the valley. Despite the ache in his heart, it felt full, confident about the plan. It would keep everyone safe.

He was met with a comforting relief when his knowledge and map accurately led him to the dusty old cabin in the tall evergreens. Joel had stocked it a few months back after EME activity hit Calka again, and the usual fights at the township hadn't gone well. It had almost pushed them into hiding had the Elemental Protection System not provided an override to the search. As grateful as they were for the EPS helping, it was merely a band-aid to a growing problem. It wasn't long after that Kon sparked the idea to Joel about leaving. By himself. Joel pushed hard to join him, but in the end, Kon stood steady on his choice. But in the silence of the log cabin, he felt the weight of the decision he had made, for himself and them.

Canned food lined the shelves while blankets and supplies sat in baskets around the kitchen. The wooden floors were thick with dust. The power hardly worked, one weak light illuminating the kitchen. As confident as he was in his decision, he couldn't help the feeling of loneliness. It wouldn't be a life for either Joel or Mallia, though. Mallia deserved the flower shop of her dreams, the garden she had always wanted in town. Joel deserved his quiet life in Calka, free from prying EME eyes. A normal life. No matter the empty spot in his heart, he was glad they weren't there.

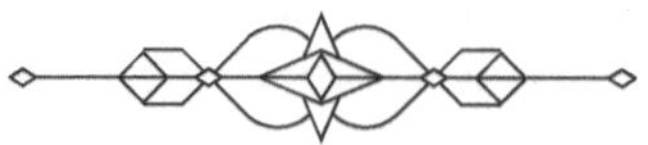

He contacted them the next day with his small communicator while sorting through the supplies. Joel had told him to call at least when he arrived. Kon worried if he didn't, they'd end up at the cabin by the end of the day looking for him. In typical fashion, Mallia wanted to visit immediately while Joel spoke more distantly of the EME at the borders of Calka again. It was in their best interest to purge the house of signs of him. If there would be a search, there could be no signs Kon had ever existed in that house. He promised he was fine; exploring the forest around him, content with his supplies. They could focus on themselves.

After hardly a month there, while traversing the mountains near the cabin, he heard it; the low roar. At first, he thought it to be thunder, but when it prolonged, drawing closer, he finally saw it for the first time. A hoverform. EME, no doubt. There was hardly any other reason to use one in Brynden Ka. It lurked over the distant trees, heading west, thankfully past the cabin. But why was it here?

In all the times they had come to the cabin, there hadn't been a single sign of the EME. Joel had been trying to call all the while, warning Kon that an Elemental safe house near the cabin had been raided. There would surely be ripples from the raid. Elementals had escaped, fleeing in all directions, including toward Kon. That night, they sat on the comms together, listening to the radio. There was a small one in the cabin, rigged to pick up the nearby chatter better than the one in Calka. It had always stayed silent until then.

Sure enough, the EME was starting to search. They would be at the cabin any day. He heard Mallia in the background, begging him to come back home. Even if the EME searches had turned up nothing, it wasn't safe.

He left the cabin the next morning, heading east from the ripple. Joel had suggested a safe house in that direction and even suggested that he could contact the EPS for Kon, but Kon had his own plans. It was his journey. To find answers, to find himself. He was heading away from the danger, but something in him knew he'd find the EME waiting for him wherever he went.

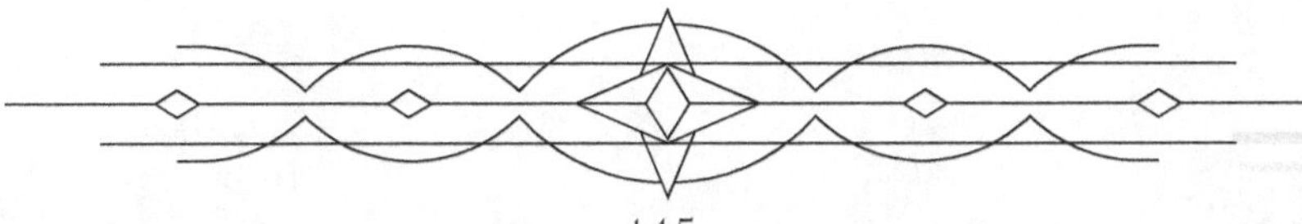

CHAPTER 14
FROZEN PASTS

Present Day

"Terrance thinks we need to up security." Para chuckled. "Someone let a cat in again."

"Does he not like them?" Alaura frowned. "I don't think that's going to stop the Stray Cats Club from letting them in."

Para gave a shrug, oblivious to the company until she peered up from the screen, where Kon waited at the door. Kon watched her expression turn from momentary confusion to a smile. "Kon, come in." Para was dressed in a casual undershirt and a cardigan, her hair in its usual braid. He only entered a few steps, his expression unwavering.

"How is Icelyn settling in?" Alaura asked, trying to spark conversation.

"What does Terrance want with her?" he asked.

Para exchanged looks with Alaura. "There were some discrepancies in her entry interview we wanted to check. Nothing serious."

Kon bit his lip as he stared down at the floor, playing with his next words carefully. He wanted answers, but there were certainly right and wrong ways to go about it. Regardless, Peter wouldn't be happy. "What's the Vinralin for?" he finally said, meeting her gaze.

Para's mouth parted slightly, as her breath paused in realization. Slowly, she let Ency off her lap and straightened. "Did someone mention it?"

He shook his head, keeping his stance steady.

She sighed, her expression falling a bit. "Where did you find it?"

"You have *more* of it?"

"I'm—not sure what you saw, but it's in the Defensive Wing for emergencies."

"What kind of emergencies?" Kon asked, lifting his chin.

Alaura interjected, holding out a hand. "Vinralin doesn't cause any adverse effects on Elementals. Sometimes, students need it to help settle their abilities."

"It was *never* here for you," Para said. "We understand its effects. We'll keep it far away from you."

"Where'd you get it?" he asked, looking between them.

"The EME used to carry it sometimes on scouting parties. Once we realized this, we started apprehending some a few years back. We got a fair bit of Vinralin away from them. They stopped carrying it in smaller groups once they realized we were after it," Para explained.

"The more of it we have, the less they do," Alaura added.

Kon stayed quiet, monitoring their expressions. Her explanation made sense. He had noticed the lack of Vinralin in smaller EME groups, something he should probably thank them for, as it had always been a hassle dodging groups that carried it.

"You're completely safe from it," Para said. "What else did you find?" Her tone was soft, different from how he expected her to react. Neither she nor Alaura held anything of warning in their movements. Both of them were steady in their seats, watching him.

He let out a sigh, frowning at the thought of his next words. "If you know who I am," he said in a calm tone, "why did you and Terrance act like you didn't?" It wasn't the time to admit sneaking into the database. At least not outright.

Para pursed her lips as she formed her response. "We didn't want to freak you out."

"How long have you known about me?" Kon asked.

Alaura watched him carefully, as though she was inspecting his movements the same way he was theirs. She reached over the back of her chair and pushed the door slightly closed. Para activated her digipad screen and started navigating through it. "Well, it was nothing beyond speculation for a while," she said, typing something into her files. "Then we got a call from someone who said they knew you and feared you were in trouble. They wanted us to intervene. That's how we found out EME had been tracking an Avari up north. When you got here, we figured it was you."

Kon met her eye now, dread slowly filling his chest. "Someone that knew me?" The words were hollow as the realization sunk deeper.

She finally found the right file and brought it up, reading it for a moment, "Someone by the name of Joel Gavins." She glanced at Kon, but after no response, she continued, "He told us that he was certain the EME had apprehended an Avari—you. He knew you well and asked us to go get you." Her head hung slightly in shame. "We didn't have the resources to get into Kain Kodan. Not at the time."

Kon winced at the name of the Northern EME base, once again feeling his breathing increase with his racing thoughts. He hadn't realized Joel even knew about those events. He must have been watching the EME radios, like he usually did, and heard the commotion. After leaving the Gavins when he was fifteen, he had only made it a year before the EME closed in on him the first time. He left to keep them safe, to draw EME away from Calka—the same reason he'd never gone back, despite missing them. He should've known Joel would find out about it and try to help. He composed himself, taking a breath as he toyed with his hands. "Have you talked to him since?" There was a pit in his stomach. What if Joel had tried to get involved?

"That was the only contact we had with him," Para said. "But it was a secure line. They wouldn't have traced anything back to him from contacting us. He just wanted you . . . safe."

Kon stifled a nod. A familiar deep wound rose to the surface of his thoughts. He took a step back, his expression a hazy focus on the ground as he moved toward the door. "Okay." His mind worked through all the ways he could check on Joel and Mallia. None of them would be safe for them—or him.

"You haven't talked to him either?" Para asked, trying to keep him around a bit longer as Alaura watched quietly.

"Wouldn't be safe."

"Well, is there anything else you wanted to ask about?" She sat up more, casting an eye on Alaura.

His gaze lifted to meet hers. "No." With a push of the door, he made his way out.

Back in the hall, Kon felt a rising anger at himself. He should've tried to keep a closer eye on the Gavins. His distance may have only blurred his ability to keep them safe. *What if they weren't safe anymore?* He glanced down the curved hall. No sign of Icelyn yet. As he looked back toward the cafeteria, a scene was arising just outside the doorway.

Peter gathered his book as he headed for the cafeteria exit. Stormy and Jyune remained at the table, reading over a folder. As he reached the open doorway, he felt refreshed. Kon was back, and it seemed like he would be staying a while. Para had little idea of their secret investigation the night before, and he felt a wave of positivity. *It would be a good day,* he thought, just as he collided with someone. Stepping back to apologize, he paused when he saw the broad shoulders and brown hair of the boy standing before him. Darren.

"Made new friends, huh?" Darren asked with a snide tilt of his head.

Peter took a step back as he noticed the band of three. Darren and his friends always meant trouble. "Uh, yeah?"

The three seemed to position themselves around him, cornering him. "I gotta admit, I didn't expect an Avari to walk in here. I bet you're over the moon," Darren said as he crossed his arms, his short messy hair spiking out above his furrowed brow.

"I mean . . . it's good that he's here. He can help us," Peter said, clutching his book extra tight.

"You think?" Darren shook his head and scoffed. "I think you've got that backward."

"What do you mean?" Peter said.

The teen looked annoyed at him as he shifted his weight. He was a good bit taller than Peter as he loomed over him. "Of course, *you'd* think it was a good thing he's here. We don't think so. Why should we help an Avari hide? They've only ever screwed us over."

Peter looked between the three nervously, but a strange defensiveness was growing in him. "Kon had nothing to do with that—"

"And when he leads the EME straight to this place? I bet you he'll act like he had nothing to do with that *either*." Darren sneered before his mocking grin faded, leaving a dark mist in his hazy green eyes.

Peter felt a pang in his chest, but beneath it, hot anger. "He's . . . here to help." It wasn't like him to entertain Darren's mocking nature, but the urge to defend his new friend was strong today.

He laughed as he loomed closer. "C'mon, Pete. I don't think even *you* believe that."

"What do you want from me?" Peter spat, frowning up at him defensively.

Darren leaned in, inches from Peter. "I want you to tell him to get out of here. Save us the trouble."

Peter's cautious expression held for a moment before it faded as his eyes drifted from Darren to slightly behind him, where defiance filled his gaze. "Why don't you tell him yourself?"

Darren drew back, confused, before a flicker of realization set in his eyes as he turned around.

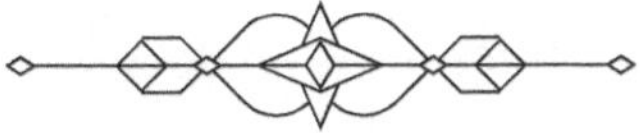

Kon stood, watching Darren. He tilted his head slightly as if asking him to repeat his statement. Darren stared, perhaps not gathering how Kon towered over him until then. His expression held stiff for a moment as if he planned to carry out Peter's request, but his deep breath didn't bring words. It simply fizzled out as his brow folded into uncertainty, and he backed away. His friends did little to hide their fidgeting as they moved. Without another word, Darren escaped down the hall.

Peter let out a smiling gasp. "I've *never* seen Darren run from someone." He turned back to Kon, who was still watching the group leave.

"I take it he doesn't like me." Kon watched the boys escape, ensuring he'd remember them should they cross his path again.

"He's always like that. The other day, he threw my book in the trash," Peter said.

Kon scrunched his nose. "Why?"

"I don't know. He's just a bully. Insecure maybe." He glanced over his shoulder as they disappeared around a corner. "Everyone here deals with their situation differently."

"Does anyone ever do anything?"

"Not really. He's got a crazy temper. Doesn't help that his element is fire." Peter shrugged. "I think you scared him, though. I've never seen him do *that*."

"Do other students want me gone too?"

"What? No! You just got here." Peter scoffed. "He's just one of those Elementals looking for someone to blame."

Kon's gaze found the floor as some students passed in and out of the cafeteria around them. "So, you're good?"

"Yeah, I'm fine. He's probably pissed." Peter chuckled, seemingly giddy.

"He can come be pissed at me next time." Kon turned to look back down the hall, still watching for the familiar pale hair of Icelyn.

"I was headed to the library. You?" Peter asked, a beam still plastered on his face.

Kon stuck his hands in his jacket and shook his head. "I think I'll wait for Icelyn. Terrance took her."

"Huh. She must know something interesting." Peter pushed his book back to one arm, loosening his stance.

"What do you mean?" Kon tilted his head as several students made a wide path around him.

"Oh, I don't know. Sometimes, they pull students back in a second time if they witnessed something useful or know something." He shrugged again. "Anyway, I'll catch up with you guys later. I've got a lead to chase. You'll see." He grinned before heading down the hall, a pep back in his step.

Kon watched him for a moment longer before he looked back toward the Defensive Wing. *Know something? What could Icelyn know?*

He headed down the hall Icelyn had originally pointed down in her search for The Closet. Checking once more to see if she was perhaps coming back, to no avail, he kept going. The last time he had explored that way, it led to a steep set of steps into the next hallway. But with the base underground, the stairs had disappeared, leveling the floor with the rest of the underground base.

It was only a short walk to the first intersection before he saw the large sign on a door to the left, "The Closet." He approached it as students filtered in and out. Some were bringing in baskets of clothes while others were leaving with bags of outfits. It seemed like it was its own small functioning clothing store. At least he knew where it was now for Icelyn. He took in some of the other doors. Most were labeled like classrooms. Some students had notebooks and binders in their hands for the start of the morning classes.

"Kon?" A voice spoke from behind him. Jasamie was coming from The Closet, dressed in a heavy sweater, dark curls in two buns. "I saw you leave last night. Is everything okay?" She joined him across the hall.

"Yeah." He ran a hand through his hair as he recoiled from the acknowledgment.

"Did you come to shop? We just got a shipment in. Probably some Rilinquin stuff that'll fit you." She pointed to the doorway.

"No. Icelyn was looking for it," he said as students eyed him.

"Where is she? Is she doing okay today?"

"Terrance wanted to talk to her."

"Oh." Jasamie blinked, a crease layering her brow.

"Is that bad?" Kon asked.

"I hope not. They probably just had more questions. C'mon, we can go check." She gestured for him to join her, watching him with her warm brown eyes. As they rounded the corner back to the main hall she said, "He's not so bad."

Kon glanced down at her. "Who?"

"Terrance. I mean, sometimes students are afraid of him, but he kind of just tries to keep that appearance," she explained. "He and my dad go *way* back. I babysit his and Para's kids all the time. Away from the Base, he's okay . . ." She trailed off as they rounded the last corner toward the med bay and Defensive Wing, where they found Icelyn walking back. They slowed as she neared, her arms crossed and head down. Kon and Jasamie exchanged glances. Icelyn's eyes were red and puffy, watery with tears. Her light bangs were slightly messy, as though she'd been wiping tears from her face. "Icelyn? Are you okay?" Jasamie asked as she approached in a hurry.

"I'm fine," she said, voice cracking. She avoided their eyes, passing by them swiftly as she rushed down the hall.

The two stood in silence before Jasamie beckoned for Kon to follow as she fell in behind Icelyn. "What happened?" she inquired as they passed the cafeteria.

Icelyn's head shook back and forth from ahead, her pale wavy hair bouncing with her quick steps. She headed past the dorms and then turned a corner. The sunroom. There was a twist of anger in Kon. *What did Terrance say?* Upon arrival, she ran up the steps into the dark room. Kon caught the door and held it for Jasamie as they fell in behind her. The theater-like room was dark, the base still underground. Tiny lights dotted the floor, marking the steps in the otherwise dimly lit empty room. Icelyn stepped down the first step and promptly fell into a seat, knees at her chest as she covered her face in her hands.

Jasamie moved to sit next to her, though Kon was slower to join. Jasamie rubbed Icelyn's shoulder gently. "It's okay."

Icelyn let out a sniffle as she collected herself in her hands. Kon sat on the other side of her, a bit farther away.

"What happened?" he asked again.

She uncovered her face and took in a deep breath. "I'm sorry," she sniffled. "He was just asking about Alinth, my dad. I should've said something yesterday."

"Said something about what?" Jasamie asked, still rubbing her shoulder.

Icelyn's shoulders dropped as her brows creased. "He's an EME officer." She wiped a tear from her cheek. "I was afraid to mention it—in case . . ."

The words were slow to sink in for Kon.

"So, he found out you were an Elemental?" Jasamie asked.

Icelyn shook her head, guilt across her face. "He already knew. He wanted me to go to an EME program for Elementals. I wanted to go into medicine. I kept thinking he would . . . change his mind before I finished school. He didn't." She folded her arms around herself. "So, I left."

Kon held back the scrunch in his nose as the words replayed in his head. *EME program for Elementals.* Of course, they had a system or school for Elementals. It was all part of their attempt at a good image: shuffle less dangerous Elementals into flashy, clean programs for the media, while the rest of them funneled into one of the larger locked-down bases around the peninsula. That was the side they didn't show the rest of the nation.

"You poor thing." Jasamie pulled her in for a hug. "It wasn't your fault. How could he have tried to do that to his daughter?"

Icelyn pulled back, an edge of iciness in her voice. "I should've left sooner. It's sick. The EME quietly takes care of the Elementals they care about while doing all of this to the rest of them. How is that fair? I was just scared to leave. I was stupid, naive—selfish." Her words spilled out like she had been holding them in for far too long as her eyes welled with another wave of tears.

"You did what kept you safe," Kon said, causing her to look at him. "It wouldn't have helped anyone to put yourself in danger."

Her eyes widened slightly before they softened on him. Silenced by his opinion, it was as if she had expected anger from him.

"What matters is you're here now, and your dad's stupid plan failed," Jasamie said, placing her hand on Icelyn's arm.

"What did Terrance think?" Kon asked as she calmed herself.

"I don't know. He seemed . . . disappointed? He wanted to know more about my dad and Alinth and that program. I just . . . felt like I let him down. Let all of you down."

"No," Jasamie said. "No. You did what you had to until you could get away. You did nothing wrong." She paused for a moment to think. "Do you have family somewhere else? Someone who would accept you? Para always tries to get students to stay with safe family first and foremost."

Icelyn rubbed her face and straightened, pushing her hair back. "No. Just my dad's family. Most of my mom's relatives are back on Makova," she said, looking at the floor.

Kon's gaze flickered to her hair at the mention of Makova, another planet. Her almost-white hair was unusual for a human. Makovan people had white hair and blotches of unpigmented skin in fancy patterns across their bodies. She didn't look full Makovan, likely part human.

"Well then, you're safe here," Jasamie said. "This kind of thing likes to sneak up on students after a day or two. It's why we recommend taking it easy."

Icelyn stifled a nod, pushing the last of the tears from her eyes as she took heavy breaths.

Jasamie tilted her head, trying to see Icelyn beneath her long pale hair. "Do you want to distract yourself with something maybe?"

Icelyn shrugged.

"Did Para mention anything? Something you could look into? Sometimes she suggests classes or activities to distract your mind."

Icelyn was quiet for a moment. "She mentioned me getting help for my . . . power. I don't know how to use it." There was still an edge in her voice.

"Okay, so let's go see Alaura about your powers and go from there? Good?"

Icelyn looked to Jasamie, then Kon. He gave her a tiny nod.

She took a deep breath. "Okay."

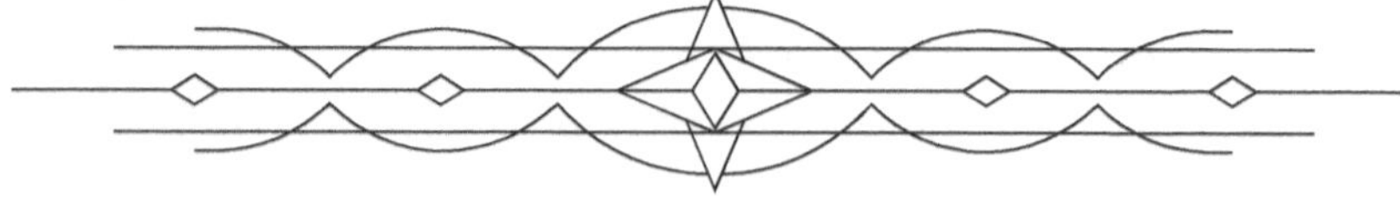

Elemental Phemone[...]
When dormant, energy stays in the body or near. Certain situations of stress or strong emotions can lead energy to stray farther from the body.
Shield
A secondary energy is also present in Elementals. It stays inside the body and on the surface, invisible to the eye. It provides a barrier, preventing Elemental energy from igniting within the body or too close to skin, avoiding bodily harm.

CHAPTER 15
ELMENDARIN

"You've never conjured anything? Used it in any way?" Alaura asked as she looked over Icelyn.

"No . . . Not knowingly. I just alerted a scanner when I was younger." Icelyn rubbed her arm, staring at the floor of the med bay. Jasamie and Kon lingered behind her. Kon kept an eye on her as she shifted back and forth.

"Come," Alaura said, directing her into the waiting room as she opened the other door, leading into a sizable office of sorts.

"Alaura's a seer; she can help with assessing your power," Jasamie said, giving her an encouraging nod. Icelyn watched Alaura while biting her lip but followed along. Kon had heard of seers—Elementals whose skill was mainly mental abilities and controlling others' mental abilities or being able to assess their brain for information on mood or truth. With it came the ability to sometimes see other Elementals' energy and even diagnose its type. It made sense that she was a medic. Seers were notoriously good at spotting injuries.

"Do you want them to join you?" Alaura asked, gesturing to the two others.

"Sure," Icelyn said as she stepped in, looking back at them with pursed lips.

Alaura offered the two tagalongs to come in before she closed the door. The office didn't hold the same medical vibe the med bay did. The walls were a warmer tone with accents of wood paneling on the lower half. There was a brown couch by the door and a desk centered against the far wall. Medical and Elemental posters lined the walls of various kinds. Alaura took a seat at her desk, grabbing a paper from a drawer as she motioned for Icelyn to sit. "Are you able to feel when your powers are around?" Alaura asked, running her eyes over Icelyn.

"I think . . . sometimes," Icelyn said, looking at her hands in her lap.

"It's faint. I see a bit of it." Alaura narrowed her eyes.

"You can *see* it?" Icelyn asked.

"Yes. I see others' Elmendarin energy," Alaura said. "Yours has settled a bit more since you got here."

"What does it look like?" Icelyn looked herself over as if she might catch a glimpse of her own power.

"It differs with each power. Yours is faint, light, like a fog. I assume it's something to do with temperature."

"What about his?" Icelyn looked back at Kon, who had his arms crossed, watching them. He met her eye with a tilt of the head.

Alaura's gaze drifted past her. "Colorful. It's strange. A bit distracting."

Kon could feel Elementals sometimes, but he had never seen the colors she described. He watched Icelyn, her shoulders still bunched from the earlier upset.

"Anyway," Alaura began, rolling the pen in her hand, "do you have temperature fluctuations often?"

Icelyn shrunk. "Yeah, I get cold a lot."

Alaura wrote something on the paper, glancing over her with cold green eyes. "Mhm. I think your Elemendarin energy is kicking up. Possibly stress-induced."

"The . . . cold is my power?"

"I believe so. Can I see your hand?" She finished writing and leaned forward, extending her hand as Icelyn scooted in and held out her own.

"Try to channel what you can. Even if you don't know how, usually your subconscious does." Alaura held her hand next to Icelyn's.

Icelyn frowned and stared at her hand, concentrating on the unseen energy. "Is it doing anything?" she asked after a few seconds of painful silence.

"A bit. This type of energy is invisible, but it's there. Do you feel the cold?"

"Yeah, I think so." Icelyn moved her fingers.

"It's faint. Your shield isn't conjuring with it, though." Alaura moved her hand back to write something else down. "Could explain why you feel cold often."

"My shield?"

"You shouldn't be able to feel the effects of the cold in your hand when you channel it. Along with Elmendarin energy, there's a second energy that comes with it. Avari called it 'Shynn,' I believe. It stays close to your body and acts as a shield against your own powers. It's how fire Elementals can conjure fire without burning themselves." She gestured up to one of the posters. It was a drawing of a hand. Closer around the hand was a line, labeled "shield." Outside the line was a second, more jagged mark surrounding the hand, marked "Elmendarin."

"Thankfully, your powers seem faint, and the only negative effect you get from the lack of shield is feeling a bit of cold. We should try and work on it, though, so you don't experience those flare-ups as bad."

"You think it can be fixed?" Icelyn asked, pulling her hand back as she looked it over as if she was still attempting to see any sign of the invisible energy around her hand.

Alaura's reply was casual. "You just need to practice with it, get your body used to how it works. It'll work itself out in time. If it gets worse, we can evaluate for Nemos Corpsa."

Icelyn tilted her head. "What's . . . that?"

"It's when the body rejects the powers, like an allergy. I don't think you have it, though." She grabbed a second paper. "I'm going to sign you up for an Elemental class. It might help. If you decide not to go—and it is your choice—just practice intentionally channeling it in your hand like you just did. See if the cold feeling starts to go away when you channel."

Icelyn nodded, still looking at her hand. "And the . . . *Elmedarin?* Energy? Is my Elemental power?"

"Elmendarin," she corrected. "The Avari shed a lot of light on how the energy works when they were still here." She glanced at Kon. "Thankfully, we now have names and science for it."

Icelyn plucked at her hair. "What all does mine do?"

"Well, temperature can range. Some fire Elementals can only heat the air around them. Some can make entire flames. I'm not sure how strong yours *can* get. You may be able to freeze things in the future. Hard to say until you start practicing." Icelyn nodded as Alaura finished up the second page and handed it over to her. It had a class name, room number, time, and a small map with directions. "These classes are open every day. Go as often as you feel you need," she said, before looking back at Kon. "Although, you have a teacher with you already. He may be able to help you practice."

Icelyn peeked over a shoulder with a small grin, where Kon lifted his chin slightly in protest but remained quiet. "Okay, thank you." There was an uncertainty in Icelyn's tone as she started to stand.

Jasamie grabbed the door as they exited. "It's time for my shift. I'll catch up later?" Jasamie said, stepping back toward the med bay.

Icelyn nodded and gave her a smile. "Sure, thanks."

"Take it easy." She looked from Icelyn to Kon, giving him a look of trust as she departed.

Back in the hallway, Icelyn toyed with the paper in her hand. "I wish I could see my powers."

Kon stayed quiet as she stepped around him, assessing her movement. She still seemed troubled, swaying slightly as she read over the paper in her hand.

"You think you'll practice?"

"I guess I should, right? What's the point of being in an Elemental safe house if I can't even use my powers?" she said with a frown.

"It's not like they'll kick you out." Movement caught his eye in the distance, where he saw the beginning of the Defensive Wing hallway.

"You don't think?" she asked.

He met her eyes. They were wide, laced with a very real, subtle fear. His casual comment was a true fear to her. He hadn't figured out what Para's plans with students were yet. If any safe house planned to train Elementals to fight back, that would be the place. Their best weapon against the EME was surely themselves. Even the EME had gone down the route of using Elementals against other Elementals, but surely Para didn't expect every student to prepare to fight. "No, you're fine."

Her gaze followed his toward the door as she inched back into his vision. "Are you leaving again?"

"I don't know."

"Want to go see what these classes are? They start soon. Might be interesting," she offered, holding the paper up.

His mind still lingered on Joel, having been thinking of the trek back to Calka since Para brought it up. He could probably get there in a few days, but the bigger issue of the rising EME groups was still a problem— the Core Sector EME that he and Para had run into, along with the various other groups he had been avoiding before that. Their movement was getting erratic again. There was an uncomfortable familiarity in the building tension. *They've done this before.* If he could even get to Calka, there was no saying if he'd manage to check on them or even get back to the base afterward. They would surely assume he wasn't coming back. "Sure," he finally said, turning from the exit. He needed time to think of a better solution anyway.

A smile spread over her face as they started down the hall. The map on the paper led back toward the classrooms. "Did anyone train *you*?" she asked as they walked.

Kon was careful to answer. "A few pointers when I was younger."

"You learned the rest on your own?" She cocked her head to the side.

"There's not many teachers around here." There was a subtle amuse-ment in his tone.

"Right." She shook her head as they reached the intersection into the hall of classrooms. She read the room numbers, turning in the direction of The Closet. Peering into the room labeled "The Closet," students were busy moving in and out. Racks of clothes sat center of the room while more lined the walls. The space was filled to the brim with clothing. Kon did his best to shrink away from the busy intersection as they passed, watching Icelyn as her eyes lit up at the busy store. It was the next door down from there.

"B2." She double-checked her paper. The door was propped open as they peeked in. It was a fairly open room, with concrete floors and markers—like a small gymnasium. Students were spread out in groups about the room. Some were talking, others practicing their powers. Kon peered in at the mix of students before checking on Icelyn, whose expression had recoiled at the sight, mouth parted in a frown. She took a step back from the door, brows creased. "They're all kids," she croaked, pulling at her shirt before her hands dropped to her side.

Kon surveyed the room again. A majority of the students inside *were* a bit younger. There were only a few who looked like older teens. "What about it?" he asked as another young student entered the room beside them.

"I just . . . feel stupid." She shook her head, kicking at the ground.

"Everyone's different. You've been hiding your powers for years, haven't you?"

"Yeah."

"So, you're new to it."

Icelyn seemed unconvinced as she reluctantly turned back to the room. Some of the kids, looking preteen, or even younger, were conjuring tiny flames, balls of light, and small warps of terrashock. It was still more than Icelyn could muster.

"Are you here for classes?" a middle-aged man said from behind them. He was tall with gray covering most of his short hair. He had on a thick vest over a flowy uniform.

"Oh . . . I am," Icelyn said in a small voice, picking at her sleeves.

"Great! We're starting soon." He smiled through a short beard before he looked up at Kon. "Para's been telling me a lot about *you*."

Kon grimaced but kept his composure, feeling the eyes of the students behind them in the room.

The man continued. "Good you showed up here. I was afraid I'd have to try and catch you."

"Why?" Kon could hear the small murmurs fall silent in the room as he checked over his shoulder.

The man put a hand on his hip. "I just feel like I can only teach these kids so much. I've got lightning, and we don't get a ton of Elementals with that. I try to teach the rest what I can about their own powers, but I would love for someone with such a broad Elemental arsenal to help." He shrugged. "Learn from the masters, right? Para says you have some good experience."

Icelyn watched him too as if they were waiting for a response.

"I don't . . ."

"Think on it. I'm sure they'd appreciate it. For now, you can just sit in with your friend . . ." He held out his hand to Icelyn.

"Icelyn," she stated, still clutching her paper.

"You and Icelyn can watch and see if you want to be a part of it. I have a few students curious to meet you already." He beckoned for them to follow him in. Several students had stopped to watch them, while others paid no mind. The man positioned himself at the front of the room, where a digital screen lined the wall. Kon moved to the back wall next to the door, crossing his arms. Icelyn followed along, crossing her arms as well, but the bunch in her shoulders didn't carry the same confidence that his did, eyes locked on the floor still.

"Alright, class, we can go ahead and get started." He rubbed his hands together as students gathered. "As always, I'll introduce myself for anyone new. I'm Phaven Margo. You can call me whichever one of those you want; most use Margo. This is a free-learning, beginners' Elemental class, open every day for beginners who want to practice with some guidance. We do group activities on Wednesdays and Sundays. The rest of the week is for free practice and help. As always, you guys can split off and find a spot to practice, and I'll be around to help."

Icelyn stared a bit longer at the dissipating crowd before turning to Kon, who was already looking at her. "I don't think I have much to practice." Her eyes traced over her empty hands.

"Maybe how Alaura suggested." Kon glanced up at a squeal of delight from a student across the room, tumbling a roll of fire in their arms. It was odd seeing Elementals excited about their powers. If anything, it felt dangerous.

Icelyn watched as well, brows creased as she held her own hands out in front of her, void of any power. "You don't happen to have cold in your 'arsenal of abilities,' do you?" She looked back to her palms.

"I don't think so." Having never attempted to train someone, he didn't know where to even begin. "Just try to feel the energy instead of seeing it."

She pursed her lips together and stared at her hands for a while.

Kon looked across the room where there were several tables set up with items on them, likely for testing skills. His attention soon shifted back to Icelyn, who was frowning in concentration. "You don't have to hold your breath," he said lightly.

"Oh." She let out an exhale. "I thought it might help."

Margo approached. "How's it going over here?"

With a defeated sigh, Icelyn dropped her hands. "I think I'm just bad at this."

"Nonsense. How long have you been practicing?" he asked.

"Uhm . . . since today?"

"Well, no wonder. You're new! What's your power?"

"Temperature. Cold. I think?" She rubbed her arm at the mention of it.

"Ah. Well, a good simple exercise for that is the water test." He beckoned her to follow, leading them over to one of the tall tables at the far end of the room. It held several bowls and cups of water. "A good indication if you're getting anywhere with your powers is ice, naturally. If you can make ice, you know you're making progress." He grabbed a small shallow cup of water and handed it to her. "Start with this. Your goal is to freeze the top of the water, then the whole thing. Then you pick a bigger bowl. Build up."

She looked over the cup, a soften in her expression. "Okay."

He gave her another smile. "Still may take time; just keep trying," he assured her before moving on to another group of students.

Icelyn moved in next to the table with her cup and sat it on the edge.

She looked back at Kon with a look of uncertainty. He gave her a shrug. A girl with curly caramel hair, looking no more than twelve, had pulled up a chair and sat herself on the other side of the table, staring at her bowl of water with furrowed concentration. Icelyn glanced at the girl and how her hand hovered near the water, and she followed suit. After a long draw of silence, she pulled back, looking at the undisturbed liquid. "I just don't know if I'm . . . actually conjuring something or if I'm just holding my hand over a cup of water," she blurted out, shoulders drooping.

"Do you feel the energy around your hand?" Kon asked, glancing from the cup to her.

"I don't know. It just feels fuzzy. I feel like I'm just imagining it." She shook her head as she glanced at the younger girl who was smiling as a thin sheet of ice spread across her bowl of water.

A boy of similar age came trotting to her side. "Shelby—you got it!" he leaned across the table to look over her bowl.

She gave a toothy smile and nodded. "Super fast this time too," the girl said, pleased with herself.

Icelyn looked back at her lukewarm cup of water, lips pursed.

The sorrow in her gaze made something in Kon sting as he spoke. "You should be able to feel it, maybe you're not channeling enough of it." He thought for a moment, desperate to give her some sense of hope. "Let me see your hand." She held out an open palm to him as he placed his hand under hers. "Can I try something?" he asked, looking over her somber expression.

Her eyes fluttered over his. "Sure, like what?"

"Tell me if you can feel this," he said quietly as his hand lightly brushed hers.

After a few seconds, she moved her fingers, seeming to feel the thick energy around them. "Yeah, what is it?" She inspected her hand, leaning in slightly to look, just as the poof of small flames ignited over her palm. She let out a gasp at the sight of the fire. It could have been coming from her own hand as she moved her fingers with the flames.

"Doesn't feel like fire, does it?" he said.

"No, it's just—energy." It was the first smile she had managed in the classroom as she played gently with the flames in her hand.

"Yours shouldn't feel cold either. You should just *feel* the energy." He pulled his hand away, the flames dissipating from her fingers.

"How did you . . . put fire in *my* hand?" she asked.

"I think the energy recognizes others. I can make it see you as a host and protect you like it would me." He shrugged, putting his hand into his pocket. "I don't know. I learned it a while ago." He had first tried it with Mallia, who had a similar reaction.

A voice piped up from behind them. "You can give your powers to other people?" The boy across the table had moved closer, watching them with intrigue.

"They're just a vessel. They can't control it," Kon explained. The introduction of a new person unnerved him, even if it was a young, eager Elemental.

"You're Kon," the boy said in a raspy voice, shaggy auburn hair covering his forehead as his green eyes watched him. The acknowledgment unnerved him even more. "I'm Samlin. Para said you're good with fire. That's my power too."

The girl had stopped focusing on her bowl, listening.

Kon only blinked.

"Margo said I need a good teacher. He and Para think I've outgrown the beginner class, but I'm too young to start the next one. I don't know why," he huffed.

"Is Para telling everyone about me?" Kon finally said, annoyance lacing his words.

"Well, I basically had to beg her to tell me anything. I just figured an Avari would be someone who can teach me," he said hopefully.

"I don't really . . . teach." Kon kept his hands firm in his pockets. No more lessons would be given out.

Samlin looked from Kon to Icelyn, then back to Kon. "Isn't that what you're doing now?"

Kon met Icelyn's eyes as she gave a subtle grin. "It's not the same."

Icelyn finally spoke up as she grabbed her cup of water. "Why don't we all group up?" She looked over at the girl, who was still watching their conversation unfold from her seat. "She and I can practice ice; you guys can practice fire."

"Sure!" Samlin straightened, smiling back over a shoulder. "Shelby already beat that cup. She can teach you how!"

"Okay," Shelby said in a tiny voice.

"Great." Icelyn flashed a smirk at Kon, a joking mischief on her face. He gave her an unamused tilt of the head as she moved to the other side of the table with her cup.

Reluctantly, he leaned against the table, turning back to the boy, who was waiting. "What do you want to know?" he grumbled.

"Okay." Samlin positioned himself against the table as well, resting an arm on it. "When you conjure fire, do you channel it from your hands or do you free cast? There's like an ongoing argument around the base over which is better. The hand is definitely easier, but I feel like free casting gets a bigger result?"

"I do both." Kon shrugged.

"Like at the same time?"

"Sometimes."

"Which one gets better results?" Samlin flicked his hand as fire sparked around it, and he fidgeted with the flames.

"What kind of results do you want?" Kon asked.

"I mean like . . . fighting EME."

A shiver ran down Kon's spine. "You shouldn't be fighting them at all." He watched the boy's expression. It made him feel uneasy—a kid so young, eager to fight something so dangerous. "You could get killed doing that."

Samlin looked stumped for a moment. "I mean, one day we all might have to fight. I can't help when that day comes, but I can be ready."

Kon let out a sigh, glancing over at Icelyn for a moment. The soft waves in her hair drifted over her shoulder as she held her cup of water, listening intently to Shelby's instruction.

It took the rest of the class to answer every question Samlin asked. From casting, to stance, to breathing—he wanted to know everything.

Samlin examined the flames in his hand, thinking of any final questions as students started to depart. "So, free casting is more powerful overall?"

"Probably, but your main goal against EME should be getting away from them. Don't try to fight them. They won't give you a fair fight."

Samlin scrunched his face in something of disappointment as he rubbed his fingers together, a few small flames bouncing around his hand. "They shouldn't just get away with it all, though. We have to stand up against them at *some* point. I'm not afraid of them."

Kon narrowed his eyes on the concrete floor as he worked out the realization that students here were different. They *were* preparing to fight—a fury he had seen in Elementals before—one that often cost them their life. His gaze flickered back to Samlin. "You should be."

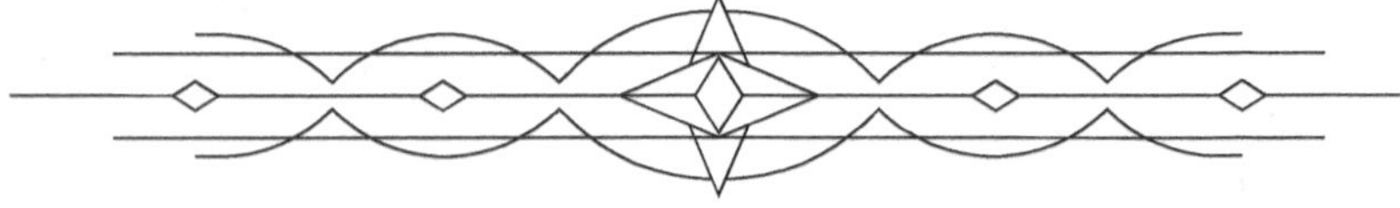

CHAPTER 16

THE PRICE OF FREEDOM

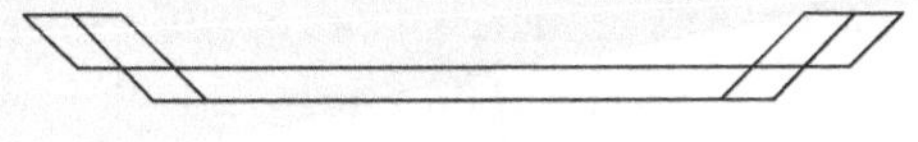

JUNE 2653

Fifteen years since Avari left.

Kon had never been east of the cabin—over the low ridges and through the valleys, following the river along its winding snake through the land. Joel had told him of a few others from the Avari Integration Program, urging him that direction after the EME had pushed too close to the cabin—people from the program who might have leads or advice. Both Joel and Mallia had suggested his best bet was relocating somewhere the EME wouldn't find him. That close to the end of Brynden Ka, back into the main continent, he wondered if life outside the peninsula would be easier.

He looked at the old, wrinkled paper in his hand, with names and rough estimates of where each of these acquaintances of Joel's might be. He had chosen Valea Taberath, a scientist from the base—one Joel had high hopes of being friendly. The unfortunate reality was that Joel had to be careful with his recommendations. Not every person who worked with the Avari years before still believed in the work they did. A scary number had turned their backs on it, some even moving in support of the EME's decision. It was risky to trust anyone, but that was always true.

Valea Taberath had been an easy choice for a lot of reasons. Her supposed location was along the river, an easy find for his emerging navigation skills. Since he had only left the cabin a month before, he was finally testing the bulk of his wilderness training. Joel had pushed it as hard as anything else, if not harder. It wouldn't matter how well Kon could defend himself against EME if he couldn't survive on his own in the woods. With the warming weather, foraging and travel had been easier.

Of course, Brynden Ka's climate stuck on the cooler end, but there was still decent summer weather. The southern region was only slightly warmer, and he hadn't felt the need to head in that direction yet. Anything he forgot relating to foraging, he could find easily within the small compact books he had. He had already stored his bag with *reecyps*, *pepron* seeds, and *pikleds*, common food plants in bloom. Reecyps could help with sickness or injury. Joel had urged him to find them early on. Pepron seeds were an easy food to ration, as long as he had the time to dry the bitter berries for their sweeter seeds. Pikleds were another fine staple coming from a stocky bush that grew the hardy purple pikleds on its roots. They lasted quite long and always grew in large groups that were easy to spot in the heaps of heavy, dark leaves.

He had even been lucky enough to find some Arypagus trees, still growing their hardy winter Arpys. The sweet pinkish fruit was Mallia's favorite. They fruited year-long, a common pick for local farms. Even harder to find, he had somehow discovered a patch of *vylaberries* on his trek. The supple plant was tricky to spot, except for the white flowers that only bloomed at night. He had gone vylaberry hunting with Seelia and Jack numerous times. It was one of their favorite activities. When he arrived at the green house, it had also been something to get him out of the house; the safety of berry hunting at night, under cover of woods and darkness. It was something he was still fond of. The sweet white and red berries only brought warm memories.

By the time he had traveled along the river for a few days to the house, he had amassed a decent collection of supplies. He gauged he could stay away from towns, as Joel suggested, for a good while. The only time he would need to interact was in times like this. He approached the small overgrown house by the water. The path to the nearby town was hardly traveled as he scanned for signs of life.

Kon checked his map and notes one last time. "Valea Taberath. Located outside Sundamyn, purple cottage by the water." He looked up to confirm its attributes before taking a breath. He had never openly admitted his identity—as he was about to do—as he stepped onto the small porch and knocked upon the old wooden door. His hands found themselves in the pockets of Joel's heavy jacket as he fidgeted in an attempt to expel the nerves from his system. After several painfully long moments, something behind the door stirred, and it clicked unlocked. The deadbolted door was pulled open slowly as a woman peeked around it. Her thin, wrinkled face grew in shock for a moment as she took one look at Kon and slammed the door shut.

He winced, blinking in confusion as his words stayed in his open mouth. Before he could draw back, the deadbolt clicked, and the door shot open again. The frizzy-haired older woman looked upon him with something of guilt—or anger. He couldn't place it. "Leave," she said, mouth pursed in her attempt to stay level. "I want no part in this."

Kon could feel his confusion melting into embarrassment. There weren't many words left to muster, so he started with the ones he had rehearsed. "Are you Valea?"

The woman's expression twisted. "Who told you where I was?" She shook her head, tone remaining sharp. "It doesn't matter. I'm not getting involved in this. Go away."

"You knew my mother—" The next line in his plan, although it was becoming clear she wasn't someone who welcomed him.

"That means nothing now. I want to be left alone." Her hardened expression stayed as she clutched the collar of her robe. Her following words sent a shiver down his spine. "Don't think I won't call them." She didn't have to say it. He knew who she meant.

Kon took an instinctive step back.

The betrayal across his face must've been evident as the slightest hint of pain showed in her brow. "I don't want to. Just . . . leave." Her eyes followed him as he stepped off the porch completely, back into the mess of weeds and brush.

"I'm sorry," were the last words he could muster.

As she started to close the door, she paused. "Gods, you really do look like Padlin."

Then he was alone again. The sting in his chest burned as though she had slashed him with more than words. *No part in this?* Kon didn't want a part in it either, but he didn't have that luxury to decide. He had chosen her because of her supposed closeness to Padlin. Joel confirmed she had been one of the scientists closely watching Padlin's pregnancy. He had even called her a friend. None of that mattered anymore.

Fearing her threats could be real, he left. Kon avoided the town as well, sticking by the river as he trailed it farther east. That hollow feeling of the event stuck with him the rest of the day. He knew many people in Brynden Ka had a short fuse concerning Avari. Joel's warmth toward him had given him false confidence.

The following days were lost to travel. Kon decided to avoid the rest of the names marked down. *Maybe Valea was right. They had no part in this anymore.*

The last thing Joel had written was a supposed safe house. Though it was only a rough location, based on his careful conversations around Calka with other Elemental families. Kon had yet to meet an Elemental. They'd likely have similar hostility to him, he would guess. They had Avari to blame for their own downfall.

The pale rocks spread out from the trickle of the river he had continued to follow. He stood on a large flat rock, gauging on his map where the turn in the river might be. It was early morning, pink skies reflecting across the low water. The safe house was supposedly nearby. Somewhere. Kon knew he was a good distance from any town. He hadn't seen any sign of used paths or trails in a while.

That made the gunshot followed by a scream even more unnerving.

Somewhere in the woods, the high pitch of the shriek nearly caused his map to drop from his hand as birds scattered from the trees. He stared toward the source, distant in the tall mix of evergreens and soft oaks. As it faded, his legs made the decision for him to move toward the sound, which was turning into voices yelling, but nothing he could make out. Only then, he could hear deeper voices shouting. His gut had a strong idea of what it was, as fire started to lick at his arms.

When he was finally in sight of it all, his stomach churned. He was right; four EME circled, shouting at the girl before them, who stood with terrashock warping at her arms. Her messy, honey-blonde hair fell over her face as she held a hand over a bleeding shoulder. "Last chance," one of the men growled. A moment later, she flung him backward with a burst. The others raised their weapons to take their shot, just as terrashock detonated beside them, sending the remaining three into the nearby trees. The energy wasn't hers.

Kon leveled himself as fire pooled around his arms. Only one of them sat up, until he sent another wave, just as large as the last, flattening them. Behind him, a shot let out from the remaining man the girl had attacked. Kon pulled the energy back, turning to land it square at him, still on the ground. The terrashock hit the man with a startling *crunch* as he fell still in the brush.

In the silence of the woods, Kon finally let the panic wash over him. He had . . . won. Joel's training worked. He had dispatched them with near ease. Though he couldn't bring himself to step close to see the damage done, there was a flash of pride in his victory . . . pride that crumbled as he turned to the girl, who wavered, hand over her ribs as blood started to stain through her shirt. A moment later, she collapsed. Kon was too far to catch her as he froze, horror setting in. When his legs finally worked, he ran to her as she weakly stirred on the ground.

"It's okay," he stuttered, dropping his bag as he assessed her. The layered sweater was stained dark as he put a hand over her ribs, trying to stop the bleeding. Her hand pushed her hair from her face, several braids intertwining her messy hair. It left a streak of blood across her face as she looked him over, silent, except for small sniffles of breath. She couldn't be much older than he was, the blush of life fading from her cheeks. "I—you're okay." They were just words to cover up his racing thoughts. He didn't know what to do. He knew what he should do, but it wasn't working. It was all happening too fast, including her fading breaths. A shaky hand pulled back from the soaked shirt as he looked into her eyes.

She coughed something of blood up, trying to form words. "I'm not—going. With. Them."

"You won't." Kon tried again, digging in his bag for something, anything. A shirt to stop the blood as he pressed it again, pushing out the thoughts he already knew. "They're gone. You're safe."

"I was trying," she struggled through a few more breaths, "to get to the border. No EME."

"Yeah." Kon nodded. "We'll get there." He choked on his words, taking a shaky huff of air to level himself. *Keep her awake.* Maybe he could still save her. "Do you have family over there?"

Her stare drifted toward the sky, her gray eyes hazing. "My sister."

"Okay." Kon swept his sleeve over his cheek in an attempt to hide his own tears as hers fell into her braided hair. His breathing was coming faster, harder. He still didn't know what to do. *Talk to her.* "Where are you from?" It was all he could think of.

She didn't seem to hear him. "Where are we?"

"By the river." He pressed his shirt harder into her ribs as it too started to stain red. "I've got you. It's okay."

"Okay." Her words came out as whispers as her face lost its twist of emotion. She looked as though she was enjoying the pink sky above—no pain. "It's pretty here."

Kon peeled back the shirt for a moment, struggling to see through his own tears. "Yeah. What's your name?" Another question to throw some form of distraction.

But no answer came that time. He finally looked up from the blood-soaked shirt, his hand drifting from it. There were only his own heavy breaths as he drew back. The birds had returned, singing in the trees overhead. Tears finally welled enough to stream down his face as he stared.

He didn't know how long he sat there, stunned, hands soaked in someone else's blood. Fighting for his own breath back as he waited for hers to return. It didn't.

The only thing to snap him out of it was the distant roaring. EME must have found the safe house. Maybe she was looking for it too. He needed to keep moving. It took the roaring coming much closer to drive him, finally, to his feet, forcing himself to leave the scene. The EME soldiers remained on the ground, unmoving, fallen with her—a fitting feat that he would've made sure of had any of them gotten up.

Everything after was a blur. All he knew was where he was heading. The border. If she believed in safety, maybe he could too. Leave the memories of Brynden Ka behind. Flee from the EME. Maybe there, Kon could call Joel somehow. He missed him. He missed Mallia.

It took another two days of nearly nonstop travel. Kon didn't want to stop. Walking was the only thing that distracted him. Even stopping to sleep brought flashes of nightmares. Part of him wanted to turn around. Go back to the questionable safety of the cabin where he could call Joel to come get him. Admit he was wrong; that he couldn't do it himself. Despite it all, he kept moving forward. He had to see the end. The end of Brynden Ka. The end of the EME.

Finally, as trees parted on a grassy hill, he came to the long open field. Removed of trees, only grass lay. But looking beyond the grass, Kon's heart sank. Across the border of Brynden Ka, the path to freedom, sat the large, towering wall. It had to stretch nearly one hundred feet in the air. The top of it contained a walkway, steel beams supporting the edges of it. Stations of watch towers sat every couple hundred feet as well. The wall spanned as far as he could see.

There was no getting over it. Of course, the nation had locked down Brynden Ka, trapping the desperate Elementals inside. Surely, the only way over was a checked entrance. He knew that they had regulated travel in and out. Joel had said as much in plotting. Taking a hoverbus back into the mainland required getting through the careful searches at the borders. For many EME, that was their sole job, keeping Elementals inside. Trying to catch a shuttle to another planet was in the least, far beyond something they could afford. Even if they could, those were regulated too. Same with water travel. The nation made it clear they didn't want Elementals in other parts of the world, and the EME graciously obliged to keep it that way.

He had thought there was a chance of sneaking past—bypassing the border checks, escaping to freedom. Staring at the giant span of wall, Kon was forced to accept the bitter reality—bitter defeat of it all. His own dream, and the dream of the girl he comforted days before, were just that. A dream.

There was no way out of the peninsula. There was no way to escape the EME.

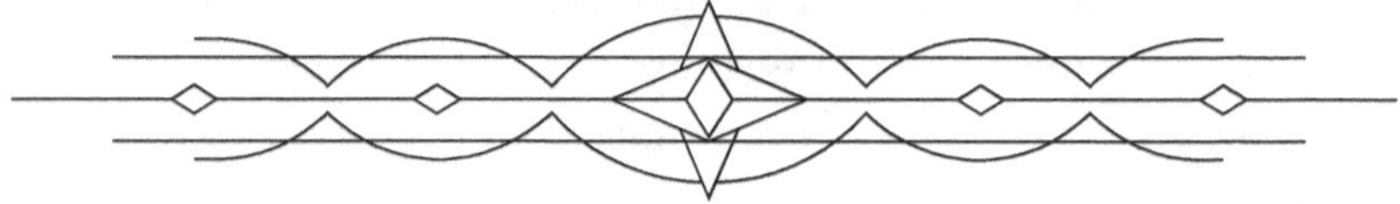

CHAPTER 17
MORALS

Present Day

"Alright, see everyone tomorrow!" Margo called out as students filed through the door into the hall.

"I guess I just need more practice," Icelyn shrugged as she exited beside Shelby.

"It was slow for me too," the young girl said quietly.

Next to them, Samlin was still buzzing around Kon with the occasional question as they entered the hallway. "Can I show you my fire burst when Para takes us off lockdown? I like practicing outside."

Kon gave him an unamused tilt of the head. "Sure." He broke off with Icelyn, fully done with Samlin's attention.

"See you guys tomorrow?" Samlin asked as he headed away with Shelby. "We have to get to science."

"Yeah, maybe." Icelyn nodded lightly as they trotted off down the hall. Out of range, she let out a sigh. "I forgot they're still in school."

Kon lingered, watching students filter in and out of rooms. "I think I'm going to go out for a bit."

"Outside?" she asked. "Can I come . . .?"

"You want to go outside?" He scrunched his nose. After her run-in with the EME, he figured she wouldn't want to be out in the woods for a while.

"Yeah. Seems like it helps you. Maybe it'll help me. I just need to swing by my room and grab my jacket."

"Okay," he said carefully as they started to walk, glancing at her for signs of trouble. Her demeanor had lightened, her shoulders pushed back as she took in a heavy breath.

Students still buzzed around The Closet as Icelyn took another glance at it, optimism in her tone. "Where's Peter?"

Kon shook his head. "I don't know. He said he had a lead or something to chase."

"Oh. You think it's to do with . . . the database? And the facility?"

He shrugged.

Upon reaching the dorms, Icelyn ducked into her room. She soon returned with her jacket, a plant in hand, and a garden trowel. The plant was lopsided in its pot, having a few scarce large leaves drooping from its stem. He blinked at her. "I had to stuff it in my bag when I left," she said. "It lost a bunch of soil . . . I figured I could go get more." Slipping on her jacket, they headed for the exit. Her movements were more fluid versus her earlier demeanor as she fell in beside him with light steps.

Several students were stretching down the hall toward the entrance, hanging posters on the walls while others removed some. A Felinian with beige and tan fur waved a hand at them as they passed by. "Hey! Events club is preparing for the dance," she spoke in a peppy voice as she held a flier out to Icelyn, flicking her tail. Her rotating ears stuck up in a friendly manner. "Come to our meetings and help us plan!" She smiled, seeming like her words were on repeat to every person she encountered.

Icelyn gave a shy smile and nodded as they walked on. "Dance?" She examined the flier, slightly amused as she read it over.

Kon paid it no mind, glancing at Para's door as they passed. Several students were in the doorway, full of conversation. Para wouldn't notice him leaving.

Icelyn read the flier out loud. "Fall Seasons Formal. Dance, party, and food. Huh." Icelyn chuckled. "Might be fun?"

He glanced at the colorful printed flier, suppressing his disdain for the idea.

"Maybe they're just trying to keep spirits high." She stuffed the flier into her pocket as they neared the entrance. More students gathered around the mural, taking notes and pointing at it as they discussed future designs. Kon glanced past it to the Defensive Wing. Terrance was approaching his office, his and Para's daughter skipping in front of him. He nodded to her in conversation as he opened the door. When he spotted the two, he gave Kon a frown of indifference before the girl called his attention back.

Kon didn't look much longer, pulling open the heavy door to hold it for Icelyn as they exited.

Icelyn watched the stairs closely as they led into the field. "We really are underground," she said as they came into the field, looking back at the bare rocky stretch of ground, void of the large base that sat there the day before. All that lay in the distance were the tall Palyra Mountains, marking where Alinth sat. She only stared for a moment longer before she turned from the snowy mountains, rather flat-faced. Waiting for them, scattered around the field, cats were already beginning to approach. "Are these always out here?" Icelyn gasped, kneeling to pet the company.

Kon scanned the tree line for any signs of trouble as he shut the hatch and then turned to greet the cats as well. The air was cool, autumn leaves falling fast from the trees after the recent flurry of snow. Kon moved away from the hatch, eyes still tracing the tree line. "This way."

Icelyn fell in next to him as they entered the trees, her potted plant clutched in her arms. "Are we going anywhere specific?" She took a last glance at the cats over her shoulder.

"Just need to pick something up," he said.

"Oh. You think it's . . . safe out here?" Her head swiveled, frantically looking through the dense trees.

"No." His gaze scanned the surroundings much more thoroughly than she did. "Just stay close." It wasn't the best idea to bring someone out with him, but he could understand her wanting out. The bustling excited life of the base was hard to grasp. Elemental students seemed barely worried about their situation. Planning parties, making clubs, painting murals. It seemed pointless to him, but maybe there was a logic behind it—one he didn't grasp, though. Maybe there was a coping mechanism amongst fretting over simple things. After all, Icelyn's mission to find soil for her plant seemed to brighten her mood as she held the pot beside him, trowel in her pocket. She fidgeted at the leaves, trying to fix their droopy state.

He roughly knew the way to his next location, another item he had hid a while ago. The wind pushed the trees above them, rustling leaves filling the air. They walked the barren floor for a while before Icelyn spoke again.

"Do you run into EME a lot? Like . . . yesterday?" she asked.

"Depends on the area."

"Do you always fight them off like that?"

Her pale hair stuck out in the barren woods as his eyes lingered over her. "No, I usually avoid them," he mumbled.

Icelyn was quiet, her next words coming carefully. "You told Samlin he shouldn't train to fight them."

"Yeah."

"Why?" She met his gaze with a cautious curiosity.

He hesitated, letting out a sigh. "I don't want that blood on my hands."

"What do you mean?"

He shrugged. "Telling him to fight them will get him killed."

"I thought the EME wanted Elementals alive?"

"That makes them look better. That's not what always happens." He lowered his tone, watching her expression twist.

"You fought them successfully though?"

"I fight them when I have to. They won't take the shot on me like they would an Elemental." In fact, they rarely took shots at him, beyond stun rounds. Sometimes, in the fear of the fight, one of the soldiers would get carried away, aiming at him to save their own life, but it never went well.

Icelyn toyed with her plant as she fidgeted to distract herself. "So, they weren't bluffing when they threatened me yesterday?"

He remembered their words the day before too, threatening to open fire. It was hard to know what type of fire they meant. In reality, it didn't matter. "Probably not." He, too, thought at one point their words were bluffs. One of his first mistakes.

Ferns dotted the trail around them, blotched with undergrowth and barren ground around the scarce trail. They could only hear the sound of rustling trees as they walked. Sharp clean air. Kon kept straight—confident in where he was headed as she followed.

"So, you've been here your whole life?" Icelyn asked after a bit, looking about the various foliage in the forest as leaves fell around them.

He figured questions would come concerning his origin. "As long as I can remember."

"Who . . . raised you? If you want to answer that."

Kon looked to the side at her, bored. "Humans. You?" An edge of humor lined his tone.

"Humans." A smile formed across her face before the glow of it faded. "But my mom was half Makovan. Sometimes, I wish she took me to Makova."

"You've never been?"

"No, but I've always wanted to." She absentmindedly traced her fingers over the pot in her hand. "Did you ever try to get out of Brynden Ka?"

"Yeah. It didn't work."

Another flurry of leaves filled the air as she paused. "For people who don't want us here, the EME makes it awfully hard for us to leave. It doesn't make sense."

"They want control of the situation."

"I hear they want Elementals for the war against Koron. Do you think . . ." she hesitated with her words, "that's why they want you too?"

"I don't know." He shook his head dismissively, keeping on the edge of the conversation. He did know. It was something he avoided thinking about.

"I also heard a lot of Elementals fled *to* Koron? They're using them now too."

"I don't think we'd be safe off planet either." He murmured, looking around at the distantly familiar terrain. He didn't know if it was true or something he told himself to make it easier to accept the reality that he was stuck there. Logic told him that whatever planet he ended up on, he'd be alone all the same.

"Maybe we can make it safer here. With the base," she said in a hopeful tone.

He gave her an unconvinced tilt of the head.

Eventually, they came to the stream he had been looking for. The rocky bed made the water dip and bend around the terrain. Kon had stopped at its edge, scanning the surroundings before he started moving upstream along the rocks. Icelyn followed behind, taking in the calm rushing water, clear over the smooth stones. Kon scanned each tree as they followed the water for a ways until he moved from the stream toward a larger tree with a split in its base. He wasn't sure how he had been so close to the base some years ago and not seen signs of it. Maybe that was the mistake other safe houses kept making. The signs of that base were subtle enough that he hadn't realized he was so close to it. If he had, he would've turned the other way.

He knelt to pull the small backpack out of the trunk of the tree, Icelyn watching with intrigue.

"Oh, my plant." She pulled her trowel and stepped off to the side. Her boot kicked a patch of moss, revealing a good soft spot of soil to dig.

Kon watched a moment longer before unzipping the bag and examining its contents. It was worn and weathered, partially saved from the elements in its hiding spot beneath the tree. It was one of the supply spots he avoided, usually having nothing of use until then. He was lucky it was so close to the base, being what it was. Icelyn patted the soil into the pot, carefully pressing it around the stem of the weepy plant before she held it up in satisfaction. As she stood, Kon was already standing, pulling something from the bag; a small communicator. Examining it, he half-heartedly pressed buttons in an attempt to bring it to life.

He had stopped carrying it years before, fearing it could link back to the Gavins if taken by the wrong hands. With stiff acceptance, he had to acknowledge at some point that the EME could catch up to him. Any bad day, any slip-up, could cost him. And with that realization, anything he had on him would be used against him, so he traveled light. Since it was a fairly unvisited part of the peninsula, he had chosen that spot to hide his bag from the green house, but it seemed age had gotten to the device before he did. He stared at it in contempt before glancing up at Icelyn, who was now dipping her pot into the stream, bringing it back up as the water soaked into the soil.

She examined her plant with a grin, pleased before her brow creased at his own look of annoyance. "Does it work?" she asked, looking at the communicator.

"No." His arms dropped to the side as he gave up on the device.

"Who do you need to reach?" She stepped closer. "Maybe the base has a phone?"

"Just an old friend." He shook his head. "Let's get you back." He dropped the communicator into the bag and tossed it under the tree again. Maybe it was better that it was dead. It kept them safer in the end.

"Do you *need* to contact your friend? Are they okay?" she asked as they started walking back down the stream.

He took in a breath, careful with his words. "I don't know. I might have to go visit."

"Oh." She was watching the water flow next to them, gentle in its tumbles. "Are they far?"

"Yeah." His eyes trailed the rocks below them in defeat as she peered down in similar disappointment.

"Do you think you'll be back?" she said in an unconvincing casual tone.

"Might be a while if I go." The idea of going, however, was enough to churn his stomach. Checking on them would only put them back in danger when they could've been well out of it by then.

"Maybe there's another way to contact them. The base?" she suggested again, only receiving a shake of the head from him as they broke from the stream and headed into the woods.

It could've been his own painful independence refusing the idea of help, but he couldn't muster the courage to ask Para, despite knowing she could make it happen.

The steady flow of leaves falling around them continued as they moved down the faint trail. When she was met with nothing but silence from him, Icelyn spoke again. "Are you ever afraid—being out here alone?"

"Afraid of what?"

"I don't know. The woods just seem big. Lonely. You're not afraid of animals or anything?"

He hesitated. "Nothing out here wants to hurt us nearly as bad as people do."

She peered up at him before turning back to the woods, hugging her plant a little closer. His answer had seemed to bring on a rift of silence, trees passing in the solemn quiet. Maybe he had been too straightforward with her. His reality might be too much to process for an Elemental just breaking out of their normal life.

"So, your dad is EME?" he asked in an attempt to change the subject.

"Yeah." She frowned.

"What does he do?" He was soft, not confident if he wanted to know the answer. He always tried to keep a disconnect from EME soldiers if he fought them. Letting his mind accept they were each their own person had only caused hesitation and problems in the past. It was best to shut it out and fight. In the end, they didn't give him a chance to plead his case as a person, so he wouldn't give them one either.

"Oh, he's not like, *out there* much. He's just data entry mostly. Still sucked hearing him talk about it all."

"He knew you were an Elemental?"

"Yeah. But according to him I *'wasn't like them.'* I wasn't *'dangerous.'* Whatever that means." She scoffed at the thought of his words.

Kon narrowed his eyes. "Anyone can be dangerous if you threaten them." He could feel her icy eyes gently set on him again.

"Maybe," she paused before she spoke again. "Do you think there's really another Avari out here somewhere?"

He was troubled by the thought. Rather it was the idea he wasn't *completely* alone or a guilt that he never found them if they *were* here. Regardless, the thought unsettled him for some reason. *It should be a good thing, right?* Or did it simply mean another Avari was facing the same thing he was? Then again, it could all be a myth, never existing at all. "I don't know." He shrugged, his voice the same tired tone it usually was, though his words came easier out here.

"I think we should ask Garik Tally, that scientist," she stated.

"We don't know whose side he's on."

"What do you mean?"

"If I walk in there and he's with the EME, what happens?" Kon said, checking the tree line again before looking down at her. Seeking answers from old Integration staff was something he stopped attempting long before.

"I mean, he was contacting the EPS . . . Seemed like he wanted to help." She fluffed the leaves of her plant.

"I don't know if it's worth the risk. Maybe he just *thinks* there's another." Kon wouldn't deny the intrigue of information, but in the grand scheme of his situation, someone telling him another Avari may still be on the planet changed nothing for him. The truth would hardly alter his path—only finding them would, and he guessed no one could point him toward that.

"Yeah." Icelyn bit her lip in thought. "We need to plan more. Maybe Peter's got an idea."

"Maybe." He watched her carefully between scanning the trees. Peter definitely had ideas.

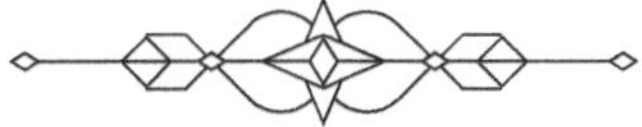

The walk back passed faster. The air was cold, likely to remain that way for the next few days while the trees shed the last of their leaves. Blue skies showed overhead as they entered the field. Kon pulled the hatch on the ground, less than enthused to get back inside.

Cats had seated themselves around the hatch, brushing against Icelyn's leg as she stood somberly, fidgeting as she watched him. "You'll tell us if you do leave, right?" she asked. The idea had likely been bouncing in her mind the whole way back.

Kon straightened up, meeting her eyes while cats brushed his boot, letting themselves in and down the stairs. "Yeah." His voice was calm, almost reassuring.

She hesitated for another long second, gauging his truth before she nodded. Following her in, he shut the hatch behind them. "Peter's probably looking for us again." She chuckled, changing the subject as she grinned at the two cats joining them.

"He usually is," Kon said as they reached the second door into the base. A few students were painting the corners of the mural, adding swirls and colors. The two of them started for the student section, both seeming to have the same idea to lay low.

"Kon." Terrance's familiar voice spoke behind them, causing them to stop in their tracks. They slowly turned to him. Icelyn had a look of guilt on her face while Kon glared at him, both prepared for a lecture. "Are you the one letting the cats in?" Terrance scowled, glancing back at the door.

Kon looked past him to the two cats in the entrance, cleaning themselves. "No."

Terrance shifted his weight, scarred brow creasing with Kon's obvious lie. "Para needs you for a minute." His lack of further comment caught them off guard.

"For what?" Kon frowned, looking back at her office.

"She's over here." He gestured toward the Defensive Wing. "Something you'll want to hear, I think."

Kon peered down the hallway behind him, a clench of dread sparking in his chest. "Okay."

Terrance headed for his office without another word. Perhaps it was time for his own second interview. Maybe they didn't want to phrase it that way. Taking a last glance at Icelyn, she stayed put, tilting her head at him. He gave her a shrug.

To Kon's surprise, they passed Terrance's office. Terrance only checked once to confirm he was following. Kon made sure to take in what he could while down there. The staff up ahead, transferring boxes into an armory—a break room of sorts in the distance, where people talked casually. His mind still lingered on the conversations outside and the pang of disappointment he felt upon finding the dead communicator.

Terrance reached the second door past his office, gesturing him in. Kon watched him closely as he ducked into the room. The light was dim, screens filling the tables and walls. The beeping of monitors and signals rang out across the array of devices. Some screens showed maps, others had text. The radio tech, Deyin, was in a chair, holding a headphone to his ear as he listened to radio chatter. He flashed a greeting as they entered.

"This is our scanner room, where we keep an eye on things outside," Terrance explained in a low voice. "We can also make protected calls from here."

"She's in there." Deyin pointed to a door to the right, spinning in his chair to check one of the many monitors before him.

Terrance nodded him into the next room. Kon looked at the mass of screens and radios for another moment before he faced the door seeing a much brighter, shorter hall that let out into a light-colored room. He could hear Para talking inside. With a last cautious look at Terrance, he entered. Terrance immediately shut the door behind him, staying outside. Kon turned around, frowning at the closed door. The cramped hall into the next room only helped to raise the wariness in him.

"It really is. The students love that program," Para said to someone as he finally came into view of the entire room. Two couches lined the walls on both sides. On the far end of the small room was a single communicator station hooked to the wall. The room looked like it had an attempt to be homey, with a small end table set up with tissues and a plant. A rug in the middle spanned the entire length of the room, leading to the device. Para turned to see him, the phone device at her ear. "Oh, he's here!" She gestured him over with a large grin. Kon was hesitant about the entire situation and lingered before approaching. "Okay, nice talking with you. I'll put him on," she said as she pulled the comm from her ear and held it out to him. "It's for you."

For a long second, he merely looked at it, then her. Her smile was eager as he finally took the line, bringing it to his ear.

Silence at first.

"Kon?"

His heart fluttered at the familiar voice. The low, calm tone. "Joel?" He looked back as Para quietly exited the room. The caution in him melted to relief.

"Are you okay?" Joel asked.

"Yeah," he breathed, unsure of what to say after all the years of silence. He had promised to call, to visit. He never got the chance. "Are you?"

"We're good." Kon could hear the smile in his voice. "We've been worried about you. I'm glad you finally made it to these guys."

"Yeah, I just got here," he said in a blank tone, still a bit stunned. Para must have called him after their earlier conversation. "Are you guys still . . . at the house?"

"Yep, everything's pretty quiet here. I was trying to keep an eye on you with the scanners until . . . I'm just glad you're okay."

"What about Mallia?"

"She's—at the flower shop right now. She finally got it up and running. Asks about you all the time."

A pit of guilt formed deep in his stomach. "So, she's okay?"

"Yeah, she's good." Joel chuckled. "Are you planning on sticking around with these guys?"

"I don't know," Kon said, looking down at the ground as the relief continued to sink in.

"You should! If I knew more about them before you left, I would've urged you in that direction."

"You think so?"

"Well, you can't fight the EME alone. I regret you leaving on your own anyway. I . . . I shouldn't have let you." His tone twisted.

"It's okay. I'm fine," Kon tried, desperate for at least Joel to believe that.

"I almost went after you a couple times," he admitted. "But I'm glad you're there now."

Kon hesitated, having mixed feelings about the base. "I don't want to put everyone here in danger." While the walls around him still felt like something of a threat, there was a growing sense of safety. Maybe it was just Joel's voice that made him feel that way.

"You're actually probably safer together. I think it's the best place for you to be."

No response came as Kon kicked at the rug underfoot.

"I just . . . don't want you out there alone anymore, you know? They almost got you once already," Joel said, causing Kon to scrunch his nose at the memories. "I know you've got a lot of talent, but let them help you."

"Okay," Kon said. If Joel wanted him there, maybe he was right. Maybe they could help each other.

"You're gonna be okay, kid," Joel promised, his voice holding the same comfort it always did. A comfort that almost stung after so many years without it. "You made it this far. Time to give the EME hell."

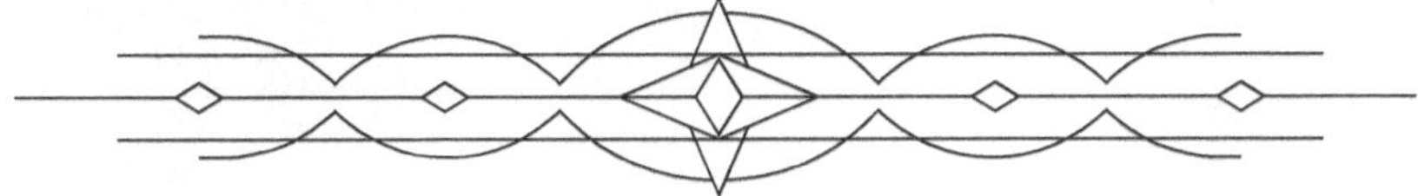

CHAPTER 18
THE BASE LIFE

"Just hold still for a second," Jasamie urged. "Icelyn, get the gel." She squinted as she held the arm of a boy who squirmed in his seat.

Icelyn opened a cabinet above the sink and nabbed the bottle of burn gel, handing it over.

"You guys have *got* to be more careful, *really*." Jasamie scolded the three young boys as she inspected the burn mark. "It's always one of you in here because of your sparring."

Icelyn moved a few cabinets down and grabbed a wrap, becoming familiar with her way around the med room. "We're going to run out of burn gel at this rate," Icelyn joked, handing the bandage to Jasamie as she finished applying the gel.

"I said I was sorry!" one of the boys yapped.

"If you can't spar *safely*, don't do it at all," Jasamie growled as she wrapped his arm.

"Keep a cold compress on it after the gel wears off," Icelyn added.

"Yeah, yeah, I remember . . ." the boy said as he looked over his bandaged arm. "Thanks."

"Be more careful. I don't want one of you back in here again tomorrow!" Jasamie called as they shuffled out of the room. She let out an exasperated sigh and turned to Icelyn, who was leaning against the counter, a grin across her pursed lips.

"I give it a week," Icelyn said with a chuckle.

"I give it two days," Jasamie muttered, prepping the exam table for the next patient.

"I guess everyone's trying to soak up the last of the decent weather."

"By throwing fireballs at each other!" She shook her head. "It's one after another lately. You came just in time. I'd go mad in here by myself."

"I'm glad I can help." Icelyn picked up the book she had been reading before. "I think I'm getting the hang of things pretty well." She started working in the med room as quickly as they'd let her, enjoying the ins and outs of it.

"Yeah, you're a natural. More patience than I have," Jasamie commented as a man walked in with a box. "Welcome back."

"Everything still in order?" he asked, pulling a pen from the pocket of his lab coat, glasses over his brown eyes. His dark hair was short and curly, graying slightly.

"The fireballs ran in here with another burn," Jasamie said with a sigh.

"Well, more burn gel." He tossed the package over to her.

"Just in time. We were getting low." Icelyn opened the cabinet, checking over the few bottles left.

"Anything else you need, Dad?" Jasamie asked as they stocked the shelf.

"No, I'll take over. Go get some food." He nodded, pulling out the chair to the desk.

Icelyn grabbed her book as they departed. "Bye, Mr. Ryv." She gave him a smile as they left. A waft of fresh air drifted from the base entrance.

Down in the cafeteria, at their usual table, Jasamie set her tray down with a huff. "So, how are you adjusting?"

"I think I'm doing alright." Icelyn shrugged, looking over the greens and sandwich before her.

"Did Para talk to you about the relocation program and all of that?"

"Yeah, she mentioned it."

"You think you'll stay or go for it? Some Elementals just want to forget it all happened, so it's good for starting fresh."

Icelyn felt the slight sting of the question. The thought of relocating again, to somewhere even farther and unfamiliar, hadn't grabbed her attention well. "I don't know. I think I like it here for now, if they'll let me stay."

Jasamie let out a snort, smirking at her with a questioning brow. "Why wouldn't they let you stay?"

Icelyn sunk in her seat slightly, pecking at the salad. "I don't know. I mean, I can't even use my powers hardly at all."

Next to her, Jasamie was amused. "You're still an Elemental. Besides, there are plenty of people here who aren't. Terrance, Peter, half of the staff. *Me?* No one's kicked *me* out."

"I know . . . I just want to be helpful in some way, I guess."

Jasamie's grin faltered. "Hey, no one's expecting Elementals to come in here and earn their place. You're here to stay safe. If you decide to help, we always appreciate it." The words hung in the air as she paused. "Plus, you're already helping, a lot. We don't get many people interested in the med bay."

Icelyn finally returned her smile, taking a bite of the leafy greens. Whatever she had thought of safe houses had been wrong so far. Of course, it was. Her only intel of them was from her EME father, speaking of them like hidden societies of Elementals bent on forming revenge. In reality, she hadn't seen much anger from anyone there. Everyone was busy plotting their next step in life. Being an Elemental surely brought a few extra steps, but here, continuing life seemed possible. Stormy and Jyune talked of their plans to open a bakery one day. Maybe it wasn't so crazy to plan a future.

From across the room, against the current of exiting students, Peter fought through the crowd. He frowned as he fixed his shirt collar, heading for them. "Are you guys going outside? It's super nice out," he asked, a hint of fluster over him.

Icelyn shared a shrug with Jasamie. "I guess we can."

"Wait for me!" Peter rushed for the line, giving them little room to argue.

"What's up with him?" Jasamie said, watching him stumble into line, tucking his book under his arm.

"He's doing some research project or something." Icelyn shook her head as he made his way back over to them. He had been frantic ever since their exploration the days before. Kon's disappearance had only stressed him out more. In recent days, he was distant. He would show up occasionally, to the displeasure of both Para and Peter. The rest of the time, there was no telling where he was. The absence forced Peter to share his ideas with her instead, talking about theories and guesses at the information found in the database. He was onto something.

There was a small stream of students headed for the doors. Cool air flowed through the open doors, chilling the halls. The base was back above ground. With the weather warm and no signs of EME, students had finally pressured Terrance into clearing it to lift again. Icelyn scanned the base of the bunker. The rim around its base was a perfect seat for students. They lined the platform, eating their lunches while others found seating on the rocks around the field or simply among the tall grass, visiting with the cats that came for attention. The air was refreshing, and Icelyn was glad her EME experience the few days before hadn't ruined her love for the outdoors, though she wouldn't dare venture into the woods alone.

"Come on over here," Jasamie called, beckoning them to an open spot on the platform. Icelyn sat her tray down on the cold steel as younger students played in the field. Jasamie was watching the kids cast fire with a lowered brow, expecting them to rush back to the med bay with another burn at any moment; meanwhile, Peter sat his stuff down, staring at his book as if his mind were reading it from memory.

The balls of fire, gusts of wind, and other Elemental practices reminded Icelyn of her own need to practice. While it was slow, she was seeing the slightest hints that her power was starting to understand her. There were less waves of cold over her, and she could almost frost her cup of water. A tiny progression but one she was fairly surprised with, being that she had never seen any signs of her abilities beyond the bothersome chill that followed her around. Her attention set back on Peter as he squirmed in his seat. "Are you okay?"

"Have you seen Kon? He stays around you the most if he shows up at all." His tone was laced with annoyance as he kept it at a whisper.

"That's not—" It was true. Icelyn scrunched her nose. "I think Para needed him for something."

His eyes hovered over his book for a second, then at her. "I've been looking into the AIP. Para has a ton of old documents about it." His tone was hushed.

Jasamie peeked her head around Icelyn. "The Avari Integration Program?"

"Yes."

"What does it have to do with us?"

Peter hesitated, biting his lip with a frown. "You can't tell anyone."

She gave him a dry brow. "Everyone knows Avari were in an Integration Program. What about it?"

"I think we should go to it."

"To the AIP base?" Icelyn asked in confusion while she toyed with her cup of water.

"Yes."

"Huh." Jasamie straightened, taking another bite of food.

"I'm still figuring it out," Peter mumbled.

Icelyn's eye had been drawn across the field where students disappeared into the woods. "Where are they all going?"

Jasamie shrugged. "Calirue. A lot go down to shop when it's nice."

"Really? Is that safe?"

"Yeah. We're close with the town community." Jasamie took in Icelyn's curious gaze. "You want to go?"

There was the smallest blossom of excitement from Icelyn as she met Jasamie with a growing grin.

"Kon?" Para huffed. "Anything?"

Kon watched the clear sky with disinterest. "No." He looked back at the group. Para, Terrance, and another woman dressed in military garb stood over the Help Key on the ground. The same device where he had met Para. Apparently, several were scattered around the outskirts of the base.

Para was kneeling down, pulling and pinching various wires while Terrance held a device in his hand, shaking his head. "Still up," he said.

"What is *up* with these things?" Para growled as the Help Key continued to blink its screen on the words "Help is on the way!" as the musical humming continued. She yanked a final wire as the screen went black and the device folded closed into the ground. She let out a sigh and stood up. "Well, there's one."

"You're sure we should take them all down?" the other woman asked. Short brown hair fell around her face, matching her dark eyes that occasionally drifted to watch the woods around them.

"They almost got us caught. If the EME is moving through this area, we can't risk them finding it again." Para sighed. "Either way, we can't safely answer them now that we know they tried tripping one. I'm just glad Kon was there the other day."

Kon looked back out into the woods. He agreed to come along as security, though he suspected Para did it simply to get him more used to them. His frequent disappearance had only made Para more eager to snag him when he *did* show up.

"Why do they keep going off like that?" Terrance said, kicking some leaves over the small folded device. "They're only supposed to activate around Elementals. This one was going off before we even got to it."

Para frowned in thought. "It thinks there's an Elemental nearby." She paused, slowly drifting her gaze over at Kon. "Unless . . . there is."

Kon turned back to them with the silence that followed to find them all peering at him. "What?"

"You think he's activating them? From that far?" Terrance asked, raising a brow.

"Well, his field of energy is definitely broader than an Elemental—" Para stared at the Help Key. "That's probably why the other one went off that day . . ."

"I didn't touch it," Kon said.

"You don't have to. It picks up energy fields. Yours just must be a lot bigger." Para put her hands on her hips. "Good to know, but it doesn't matter. They still need to go offline."

"On to the next one?" Terrance said with a sigh, pulling up his map.

"Yeah," Para muttered.

Terrance started tapping on the digital map to the next Key. "Ashdyn, tell Deyin to check the relay on this one, just to make sure."

Ashdyn turned to the side as she activated her earpiece while Para took a last inspection over the Key, checking to make sure it was hidden. Her gaze drifted to Kon, who was still peering at them in confusion. He moved closer as she beckoned him over. "Have you been down to Calirue?" she asked, catching her breath.

Kon gave a grimace and shook his head. "I don't go into towns."

"Well, they know about us," she said. "A lot of Elementals go down there to shop."

"I'm not an Elemental." Kon tilted his head.

"I know. Calirue is a long-standing ally with us. They have as much reason as we do to keep the EME away. A lot of Elemental families live there, including the mayor. If you do need to go into town for anything, Calirue would be good for you."

His frown persisted, unconvinced.

"I wouldn't tell you to trust them if I didn't trust them myself. There *are* people you can trust."

"And people you can't." He pushed his hands into his pockets.

Para studied him as she pulled her braid over her shoulder with a sigh. It was one of the few decently warm days left of fall. Leaves crunched as they traversed the woods, working loosely in a circle around the base to each of the Help Keys. Despite the previous flare-ups with the EME— meeting Para and rescuing Icelyn—the EME had gone strangely silent. Kon was sure the two encounters would raise EME activity, but as far as Para and Deyin had reported, there had been mostly radio silence in the area. Para had lightly explained the base's tactics to draw the EME away; something of planting false calls to push them farther from the base.

He contemplated how true that was, or maybe Para simply didn't want to bother him with the truth. However, with his own investigations around the area, he could confirm the lack of EME movement. It was unnerving. He never knew them to back out of an area that had unresolved Elemental activity. Especially with them having followed him that way. It was as if the base's presence itself was deterring EME from searching for him there.

It didn't make sense.

The next few Help Keys went at the same slow pace until they had circled to the last one. Kon positioned himself away from the group again, crossing his arms as he watched the woods. He was fairly certain there was nothing out there by the time they got to the last Key, but he kept his watch anyway as they fiddled with it. Terrance was kneeling, pulling wires from the panel. Para held the digital screen, watching the map as Deyin talked over the radio in Ashdyn's hand.

"They were going to get glitchy over winter anyway. They always do," Deyin explained.

Para had seemed disappointed about deactivating the Keys, explaining how they've helped in the past. Elementals traveling to the coast would often stumble across them, where the Key would give them information and alert the base. It wasn't a large number of students brought in, but Para insisted if they helped even one student get to safety, they were worth it. "We'll just have to think of a way to drive Elementals into Calirue. They can contact us from there," she said, glancing over to Kon as he lingered.

"Maybe send some locals out periodically," Ashdyn suggested.

Terrance pulled the last wire as the device folded into the ground before looking up at Para for confirmation.

"Offline," Deyan said through the radio.

"Yeah, it's down," Para confirmed, watching the last dot on the map disappear before she dropped the device to her side. "They're all offline."

Kon started to fall back in with the group as they prepared to leave but stopped, staring into the woods.

Para noticed his sudden pause. "What?" she asked as Terrance stood quickly.

He hesitated. "Hovercraft. That way." He watched through the trees where the faintest buzzing could be heard from the sky.

"Deyin? Is there a Hovercraft nearby?" Ashdyn pressed.

"That's by Calirue?" Terrance scrutinized as he tried to listen for it. "How do you hear that?"

Deyin picked up on the radio after a moment of silence, causing them to jump slightly. "What direction? I don't see anything on the radar."

"By Calirue," Ashdyn muttered, running her hand through her dark hair.

"Nothing. They might be flying under the radar."

"Are you sure it's one?" Terrance asked with skepticism.

Kon glared back at him. "Yes."

"Okay, let's get back." Para pulled at her bag. "We can call Calirue from the base and see if they know anything about it. It's not getting closer, is it?" she asked, looking to Kon, who was still sharing glares of contempt with Terrance.

Kon broke his gaze, finding his eyes back at the woods around him. "No." The humming started to fade as they gathered themselves and headed toward the base.

"If it's flying below the radar, that's not a good sign. We might have to get the relay scanner going," Terrance said, watching around them.

"Could they still be looking for the girl we found?" Ashdyn asked, pushing her supply pack behind her.

"I figured they would've given up searching for Icelyn in this area. It's been a few days." Para shook her head. "And that doesn't explain why they would be flying that low."

"Calirue doesn't have a docking station or something?" Kon suggested.

"No, they use regular air travel for supplies," Terrance said.

"It's probably nothing. They like to sweep around Calirue all the time," Para said, though her tone was unconvincing.

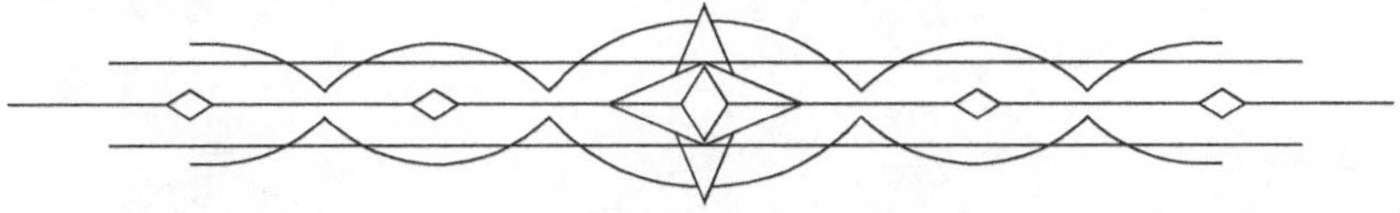

The path down to Calirue was likely the only worn trail around the base. Students filed to and from town as Icelyn peeked at each thing they carried back. Some carried bags of clothing, others held books and fresh food. Icelyn couldn't determine the true reason for the pit in her stomach. "Are you sure it's safe?" she asked, pulling at her satchel. "I don't know if EME from Alinth are still looking for me."

Jasamie nodded, stepping around the roots and ferns along the path. "Trust me, no one in Calirue is calling the EME. It's a small town with a lot of Elemental families."

It was hard to accept she'd be free to enjoy an outing after so many years of hiding in Alinth. Many of those years she hardly knew she was hiding. Soon after discovering she may have been an Elemental from the buzz of her dad's scanner, he all but yanked her from every school activity and anything that would lead her to be away from home longer than necessary. His anger toward it all might have been at her powers, but it never felt that way. It felt like a fault of her own, in that distant scowl he'd give her.

He never did look at her the same.

"Do you come down here a lot?" Icelyn asked as Jasamie gave a few waves to passing students.

"Not really. Never had anyone to go with."

Icelyn tilted her head. "Really?"

The path underfoot had evened out, trees starting to thin. Jasamie only shrugged, pulling at her yellow scarf. "When you're friends with everyone, you're kinda friends with no one."

Icelyn's lips pursed. Most of her own friends had forgotten about her years before when she stopped going out. She managed to rekindle tiny friendships in her nursing classes but then her dad pulled those from her grasp. Even now, forming small friendships at the base, there was the fear that somehow, her father would take them too.

Entering the main street of town, a large archway welcomed them in, leading to the string of storefronts along the stone street. It was buzzing with students, or what Icelyn could only assume were base students. She only recognized a few of them, traversing up and down the street. There was a bakery, thrift store, barber, and more businesses in town. Icelyn could only swivel her head in all directions, trying to take in the possibilities.

"Are you good?" Jasamie asked, shifting into Icelyn's vision.

"Yeah," Icelyn breathed. The air was fresh, smelling slightly of baked bread and flowers as her eyes panned down the brick storefronts decorated with colorful hanging plants.

"Where do you want to go?"

Icelyn circled another time or two before her eyes found it. "They have a bookstore?" The store sat across the street. Plants hung in the windows, decorated with piles of books. A sign on the window read "book sale" in large red letters.

"Yeah. C'mon." Jasamie beckoned for her, heading for the quaint store.

A bell chimed as they crept inside. The store gave no waste of space. Bookshelves lined the relatively tight hall, greeting them in the small entryway. The air inside was cold and dry, the smell of incense somewhere in the dusty air. Icelyn immediately entered one of the halls of bookcases, running a hand over the spines of the dated books. Reading was about the only thing she kept up back home; hiding away in her room, reading of a better life. Part of her wanted to draw away from books in an attempt to free herself from that life, but another part of her couldn't help the draw of it.

The store was mostly empty of other customers as they browsed. Icelyn picked out a few books, something new to try along with a large old book nestled at the back. She had almost missed it in the dim light of the back corner: a book on Avari. Coated in dust and yellow pages, it looked hardly opened in twenty years. She and Jasamie agreed that Peter would be ecstatic over the find, hopefully enough to bring him out of whatever edge he had grown lately.

Back out on the streets, they discovered a plant store to Icelyn's delight in their cruise of the town. Elbows linked, they enjoyed the small colorful street. No one questioned them, no one batted an eye. It was the first time Icelyn had felt safe to leave the comfort of her space. A place where she could belong.

Back into the woods, heading up the trail to the base, Jasamie let out a sigh. "That was fun, right?"

Icelyn's grin agreed. She clutched her satchel of books. "Yeah."

"Have you been working on those special little ice powers of yours?"

"At best, I can keep a drink chilled," Icelyn joked.

Jasamie cocked her head to the side with a coy brow. "So, your name is Icelyn—with ice powers. How'd that come about?"

Icelyn chuckled. "Yeah. It's . . . odd." Her eyes found the dirt path below. "There was this huge snowstorm the day I was born. My mom wanted to name me after it, in Makovan tradition. She always said I reminded her of winter back home. That my eyes were like the ice of the lake she grew up by, back on Makova." Icelyn had never gotten to see that lake by the ocean that her mom talked about. She let out a tiny breath. "After she died, my powers came in. Ice. I guess the cold has followed me my whole life."

"I'm sorry," Jasamie said before falling silent. The trees around them swayed in the early autumn breeze. "Kind of sounds like your powers were meant to be."

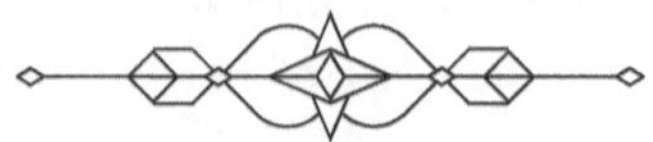

After Kon had heard the distant hovercraft, the short walk back to the base was filled with tension. Para and Terrance made conversation, but there was a clear bother in their tones. They threw out mentions of doing a sweep or even starting up the hoverform for a test run. Kon still questioned if they had one. In his wide and thorough search of whatever part of the base he could access, he'd never found signs of it.

As the field came into view, students were still out. Some sat upon rocks while others practiced their abilities a bit farther from the large base. They had just cleared it to rise back above ground. Kon wondered if they'd move it back under with the notice of activity. Of course, their standing with the EME seemed much more confident than his. Subtle signs of EME were always his first indication to leave, though he supposed the EPS didn't get its reputation by running from the EME. They were the only force on Brynden Ka that fought it.

Several students waved to Para. Some sat in the grass having club meetings, while other younger students zipped up and down the field. Para had explained that the base's defense system would alert them of any hovercrafts that came too close, allowing at least some peace of mind for students to enjoy the field. Other base staff had stationed themselves in the woods, watching for danger there as well.

Kon broke from the group early in hopes of slipping away unnoticed—hopes that were quickly dashed by Samlin blocking his path.

"Kon! Can I show you my fireball now?" he asked with a toothy smile. Kon could barely get a word in before Samlin turned and beckoned for him to watch. "It'll take a second. We won't get many more good days!"

Kon sighed, taking a few paces closer to watch.

"Okay, Wyatt, get it ready!" Samlin called to a boy in the distance who was straightening a stick they had poked into the ground and craftily placed an empty box on top as a head. The boy ran for cover as Samlin conjured the flames around his arms, squaring up the makeshift enemy. After a moment of preparation, he threw up his hand, a bolt of fire zipping through the air, igniting the energy around the box as it went up in flames. He then lowered his arm, freely casting a final burst to knock the charred box onto the ground, where the boy nearby quickly ran to stomp the rest of it out. "See?" Samlin turned to Kon with a grin, shaking his curly brown hair from his face.

Kon couldn't deny the power was impressive for a kid his age, though his confidence only brought worry for Kon. He nodded, looking for words. "It's good," he said with a casual tone.

"And I've still got a ton of energy!" Samlin boasted. "You should show us some of your stuff!"

"Yeah!" the other boy agreed, carrying over the burnt box. Their eyes watched him in eager excitement.

Kon shook his head, keeping his hands in his pockets. "I'll save that for the other guys," he tried to joke as Samlin sighed. The other boy ran back to the stick to set up the burnt box for himself. Kon didn't find interest in "showing off." There was nothing that made him feel good about using his powers. They had always been a danger to him. Something for emergencies. His training wasn't done lightly, and never for people to watch.

Kon made his escape for the door again, scanning for Para and Terrance, who were nowhere in sight. He was curious if they would find a trace of the hoverform. Their attitude toward it was strange. Among the crowd, he noticed her pale hair first, as Icelyn sat at the platform of the base. Her eyes found him at the same moment, a smile forming as she stood up. She was alone, holding a bottle in her hand as they approached each other. In the few days being there, she had been the only person he didn't find difficulty talking to. She made little fuss of his appearance—or disappearance—only happy to talk when he showed up again. She was maybe the sole person there that trusted him to reappear.

"Where is everyone?" he asked, rubbing his neck as he looked around.

"Uhm, Peter and Jasamie went to the library. I stayed out here to practice," she said, looking down at her clear bottle of water. "Look!" She held it up to show the hazy signs of ice forming on the outside of the cup.

His expression softened behind his wavy hair, and a small grin formed.

"You're learning fast." Tilting his head, he examined the layer of frost over the cup. "Does it still feel cold?"

"A little, but I think there's *some* shield there. I didn't even need my jacket today." She masked her grin, looking back down at the cup, seemingly satisfied with his reaction. The top half of her pale hair was pulled back, secured in fabric of blue as she trailed her hand through the waves over her shoulder. She gave a hopeful breath. "Anyway—uh, Peter was wondering where you were."

"Isn't he usually?"

"Yeah, but he's doing some research or something. He wants to meet tomorrow morning," she said as they passed through the open doors. "Did you guys get everything shut off?"

"Yeah."

"No EME still?"

"Not that I saw," he said, holding back the mention of the hovercraft. Para was right, it could easily be nothing. He heard them often in the distance when he was traveling, and they rarely amounted to anything. There was no reason to freak out students.

"Well, that's good." Icelyn shrugged. "When I got here the other day, I thought for sure they'd find us."

"Me too." They walked through the mass of students heading outside. His wariness of the situation hadn't worn off, but things had calmed down over the days since he arrived. The base's overall confidence in their own safety was hard to ignore. Whether by ignorance or knowledge, it was hard to tell.

"Me and Jasamie went to Calirue," she explained, stuffing her bottle back in her satchel of books. "There were a ton of students down there."

"Yeah, Para mentioned it." Kon pushed a hand in his pocket, stone-faced over the idea of entering town. "How'd it go?"

"It was good," Icelyn said, a higher shift to her voice as if she already knew he wouldn't believe her. "It felt safe enough for us."

A group of students passed as Kon returned their stares. Many hadn't completely settled yet with his appearance at the base, still wide-eyed any time he'd turn up again. "Huh." He tried to hide the disagreeing curl in his lip. *By "us," she must've meant Elementals; everyone else at the base.* In his eyes, there was no benefit of the doubt to give towns anymore. It only took one person to be curious. One person to glance a moment too long and question the inky marks over his skin. His other attributes could be any mix of species, but not the markings. Those were damning if the right person recognized them. Para's glint of confidence meant nothing to him. He had all but stopped going near towns years ago.

Past the cafeteria and common room, they turned for the sunroom through their mix of casual talk. It remained a place they went to often. If Kon was anywhere in the base, it was the sunroom or his own room. Icelyn discussed her med bay adventures, enamored by the job she had achieved there. She was fitting in well.

The small round room was bright, illuminated by the tall window. Elementals played in the field behind the base, enjoying the cool fall air. It was a stark contrast from the recent flurry of rain and snow.

Icelyn plopped down onto the first step with a sigh. Kon was slower to approach as she watched him. Her voice had shifted, ever so quiet. "I can never tell if you like coming back."

Pulling at his jacket sleeve, he gave a tilt of his head as he joined her. At first, he simply watched her wavy hair fall over her shoulders. "If I didn't, I wouldn't." It wasn't as simple as staying or leaving; at least, it wasn't in his mind. Kon had known for a while that something needed to change, that he was entering a dangerous position with the EME again.

Staying here was more so a desperation or maybe a long, deep exhaustion. Some vague hope to rekindle. But even if he could find that here, his body wouldn't allow him the grace of dropping his guard and truly rebuilding, so he split his time. He liked to tell himself that his pacing around the few miles by the base was useful, that he was watching out for danger. That wasn't the reason. In truth, he only felt safe on the move, therefore, he needed the imitation of it if he had any hopes of sticking around.

"I'm sorry," Icelyn said, seemingly out of nowhere.

Kon blinked at her. "For what?"

She folded her arms, resting on her knees. "It just seems like it's hard for you, or maybe scary, being here." Her eyes traced out the window where Palyra Mountain sat in the distance. "But you're trying, and I'm glad. I'm just sorry it's difficult."

Others didn't share the same opinion—at least not openly. From Peter's disgruntled comments about his disappearances to Terrance's frown at him anytime he headed for the door, it felt like more of an inconvenience to them; that they merely thought he was being unsociable, cold. But Icelyn never blamed his distant nature.

"It's not so bad here." He let his eyes wander to her cheek where the soft whisps of her bangs curled.

Her next question came as the laughs of Elementals let out in the field. "Have you always liked being alone?"

Did he ever truly like it? "No." There was one point that it terrified him, the thought of having only himself. But he didn't grow to like the solitude; instead, he merely chose it for his own safety or others. It was all just weird. Most times, he would be tailed by EME, not a single soul around to help him. Then, surrounded by Elementals, there wasn't a single sign of the EME since he'd been here. It was as if they had vanished as a whole. Maybe that's why he searched the woods day after day, to try and make sense of their silence. A rotten twist in his stomach made him ask himself if he missed them somehow. But that couldn't be it; their absence wasn't something to be missed—it was something to be feared.

Icelyn changed the subject after that, recounting her day in the med bay and anything else he had missed in his departure, as always. Most of it was trivial, but she seemed to take pride in filling him in each time. Her care to include him regardless reminded him of Mallia. Someone who was happy to have him nearby.

Icelyn finally grabbed her satchel. "We found this book for Peter," she explained, pulling the large worn book from the bag. "He told us to look for anything to do with Avari."

"Of course."

Icelyn paused, cracking open the book. The old pages turned over one another as she skimmed. "I should get it to him while he's in the library." As they stood, Icelyn flipped another page. "It's got all these drawings."

He finally inched closer, looking over her shoulder at the contents of the book. Thick pages showed scientific sketches and information. Loose paper of magazine articles dotted the book, as though someone had thrown out all they had regarding Avari into the single book.

Icelyn stopped on a drawing of an Avari. "It says here Avari have a third breathing port?" Her finger traced over the image where it circled the three gill-like lines on the Avari's ribs, directly under the breast. She read from the paragraph. "A third breathing port capable of filtering oxygen directly to the lungs—Do you have that?" She turned to look at his shirt, about where it would be.

"Never really used them," he frowned, instinctively folding his arms around his ribs.

"Really? You don't need to?" She looked back at the page.

"Regular breathing works fine for me." One of the many small details about himself he avoided.

Icelyn read over his deadpanned face a moment longer, then she closed the book. "Think he'll like it?"

"Surely." He unfolded his arms, still acutely aware of himself. "What is this for again?"

"Peter's meeting tomorrow. He says it's important."

"Important?"

"Yeah, I don't know." She shrugged. "He was really stressed out about it."

"He explained Avari marking patterns to me for fifteen minutes yesterday." He gave her a dry tilt of the head. "More important than that?"

A breathy laugh escaped her lips. "I don't know. I think it's about that facility."

"The Integration facility?" He still had hoped to get to it one day. Until then, the base was a comfortable enough spot to stay—a thought that bothered him—even as Icelyn met him with a warm grin.

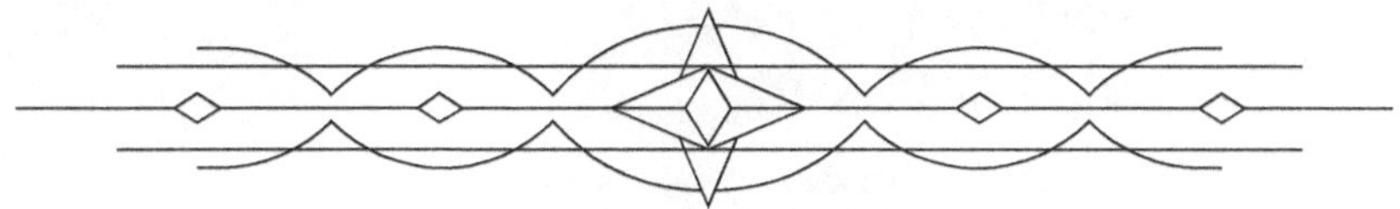

I believe in you.
I know you will make the difference.
B21
1010371071
BRYNDEN KA
West Weekly
Friday, March 3rd, 2636
News for the Western Sector of Brynden Ka
Weekend Weather
B21
AVARI INTEGRATION SPARKING
GALACTIC ATTENTION
Government hopes to keep Avari program under wraps fails after the new species was recognized in Galaxy Magazine, across multiple planets. Perhaps the most attention Brynden Ka has attracted, the Avari Integration Program has quickly been building interested in the overall quiet peninsula. Scientists have made towering strides in the investigation of the new species, including rumored medicinal magic found within
Mentor And Guvint with partnered Avari
Town of Dar
holds massi
spring mark
Starting off the fast approac
Summer, Darnar has announ
their 5th annual market. A to
of trade, and eager farmers
Darnar has been slowly but surely
raising their local trade market,
expanding their in town market
with a new addition across the
River. A ceremony was held
recently announcing the new
large bridge across the water,
made specifically for farms and
carts. Bring your precious crops,
and Darnar promises you a
fruitful event of selling and trade
to start off the new year.
Earning its reputation as a busy
trade town, Darnar continues to
provide location for local farmers
to buy and sell. Over recent years
trade has even expanded into the
Southern Sector, with addition of
the new Hoverdocks, fitting even
the largest carriers. This has since
marked Darnar as a familiar hub
for many hoping to trade their
crops off to farther Sectors, or
even off the peninsula entirely.
Local Darnar mayor executive

CHAPTER 20
THE LEAD

Peter sat in the empty library meeting room reading page after page of his old, worn book. The reading was almost a memory at that point. Habit. He must have read it a hundred times over the last few years. He flipped to the next page where the picture of him and his father spilled out. It was frayed and cracked. With a hesitant pause, he lifted the picture, turning it over to read the note again:

I believe in you. I know you will make the difference.

B21 1010371071

Those numbers had always plagued him. He had searched every possibility, every page number, article, and address with that series of numbers. Nothing. Had his father left him the answers to everything? His disappearance? The Avari? Maybe he wasn't smart enough to decipher it. He slapped the picture back down and closed the book, looking over the table of books he had collected over the last few days. Piles of organized magazines, articles, books—anything concerning Avari.

Jasamie appeared at the door carrying two newspapers. "Missed some," she chirped, setting them down on the table amongst the piles of evidence. "Haven't you read most of these already, though?"

"It's not about what I've read." Peter shook his head. "It's about . . . finding the connection between it all." He lifted the book Icelyn had presented him earlier, skimming the pages. Most of it was nothing new to him as he skimmed through, searching for a key difference.

Jasamie plopped down in a chair and scooted in, picking a random book from the pile. "What . . . type of connection?"

"A location, a name, *something* everyone's leaving out. None of these even say *which* Avari in the program was pregnant . . . Who are Kon's parents?"

"It doesn't say?" Jasamie asked, pausing to read a page of her book. "Were they hiding it?"

"None of them do. There's something missing." He frowned, flipping the pages as they led him to a bump in the book where an old newspaper flopped out. The cover was a picture of an Avari and a human, posing in the halls of the facility. He skimmed the paper, one he hadn't recognized in his collection of newspapers. It talked of Galactic media, advancements in knowledge, and new foods being introduced; the usual. Just another old news headline from the Avari Integration Program's prime.

"It's getting late, Peter." Jasamie yawned.

He tossed the magazine onto the table, leaning back with a loud sigh. *What was the point of this?* How many hours had he spent trying to solve the elaborate mystery of his father? He rubbed his eyes, looking down at the newspaper with a scowl.

There it was.

He grabbed the paper, fixing his round wire glasses as he pulled it closer, inspecting the entire picture.

"Peter?" Jasamie said.

The Avari and the man posed loosely for the picture, smiling. On the door behind them, like a haunting stamp placed just for Peter: B21.

"Oh, my God." Grabbing his book, he rushed back to the page he had been on.

"What?" Jasamie urged.

Peter quickly fumbled with the old picture, turning it over. *B21.* "It's a room number," he breathed.

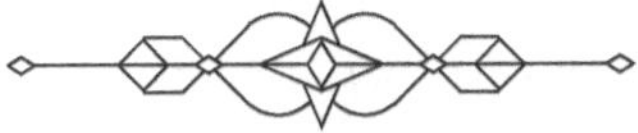

"Okay. I gathered the rest of the information last night with Jasamie," Peter stated, standing before a mildly confused Icelyn and Kon.

"Yeah, I'm still not sure what this is really about," Jasamie added in a casual tone as she leaned in her chair.

Kon took in the pile of books in front of them nearly spilling over the table. He didn't know why Peter seemed to be fraying at the edges in anxious energy as he paced the room. All he knew was it surely, definitely, had to do with Avari—a thought that made Kon regret showing up at all.

Icelyn stepped a bit closer, scanning the various old articles. Plucking one off the top, she inspected the photo of the Avari, glancing back at Kon with a raised brow. "You found all of these here in the library?" She pulled the sleeve of her cardigan over her hands as she read.

Peter peered over his stash of books, adjusting the position of the newspapers before him, something Kon had counted him doing at least five times since he arrived. With a step back, as if the papers had to be just right, Peter sighed. "Para likes to gather books about Elementals and Avari. The EME has been trying to get rid of information on them."

"I heard people off planet think Avari are a myth," Jasamie added.

"Yeah?" Kon smirked, arms crossed. Peter had gathered them all early that morning. He assumed it was about Peter's grand scheme Icelyn had mentioned the day before, but for some reason, he hadn't expected that level of energy from him.

"We're getting off-topic!" Peter snapped, cutting off Jasamie. "I called you all here to help me—" The door to their library nook slid open as heads turned to see Stormy and Jyune peek in.

"Are we late?" Stormy asked.

"We brought snacks for the party." Jyune held up the bag of cookies from her seat on Stormy's shoulder.

Peter ushered them into the room. "Get in, and it's not a party." He craned his neck out the door with a last paranoid check into the library before he shut the door. "This is serious!"

"Just tell us what you found," Icelyn urged.

"This is *top secret.* We can't tell anyone. Not yet," Peter hissed, the third time he had said that. His tone stayed at an urgent whisper as he ran his hand through his abnormally messy hair.

Stormy and Jyune took a seat at the table as Icelyn lingered nearby, placing her article back on the table. Kon stayed at the back, avoiding looking at the images before him. The room had gone silent as they waited for Peter's grand plan to spill out.

"I think we may be able to uncover why the Avari left," Peter announced as confidently as he could without speaking too loudly.

Stormy tilted her head in confusion. "Didn't they just leave because the government wasn't agreeing on integration terms?"

"That's what they told everyone. That it was diplomatic. They agreed it wasn't working and left . . . but *no* evidence supports that."

"I think everyone knows it wasn't very diplomatic," Kon mumbled.

"Kon, as the only Avari here, what do *you* know about them leaving?"

Kon frowned, recalling the hazy information Joel had given him years before. He was always vague about the program, speaking of it distantly. "Government wanted control; it ended in a fight."

Peter laid his book down on the table. "I have reason to believe it was more than that. I think the answer is in the AIP base." He flipped open his book, pointing at the pile of evidence. "I went through each of these recollections of events that happened, written by news, mentors, EME, everyone . . . and they all have a different story. None of them match the story of Andren Day." He jabbed a finger into his book.

Jyune was seated on the table now, looking over her cookies, while Stormy peeked at the book, a crease of concern across her patterned Rilinquin brow.

"What's his story?" Icelyn tilted her head.

Swiping his book into his arms like it was second nature, Peter began, "November 2637, he mentions that the Elemental Investigation Forces, now named the EME, believed the Avari Integration Program was with-holding information from them. Vital information." He cast a glance back at the rest of the books. "No other recollection states this. I asked Para. The base doesn't have anything on it either. No mention of this. You know what else no one mentions?"

There was silence in the room before Icelyn finally caved. "What?"

"Him." Peter pointed at Kon, who gave him a frown.

"Well . . . was he even born yet?" Stormy asked, reaching for a cookie.

"We know he had to be born *before* they left, but not one of these issues mentions a child being born. No one even knows Kon exists. *He's* what they were hiding, but why?"

"If they were hiding him, why hide him *here*?" Icelyn questioned. "Why didn't they take him?"

Kon shrugged in the back as everyone watched him as if he could give them some play-by-play memory of the day he was born.

"It's like everyone's retelling of the program is missing something. I think whatever's missing is in that base . . ." Peter explained, voice quick-ening with every word. "And we can go to the facility—"

"We?" Kon interrupted.

"We can find out what the program was hiding," Peter continued.

"All of us?" Jasamie asked.

"Find out if another Avari is here—" Peter said.

"Wait, what?" Stormy questioned.

"*And find out where my dad went!*" Peter blurted, before finally stopping.

Eyes stuck on him in shock. Icelyn's brows creased. Jasamie looked lost, while Stormy and Jyune stared at Peter with large eyes. After a long draw of stunned silence from the group, Kon sighed. "No one's going anywhere."

"What?" Peter cried.

"I'm not putting anyone in danger to find old answers. It won't change anything happening now."

"It could!" Peter stuttered, sighing in distress. "Look!" He yanked his book open, pulling out the picture and slapping it on the table near Kon, the note on the back showing. "Look at this." He stared at Kon, clearly concerned most with him seeing it.

Kon half-heartedly moved closer, looking over the note.

"My dad wrote this letter to me. It says 'B21,' and then numbers. I've spent years trying to find out what it was—" he grabbed the newspaper, walking around the table at Kon's reluctance to get any closer than he already had. "Look at this picture. 'B21.' It's a room. He wants me to go to this room . . .in the AIP Facility. It could answer *everything!*"

Kon sighed at first, looking at the picture with disinterest—until he saw it. He took a step forward, taking the paper from Peter. His eyes narrowed on the image. Joel. He stood next to a male Avari who held a lopsided grin. Kon couldn't linger long on the Avari, the clear show of their dark markings made something twist in his stomach. He knew Joel was a mentor, but he rarely heard about the program, let alone saw images from it. Peter was right, the door behind them read 'B21." *Did Joel know?*

"See?" Peter urged. "Whatever is in there could answer things for you—*and* me."

Kon stayed quiet, eyes locked on Joel for another moment before he tossed the photo back on the table. He already knew Joel was a mentor. It still meant nothing.

"Who were Kon's parents?" Icelyn interrupted the tension as she picked up one of the magazines, an image of a group of Avari on the cover. "Do you know?" She looked back at Kon, caution in her pursed lips.

"Even I don't know," Peter scoffed.

Surprisingly, Kon knew something about himself that Peter didn't. He hesitated. "Jarauk and Padlin." Two names he held in his mind, though he had never gotten a face to pair with them. Joel was always hesitant to tell him much about them, besides simple things like how they were similar. He would always say, "*Maybe they'll come back and tell you themselves.*" Maybe he avoided it so Kon wouldn't go looking for answers. He still wondered about the statement. Did Joel really believe that? Or was it just to comfort a kid alone in the world?

"Jarauk?" Peter grabbed the newspaper, investigating it closer before he thrust it at Kon again. "That's him! Number one. See? It's connected!

I should've known it was him! How do you know that?" He was entirely frantic.

Kon looked at the image again, that time at the Avari. Joel didn't have pictures of them. Kon never knew which one of them matched the names. He had never seen Joel with an Avari—let alone his supposed father. It made something in him sting, looking at the Avari, who did look eerily like himself. His father. The father that left him there, alone. His cold gaze fell past the paper to Peter. "What does it matter, Peter?"

"It matters to me. Those answers could help *me* too. My dad left because of something he knew. What if it's the same reason you're here?" he urged. "We could both find out why our lives ended up like this."

Kon broke his gaze with a shake of his head, looking off to the side.

Across the room, Jasamie sat up, more serious as she laced her fingers together. "Okay, I understand it's important to get closure, but Kon has a point. Something like this could be dangerous. Does Para know anything about this?"

Peter shook his head rapidly, facing the table again as he took in his mountain of evidence. "No. I don't want to tell her—not yet. They have enough to worry about."

Jasamie held out her hands. "So, we all just disappear for a few days. You think she won't notice? She won't get concerned?"

"I don't know. I just think we should talk about it." Peter leaned on the table, brows furrowed in his stress. "So, here we are."

Stormy and Jyune had been unnaturally quiet, watching the situation unfold. "Where *is* this base?" Stormy asked, her voice slightly quieter than usual.

"It's by Darnar," Icelyn said.

"We know how to get there," Jyune piped in.

"Darnar is also where Garik Tally is, a scientist from the program," Icelyn added. "I think he could tell us a lot."

Jasamie rested an elbow on the table, frowning. "How do you guys know all this?"

"The database," Kon said, while Peter whipped his gaze to him, bewildered at the admittance.

"You went into the database?" Jasamie lowered her tone. "When?"

"That was a secret," Peter defended.

"The—night I got here." Icelyn rubbed her arm.

Peter pulled his hands to his head as their secret mission now lay on the table of events.

Jasamie blinked, a partial smirk in her tone. "And Terrance didn't find out?"

"Not yet," Peter breathed, angry gaze locked on Kon.

"Wow, you guys have been planning all week, haven't you?"

"We aren't planning anything," Kon said, his voice low in a growing agitation. "I just went looking for answers."

"But *now* you don't want answers?" Peter argued. "We have a lead! You said it yourself that you wanted to get in there!"

"Alone. You two tagging along that night didn't put you in danger. This would." Kon stared back. "I shouldn't have mentioned it."

Peter's arms dropped to his side in defeat.

Icelyn glanced between them, biting a lip as her hand ran over her wavy hair. "Maybe we can figure out something. I mean, you brought us here to talk about ideas. Maybe there's a way that everyone can be happy."

"Maybe it wouldn't hurt to include Para in this discussion?" Jasamie noted.

Peter and Kon spoke with a simultaneous, "No."

Kon glanced at him before continuing. "He's right; she's got enough to worry about. If it doesn't amount to anything, it's just a waste of time."

"But we can't all just disappear," Jasamie argued. "That would cause more problems than it would prevent."

"Maybe someone can cover for us?" Stormy suggested. "Make up some alibis?"

"I don't think that would work for all of us," Icelyn said. "Jasamie and I work in the med bay. If we don't show up, her dad and Alaura will know—and Para is always checking on where Kon is. She'd notice too."

Jasamie nodded. "What if Kon went alone and took a radio? We can keep in contact, and he could probably get in and out faster without us. Para already knows he leaves a lot. It's less suspicious."

Peter's brows furrowed, though he stayed quiet. Stormy shrugged. Kon didn't bother giving input either. The idea of being called on a radio every five minutes didn't seem ideal. He'd likely throw it in the river within an hour of leaving.

Icelyn stared at the carpeted floor before she spoke. "Why don't we all think on this? Meet here again tomorrow and see if anyone has any ideas."

Peter nodded stiffly. "Yeah, but no one discusses this outside this room," he said. "Okay, Jyune?"

Jyune chuckled. "Okay, Stormy?"

"Hey, I'm not a chatterbox like you," Stormy sneered.

"Good. Tomorrow," Peter said, taking a last look at them all before picking up his book and rushing out of the room. Icelyn turned to Kon as Stormy and Jyune departed as well.

"Lousy party," Jyune mumbled on the way out, cookies in hand.

Jasamie stretched. "I knew he was up to something last night, but I didn't expect *that*."

"You think he's right?" Icelyn asked, lingering near Kon.

He could feel her eyes on him. "I don't know," Kon said, glancing at the newspaper on the table. He didn't know why the eyes of those old images stung.

With a last glance at the pile of evidence, Icelyn joined him on the way out. The rest of the library was fairly empty, only a bluish-Rilinquin girl scanning the tall wooden shelves across the room. The nook they had just left was often reserved for reading or study groups. There was another parallel across the library. The carpet underfoot helped to muffle footsteps as they departed into the hall.

"Should someone check on him?" Jasamie asked. "He seems really high-strung lately."

"I think he needs to take a break." Icelyn pulled at her cardigan, glancing up at Kon, who was still silent, his gaze deep in thought. He could admit Peter's idea wasn't crazy, though the logic of it rested on emotion. The idea that he could find answers about his father while unlocking secrets about the Avari was certainly enough to bring Peter to that level of craze. Though, it would need far more planning than a short library meeting.

"I've got to get back to the med bay." Jasamie shook her head. "I'll check on him later if I can find him."

As they rounded the corner into the next hall, they all slowed to a stop at the scene approaching them.

"Well, that was easy," Icelyn said as they looked upon Peter, his face laced with a scowl as he approached. Para and Terrance trailed behind him, their expressions twisted in trouble.

"See? He's right there," Peter said.

They stopped short of the group, Para looking over Kon in pure . . . confusion. "Kon," she started. Her mouth remained open, looking for words before she turned to Terrance, brows creased.

"What?" Kon asked carefully as they stared at him in something of dismay. His stomach was starting to knot into a familiar pit in his chest, mainly over Terrance, who wore a thick military jacket. Dressed for the outside, it was a new look for him, but most concerning was the pistol on his side and the strap of a rifle over his chest.

In the mess of concern across Para's face, she finally spoke, a tone laced with fear. "We have a problem."

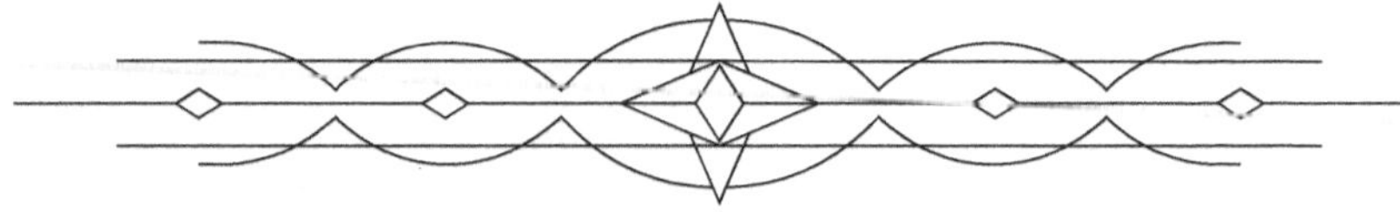

JOLLY FISHER

CHAPTER 21

TRUST

MAY 2654

Sixteen years since Avari left.

Leaves above gave way, dropping nets of water onto the map below. Kon attempted to wipe it with his sleeve as he kept his eye on the smeared 'X.' He had never been that far; the map was confusing enough without the strange terrain—flat outstretches of marshy woods, leading to cliffs of long winding lakes and canals. The only form of height in the land being the large, strange rocks jutting from the ground and the tall trees.

After leaving the cabin, it had taken him months to get that far south, the EME trailing him every step of the way. There were times of grace periods, a good week or two with no sightings, but they'd always show up again. Closer. He had several fights under his belt by then. Small EME scraps followed by him darting into the woods. While he was good at fighting, he was better at hiding.

He walked a bit farther, preserving his map in his coat until he could get to a clearing or shelter, whichever came first. It ended up the same, however. His path was blocked by the water again on the edge of the trees. The rock formations in the distance appeared to defy gravity, the towering boulders balancing themselves on small slivers of rock. Kon was cautious and looked out over the water. It was common for hovercrafts to float over the waterways for easier travel, something that was more seen in the south with the broader, calmer canals.

He rattled the wrinkled map out once more and scanned it. Times like these were when the silence would set in the deepest. Joel had taught him everything about navigation. Looking at the map, he could almost hear his tips and tricks. Joel would've known how to navigate the maze. Instead, Kon stood alone, frowning at the map in the dipping summer sun.

There was a town straight south. Maybe he could head that direction for the night—try to move north in the morning. Back in the woods, it was darkening with the setting sun. The town was close, and although his hope had been to avoid it altogether, the twists and turns of the water were leaving few choices.

The haze of traveling all day was wearing on him. The EME pushing him into uncharted land hadn't given him much rest in days. There was no telling what they were attempting to do. He only hoped he wasn't heading where they wanted.

Street lamps came into view up ahead, and he could see the beginning of a small bridge into town. He quickly found what he was after—the information sign and map detailing paths to and from the town. Maybe with luck, he wouldn't even need to head into town.

Illuminated by the yellowish sky, there were two forms on the bridge, looking out at the water as Kon approached quietly, hoping to avoid any notice at all. He pulled out his map again, comparing the two as he marked down the roads and bridges not labeled on his own. There was a path north. He took another glance around and noticed the forms on the bridge were now watching him—a girl and a boy, both carrying traveling backpacks like his. Kon didn't stick around, quickly folding his map and turning back toward the woods.

If he could make it to the Hyeva Mountains by nightfall, he could be back in the Western Region by tomorrow and heading north. He suspected the EME would stay south for a while looking for him. It was a favorable plan, aside from the fast-growing fatigue clouding his mind. He hardly noticed the two travelers following behind him—until the snap of a twig made him turn.

They stopped with him, staring, both in tattered clothing. The girl was human with brown hair that was pulled back loosely. The boy was a taller Rilinquin of a muted purple hue and dark burgundy hair, short over his forehead. There was silence as they faced each other.

"Are you going north?" the boy finally asked, as the girl hugged the straps of her bag, her large, dark eyes watching Kon with something of . . . nerves.

Kon weighed the option of saying nothing, slowly studying them as he finally spoke. "Trying to get to Keylon," he lied. It was a fishing town northwest of there, by the coast. Believable enough in the direction he was headed.

"Do you know if there are any safe houses around there?" the boy said, head tilted in a shy demeanor. They *were* Elementals. Kon had figured as much when he saw the backpacks and careful expressions. They must've figured he was as well—if they didn't already notice the markings, growing ever darker by the year.

"I don't know," Kon said, turning to leave.

"Can we travel with you?" the Rilinquin asked. "I'm Rin. This is Sadie. We're just trying to get to a safe place."

Sadie shifted, rubbing the straps of her backpack as her eyes darted the floor.

Kon glanced between them. "I don't travel in groups."

"Just to Keylon, at least? We don't even know where to stay for the night," Rin insisted.

"That town has inns probably." Kon gestured back to the town they were leaving.

"No money," Sadie spoke, her voice tiny, matching her jittered movements.

"It's too risky anyway," Rin explained. "Two teens traveling alone . . . it's probably obvious what we are."

Kon sighed as the sky was glowing orange, clouds from the rain in the far distance. "To Keylon, that's it," he stated. It would only slightly disrupt his path. It couldn't hurt to let them follow him that far, then lose them in town.

"Okay," Rin said with a small grin. Their clothing indicated they had come from the north as well—layered gray clothing and wearing scarves of worn cloth.

Kon reluctantly turned and started walking again, figuring the best plan would be to keep his pace. They followed without another word. There wasn't even conversation with each other as they kept behind him. His only indicator they remained on his trail were the footsteps. The silence stayed for most of the setting sun until the sky was turning pink with the last bursts of sunset, the woods already dark.

"Should we set up for the night?" Rin finally asked in a strangely casual tone.

Kon slowed, worried they would request a stop as he turned to them. They both fidgeted as they watched him.

"Maybe over here?" Rin said, after the lack of response from Kon.

"I'm gonna keep going," Kon said. "Just go northwest in the morning until you hit the coast. Keylon will be there."

There was a look of panic from Sadie, more so annoyance from Rin. "You're leaving?" he asked with an edge.

Kon shrugged. "You'll be fine." He gripped the strap of his bag, turning. There was a subtly growing urge to leave them; one he couldn't place yet.

"Wait—" Sadie said. "Can you at least help us start a fire? I . . . I don't want to be here in the dark," she stuttered.

Kon sighed, guilt sticking in his chest at her pleading eyes. "Where?"

They looked around quickly, pointing to a small open space amongst the brush. "Here," she pointed, putting her bag down as she pulled at her scarf.

"Okay." Kon lingered closer as Rin dropped his bag as well, watching him in silence.

Sadie crouched to gather some small sticks and piled them together, looking up every few seconds to make sure Kon was still there.

"I'll go look for some dry wood." Rin moved away from the clearing into the dark woods.

Kon watched him for a moment before he looked back at Sadie, who was still pushing sticks together on the ground in a rush. He moved closer, kneeling to help. Her hands trembled as she gathered each stick, pausing only as she reached for the same one as he did. Her hand hovered, shaking, before she pulled it back. Kon paused with her, a sinking in his stomach forming, ever so slowly.

"Will this work?" she asked through a sniffle.

"Yeah. Just keep adding to it through the night. Wood, not many leaves," he explained as he took the stick in his hand and began heating the air around it until it *poofed* into a small bundle of flames. He nestled it under the others, kindling it with his own energy until the fire was supporting itself. Sadie watched the flames, her eyes glazing over. Kon started to move back, reaching for his bag to make his escape.

"Wait—" she grabbed for her own bag. "You don't want to stay? It's getting dark."

Kon opened his mouth to defend himself. Everything in him was telling him to leave as she pulled her bag around, faster than she meant to. It flopped to the side, her belongings spilling out. Some wrapped bread, a cloth, part of a jacket—and a tracker. Not a digital map to perhaps navigate, but a new tracker. Small and shiny, it stuck out from the rest of the items. It wasn't something most people in Brynden Ka carried, or could even get. It was a military device. Kon had stopped moving, looking at her in confusion.

"I'm sorry," she cracked, tears welling in her eyes. "I'm sorry." She pulled at her scarf again, that time hard enough that it revealed her neck. There was a device around it—a metal collar with a ring of light glowing green in the center.

Kon grabbed his bag and stood, the hair on his neck standing up as a shiver ran through him.

She stood as well, inconsolable. "I'm sorry—I'm sorry," she continued to repeat between huffs of tears.

"What is that?" Kon asked, taking a step away from her. Fear was creeping through him.

She partially froze, meeting his eyes. Her expression folded as she whispered again, "I'm sorry." Her eyes drifted from him to something behind him.

Running sounded from the woods as someone rammed him from behind, full force, knocking him to the ground. Rin was on top of him, fist pulled back in preparation to punch. His expression sat blank, something of stiff contempt as his eyes had turned dark. Everything spun for a moment. Kon's arm went up to block the first blow, fire surging up his sleeves as Rin curled back away from the flames before he pulled a knife from his belt.

"Put it out!" the Rilinquin warned, slashing the knife and slicing through Kon's jacket, into his forearm. Rin channeled his own fire to prevent another burn as he forced one of Kon's arms to the ground. *He had fire too*. They never needed Kon for a fire. Through the struggle, Rin tried to hold the knife at his neck. "Stop," he warned.

He was larger than Kon, who had yet to grow into his height. Panic was too heavy to think of another way to get him off. Terrashock detonated between them, sending Rin flying backward next to the fire. Kon scrambled into a sitting position as the Rilinquin rolled on the ground, grasping his burnt hand as he stared at Kon in surprise. Kon quickly stood, looking between both of them as fire licked up his arms.

Sadie was sobbing uncontrollably, frantically pulling the scarf off and fully revealing the device around her neck. "They told us to! They told us to!" she cried.

"Who?" Kon asked, though he already knew. The Rilinquin started to stand. He was realizing the physical advantage Rin had over him. He was older, taller, and stronger, as he stood, sizing up Kon. Kon couldn't let him get that close again.

"We bring you to them. We go free. That's the deal," Rin spat. "It's nothing personal." Fire sparked up his arms as he shook himself out. Kon could see the edge of the same type of collar under his scarf. The work of the EME. It all clicked in his head.

As the first blast of fire came at Kon, he realized Rin was fighting for his life—a fruitless effort. So was Kon. He only hesitated for a moment, as guilt flashed through him, before he sent another wave of terrashock surging back, much larger that time—larger than he meant as fear clung to him. It rippled through the fire, dissipating it until it reached the Rilinquin, sending him flying back once more. That time, he hit a tree with a *thud*. There was a pang of remorse as Kon turned to Sadie, who was still sobbing.

Upon realizing Kon's attention was on her, she dropped to the ground. "I'm sorry . . . please . . . I don't even know him," she wept. "They . . . they just told us to find other Elementals . . . to find you." She held her hands across her face, preparing for his attack.

Kon was frozen. Something in his chest burned at her fear that he would attack her next. He had only looked to her for answers. "Where are they?" Kon inquired, trying to keep his shaky tone harsh as he kept an eye on Rin, still curled up at the tree.

"I don't know . . . Probably coming . . . soon. I'm sorry . . ." she cried. "They said we could go if we found you. They showed us pictures. I didn't want to." Her words kept spilling out as Kon stood in shock. Even other Elementals were unsafe. Of course the EME would use them against him too.

"This is your fault," Rin coughed, clutching his ribs as blood pooled in his mouth. "We're dead because of you," he snarled as the girl soothed herself with heavy breaths. The words stung in his chest.

Kon's gaze lingered on him, brows creased, until he saw a light in the distance behind him. Then another. It was their plan all along.

They were here.

There was no time left. He darted into the trees, leaving the two Elementals by their fire as the lights of the EME soldiers grew closer. Trees blurred in the approaching twilight. Everything was dark as the sky was stained a soft-purple hue. Kon didn't know what direction he was running. It didn't matter as long as it was away. All the days spent carefully trying to separate himself from the EME. The sleepless nights, the exhaust. For nothing. He skidded to a stop as he saw more lights to his left. Multiple groups. He veered off, passing through unfamiliar trees, before finally forcing himself to pause.

He ducked behind a tall evergreen, slowing his breathing to listen. It was hard to tell how far he ran. There was a hoverform in the sky, coming closer. Voices in the woods drifted around him. He could still hear the far cries echoing from the girl. The path straight ahead seemed clear, but the nearing hoverform wasn't a good sign. There was a growing burning in his arm and an ache in his head. He pulled at his sleeve to look at the gash. The knife had sliced clear through his jacket, leaving a sizable wound, though it was hard to see through the seeping red. He covered it with a hand and took one more glance around before he moved forward, slower that time, watching his steps. The lights in the hazy woods were scattered but closing in as they swept.

He didn't have much time.

Kon shuddered at the distant barking of a dog somewhere behind him—the EME had only recently started using them. It was an added threat he still hadn't found a solid solution for. Then he had the problem of undercover Elementals.

Elementals had been some of the kinder people to him in the past. Maybe the only people that half understood him. Ever since the river, the girl with the blonde braids, there had been guilt left deep in his chest. A yearning to prevent the same outcome. While he still avoided staying too close to Elementals, in fear that it would only lead to their danger, he tried to help where he could in the rare chance he ran across them. Maybe the EME discovered that somehow—that weakness in him. This is what became of it. But that was always how the EME played. Tainting the things he cared for until there was nothing left but distrust.

The trees were thinning as another waterway appeared before him, a wide, slow canal next to a cliff of jutting rocks. He headed for the water. If he could get across, maybe they'd lose him, expecting him to stay in the woods. He scanned for signs of EME. Nothing. His hand held steady on his sleeve as he quickly started along the bank. He could deal with injuries later. It was the time to make distance. Due to one particularly close call in which Kon attempted to hide out from the EME in the area, they grew to have a keen sense to search the entire radius more carefully. Therefore, beelining one direction might give him the space to escape the radius of their search.

Purple skies had all but turned to night by the time he could no longer hear the hoverforms. There was no telling where he was. It didn't matter. A problem for another day. The pain in his arm had long been clouded by exhaustion. He needed to stop soon. Each step almost landed in a stumble as his awareness of the ground below him started to drift. He hardly noticed the dark form in the water, a hovercraft of some kind, powered off and floating in silence.

It wasn't until a voice spoke, jolting him out of his haze. "Didn't think I'd see anyone out here." A man chuckled, raising a hand to wave. "Almost missed ya' passin' by."

Kon was frozen as his eyes adjusted in the dark to look upon the heavyset man with a fishing hat and thick mustache, seated comfortably on the porch of what appeared to be a hoverhouse. It was silent and dark in the water. Only a dim light on the porch gave it away. He cursed himself for being that tired to wander that close. If it weren't for the gnawing fatigue, he would've bolted, but his legs were stuck to the rocky shore, staring at the man like a startled deer.

The man stared at the night sky, not yet acknowledging Kon's fear. "It's awful late for a walk. Where ya' headed?"

Kon didn't have the energy to calculate his response. "North." Was he even headed that way? Probably not from the look on the man's face.

"North?" the man asked, glancing up at the purple sky. "Ah, I'm takin' a shipment that way. I don't mind givin' rides."

Kon could feel his body rocking as if it were trying to doze itself to sleep without him. Normally, a ride with strangers was off the table. There was no telling if he'd be spotted. But then again, talking to someone while he was running from the EME was usually off the table too, yet there he was. Maybe the only thing pushing him to trust the man was pure desperation.

"Come on, ya' look tired. I was just about to start up and get on the airway." The pudgy man stood with a beckon, sliding the door open as he entered, leaving the small porch for Kon.

He looked back into the woods, his chest still fluttered with emotions from the Elementals that had just betrayed him—but he was faced with another decision. He could try his luck getting away on foot, escape the squadron of EME and hoverforms, nearly ready to drop with exhaustion already, or . . . trust someone.

Kon slowly appeared at the door. The man moved some boxes off a table. Hoverhouses were small, portable homes, capable of floating on water or hovering on lower-air highways. They usually contained the necessities of a house in a compact form. There were boxes piled up by the door and a narrow walkway to the front of the craft.

He gestured Kon inside again. "Sit, I'll get us goin'." The control room ahead was lit up with lights across the control panel as the man plopped down in the chair, spinning it around to tap away at the controls.

Kon slid the glass door closed behind him and approached as the craft began to hum to life. There was a sink across from the table and a tiny kitchen. A musty smell stuck in the air, reminiscent of his old cabin. Everything was outdated, including the model of hoverhouse. It was an older one, from the looks of it. Light yellow wallpaper lined the walls as wires dipped around the ceiling of the craft. Fish trophies and flags decorated the wall alongside old photos and dated soda brand posters.

He was careful to scan every detail for signs of trouble, but there were only more fishing supplies. No weapons, besides silverware and a fishing knife. No odd EME radios or trackers. He convinced himself he had looked carefully enough as he finally sat on the red leather booth at the table, watching out the wide window as the craft began to hover quietly. His eyes scanned the woods as they turned. No EME. He prayed they were still around that fire, checking every rock and fern for him.

Tall rock formations balanced large boulders in the distance. The marshy land opened more as the craft hovered over the water. Crafts that heavy usually couldn't get very far off the ground, hence why they used water travel often or the few lower airways.

"I'll merge us onto the airway. Should be smooth sailin' after that," the man called from the control room, slightly visible from the booth. Kon stayed put, hand firm on his sleeve. He sat still for a while as the sting of shock wore off, being careful to watch every move the man made up front. When the adrenaline was gone, he finally began to remove his bag. Unzipping the front pocket, he looked for a bandage. His stare was blurry as he pulled it out.

Trees dashed past the window as the hoverhouse bounced onto the airway from the water's edge. A long straight channel full of various other hovercrafts floating above the barren ground cleared for the airway. Kon never went near them. Brynden Ka didn't have many, but the ones it did have were large, mainly for commercial transportation to get from one side of the peninsula to the other. He had never been on one. The travel needed never warranted entering that type of airstream. It could get him all the way north in a matter of hours—a feat that would take weeks, or more, to walk. He watched the craft slowly gain speed, lifting off the ground more until it was matched with the others.

The man finally stood, stretching, and lumbered back into the room. "Might be a while," he yawned as Kon watched him, partially curled up against the window, the wrap stiff in his hand. Disappearing into a room right off the cockpit, he returned moments later with a cloth and a bottle. "Should disinfect that," he mumbled, placing them on the table, gesturing to Kon's arm before he sat on the other side of the table, keeping his distance.

Kon looked over his sleeve, soaked in drying blood by then. In the dim light, he could finally see how bad it looked.

"Get into some trouble?" the pudgy man asked. He was human, with a round face, fishing overalls, and a wide bucket hat decorated with hooks and tassels. His expression read with worry as he took a moment to look over Kon and the state he was in.

Kon didn't respond, just cautiously reached for the cloth and bottle. Carefully, he pulled the bloody sleeve back, exposing the cut on the side of his arm. Working messily, he kept an eye on the man's movements. The worry on the fisherman's face was probably warranted. Kon had been traveling nonstop for days.

"Are ya' runnin' from someone?" the man asked again, a bit softer.

Kon shrugged as he wiped the blood from his arm, a scowl on his face.

The man grinned, taking amusement in his next words. "Ain't nothing wrong with runnin'. I ran from lots of things when I was young." He chuckled. "I was quite the trouble back in the day. Where is it you're tryin' to go?"

Kon was wrapping the cut, the red-stained cloth on the table. "I don't know." It was a messy job for wound care, but he was too fatigued to get himself to work any more diligently.

"Well, don't ya' got family somewhere? Friends?" the man asked, fidgeting with the fingerless glove over his hand. "Someone you can get to?"

Kon's expression stayed on the man for a moment longer before it fell. "No." He fixed his sleeve over the wrap before looking out the window at the trees below them.

It remained quiet for a while until the man promptly stood. "Well, I think I'll cook something up. Hungry?" The man went about his business, pulling out some bread from the cupboard as Kon watched his every move. When he was certain the man truly was making his food, he allowed himself to look back out the window. The trees and mountains were hardly visible in the dark below them. He was sure he had never been that high up, floating along with other Hovercrafts. Most of the ones as low as this were other hoverhouses, a few being supply carriers. There might've been more awe in him if he wasn't in such a state.

Despite his lack of answer, the man made an extra sandwich anyway, scooting the grilled cheese to Kon's end of the table before he took his to the cockpit, promising that he'd leave him alone for a bit. Whether Kon believed him or not, he was nodding off. It might've been months since he was *inside*. He didn't remember. But the warmth of the ship and the strangely soothing hum of the craft was lulling him to sleep. He managed a bite or two of the sandwich for his own good.

The calming hum of the craft eventually rocked him into a slumber. Maybe he was just delusional from fatigue and blood loss, but it was the first time in a while he felt some form of *safety*, though, as he drifted off, he clutched the knife in his jacket.

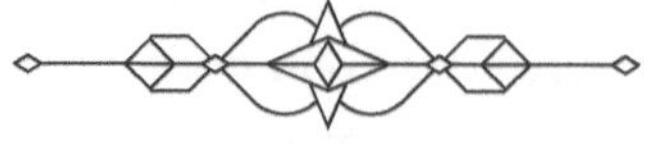

When Kon woke, it was light out. The sun was already well into the sky, the first thing he saw out the window. It illuminated a vast view from over the trees; the taller, denser mountains spanning higher than they were. They were definitely back in the north. He stretched slightly as he looked about. It had been months since he slept that deeply. His body was functioning again after the much-needed rest. He scanned from the cockpit to the back door. Nothing he overlooked. It was still the dated, old fishing house.

The man was in his chair in the cockpit, leaning back as he listened to a tiny radio playing fuzzy music. Kon's plate from the night before was gone, along with the soaked cloths, meaning he must've slept deep enough that the man was able to clean up around him without waking him. In their place was a bowl of crackers. Another offering.

Kon examined the wrap on his arm. The sleeve of his jacket was still dark with blood as he tried to examine the rip in it. The knife had left a sizable gape, easy enough to fix with the thread in his bag. It hadn't been the first time he patched the old jacket that Joel had given him.

"Had a good sleep?" the man asked as he finally noticed Kon. "I swear, this is the only place I get a good night's sleep. Puts me right to bed, this craft purrin' like a kitten. Nothin' beats it if you ask me." He stretched as he stood, joining Kon across the table again.

Kon's gaze out the window shifted to him, still wary.

The man took another approach. "We'll be at my stop soon. I reckon you don't want dropped off in town, eh?"

It may have been the state the fisherman found him in or maybe he had noticed the obvious signs that Kon was running from something big. Kon didn't know if he knew, but he made no signs of bother. Avari had been gone for sixteen years. They became less and less remembered to the public. It only aided Kon for them to be forgotten. Kon shook his head in response.

"You got somewhere specific you're goin' to?"

Another head shake. Just north. Away from the EME.

"Well, I can pull off the airway a few miles off Dashtyn. Is that around where ya'd want to be?"

Dashtyn. That was as far north as you could get. They were on the other side of the peninsula. If he was lucky, it would take the EME weeks to find signs of him. Maybe months. "Yeah," Kon said, masking his relief.

"And I reckon you still don't wanna tell me what you're runnin' from?"

Kon shook his head. The more anonymous he remained, the safer. For him and the stranger. In his mind, he needed to remain as no one in the world.

The man continued. "Back in the day, gosh, I'd say I ran from just about everything. Responsibility, love, myself. I took this job young, let me move around a lot. It gets easier."

Kon finally met his eye for a reason that wasn't distrust. "Did you ever stop?"

"Running?" The fisherman gave a casual shrug. "I reckon we all stop runnin' when we find our place."

The man did as he promised. They traveled down a river for a bit, escaping the business of the airway for a few miles until they came to a stop. It was all woods again.

"Dashtyn is straight that way, 'long with the coast. You sure you've got your own out here?" The man inquired as Kon fixed his bag.

"Yeah. Thanks." He stepped off onto the rocks of the bank, looking back as the fisherman stood in the doorway.

"You take care, kid, alright?"

Kon lightly smiled—perhaps the first one he'd given anyone in months—before he turned for the woods.

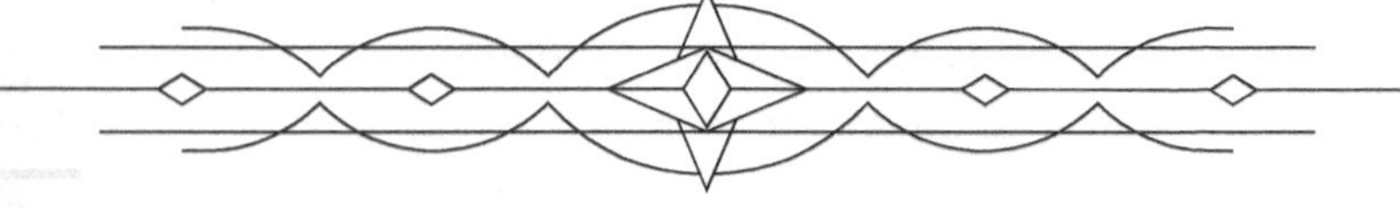

22

SMOLDERING TRUTHS

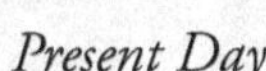

Present Day

Kon and Icelyn exchanged looks of confusion as they followed Para and Terrance down the halls toward the front of the base. She ushered the two of them into her office before shutting the door. As it latched closed, Para turned to Kon. "You've been here all day?"

He drew back, never seeing worry like that from her, even in the situation that they had met. Was it concern? Fear? "Yeah?"

"When is the last time you left?"

"I—yesterday?" He shook his head. "What's going on?"

"Icelyn, you've been with him?" Terrance asked, arms crossed. He spoke low, eyes staying on Kon.

"He's been here all morning," Icelyn backed him up. "What happened?"

Kon changed his gaze to Terrance, whose comment sounded more like an accusation. "What happened?" he repeated when Icelyn's question only brought silence.

Para put a hand on her head, taking a deep breath. She toyed with her words for a long moment. "Calirue . . . sent us an emergency alert."

"Okay—EME?"

"They said an Avari was attacking them."

Kon froze, only one word escaping his lips. "*What?*"

"An Avari. They said an Avari is down there . . . attacking them," Para repeated, trying to believe the words herself.

"An Elemental?"

"No," Para breathed. "They saw the markings. Using fire and terrashock."

Kon looked between the two of them. They *were* accusing him.

Terrance pulled his chest strap around him, sighing. "We don't have time for this. We need to get down there."

"Will you come with us?" Para asked.

"What if it's a trap?" Kon pressed as Terrance opened the door. It had to be.

"What if it's not?" Somehow a much scarier thought.

Kon followed them into the hall toward the exit as Jasamie and Peter ran to catch up.

"What's going on?" Jasamie asked as Peter clutched his book, brows still furrowed.

"Stay here. We'll be back," Para said without turning.

"Para . . ." Icelyn started, rubbing an arm as she fought for words. "Is there anything I can help with?"

"Get the med bay ready with Jasamie. Just in case." Para's usual cheery demeanor was nowhere to be found.

Icelyn slowed as Jasamie and Peter finally caught up. Kon glanced over his shoulder at her as she stopped. "Be careful," she blurted out as the group left. Kon could hear Jasamie and Peter asking Icelyn what had happened as he turned back to Para, looking toward the door to a group of Terrance's Defensive Wing people, all dressed in full uniform. It was only then he noticed the rifles across their shoulders and heavy vests. It was uncomfortably similar to EME uniforms, though lighter in color and lacking the masks.

"Okay, let's head out," Terrance called to them as Deyin opened the doors.

"I'll watch the comms. Be careful," Deyin said as they passed.

"Get any students outside back in," Para added quickly.

"Yep," he nodded, giving Kon a nervous grin.

Outside, the weather was still fairly nice, though dark clouds were moving in as Kon fell in beside Para. "Run me through it again." Kon pushed the anxious energy away at the sight of the group. *They were on his side, right?*

Para sighed. "Calirue's mayor has our signal. They can send distress signals through it. We use it for EME calls, mostly. This time, we assumed it was that again, but when we got him on the phone, he said it was an Elemental—an Avari. In town. When people approached, he lashed out or something."

"And you thought it was me?"

"I didn't know *what* to think, Kon," she said. "I still don't."

"Is he still attacking? What do you plan on doing?"

"He destroyed a few storefronts and was heading farther into town, last we heard. I don't know."

"Maybe they just mistook what they saw. An Elemental or some-thing?" Kon glanced toward the front of the group where Terrance was talking with the others.

"I don't know. The mayor said he recognized the markings," Para said. "They approached him to offer help, and he lashed out. Whoever it is, we'll try to talk them down. I'm hoping your just being here will help."

"Don't you guys have a hoverform?" He asked, looking back at the base as it fell from view.

"Too loud. They'd hear us coming." She sighed. "Are you *sure* you don't know another Avari?"

He tilted his head slightly at her. "I'm sure." It wasn't a good situation for him.

Para still didn't look convinced, but she accepted his answer regard-less. If it were true, an Avari showing up mere days after he arrived at the base, maybe nothing could convince them he had nothing to do with it. He chased his mind for any instance, wondering if he could've over-looked the encounter, though it was obvious he wouldn't forget such a thing. Paranoia stuck on him as they walked—especially with the glances Terrance and the others were giving him like he was hiding something. Part of him hoped it was an Elemental. Just an Elemental. Maybe even

EME. Anything but an Avari. He could fight the EME. He could even fight Elementals—he pushed the thoughts from his head. There wouldn't be a fight. It was all a misunderstanding, surely.

As they neared Calirue down the rocky slope, faint smoke filled the sky. They quickened their pace, the trees starting to thin near the edge of town. Terrance glanced over his shoulder. "Remember, stay alert. We don't know who this is or what they want."

The trail they followed widened into a road leading straight into town. They slowed their pace down the path, leading to the line of shops and storefronts across the main street. As they entered, there was a crowd of people farther down the road gathered around one shop. A man broke from the group quickly upon spotting them. His graying hair suggested he was middle-aged, and he wore a neat suit that lay partly wrinkled in his anxious fidgeting. There was a nervous greeting before the thin man spoke. "We're not sure what happened." He shook his head.

"Is everyone okay?" Terrance asked, looking behind him at the crowd.

"Yeah, yeah. He just came into town, wandering around. We thought maybe he needed help. But when Lorin offered him to come into her shop for a drink, he just—"

"Can we see?" Terrance asked.

Kon glanced around the clearing at the frenzy of destroyed shops. The attacks were random—one store hit, another untouched. To his relief, or Icelyn's, the library was one of the ones untouched. She had mentioned her joy in finding it yesterday. The street was empty except for the huddle of people murmuring amongst themselves.

"Yeah." The man nodded, gesturing them to follow him to the group. "Lorin said he shattered the whole front of the store in a moment—she barely saw it coming."

They looked over the store, glass broken on the ground as well as the stores around it. The window frames were bent in slightly with the blast, and charred marks painted several of the pieces of furniture in the window. Some of it still smoldered out of the store into the sky.

"Where is he now?" Terrance asked.

A woman approached, her pale hair in a bun with an apron over her layered dress. "I just offered him a drink. I've done it before for new-comers. A lot of Elementals, y'know . . ." she explained in a small voice. "He was mighty tall. I wondered if he could be one of those—Avari. I read about them in a magazine. But he was just . . . off. I've never seen it before. He walked off that way." She pointed down the street toward the divide in the road where more stores were shattered, and the ground was charred and smoldering. "He started throwing fire and terrashock at everything like he didn't even hear me—"

"Did he look like him?" Terrance pointed to Kon at the back of the group. To his horror, the group parted to reveal him. Kon looked to Terrance, first in anger, then reluctantly, at the woman, who narrowed her gaze on him.

"Yes, a bit. Same height and look. Different clothes. I think he was older," she said, eyeing him carefully.

He had seen that scared look from people before. His stare found the ground, hoping to appear smaller or disappear altogether.

"You have an Avari with you?" the man asked, drawing back. "Was this one with you as well?"

Kon felt his face flush with embarrassment as he traced over the path of the dusty stones below to the charred storefronts. In the distance, he noticed the corridor by the library to the next street.

"He's here to help, Mr. Dawn. Whoever this other Avari is, he's not with us," Para said as she moved next to Terrance. "Do you know if he's still here?"

"I . . . I'm not sure. We didn't want to follow him—" The man was cut short by an explosion in the next street over. A scream came with it. The crowd turned as smoke began to billow out above the stores.

"Get everyone inside," Terrance ordered, grabbing the strap on his rifle. "Haden, Clys, stay with them."

A strange pull drew Kon down the alleyway toward the billow-ing smoke. The remainder of the group followed. The warping sound went off in succession, one after another of terrashock blasts as they approached. *It couldn't be. It couldn't be what they thought.* Kon rounded the corner. As the street came into view, the source of the explosions was finally revealed. The tall figure stood in the center of the road, his back to them as he stared down another store window that detonated moments later in the rippling blast of terrashock. A woman ran toward them, away from her destroyed cart in the road as several others ducked inside buildings. It seemed his focus wasn't on the citizens but on overall destruction.

Kon was frozen as he stared. He didn't want it to be true, but he rarely saw that type of power from an Elemental. With the figure's back facing them and his high collar, Kon couldn't yet see if he had the same dark marks across his skin.

Terrance called out. "Hey!" His hand found his rifle as he slowly stepped forward.

The figure paused, having heard him, and then a long, painful silence followed before he turned. The stranger was dressed in a black, flowy uniform, a high collar on his jacket, covering most of his body. The inky markings around his neck crept across his face. Kon's heart sank. Pointed ears, dark hair, and tanned skin; it *was* an Avari.

Kon wondered if he was that obvious to spot. If he were that scary—

The Avari stood unnaturally still on the road. He stared, his gaze watching each of them until he locked onto Kon, head tilting in recognition.

Para stepped forward slightly. "If you need help, we can help you. Why are you here?" Para called out, but his eyes stayed on Kon.

Kon knew that look. There wouldn't be a conversation. "Para, get back," Kon said in a low voice, stepping toward her slowly.

"Are you okay?" Para called again, her tone indicating she didn't see the warning. She took another small step forward, her arms out in a non-defensive posture. Her desperation to help clouded her vision toward the stranger.

As Kon set back on the Avari, he saw the hazy warping of the air skewing his vision. Subtle purple hues, like melting, crinkling glass.

Terrashock.

"Para—" Kon pushed himself forward just as Para saw the terrashock herself. It detonated. With hardly a second to spare, he shoved Para behind him, catching the blast in his own terrashock. The two energies pushed against each other, twisting and compressing the air for a moment in colorful bends before deflecting away in a fiery mass. Kon dispersed the energy to see the Avari again. He waited for an answer as if the attacker would explain himself. However, the betrayal across his expression brought nothing from the stranger, who sparked fire up his arms as he took a careful step their way. "Get out of here." Kon glanced over his shoulder at the group. "Now." It was clear who the Avari had come to pick a fight with—but why? Was it even a fight he could win?

The stranger recoiled with another wave of terrashock, manifesting from Kon's front and left. Kon channeled his own again to counter the blow, arms extended to hold the energy in place. Fire sparked in the air as they collided in warping hues of purple. His energy hardly held through the block, feeling the pressure in his head, a clear sign his powers were stressing.

Someone could match him, and they wanted a fight.

He looked back at the Avari, who was moving, steadily walking along the far side of the street toward him. Kon pushed the energy down and made an attempt to talk. "Who are you?" he urged as the Avari moved closer still, raising an arm to send a quick bump of terrashock, too fast to stop. It pushed Kon back slightly as he caught himself in the energy. That was a clear enough response. No more talking.

Kon took a deep breath as he readied himself. The energy was already far more than any Elemental he had fought. He checked behind him where the group was back down the side street, a safe distance away. Kon let the energy seep around him. Attacking felt . . . wrong, though the Avari approaching him had already launched several blows. He was closer, almost directly across him in the road. Kon stayed put, blocking his path into the side street where the citizens and group waited.

He kept up his guard, waiting for the next move. Conjuring another mass of terrashock mixed with fire, Kon held the energy, ready to detonate or shield. He tried to get a better look at the attacker as he closed in. Messy black hair, rippling markings across his skin, and a glare of contempt as he slowed. The scowl on the attacker's face contorted and bent as terrashock blocked Kon's view, erupting a moment later.

Raising his arms, the attack collided with Kon's energy. The collision triggered a spark of electricity within it—one that grew and warped as it latched onto Kon. Lightning. He rarely used that ability. It was too iffy to channel. Something he scarcely practiced. It was too dangerous to use around Joel when he was trying to hone the rest of his abilities, but not then. From within the fire flowing over his arms, the lightning trailed as it bounced from his arms to the cloud of energy around him. He gave the attacker one last chance to back off, but his slow steady steps toward him remained.

His energy always got unsteady when using it that aggressively. There was no telling what would come out if he fought back. He just wanted answers, but he felt like he was running out of time—and space—to launch his own attack. Maybe he needed to make himself known.

Kon pulled the drifting energy back with an arm before he shot it out at the Avari, a mix of terrashock, lightning, and fire. The terrashock ricocheted off the storefront, shattering the glass as it exploded next to the Avari. Ripples of fire came sundering out, as the lightning tunneled behind it, sparking and whirling around him, latching onto anything the electricity could find, including the enemy who was before him. The Avari took a step back, shielding himself from the terrashock. As he turned to see the lightning quickly approaching, he folded in on himself for a moment. Energy warped around him in a shield and then erupted. The blast knocked out any remaining windows as Kon fought to block the ricochet from himself and the rest behind him in the alley.

He took a few last steps with the remaining energy dissipating in the air, then the Avari faced him. He was a good bit older, with dark, violet eyes. He was covered in nearly black armor, his closed fists covered in a hard, armored fingerless glove—the same protective gear covering the rest of him. It was definitely Anaiess clothing. *Brynden Ka* clothing.

The Avari paused for a moment, examining Kon with a tilt of the head, expression remaining unsettlingly blank. There wasn't even a twitch in his eye. It was as if he looked through him as fire flowed up the attacker's arm, drawing it back as the flames grew. He moved in odd, erratic movements, no show of emotion on his face, even as he pulled back the growing flames. With a gust, he swung out the fire. A large blast filled the air in flames. Until that moment, he had mostly been using terrashock, but the fire had engulfed the surroundings. Kon pushed it away in confusion, only to realize the reason as the flames started to peel back. The Avari was gone.

The fire was a cover.

The second it took him to realize was a second too late. As he noticed the movement to his left, a round of terrashock detonated at his shoulder. Kon only had time to brace for it as it knocked him backward onto the ground. Landing on his hands on the rough stone street, he spun back to face the attacker. In his head, pressure mounted as his powers screamed at him to stop. The Avari was overpowering him.

"Kon!" Para yelled from the alley as they stood helpless to intervene. Several others were calling out, trying to draw the Avari's attention from Kon. There was an attempt to put terrashock between them as he tried to shake out the blast, but the Avari passed through it, marching toward him. He was only a few feet from Kon, who held fire at the ready.

A bolt of lightning struck out from behind, hitting the Avari square in the back. Kon watched him freeze with a wince. The fire in his hands depleted as he turned to the source.

Para stared at him in defiance, arm raised in her position outside of the alleyway. "Get away from him," she growled.

Kon took this chance to climb to his feet, realizing the height the Avari had over him. Fire was spreading up the Avari's arm again. His next blast of fire was going to be at Para, and she couldn't stop it. Kon didn't know why the next sudden bad idea came to him. Joel hadn't just taught him how to use his powers. He had taught him other ways to fight, too. As the Avari pulled an arm back, aiming at Para, Kon grabbed it, yanking him around to face him before he sent a fist to his cheek. The Avari recoiled to the side, stunned by the punch. Even Kon was stunned, mostly that it had worked at all. As the Avari flinched back, for just an instant, Kon noticed his pointed ears. Something was wrapped around them—*an earpiece?*

The Avari recovered fast and swung the arm of fire at Kon, causing him to pull back, ducking before he sent another swinging fist at the assailant.

The Avari caught that one.

Kon tried pulling his arm away, but it was locked in the Avari's grasp as he came face-to-face with the only other member of his species he'd ever seen. His eyes drifted from the Avari's stark-violet slit eyes to his neck—a metal collar with a ring of light glowing green in the center. Flashes of memory hit his mind. In a moment, the realization swept over him. That wasn't an Avari who'd come back to find him.

It was the EME.

Lost in the realization, Kon missed the fist aimed at his cheek, followed by a hard push, landing him on the stone ground.

"Stop!" Terrance called behind him, his rifle aimed closely. Ashdyn was beside him, aiming as well while Para stood with lightning etching around her hand. "Step away from him," he warned, but the Avari didn't turn. He only stared down at Kon.

Kon shook his head from the blow, feeling the cut on his cheek from the armored fist. His head spun as he tried to steady his blurred vision. He wasn't winning.

"Don't make us shoot," Terrance called again. Kon could only hope that Terrance knew not to shoot terrashock.

The Avari had stopped. He stood over Kon, frozen, and while his eyes lingered in Kon's direction, they weren't looking at him. They looked . . . past him. Kon didn't dare move. Fire pooled around his arms in an attempt to look more ready than he was. He waited for another attack. He would have to accept his unstable energy and fight anyway. But it didn't come.

Instead, the Avari hovered over him for another moment, expression blank, before he stepped past him, down the road. Kon turned to watch him, the numbing in his cheek starting to melt to a dull ache. Terrance lowered his gun slightly in confusion. There was silence across the street until the figure was out of sight and around a building.

"Find out where he's going, Ash. Be careful," Terrance said.

Ashdyn nodded, wasting no time as she pushed her gun behind her and rushed down the street in the direction he went. Even Kon was shocked at her confidence, chasing after something that had just left the destruction he did.

Para went straight for Kon, kneeling to his level. "Are you okay?" she asked, reaching out, careful not to touch the flames around his arms.

He winced slightly as he drew away from her. "Yeah," he said with disbelief before slowly looking at himself as the fire started to retract down his arms. His hand stung from the hard ground as he pulled it up to assess the scratches as the last flames around his fingers dispersed.

He had lost.

"You're bleeding," she said gently, hovering her hand near his face.

He drew away from her hand, again lifting his own to confirm. The good-sized cut on his cheek from the armored fist stung as he pulled it away to inspect the trickle of blood.

Terrance approached, pushing his rifle back over his shoulder. "What the hell was that?"

"Well, now we know it wasn't Kon," Para said, lowering her hand with a deep breath.

Kon could at least be glad *that* was cleared up, but in its wake, it left a million new, terrifying questions.

"Where did he come from?" Terrance asked, watching down the street for Ashdyn.

"EME," Kon almost whispered.

"What?" Para stared at him.

"He's with the EME," he breathed, a pit in his stomach swallowing up his breath. "He had the . . . collar."

"An Elemental collar?" Terrance asked, looking down at him.

Para drew back slightly, her expression matching the dread he felt. "You're sure?"

With a nod from Kon, Terrance cursed under his breath in a language Kon didn't recognize. Terrance met eyes with Para. "They set a trap." He shook his head, scoffing. "We fell for it."

Kon was grasping the same realization. If that Avari was with the EME, they knew Kon was there *and* with the EPS. They would send everything. Kon didn't know what to be more afraid of. Despite the realization, however, Kon felt a deeper fear for who he had just met, for a reason he couldn't say.

Ashdyn reappeared in the distance, jogging back, slightly out of breath. "He went into the woods, but he's headed away from town and away from the base. I lost him in the trees."

"We need to get back. Now." Terrance growled, watching the sky.

Kon started to get up, still in shock. Para rose with him, offering to help but to no avail. His head spun from the blow to the face or the large use of his powers. He could feel the familiar drop of blood from his nose as it stained the stones below with a splatter. It was the risk of pushing his powers too far as he cupped his sleeve over his nose.

"Are you okay? What are you feeling?" Para asked.

With a shake of his head, he wiped the blood from his nose, trying to clear the dizziness. It would pass.

Para glanced at the gathering group. "Who has the medical kit?"

"I'm fine." He stabilized himself, shaking out the soreness. "Let's go." The worst pain would come later when it fully sank in that he had just fought *another Avari*—working for the EME.

Terrance only exchanged a handful of words with the mayor, promising to call from the base before they headed out. Anxious murmurs of the townsfolk followed them out. Nothing good would come for Calirue, except for the small assurance that the EME's focus wouldn't stay on them for long. Their sights had been set, perfectly tricking Kon and the base right into position.

Rain had started to fall from the darkening skies as they headed into the trees. The group was much quieter, with a nervous stillness over everyone as they walked with their guards up. The Defensive Wing arsenal kept their heads on a swivel as they trailed back toward the base. Kon expected to hear the distant roar of hoverforms at any moment, but it never came. An occasional rumble of thunder triggered more fear in him than it should've as they headed up the trail. Kon stuck in the back again, where Para stayed close to him.

When she finally spoke, her voice was light. "I didn't know you had lightning and . . . did I see light?"

"Sometimes they spill over onto each other," he murmured.

"It was impressive. You did good."

He looked at her with a scrunch of the nose, an ache radiating from his cheek. "He flattened me."

"No—you held your own," she said, watching him. "For the first time ever fighting an Avari? You did better than anyone else would've."

He let out a sigh and shook his head, reaching up to his nose again at the wet feeling of blood. It had been doing that since they left.

Para kept her gaze as he wiped it away. "Does it normally do that?"

He shrugged, not having much of an answer for her that wouldn't elicit more worry. "Sometimes. I don't know."

"Huh."

"What?"

"I don't know, I just don't see that in Elementals," she said. "We'll get you checked out at the med bay."

"I said I'm fine."

"We should've tried to step in sooner," she mumbled.

"You did." He gave her a frown. "And it could've gotten you hurt."

"I had to do something." She sighed, her shoulders drooping as she pushed stray hairs out of her face. "I'm the one who asked you to come down here. I'm the one who brought you here. This is all my fault—"

"Stop. Neither of us could've known." The thought that an Avari was most likely looking for *him* unnerved him. Previously, the idea of an Avari out there with him would've been one of hope. But a dread festered deep in his stomach now.

He considered his options. If he left, would the Avari still find him? If he did, the chances of beating him were slim. Leaving might be an even worse decision, the prospect of meeting the hostile Avari in the woods, alone.

The EME could catch him with one source.

They didn't need hoverforms and squadrons. They just needed one Avari.

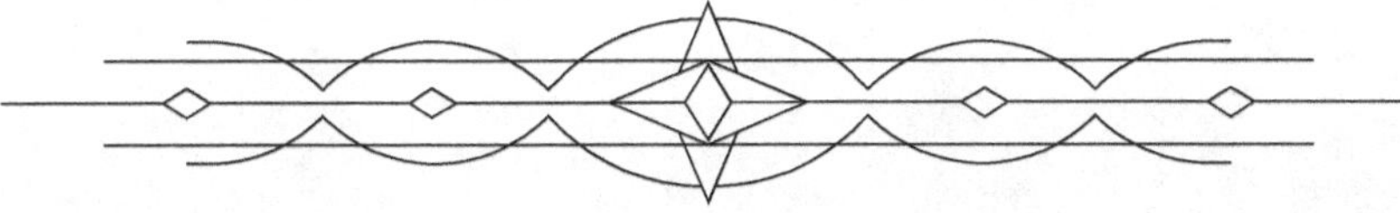

CHAPTER 23
THE PLAN

I celyn kicked her legs as she sat on the med bay counter next to the bookshelf. Jasamie had taken the desk while Peter paced around the room, deep in thought. Messing with the bandage on her hand, Icelyn replayed the words in her head. *Avari? Attacking Calirue?* It didn't make sense. She then recalled the look on Kon's face when he realized the accusations, almost like he was expecting the base to turn on him. It was a weariness across his face. One that showed a long, deep . . . defeat. She shook the thoughts out of her head.

Peter must have been thinking similar things as well as he suddenly spoke up. "You're sure they said Avari?"

"Yes," Icelyn said, having lost count of how many times she confirmed it to him.

"And they think it was Kon?"

She shrugged. "It seemed like they might? At least Terrance did." Her books sat beside her as she glanced at them, having tried to read it several times already. The words always became hazy as her mind wandered back to the situation at hand. That time, she didn't bother picking it up.

"That's crazy—How could they think—?" he scoffed, just as Alaura entered.

"They're back," Alaura said, lacking any form of urgency.

Peter stopped in his tracks, staring at her. "Well? What happened? Who was it?" he demanded, while Icelyn hopped down from the counter.

Alaura raised a hand at him, giving him a stern look. "Let them get settled. We need the med bay, Peter. Can you wait outside?"

Peter's body drooped in disappointment. "But—"

"Outside," she said. It sounded like a warning.

Icelyn's brows creased at her comment. *Need the med bay for who?* Fearing she'd be sent out as well if she asked too many questions, she took a breath and composed herself. "What should I get ready?" she asked, hoping the anxious tone in her voice wasn't noticeable as she started to pull up the sleeves of her thin jacket.

"Disinfectant, bandages maybe." Alaura propped the doors open, exiting back into the hall. Icelyn exchanged glances with Jasamie, who stayed in her chair for a moment longer before standing to look for the disinfectant. Icelyn rushed to the sink to clean her hands, drying them quickly before she got out the bandages and a few gauzes, looking over the collection as her heart pounded. Turning toward the door at the commotion, Peter's array of questions marked their approach. Moments later, Alaura reentered, followed by Kon with Para close behind him.

"Just let us clean it up at least," Para fussed to him.

Icelyn's heart sank at the sight of blood on the side of Kon's face. A fluttered hand ran through her hair as she worked to hide her worry.

He glanced down at Para in annoyance. His hair was a bit messier than usual; blood and dust coated his clothes. Gaze on the floor, he sighed. "Para, I'm fine."

"Guys." Para looked between Icelyn and Jasamie. "Patch him up, will you? I need to check on something. Don't let him leave until he's good." She gave a small, joking grin, a tiny bit of her usual personality coming back.

Alaura nodded at them, a trusting look, before she followed Para, closing the door.

"Okay . . ." Icelyn said, a bit stunned as she watched the door before looking at Kon. He watched over his shoulder as Para left, as if he might make a run for it after all. "Come sit." She pulled out the desk chair. "It's lower so I can look at your cheek." She half expected him to decline, but to her surprise, he moved across the room and sat. She glanced back at Jasamie, who nodded for her to take the lead as she leaned against the counter. Turning back to Kon, they were nearly at eye level. His golden eyes watched her, clouded in fatigue.

"Hi," he said after a moment.

"Are you okay?" she blurted as she finally broke her act.

"Yeah." His tone was calm, almost bored. She couldn't gauge if he was telling the truth, as always. He was probably tired of being fussed over.

"What happened?" Jasamie asked as she wet a rag and handed it to Icelyn, keeping her distance.

Icelyn took it and moved closer. "Was it really . . . an Avari?" Her voice was low as she assessed the cut. The skin around it was already stained red, shifting purple as a bruise formed.

"Yeah," he repeated in the same tone.

Icelyn sighed, trying to compose herself. "Well . . . let's get you cleaned up first," she said lightly, carefully reaching the rag toward his face. His stillness told her she could proceed as she gently started wiping the farthest of the blood trail before moving to the cut itself. He winced slightly as she reached the wound and the bruise around it. "It's not too bad," she said.

"That's what I told Para." His eyes watched the far wall, maybe at something even more distant, maybe at nothing at all.

She touched his chin with her other hand. "Look up a little." She examined the cut once it was clean. He tolerated the treatment. Cleaning it had caused it to bleed a bit more as she dabbed it. Wiping away the blood had revealed the full effect of his markings, dark and shaky across his cheek, coming to a point halfway across. In the bright light, they carried an almost red hue in their color. Something she noticed outside as well, when the light would hit them. They appeared black, but in the light, they would shine a deep red.

She only let her gaze linger on them for a moment. They were even prettier up close, but she knew he wouldn't like her staring. She had noticed, early on, his constant hiding of his markings, especially the ones on his hands and arms, always wearing long sleeves or his jacket. He had yet to reveal the markings anywhere else. "Well, I don't think it needs stitches," Icelyn said, stepping back to look at it.

Jasamie peeked over her to look as well. "Yeah, probably not," she agreed, handing Icelyn an ointment.

Icelyn applied it lightly, careful to not touch it more than she had to.

Jasamie stood back, letting Icelyn handle the treatment as she asked more questions. "So, what did Para and Terrance think of it? Why was one down there?"

"EME sent him," Kon said, his tone a bit deeper at the mention of it.

Icelyn took in a sharp breath. "What? How? Why?" She stepped back.

"I don't know," Kon said, turning his head to look at her, his golden eyes even more stunning up close. The unnatural slit pupils somehow looked perfectly natural on him as they dilated ever so slightly.

There was a tiny grin over her lips as her stomach fluttered before she looked away. "Does anything else hurt? No signs of a concussion?" she asked, distracting herself.

"No. Para checked a few times," he grumbled.

"What about your hand?" She gestured to the bloody sleeve around his closed palm.

"It's just another cut." He stood. "I can handle it."

She held out her hand. "Let me see."

His head tilted, the bags under his eyes more prominent, before offering his hand.

She took it, examining the bloodied sleeve. "Your efforts to hide this stuff won't work as long as I'm here."

"Yeah." Jasamie narrowed her eyes. "You don't want Para dragging you in here again, do you?"

Icelyn pushed his sleeve back, revealing the deep scrapes across his palm, which had stopped bleeding. His hands were warm against hers, freezing in the moderately cool room. "Can I see the disinfectant?" Icelyn called to Jasamie as she looked over the mix of dust and blood.

Jasamie passed over the bottle. "We're almost out. There should be more in storage." She stretched. "I'll go get some. You can handle this, right *Doctor* Icelyn?"

"Yeah," Icelyn chuckled as she dabbed a new rag in the disinfectant and returned to her spot, holding his hand again to see the damage. He watched over his shoulder as Jasamie left, closing the door behind her. She could feel his gaze set back on her as she wiped each cut.

"Your hands are cold," he said, voice ever so soft.

"Yeah . . . sorry." She folded her hands together to try to spark warmth back into them.

"Your powers are acting up again?" he asked. His voice was calm. She didn't know how he could sound that stable after what he had explained, but she was grateful for it. It grounded her better than her rushed thoughts did.

"Probably. I just got worried. I don't know." She tried to focus on her task, wiping the blood off before she nabbed the bottle of ointment on the table and applied a bit over the deeper scrapes.

"Everything's fine. Try breathing to calm it down," he said as she finally drew back, taking a deep breath.

"I'm just glad everyone's okay." She gave a pursed smile after a moment, her emotions toiling.

The attack was surely just the beginning of something messy, or maybe she was freaking herself out. She shook her head and turned to grab the bandages out of the drawer, returning again to look over his hand. Pulling his sleeve back a bit more to apply the wrap, she noticed a faded scar of a burn on the side of his wrist, wrapping around the entirety of it, overlapping a few of his markings. He pulled his hand back, his sleeve falling over it as she met his eyes. His expression had turned defensive, a hurt in his eyes as he recoiled, barely.

With a careful hand, Icelyn pretended she hadn't noticed it, wrapping his palm quickly before drawing back. "There. Now we match." She smiled, holding out her own wrapped hand next to his.

"Thanks," he said, the smallest grin forming for a moment as the door opened again.

Alaura entered just as Icelyn pulled away, grabbing the supplies to store. "Everything good?" she asked, looking between them. "He looks better."

"Yeah, just some scratches. I think we got everything," Icelyn said, her heart still unsettled in her chest.

"You're sure nothing else hurts? Para said you took a pretty good hit." Alaura looked over Kon, who had retracted his expression back to one of distrust.

"I'm fine," he said before he moved toward the door, toying with the wrap on his hand.

"Okay." Alaura's tone was unconvinced as she looked at Icelyn with an expressionless brow. "Your powers are acting up again. I'll take over."

Icelyn's stomach almost flipped into her throat. She had forgotten Alaura could *see* Elemental energy, and her nerves were bringing it out, an obvious cold cloud hanging around her. "Oh—alright," she said, following Kon as she tried to settle the anxious energy.

"Make sure he takes it easy." Alaura gestured to Kon as he dodged Jasamie coming back with the box of supplies. Icelyn gave a quick nod before she trotted after him.

As they entered the hall, Peter looked almost ready to throw up, bent over against the wall, clutching his book in agony. He glanced up, almost falling as he regained his balance. "Kon!" he exclaimed. "What happened?"

Icelyn glanced back into the med bay, worried who might overhear. She shushed Peter, holding up a finger. "Not here, Peter," she whispered.

"Okay, where?" he responded back in a hushed tone.

The floor shuddered as metal gears sounded out somewhere above and below them. They were taking the base underground again. It wasn't a good sign. Kon lingered, his expression flat as they all looked back down the hall where the Defensive Wing buzzed with people.

Icelyn watched the mess of Defensive Wing personnel move, carrying crates and guns in the distance. Her breath was thin as she spoke. "The library."

"Okay, tell me now!" Peter cried as he shut the door to the library. Jasamie sat back in her chair as Icelyn and Kon lingered around the table.

Kon squinted, his cheek still aching, along with the rest of his body from the altercation. Peter's energetic energy only seemed to make him more tired. "It was an Avari," he said plainly, arms crossed. "Para's going to be looking for me soon. We don't have long."

"An Avari? Who?"

"How should I know?" Kon growled.

"Well, what did he look like?"

"Me, but taller—and older."

"Taller?" Icelyn asked, panning over Kon's height.

Peter took a seat, hand on his head. "*Two* Avaris," he said in disbelief. "What does that mean?"

Icelyn had her arms crossed as well, frowning as she kept an eye on Kon. "Remember that letter we found in the database?" she started slowly. "Garik Tally said he thought there were two Avari here. He was right."

"Do you think this one just got here? Or has he been here?" Peter asked, looking up at Kon from his slump at the table.

"He's been here."

"So, an old AIP member? Where was he this whole time?"

"With the EME," Kon said, looking down at the ground.

Peter paused, looking down as well in despair. "Did he escape . . .?" he asked.

"No. They sent him."

"For what?" Peter breathed.

"For me."

There was a defeated silence over the room. Jasamie looked lost in thought, Icelyn was cold and worried, and Peter sat back against the chair, his arms in his lap. "This isn't good," Peter croaked.

Kon sighed. "I couldn't beat him. They're going to keep sending him until he brings me back with him."

"Why only use him now?" Icelyn asked. "Why not before?"

Kon shrugged, realizing the EME must have known more than they let on. "I wasn't with a group before. This is the only time I haven't been moving." He fought to ignore the thoughts in his head, the feeling that he should've left; should still leave. The EME had been waiting all those years for him to settle with a group, to lure him in with a trap. Another Avari. Something they knew the EPS would never ignore.

"There has to be something we can do." Peter sat up. "We can't just let them get away with stealing *two* Avari. Maybe we can save him."

"Save him?" Kon repeated.

"I mean . . . we can't leave him with them. Maybe if we get him out of their hands, we can save him," Peter said.

"That requires *winning* the fight," Kon said. He had been working through the fight ever since, replaying what he should've done differently. The Avari's powers were honed in well, but there was a chance he could outsmart him in better circumstances. If he had let his powers go to their fullest, maybe he could even win. Regardless, it would be close. Having to protect the rest of the group had hampered his full range of ability. There was also the thought that his opponent was simply better. More powerful. Smarter.

"Well, what does the EME always do?" Peter asked, slapping a hand on the table.

"Ruin everything," Icelyn grumbled.

Peter stood up. "They don't play *fair*. So, neither should we."

Jasamie spoke up. "We know nothing about him, though. We have no advantage." She was right. The advantage of surprise had been on their side. At least he knew there was an Avari. Any notion of who he was, or how to beat him, wasn't there . . . yet.

Kon's stare lifted from the floor. "But we know where we can get one." There was reason to search. A reason to find answers. He met Peter's gaze. "I need to get into that base."

A wide grin spread across Peter's face.

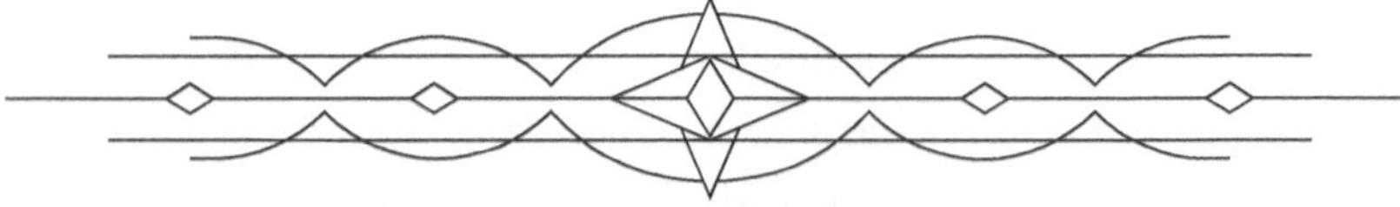

CHAPTER 24

LOCKDOWN

Kon had never been that far into the Defensive Wing. Para had finally called him in after locking down the base and prepping the scanners. It was time to discuss. Para led him into the small gray office toward the end of the hall. Alaura, Terrance, and Deyin were already inside. Kon positioned himself against the wall with crossed arms.

"Okay. Run us through it again," Terrance began, looking at Kon. "Why do you think he was with the EME? We need to confirm that first and foremost."

Kon sighed, replaying the vision in his head. "He had the collar."

"Right. What if he escaped?" Terrance argued.

"It was green. That means it was online," Kon said. "He had an earpiece in too. I think they were giving him orders."

"Orders?" Para asked, hands on the table in the middle of the room.

"Yeah, he was acting weird, wasn't he?" Kon looked between them. "Like he was . . . being talked through it . . ." He faded off as he noticed everyone's eyes on him and then looked down with a scowl.

"Yeah. His movement was off," Terrance said, typing into the digipad in his hand.

Para shook her head. "Which means EME were probably watching it somehow—through a camera on him or something. They definitely know Kon is with us now."

Kon looked back up at them, a scrunch in his brow. "If I leave now, I can draw them north. They won't have an interest in this place if they're on my trail—"

"No," Para interrupted. "No, Kon. You're not sacrificing your safety for us. You already did that today. We should've been more ready for this." A tiny breath escaped her lips as she leaned forward on the table. "We owe you an apology."

"They've been tailing me for years. I'm used to this. I can get away from them." Any confidence in his statement was missing.

"But can you get away from *him*?" Terrance asked and was only met with a lowered brow from Kon.

Para straightened. "No, now isn't the time to separate. This is what they want. It's probably why they're pressuring us so hard now. If they can push Kon back out on his own, it's an easier fight." She watched him with sympathy. "We need to stay together."

Kon didn't respond. He just kept his gaze on the floor. "Do we know *anything* about him?" If they had information on Kon, maybe they had information on the new stranger.

Terrance shook his head slightly as he flipped through his digipad. "We're looking into the files we have about the AIP, seeing if we can connect any of it to him. He has to be from there."

Alaura spoke up from the back. "You think they've had him for almost twenty years?"

"It's all that makes sense."

Kon squirmed at the thought. Did he just face a version of his future self if he fell into the hands of the EME again? He felt sick to his stomach as he looked back up at the group, only to find Para staring.

Worry laced her expression as she watched him. Maybe his fatigue was disrupting his ability to mask his discomfort. "Okay. We can talk more about it tomorrow. Kon, you should go rest. Let us handle this now, okay?"

He looked at them all with tired eyes, only to be met with nods. After hesitating for a long moment, waiting for any objections, he reached for the door. "Okay." There was no point in arguing. He let himself out.

There was a small dining hall across from him where a few of the base security were resting. Ashdyn was seated at the table alongside another woman with short red hair. Kon took in the rest area as conversation carried around.

"Are you sure you're okay?" the other woman fussed, brushing Ashdyn's hair from her face.

"Yeah. Everything's fine." Ashdyn grinned as she leaned in. A few poured coffee in their mugs for the night shift while others from Calirue retold the story from earlier. Kon only watched a moment longer. He rubbed his face before someone exited behind him.

"Kon," Para said gently. He looked over his shoulder at her as she continued. "Feeling okay?"

"I'm just tired," he mumbled.

She looked at him with a tilt in her head, a light grin on her face. "We should've waited 'til tomorrow anyway. Thank you for coming." She toyed with her hand before looking back at him. "And . . . we're all very grateful that you're with us. Don't ever think you're burdening us here."

He tilted his head the same way she did. "Is Calirue going to be okay?"

There was a subtle shrug in her shoulders. "We're keeping an eye on them. We'll keep the EME away as best we can."

He pushed a hand in his pocket. "I still think you'd be safer if I left."

Para chuckled. "You're the only one who thinks that. Go rest." She opened the door.

Kon's limbs felt heavy as he started back toward the student section. A few more base staff passed him, casting careful glances as he exited into the mural room. His mind still whirled with possibilities. For as long as he could remember, he was told he was the only Avari left on the planet. But there was another, and in a twist with a bitter sting, the Avari was the biggest threat he'd yet faced.

As he passed the med bay in a haze, he hardly noticed Icelyn leaving. "Done already?" she asked as he slowed.

"I guess," he said, looking her over. She had a sweater on, her hair pulled back partially. Her bangs fluffed across her forehead where her soft eyes watched him. He hesitated. "Are you done?" He glanced back in the med bay.

"Yeah. Nem should be here soon for the night shift," she said, a book in her hand as they continued down the hall. His demeanor must've been evident as her gaze stayed on him. "Did they seem worried?"

"A bit."

"Oh." Icelyn clutched her book.

"We're okay. For now," he said in hopes of reassuring her. "Where's Jasamie?"

"Babysitting since Para and Terrance have been in meetings all day." Icelyn shrugged as they approached the cafeteria. The looks from students had amped up. Wide eyes; some confused, others worried. The news had gotten out about an Avari attacking Calirue. It was likely some students still thought it was him. Even with the truth, the situation was one to elicit worry. Whatever rumor sparked—that Avari had returned to cause war, that the EME was lurking behind it all—they all ended in the surefire fact that danger was evident for the base. The mood among the halls had shifted all day in the realization. Their pace quickened to escape the cafeteria.

Out of the buzz, Stormy and Jyune tailed them. "Wait up!" Stormy called, trotting to catch them. "What the heck did we miss earlier?"

Icelyn and Kon exchanged glances as they all walked down the hall.

"It's . . . hard to talk about it here," Icelyn said.

"Peter said we missed a secret meeting," Jyune retorted, nuzzled into Stormy's hood.

"No—I mean, kind of? Earlier."

"He filled us in a bit; he says we have a plan?" Stormy urged. "We've been hearing crazy rumors all day. Kon looks awful . . ." They turned into the hall of rooms, a few students moving about.

Icelyn and Kon stayed quiet, carefully watching the students around them as some glanced up at them. It wasn't the place to talk. Icelyn tried to fight off their questions as they worked down the hall. "It's a lot to explain," Icelyn said slowly.

Kon finally stopped at his door where his annoyed gaze finally set on them as they stood, awaiting answers. He sighed, pushing the door open. "Get in."

The group rushed in, stopping just inside to take in the empty room.

"You haven't decorated?" Jyune asked as she perked up from her hood, hopping down onto the bed.

"Yeah, you really haven't touched your room at all?" Stormy said. The dark sheets of the bed looked undisturbed while the only sign of occupation was the two bags on the floor.

He gave them a dry look. "What do you want to know?"

Jyune sat down at the end of the bed, hanging her legs off it. "Everyone says you attacked Calirue."

"*Jyune!*" Stormy scolded. "*Some* people were saying that. Obviously, you didn't. Peter said it was another Avari? Working for the EME?"

Kon nodded.

"What is Para planning to do about it?"

"I don't know. She wasn't saying much," Kon mumbled as he watched them.

"I'm sure they have a plan." Icelyn added. "But maybe we can help them in our own way too. If we can find out more about him . . . maybe we can get that info back to them."

"We can navigate!" Jyune stated with confidence, curling her tail as she looked about the room, likely planning her own renovations for him.

Kon glowered at the idea. "I can't protect people out in the woods when that Avari could be anywhere. It's best if I go by myself."

"But you shouldn't be out there alone either," Icelyn protested as her eyes flickered up at him. "He could still be out there."

"They put us on lockdown. Full lockdown," Stormy explained. "That means no one is even allowed out of the door—especially not you." She looked at Kon before plopping down next to Jyune. "The doors are locked. The Stray Cats Club had to basically beg Terrance to let them outside. They're not letting you just leave."

The words unnerved Kon.

"We need to get down there before he attacks again," Icelyn said. "You have to have more knowledge of how to beat him for next time."

Kon sighed. "They're not just going to let us leave. The woods around here aren't safe anyway." The EME were surely in full search mode knowing that Kon *and* the EPS were nearby. Any attempt to leave the base could end with the EME or the Avari.

Stormy's mouth parted in realization. "The tunnels."

"What?" Icelyn said.

Stormy sat up, meeting the eyes of Jyune, repeating herself. "The tunnels!" Jyune met her grin with a wide one of her own as Stormy continued. "When we want to go to Darnar, for cooking supplies, Para always tells us it's too far to walk alone, but sometimes, she lets us use the tunnels to get part of the way there and avoid the EME heavy traffic areas!"

"What tunnels?" Kon asked, straightening as he tried to dispel his exhaustion long enough to listen.

"Under the base!" Jyune yipped, standing up on the bed.

"There's a few. They go in different directions, a few miles or so. I think they're an escape route if we ever get attacked," Stormy said. "Students don't have access to them, but they let us down there when we need to get to Darnar. It lets out a few miles from town!"

"How do we get in?" he asked.

Stormy thought for a moment. "I doubt Para would give us clearance, but I think I know where they keep the keys." She fiddled with her tail. "But once you leave the tunnel, it locks. We would need to find our own way back . . . but Jyune and I know the safe way."

"Never seen any EME on our walk back," Jyune confirmed.

"That would get us to Darnar safely, and then from there, we can be in and out before anyone even knows we left!"

"We?" Kon questioned in a curt tone, scrunching his nose at the idea of them tagging along.

"Oh, come on," Stormy squinted. "*You* need us to get down there. We know the way through the tunnels *and* back."

Kon frowned at her.

Icelyn took in a breath. "I know you want us safe, but this concerns all of us now." She looked at Kon with a careful plea. "We're strongest together."

Para's similar words rang in his head, overlapped by distant memories of the fiery safe house he had left years before. It was his fault. The EME wouldn't have been up there if he wasn't. And an Avari wouldn't be by the base if he wasn't. In the end, it was always his fault. The one difference was their reaction. Before, in the hazy chaos of EME approaching with Elementals rushing to prepare for a fight, he was told to run. That his presence put them in even more danger. Words that haunted him ever since. It was a stark contrast from Para's words of encouragement. Maybe there *was* strength in numbers or those distant words were right.

"We'll talk about it tomorrow," he said, reaching up to rub his eye.

"Peter said we should leave early anyway. We'll be ready. I'll try and get a key card tonight." Stormy held an arm out for Jyune to climb on. The two headed for the door. Jyune looked back at the two of them with a mischievous smirk as they closed the door on their way out. Silence overtook the room.

Icelyn lingered. "How's your hand feeling?"

"It's fine."

"Your jacket's all dirty," she said lightly as he finally turned to look at her, his demeanor a bit softer.

He looked down at the sleeves, dark with blood, other spots still dusty, and layered with sewn lines from years of wear and rips. "Yeah," he grumbled. "I'll clean it tomorrow."

She looked like she was hesitating with her words, her weight switching from one leg to the other. "I could go clean it. Let you get some rest."

"It'll be fine," he started as she took another approach quickly.

"I'll get it back to you tomorrow, first thing. Jasamie showed me the laundry room. I'll be careful with it. I just want to . . ." she paused, "help."

He watched her for a long moment; her expression seemed desperate to feel needed. It was probably the reason she was so steadfast to start in the med bay. She acted as if she had to make up for her small Elemental powers somehow. That she had to be useful in other ways. Kon took another look at his jacket, worn down since Joel had given it to him years before. One of the only things he still had of his and probably one of the only possessions he cared for. A sigh escaped his lips as he reached into his pocket and started pulling things out. "Be careful with it," he mumbled, tossing the AIP base map on the bed, then a knife from the inside pocket, a compass, and a few other items.

Icelyn perked up. "Of course, I'll be extra careful," she agreed as he removed it. He held it out to her, where she took it gingerly, a grin across her face as she folded it in her arms. The size of it engulfed her. "I'll get it back to you first thing tomorrow."

"Okay," he said, an edge of amusement in his voice.

She gave a last smile before reached for the door. "Goodnight," she said as she headed out.

"Night." He lingered in place as she closed the door, sighing. The various items sprinkled the bed as a familiar feeling overcame him. A lightheaded burning in his sinus as he pulled his hand from his nose to see the trickle of blood. It had been doing that since Calirue. He stared at it in a frown of hazy acknowledgment. It wasn't the time for his powers to be acting up.

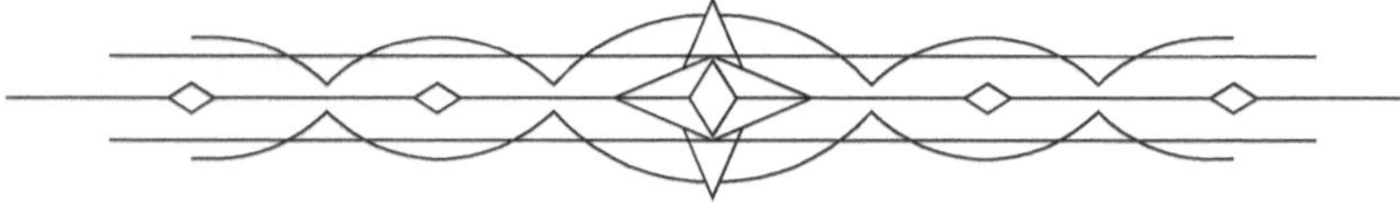

EARLY NOVEMBER 2654

Seventeen years since Avari left.

The woods far up the mountain were sparse. If Kon had known the danger he would face, he would've stayed in the thicker evergreens. He stood before the three EME soldiers, a scouting party no doubt. They were in full EME gear, angular helmets watching him through their visors.

"Stay where you are," one warned. He wouldn't have much luck losing them in the terrain. There would be another fight—the second in a week.

Another raised the triangular radio to his helmet. "Code Alph—"

Fire surged over them, followed by a hard blast of terrashock. They hit the ground and trees around them in *thuds* as Kon moved closer, looking for the radio in hand. It played static a few feet from one of the unmoving soldiers as he picked it up.

"Repeat that. Over," the radio spoke, voice rough with interference. A shuffle to his left brought him to face the movement, fire still sparking at his sleeves. One of them was still awake, nearly in a sitting position as they buffered, stunned. The large crack in their helmet visor caused them to pull it off, revealing the face of a young Human man.

The man looked at Kon with terror, a hand on his ribs, raising the other to Kon in peace. "Please—"

The radio spoke again as Kon stared at the man. "Did you say Code Alpha, B team? Respond. Over." It was rare to see them without helmets. Just ordinary people. It had happened a few times. He never knew how to proceed once the EME soldier sat on the ground, trying to talk him down with promises of surrender.

"I'm—" the man started, catching his breath. "I'm not going to hurt you. . . I swear. Just go." He held both arms up, wincing.

"Sending emergency team your way. Over," the radio warned. Time to go.

With a last glance at the man, EME weapons strewn over the forest, Kon finally crunched the radio in terrashock and dropped it, heading away, leaving the man in the fallout of the fight. He had spent a few relatively safe months in the north, ever since he got the ride from the fisherman in the hoverhouse. It took the EME the entire summer to decipher where he was, surely tipped off because the coming fall had pushed Kon back into towns in search of winter supplies. Winter that far north would prove dangerous, something he was willing to attempt with the months of success he had faced—as long as the EME stayed at bay.

Along the ridge of the tall mountain range, trees in the distance cascaded the rough terrain. The sky shone with hues of purple in the morning air. It would be a long day of travel weaving away from the fight. They knew he was there. He needed to make distance.

It was well into midday by the time he stopped along a rushing, rocky stream. His backpack hit the ground with a *thud* as he sighed, rubbing his cheek. He was running low on food. The old patched tear in his sleeve caught his eye; the damage done from events that felt like years ago. He hadn't run into Elementals since then.

He didn't stop for long, heading uphill along the stream. Trees were a bit denser in that part of the mountain. A rainbow of yellow-to-red leaves fell around him in the breeze. The white bark of the trees contrasted with the piles of warm leaves on the ground. Though a bit colder, it was peaceful up there. He had planned to reach a high point to see if he could pinpoint his exact location. It might even be fair to stay that high for a while. He had heard rumors that EME hoverforms had trouble with mountains—a small chance at safety.

He had been following the sheer rock facing his right side most of the day, attempting to find its top. Surely, it would be a view to suit his needs. Ahead, the stream veered along with the wall of a cliff. As he rounded the jut of stones, he found himself on a faint dirt path. He hardly knew there could be paths that far up. Was there a town nearby? Following the bend in the rocks, he came face to face with a woman on the trail. He nearly turned to bolt, had it not been for her reaction.

"Oh, I was hoping I'd find someone here. It's been quiet," the woman called. She had on a long, worn dress overlapping several layers of clothing, topped with a pale hooded shawl that contrasted her darker skin. She pushed the hood down to smile at him. Human. She appeared middle-aged, her dark coiled hair starting to shift gray. The warmth in her grin confused him as she set down the several large bags in her arms. "Have you been traveling far?" she asked as if expecting him. Kon hardly realized he was backing away until she held an arm up gently. "It's alright. You're safe. I get a lot of traveling Elementals up here." She kept her distance, pulling her hands together as she faced him.

So, she knew he was an Elemental—or maybe she guessed from his age and demeanor. Or perhaps, the markings across his tanned skin were dark enough to make it obvious what he was, though she didn't call him an Avari. She merely said Elemental. Not everyone instantly knew what his markings meant. Especially younger people, who had never lived in a world with Avari.

The woman seemed confident in her questions, no matter what she thought he was. "Were you passing through or looking for the safe house?"

Kon felt his stomach rumble as he checked the woods around him cautiously. "Safe house?" Joel had mentioned safe houses in the north. Though he had seen signs of them, he never came close to any of them.

"Yes, safe house," she said plainly, maybe even with pride. "We've been getting more Elementals looking for us specifically. I suppose you've just ended up here then?"

"I'm just passing through," Kon said as he started to turn.

"Nonsense. You look half-starved to begin with. Come." She bent to pick up her bags again, gesturing him to follow her up the twist in the trail. "If you plan to pass through, at least pass through my safe house and gather yourself for a bit."

Kon swayed on the path for a moment, weighing his options. She was headed up the path, the way he had planned to go anyway. Perhaps it wouldn't hurt to gather information. Or maybe it would be better to turn tail and run—

"Come. I have dinner on the stove!" she called. "The stew's been cooking all day."

It had to be the sheer hunger that got his legs moving as he started to trail distantly behind her. The walk was quiet. She must've trusted that he was following, only checking once early on. It wasn't long before the small path revealed flowers along the trail, leading to a house decently hidden by itself in the crook of the mountains on a ledge up the hilly terrain. It was a low cottage, overgrown by tall bushes and shrubs. The path underfoot had turned to round stones.

Kon wondered if he could've even found it on his own, so blended in to the forest. He hardly had time to decide if he wanted to stick around as the door to the cottage swung open, three young children coming to greet her. They all looked early tweens—two humans and a Rilinquin— and they approached with grins.

"The stew is nearly done," the Rilinquin girl said. "Did you find the spices?"

"Who is this?" another human girl asked as they noticed Kon, who had frozen.

The woman glanced at him, ushering the kids away. "Never mind that. Take these inside." She handed the bags to them, and they rushed back to the door. She then turned to Kon with another warm grin as she approached. "It's alright. They're Elementals too. They all are." She gestured to the eyes at the window, peering at them. "I'm Lyanne. Come. Let's get you settled in for dinner." She offered an arm behind him, nudging him toward the door.

Kon tried to remind himself that Joel had mentioned safe houses before. That he may find answers—and even allies—at them. At the very least, safety. With that thought in his mind, he let her lead him inside.

"How long have you been traveling?" she asked as they entered through the low door. Inside, there was a dusty checkered floor with a kitchen to their right. It was much warmer inside, and the scent of cooked stew hit him. Something of vegetables, and meat, mixed into one divine smell that made his stomach churn with intrigue. He hardly heard her over the hum of voices. The three younger teens stood in the kitchen, fretting over the large stew as the one older girl directed them.

"A while," he managed to get out as his eyes traced up the wooden cabinets and old scenic paintings on the walls. The left led to a dining room, where several more Elementals sat. Some talked amongst themselves while others glanced at him with sympathy.

Lyanne brought him through the dining room and into the next room, a much wider room of old couches and chairs laid on thick carpet. A small screen against the wall played a cartoon as a few younger children watched. "I started expanding a while back," Lyanne started as they entered a narrow hall with several rooms. One was full of children's toys and games, another had racks of clothing piled throughout the whole room. At the end of the hall was a set of stairs. "I had some help adding on over the years." The steps went both up and down. She headed down. "We've just finished most of the basement. Plenty of rooms for everyone. We usually have a room or two to spare for passersby like you."

He couldn't help but feel claustrophobic from the narrow staircase but remained stone-faced as they came into a sizeable hall. It appeared to have been a normal basement at one point, as shown by the concrete floor. It was covered in a long series of rugs that spanned down the hall. Walls had been built, forming a hall of small rooms on both sides. It was quiet down there, only a person or two that he could see, cleaning up in the rooms. The rugs and plants attempted to make the place look homey. She led him into a room toward the end of the hall.

"Of course, if you change your mind and want to stay, we can find you a more permanent spot," she said. "But hopefully, this will do for now." The room was rather plain with a round woven rug in the center of the room and a small bed and dresser to the side. On the wool blanket over the bed sat several pamphlets. "We can talk over everything after dinner? Your stuff is safe here." She patted the bed as he stood somberly, still anxious about his own motives.

Being driven anywhere in desperation was always a bad sign. Whether it was a good place to be or not, he was still forced to come there out of necessity. But it was this or wander into the nearest town, where someone would surely notice him—where the EME may already be waiting. He wished things were as easy as the summer months, with food in the forest plentiful between fishing and foraging. The winter months were the riskiest for him. It drove him into situations he was unfamiliar with, like arriving at a safe house in the northern woods.

He kept his bag with him, jacket on, despite the warmth inside. He hardly matched the others, who were dressed in cleaner outfits. No sign of travel on them but subtle signs of wear. His own outfit was tattered.

Upstairs, the stew was being served, the sweet smell of it reaching every corner of the house. Lyanne made careful consideration to fill up his bowl with extra chunks of potatoes and other ingredients. He avoided the eyes of the others, retreating to his room as quickly as he could. His fear of being recognized remained steadfast, even in a house full of Elementals. It was hard to tell if anyone noticed, but he felt their gazes, so he stayed in the small room Lyanne had given him, plotting his next movement. He had to be nearing the top of the ridges soon. Maybe another day's travel.

The pamphlets beside him on the wool blanket caught his eye. They were folded, looking partially aged. One was for food resources in the north. It highlighted towns that had donation programs for travelers. The other one was for safe houses, specifically the Elemental Protection System. It noted the wide connections the EPS held over many safe houses in the peninsula and had suggestions on reaching out to the EPS for relocation for families or individuals. Kon was suspicious of such a claim. Surely, no safe house had the level of power they claimed. The idea that a group of Elementals could help him get somewhere safe—there was no such thing.

A knock at the doorway cut his thought short as he found a Felinian girl peeking around the doorframe. Her long, creamy-beige hair matched her fair skin, covered in the classic Felinian patterns of color. Her mouth formed a line, and she bit at her lip anxiously. "Did you want more?" She held a few empty bowls in her arm as her tail flicked around the door. "I can bring you another bowl." Kon shook his head as she crept into the room. Her soft skirt fluffed over her legs with each tiny step while a baggy turtleneck covered her arms up to her hands. "I can take your bowl." Her voice was quiet, almost a whisper as her pointed ears rotated toward him, her bright amber eyes watching him.

He handed over the bowl without contest. Her eyes remained on him as she added the bowl to her collection.

"Are . . . Are there EME out there?" she asked.

Kon hesitated. He forgot they had the same fear as he did. Sometimes, it felt like the EME was solely after him, but everyone there was in danger. "Not close."

She nodded, seeming pleased with the answer as her eyes finally drifted off him. She exited without another word.

He hardly had time to process the interaction before Lyanne was at the door. "I figured you came back here. It can be an adjustment with the new people," she said, entering. She was wrapped in a lighter shawl. "I wanted to give you some information and ask for some in return."

Kon watched her with narrowed eyes, trying to hide his recoil as she drew closer.

"What's your name?" she started.

Kon looked past her to the door, where a set of younger russet eyes peered around the corner; the Rilinquin girl from the kitchen. He met Lyanne's gaze again. "Kon."

"Well, Kon, this safe house is partnered with the EPS. Have you heard of them?"

He shrugged, pulling at his hands as he tried to settle a bouncing knee. "A little." Joel had mentioned them in passing remarks.

"The Elemental Protection System. They're a widespread organization seeking to help Elementals. They have a base in the west," she explained.

"While we may not have a ton here, we can contact them if you need to get in touch with family. They can help."

Family. Joel, Mallia. Kon hoped the wince he let out wasn't noticeable as he shook his head. It had been over a year since he left. Reaching out would only make the pain of leaving fresh again. For him and them. He had stashed his communicator away a while before, fearing what carrying it could bring. If they had been trying to reach him, it was met with silence. It was for the best anyway.

"Well, what else can we do to help?" she asked.

What could anyone do to help? It wasn't safe to reach out to the Gavins. He had nowhere to go. Nowhere to be sent. No home to get back to.

An older human girl appeared at the door next. She looked a few years older than Kon. Her green eyes were wide as she watched him, dressed in the same layered dress style as most people there. Combing through her long brown hair with her fingers, she looked from Kon to Lyanne. She had been the one cooking earlier, if he remembered correctly. "So, it *is* true." She moved in next to Lyanne, looking him over for another few seconds in confirmation. "Do you know what he is?" Her tone was hushed.

Lyanne clicked her tongue, directing the girl back into the hall. "Now, Enis, don't freak him out." She checked Kon's expression as he started to draw away. "It doesn't matter what he is. He's in the same situation as we are."

"Shouldn't we tell the EPS? I mean—he's an *Avari*. I thought they were . . . gone." The girl couldn't take her eyes off him, despite the shushes from Lyanne. Even though her voice was laced in excitement, the word still stung in Kon's ear. One specific word.

"Are you sure?" someone from the hall asked.

"I'm sure. Look at him." Enis looked him over in fascination as the head of a second girl appeared, making Kon shrink back even more.

It sounded as though the entire house was behind the door, waiting in the hall, trapping him. His face must've flashed fear as Lyanne started to push the crowd back.

Enis was grinning. "We have to let the EPS know."

"We'll do no such thing, unless he wants that." Lyanne shook her head. "We'll help him how he wants."

"Ask him about the others," a deeper voice in the hall whispered.

"Where did he come from?"

"Are the EME looking for him?"

Kon wanted to disappear completely. He hadn't been there long, and news had already gotten out about what he was. Excitement or fear, it didn't matter. It was dangerous.

"Everyone, away. Now, leave him be for tonight," Lyanne spoke, voice still gentle, even with the edge in it. "I don't want anyone bothering him. Go back to your activities." She shooed them away with a hand. The gathered crowd outside the door dispersed, known only by the shuffle of footsteps. As she looked back at Kon, her expression twisted in sympathy. He watched the emptying hall, anxiety tight around his throat as his arms folded around his stomach.

"They're only curious about you. They do it to every new arrival," she said, moving close to sit at the other end of the bed. "You think about it tonight. If you do want help, we can help." With silence from Kon, she left without another word. She closed the door halfway, in an attempt to give him more privacy.

Only one other person appeared that night, the pale Felinian girl, who brought him a cup of warm tea. She asked no questions and behaved in the same stiff, quiet manner as she had before.

He convinced himself to stay the night, thinking that sleep and food were needed if he wanted to keep going. There was careful precaution taken, rigging the small vase on the table over the cracked door to ensure any attempt to open the door would land in a loud crash. No one could be trusted fully. Elementals or not, he had already seen that it didn't matter; they'd betray him all the same. His mind wandered to what Joel would think of their proposal. It didn't seem like a good idea for anyone to be informed of an *Avari* being there. But what if their claims were true? If they truly could get him somewhere safer.

As the next day came, Lyanne found subtle ways to keep him around;

giving him a tour, asking for help in the garden . . . The others at the safe house seemed generally intrigued by him. By the end of the second day, he still hadn't met everyone there or even knew how many people there were. Some came and went. Some traveled to the nearby town. Others stayed to themselves.

As evening stretched into nightfall, the pale Felinian finally worked up the courage to approach him again as he sat in the garden, looking over his map with the company of a fat tabby cat. His bag sat next to him. He weighed what options he had: continue on his own or accept help from the alleged "EPS." Maybe it wouldn't hurt to let them try and help him.

"You really are one?" the Felinian asked, crouching near him as her soft pinkish-gray dress bunched around her.

Kon looked up from the map. "One what?" He knew what she meant.

"Avari." The only word she responded with as she picked at the tiny flowers.

Kon's eyes crawled over the grass and weeds around them as his hand dismissively stroked the cat's head. He shrugged. Part of him hardly believed it himself. He didn't *feel* like one. What even was an Avari? Nothing *he* knew.

"I heard . . . you're here to help us."

Kon didn't know how to respond. Did people truly think he was there to save everyone? He could hardly keep himself from danger. How could anyone else rely on him? "I'm just . . . here. Like everyone else," he said. It wasn't her fault. He had heard the whispers from Brynden Ka. That the only hope for Elementals was Avari coming back, them returning to clear the accusations and make things right. Maybe they'd come for him too. Take him back to his home, if such a thing even existed.

Her ears flattened a bit in thought as her tail swept the grass behind her. Her words came in the same slow rhythm as before. "*I* think you'll help us."

He stared at the map, pain somewhere in him.

When no response came, she carried on as though the topic hadn't been tough. "Did you like the tea? I picked the flowers myself."

Kon suppressed the burning in his chest, a deep sinking guilt. "Yeah."

He might've asked her name next if Lyanne hadn't come from the front door, wrapped in a burgundy shawl. Her face was washed in worry. "Get inside. Both of you."

"What's going on?" Kon tried to ask as Lyanne closed the door behind them, latching it. Others were gathering in the dining room as she peeked out of the blinds before shutting them.

She clenched a communicator in her hands. "Dyn and Marco were heading into town for their shifts. They said EME were coming up the trail. They barely got away in time to hide."

"Coming—to us?" Enis held her hands at her apron, stepping away from the pot on the stove.

"We have to assume so." Lyanne shook her head. "Get ready. Pack your bags. Be ready to run or fight."

"Maybe they're just scouting?" someone offered from the gathered group.

"They said there were a lot of them—they don't scout in those numbers. Get your stuff. *Go.*"

At that, the group broke as chaos swept over the house. The younger Elementals were huddled on the couch, already in tears as Kon stood numbly. *EME headed this way? Why?* He was *certain* he had gotten well away from the previous group. Certain that they didn't know where he was. *Code Alpha.* He had learned a while ago that meant him. The code they called when they had his location. The certainty started to churn and spoil in him as guilt took its place. He should've kept moving. Maybe they could fight them. Fight and get everyone away in time. The rush of people was a blur as he turned to Lyanne. She was pulling bags of extra supplies out onto the tables as a few others helped her.

"I see lights," Enis whimpered, peeking through the kitchen window. "They're here."

"Rannon, get the fire ready," Lyanne ordered to the man at the door. He watched out the corner of the window as fire started to bloom around his arms.

Kon stopped next to Lyanne as she pushed the supplies onto the table. He had never fought a group of more than a few, but he could try. "Maybe we can fight them. Get everyone out together . . . I can—"

"No," she cut him off. "More will come. *You* need to go. They can't see you." She started pulling him toward the back door, shoving an arm full of bagged supplies into his arms; something of a wrapped blanket filled with food and water.

"I can help," Kon pleaded as she opened the door, directing him out.

"No, honey." She held her hand to distance him. "If they find *you* here, it'll be worse for all of us. This isn't your fight." The sky was stained purple with nightfall as crickets chirped. But in the distance, sure enough, Kon could hear the familiar roar. They were coming.

"I'm sorry," he blurted. The EME wouldn't have even been there in the numbers they were if it wasn't for him. One way or another, it was his fault. His gaze fell past her, where the fair-haired Felinian stood, watching him.

Lyanne smiled the same warm smile as when she found him. "Go."

Kon stumbled back, staring at her in defeat. Was that really his only choice? The best thing he could do for them? She didn't give him a chance to question it before she disappeared back inside, leaving him facing the large amber eyes of the Felinian. Her mouth barely formed the words. "Help us."

He had to listen to Lyanne. Leaving *was* helping them. He couldn't stay any longer, and he turned for the woods. There was the commotion of a few others leaving behind him. Some of the older teens were taking the younger ones to run for safety. He didn't look back. Others would surely remain to keep the EME near the house. To give the rest time to flee before EME swarmed every inch of the woods. And if they found Kon, they would send every ship there. They were probably already doing that. The mistake he had made the days before, giving the EME group time to call in Code Alpha. Of course, they would all be there.

How could he be so stupid?

He didn't look back until the sky was nearly dark. It was the only thing that would keep him from returning. He ignored every sound behind him between subtle gunfire and a hoverform somewhere. Something deep inside him ached; a longing to belong. All he ever found was reasons why he *didn't* belong. Reasons he was a danger. Maybe the EME was right to search for him if all he ever brought was destruction in his wake.

When he finally reached a high ridge, nearly at the peak of the mountain, he allowed himself to look back. Only once.

His heart sank.

Fire. The cottage was a blaze of fire in the woods. The shadow of a hoverform lurking overhead with its long metal tail turning as it searched the woods.

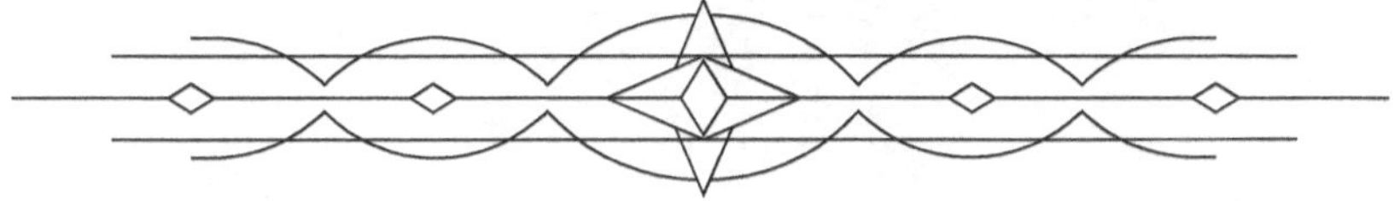

CHAPTER 26
MEMORIES

Night brought the twisting darkened nightmares—the same ones as always; flashes of memories mixed with made-up horrors of the EME. Were they made up? Maybe they were memories he had blocked out. They never made much sense. They were just glimpses of images and an overwhelming fear in his chest. However, there was a new image in the mix: the fiery figure of the Avari looming over him as EME soldiers closed in all around him. Looking at the strange Avari, he realized—it was himself. The Avari he faced was his own fate. If he failed, he would become the same . . .

Kon shot up. The room was dark, a small light illuminating the bathroom across the room. Everything was still again. Quiet, except for his own rapid breaths. He rubbed his face, trying to push the lingering feelings of the nightmare away. His cheek still stung as his hand ran over it. The clock on the nightstand read 4:30 a.m., but his racing heart told him he'd only find himself back in a bad dream should he try to sleep again.

There was a reason he rarely stayed the night at the base.

He wasn't used to the room yet. Waking up in the cold gray dorm only panicked him. Each time he attempted to sleep, it ended the same.

Peter and Para surely thought he was crazy the first few times he left for the night to sleep in the woods, but the walls of the room felt smaller at night.

He pushed himself up, groggy as he ran a hand over his side, still sore from the blast of terrashock. The room did little to comfort him. He needed to walk. He noted his missing jacket and paused at the door, feeling the lack of comfort with its disappearance. There would only be Luneduine out that early anyway. Pulling his sleeves up onto his hands, he exited into the hall. The lights were at their dim level, leaving the halls in a hazy red hue. There was no one in sight, just the long stretch of hallway as he made his way out of the student rooms.

The main hall held a bit more life with several Luneduine about. One was switching out posters while several talked outside the cafeteria. He made his way in the direction of the entrance. It seemed like a place where few people would be at that hour. He also wanted to confirm Stormy's previous comment about the base being on total lockdown. He had heard the announcement earlier over the intercoms—which were only used during emergencies—explaining the base was retracting again and no students would be allowed to leave. He hoped it wasn't true, but Stormy seemed to think otherwise. As dangerous as the woods were around the area, there was a certain suffocation he felt in the base, especially in times like these. As he passed the med bay, he heard conversation inside; the warped, bubbly voice of a Luneduine. The mural was loosely illuminated around the edges. In the dim light, he could see some of the paint was even glowing, giving it a new look aside from its daylight composition.

He tried the heavy door. Locked. His hand dropped from the handle to his side in disappointment as he backed up. The thought of being trapped in the base only made his chest hurt more, no matter how hard he tried to convince himself that he wasn't "trapped." The base was just being cautious, no doubt the doing of Terrance. He could leave at any time. If he wanted to, he could open the door, his own way. There was no reason to panic.

"Kon?" The voice was familiar. Gentle and quiet. He faced Icelyn, peeking out of the student hall. "I thought I saw someone go by the med bay."

He gave her a tired tilt of his head. "Couldn't sleep." There was something comforting in seeing her, accompanied by confusion over why she was there.

"Are you okay?" she lingered. "Come, let's walk." He didn't object much as he sauntered over to her.

"Why are you up so early?" he murmured, voice rough in his groggy state.

She wore a tank top undershirt tucked into sweatpants and had her hair braided loosely over her shoulder. "I couldn't sleep either. Decided to go check on the med bay." She looked up at the doors where a Luneduine lingered. "Nem was telling me about the nightlife."

They approached the doors, where the Luneduine, Nem, straightened. "It's nice to finally meet the two new arrivals. Usually, I just hear about everything the next night," she said, her voice having the signature strange Luneduine tonal shift. Their voices always sounded something like a radio, slightly distorted. Her large black eyes watched them both.

"Yeah, I'm glad I stopped by. Jasamie talks about you a lot," Icelyn said.

"I do my best. We don't get a lot of night traffic," Nem said as she pushed her short pink hair over her curled ear. "Is there anything you guys need?"

"I don't think so. It was nice talking to you," Icelyn said as Kon lingered.

"You know where to find me." Nem grinned as she toyed with her necklace resting on her translucent chest, one of their species' more interesting attributes. She stepped back into the med bay as they continued back down the hall.

Icelyn hesitated until they were a bit farther down before she spoke again. "Are you sure you're okay?"

"Yeah," he said. "You?"

"There's just a lot going on," she said. "I got your jacket washed. It's in my room. Did you want it now?"

He shook his head. "It's fine." They turned down the hall toward The Closet, the area quiet in the early morning.

"So . . ." she began, as they passed empty classrooms. "How do you feel about our plan?"

"I still think I should go alone." He grimaced at the idea of taking a group.

"Well . . . I mean, Stormy and Jyune know how to get to the tunnels," Icelyn started, fiddling with her hands. "Peter is a brainiac about Avari and the facility. I know medicine. If Jasamie goes, then we'll have two medics. I think it's a good team."

"I don't want anyone getting hurt—or worse. That comes back on me."

The corner of her mouth pulled back in a scowl as she watched the ground. "If you're allowed to risk your life with this, so are we. This concerns us all." Her expression turned light again with a grin. "And you know you won't keep Peter from going—or me."

He watched her, having no other comfort as they paced through the narrow back halls. His gaze fell to the floor. "If I just left now, the EME would leave too," he said. The idea wasn't crazy to him. Either way felt like a dangerous situation, but only one included an entire base and town of lives in danger.

"You don't know that," Icelyn said, her tone shifting again.

"I know it would buy you guys time."

She stopped, staring up at him. "We don't need time, Kon. We need you. I wouldn't even be here without you."

Instead of annoyance, his eyes softened to pain.

She took a slow step forward, her gaze set on him. "Why are you afraid of us?"

He lingered for a moment before he gave a nod down the hall, gesturing for her to follow. She stayed put, stubbornly, before joining him again. The gray walls were more exposed down that far, posters on the walls being slimmer. There were only a few and most of them looked old. He didn't realize how much the posters helped to ease him, until there were none. The classroom doors were dark inside as they walked along the light tiles. He finally spoke. "Every place I've stayed, I've put people in danger." As they rounded a turn, exposing a long stretch of empty hallway, he continued. "The people that raised me, EME got to them—I never saw them again."

Icelyn watched him, her hands on her chest.

"The people I stayed with after that, I didn't want it to happen to them. So, I left. Anywhere I went, the EME followed. I saw people die because of that." He didn't let the memories seep into his mind. He simply let the reality of it out. "I found a safe house. I thought it would be okay. The EME tracked me to it and burned it to the ground." He sighed, avoiding her gaze as he stared at the tiles below them. "It's always been safer by myself. For everyone."

Icelyn was quiet at first before her next words came carefully. "Why'd you come here?"

He pursed his lips together. "I was just passing through." The real answer felt too stupid to say out loud; the guilt he had felt—like he led the EME to that Help Key—where they surrounded Para. It was all too familiar of an incident. The last time, he had been too late. "I didn't think I'd stay this long."

"I'm glad you did." She smiled lightly. "It feels safer when you're here." Her cold blue eyes met his. "Not just for us, but for you too. We worry about you, you know."

"I know." He shook his head. "I don't think I can sneak out at this point anyway," he joked.

"Exactly." She grinned as they traversed the long hall. There were no doors down the final long stretch of the back hallway. "I've never been down this far." She took in the sparse banners lining the walls. Some were words of encouragement, others were simple music covers and movie posters—things the busier halls didn't have room for.

"Why do you want to go? It's safer here," Kon asked as they neared the turn ahead.

"I don't know. I just want to help," she said. "If we get the upper hand on the EME—maybe things will change." Something in the gentle, smooth tone of her voice was . . . easy. Easy to listen to. Easy to talk to. "I have dreams for the future. I'm sure you do too. I want to see a life where we can achieve those."

"It could be dangerous."

"All the more reason to stick together."

The turn back into the busy of the base started with the theater, doors open and dark inside. A video played, a good group of Luneduine seated inside watching. Ahead was the library. Kon half expected Peter to be inside, reading away at his piles of evidence.

"Dreams for the future?" he finally asked, casually.

"Just normal things." She shrugged. "A house by the ocean, get my nursing degree. Have a garden."

"The ocean?"

Across from the library was the common room as they approached the main hall once again. Besides Luneduine being busy in conversation, Kon noticed a familiar face leaning against the doors to the lounge area. Darren. He hardly recognized him from the earlier encounter of him cornering Peter. He hadn't seen him since. The boy's expression was locked on Kon, a frown across his face. Had he learned his lesson? Kon didn't give much mind to it as they passed, feeling his eyes follow him. Icelyn turned as if she were about to answer him—before the voice behind them sounded out first.

"Is it true?" Darren said, a smirk in his tone as they stopped to face him. Maybe he hadn't learned.

Kon met his gaze. Part of him figured no good would come from entertaining him, but he faced Darren anyway.

"Your own species just rejected you too? I mean, that had to have stung." Darren sneered, straightening from the door frame. "What hurt more? That or the punch?" He pointed to his own cheek with a grin.

Kon's expression remained the same as he tilted his head in boredom. "Is that it?"

Darren's friends lingered inside the common area, watching with far less confidence. A few Luneduine had looked up too, confusion on their round faces. "No, I just want to know what you're waiting for," Darren continued. When he was met with Kon's unwavering silence, he pressed on. "We all know it's a matter of time before you bolt. What's the plan?" He started to step closer, arms swinging in his monologue. "Maybe just wait until the EME is on our doorstep? Then we can be a distraction while you get away? Is that it?"

Icelyn had finally gotten over her shock, a frown hard on her face. "What is your problem?"

Darren ignored her, his eyes remaining on Kon. "Did I get it right? You'll abandon us when you're ready?"

Kon let out a small sigh. "You seem capable of taking care of yourself. Why do you need me?" He started to turn.

Darren's expression went cold. "Is that what you told Lyanne?"

Kon froze at the name. The memories of the woman, the safe house. The EME. He felt his breath quicken with a mix of emotions.

Darren must've caught his shift. "Yeah. I was there. That entire safe house went up in flames because of you. Hardly any of us got away."

Kon's expression had transformed into something of sorrow. Memories played back, searching his mind for the familiar face. He had only stayed for a day before they came. Lyanne had taken such pride in her assistance of Elementals. Her warmth had been no different with Kon, insisting he come and stay. Even as the EME closed in, surely brought on by his presence, she merely ushered him to safety. He wanted to believe her words, that leaving was the best thing he could do, that the EME's failure to find him would help them in the end. Maybe she had lied to protect him. The searches had only gotten bigger after that.

"I didn't mean for it to happen," he said in a low voice.

Darren tilted his head with a lopsided grin. "Don't be too hard on yourself. It's in an Avari's nature to leave messes they made."

Kon felt something twist in him. An anger. As the air around him started to heat, it was cut short.

"Darren." The harsh, cold voice came from around the corner. Ashdyn had appeared from the hall by the stairs. Her hardened gaze was locked on him as she approached, her short brown hair pulled back. "What's going on?"

Darren shrunk, taken aback that a member of the base staff had intervened, or maybe he was afraid of Ashdyn specifically. "I—he—" he began to fold.

Ashdyn stepped closer, ice in her dark eyes as she stopped, folding her arms together. Nothing else needed to be said.

Darren hovered for another moment, glancing at Kon one last time with fiery eyes before he stormed down the hall. The spectators quickly pretended they hadn't witnessed it, looking back to their books and activities.

Ashdyn took in a bored breath. "Best not to entertain that type," she said, but Kon had already started heading in the other direction, back down the hall, Icelyn on his tail.

The seeping energy around him dissipated. The anger at Darren's words was turning into anger that he even let such comments in.

Icelyn was quick to catch up, letting out a large huff as she balled her fists. "What a jerk!"

Kon shook his head dismissively.

Her steps got heavier as she looked over her shoulder with a frown. "Unbelievable. Are you okay?" She looked back at him.

His gaze on the floor lifted to hers. "Yeah." Nothing in his expression wavered, despite the sting in his chest. "It's nothing." They were approaching the turn to the dorms.

"I should go find him, give him a piece of my mind," she snorted, checking her shoulder one more time with narrow eyes.

"No point." He slowed as his door neared. "We have bigger things to focus on if we're going to Darnar."

Icelyn softened a bit, nodding. "Yeah."

"It might help if someone stayed here, though. Cover for us." It was his last attempt. He still planned to try and talk them down in the morning.

Icelyn let out a breath of a laugh. "You'll have to try that on the others. It's not working on me." His brows creased in a humored stare as she started to back down the hall to her own room. She met him with one last lopsided smile. "You're not getting rid of me."

He hardly noticed that he smiled back.

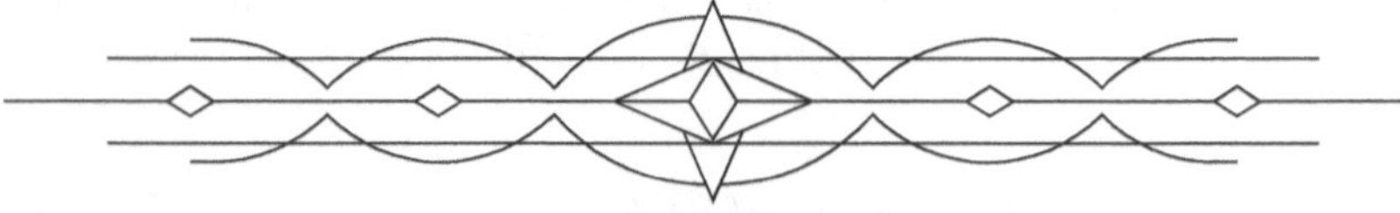

CHAPTER

27

TUNNELS

"Of course, the tunnels!" Peter exclaimed as he sat on the steps to the sunroom. It was void of students, with little need to worry about prying ears. "And there's one right to Darnar?"

"Almost a straight shot," Stormy said, taking another swig of her juice.

"Well, that's perfect. We can get down there and back in a day probably!" Peter said.

Kon watched him, a dry look across his face. "*You* didn't like our last venture in the database. You really want to go?" He knew Peter would want to go, but the logistics of it raised questions. Regardless, he had been subtly pushing them to stay all morning to no avail.

"Well . . . yeah!"

"This one is *actually* dangerous," he grumbled, rubbing the tire from his face.

"Do you think I'd miss getting into that base for *anything*? No way in hell I'm passing that up," Peter said in a shrill tone as he pulled his backpack close. "I packed everything last night. When do you think Jasamie will report back?"

Kon sighed. "The sooner the better." There was no telling how long the EME would wait before trying something again. It wouldn't be long. Jasamie had agreed to watch for a time when the Defensive Wing seemed particularly distracted, as she was the one more often around. As soon as Para and Terrance were busy, that would be the time to go. If there was information to gather, they had to get it right away. He had learned early to act before the EME did. Stay a step ahead of them.

It was only him, Peter, Stormy, and Jyune by the sunroom. Kon usually wasn't around there that early in the morning, favoring the woods in the morning air, but the doors remained locked. Night had only brought a mix of nightmares and little sleep—something he saw coming with the recent encounter. Icelyn hadn't turned up yet. He stood near the steps in a long-sleeved shirt. He wondered if her swipe of his jacket was a ploy to keep him from sneaking off. His missing jacket hadn't gone unnoticed.

"You look different," Jyune hummed as she sat on the step, peeling her orange and lounging back against her bag.

"Is your face feeling better?" Stormy asked, glancing him over as he crossed his arms. His cheek had improved, the redness dying down a bit as the bruise came to color.

"Why'd he hit ya'?" Jyune asked.

"I punched first, I guess," Kon grumbled, looking down the long hall.

"You *punched* him?" Peter questioned, intrigue in his expression.

Kon shrugged. "Fire wasn't working. He was going after Para."

"I wish I could've seen it," Peter swooned before Kon's glare brought him back down. "I mean . . . I'm sure it was scary. That was probably the first Avari duel ever on Anaiess! I wonder if Terrance got any of it on recording. It would be fascinating to see the fighting styles clash between two Avari . . ." he faded off as Kon's expression stayed on him, unamused.

"You don't think we'll run into this guy while we're out, do you?" Stormy asked.

Kon shook his head. "If they know we're in the area, he'll probably stay around Calirue." He and squadrons of EME.

Jyune scrunched her round face. "And if he does follow us, Kon will *mess* him up!"

Kon winced at her confidence. What if the Avari did follow them somehow? Could he face him alone? The answer was already in his mind, but he didn't want to accept it, still searching for the key he was missing—the one thing he could've done differently to change the fight in Calirue. Just like the dreams the night before, his mind stuck on the replay; the Avari, coming for him. If he couldn't win, he'd end up the same, a weapon to experiment with at the hands of the EME.

"Kon?" Stormy said.

Kon snapped back to reality. "What?"

"I said, do you have a plan?"

He tried to clear his head from the loudness of his own thoughts. "Hit Darnar first. Go from there."

Peter sipped on his juice, thinking. "Do we even know this guy is still in Darnar?"

"I can ask around. Another reason you need us." Stormy smirked. "It's not that big a town. They know me and Jyune. If he's there, I'm sure we can get directions."

Peter raised a brow. "Do you think Kon can get into town unnoticed?" They all frowned as they sized him up.

He looked between them. "I can just put up my hood. We won't stay long." While he didn't like entering towns, on rare occasions, it was necessary. If he was fast, he could usually go unnoticed.

As they sat in the silence of the plan, Kon noticed Icelyn coming down the hall, his dark jacket in her arms. She clutched it close to her, as she had last night. Her grin grew as she presented it to him. "You guys are all here already?" she said lightly as he took the jacket. The faded fabric of it looked dark again, no longer coated in dust. She had taken care to fold it neatly.

"Thanks," he murmured as she let out a satisfied huff. There was still a smile on her face as she pulled her hair over her shoulder. It was messily folded into a loose braid, small wisps of hair falling from the sides of her face around her bangs. She started to put on her own jacket on top of her gray halter top, over a flowy shirt.

There was always the chance someone would notice them dressed in outdoor attire, backpacks on. It was the reason they all huddled at the end of the hall by the sunroom, a place rarely visited by others.

"We didn't want to miss it," Jyune said as Icelyn sat down her backpack.

"Well, I grabbed some supplies. A few things from the med bay, some food—" she kneeled as she moved supplies around. "How are we getting to the tunnels without being noticed?"

Peter was anxiously fiddling with his jacket. "Staircase to a less populated floor is our best bet. Maybe elevators?"

Stormy pulled at her hat. "I couldn't get the tunnel key last night. The Defensive Wing was *swarming* with people."

"We'll figure it out." Kon started to fill his jacket pockets with its previous contents as the rest fretted over details.

"How far is that facility from Darnar?" Stormy asked as she looked over the map Peter had rattled open.

"A decent walk, I think. It's up in Benova Mountains." Peter's finger traced over the red drawn circle in their best estimate of the facility's location.

Jyune sat up, still nibbling on her orange. "I packed our cookie supply!"

"Don't tell me you're just bringing cookies?" Peter said.

"Well, there's a muffin in here somewhere . . ." Jyune began digging in her bag.

"You think we're missing anything?" Icelyn said as she stood.

"Probably," Kon said, looking off to the side with feigned disinterest.

Peter was writing something on his map, a list of sorts, while Stormy discussed the proper supplies-to-cookies ratio with Jyune.

Down the hall, Jasamie hurried toward them. She stopped for a moment, out of breath. "Okay," she began with a sigh. "They're going into a big meeting about base security any minute. Most of the people we need to avoid will be in there." She had a messenger bag on her hip, thick with supplies.

"Is everyone ready?" Peter said.

Kon sighed. "This is a bad idea."

"We don't have a choice," Peter stated. "We *have* to get answers before the next fight. We can't risk you going alone and running into him!"

Kon panned over the group of eager faces. "You're sure you want to do this?" They all nodded in agreement. "Let's go."

The group sprang into action. Jyune climbed into Stormy's backpack while Peter zipped his book into the safety of his bag. "We have to be careful," Peter said in a hushed tone. "Terrance will kill us if he catches us trying to leave."

Kon shrugged off the warning. "Then don't get caught."

They peaked around the corner of the hall into the common area. There were only a few early-morning students moving around. Kon took the empty hall as his chance to head for the staircase. The rest tailed behind him. The camera pointed at the staircase had been fixed from the other day. He gave a defiant glare at it as he moved into the staircase. There was no point wasting his energy to mask cameras. It was only a matter of time before they would realize the group was gone, whether the others knew it or not.

They stopped inside the staircase as Kon turned to Stormy. "Where would the key cards be?"

"We usually have to grab a level four key card on the first floor . . . but we can't go through the mural area—they'd see us. I tried last night. Too many people."

"There's key cards on the second floor," Peter whispered.

"Where?" Icelyn whispered back.

"Why are you whispering?" Kon grumbled. "Can we get there from this side?"

Peter clutched the straps of his bag. "They're hanging in an office. I mean, maybe we can get to them. It'd be risky."

"Lead the way."

Peter hesitated, his brows creased, before he turned and started down the stairs to the next door. "Are . . . Are you sure we need them?"

"The doors to the tunnel won't open themselves." Jyune peeked over Stormy's shoulder.

"But they're on the other side of the base. There's no way we're making it that far unseen." Peter stood frozen at the door.

"We have to." Kon watched him, waiting for him to move.

Peter took a deep breath and turned. "No, we don't." He hesitated as the group stared at him before he reached into his coat pocket, pulling out a key card. "This might work. It'll open most doors. We can test it on the elevator." He turned to exit into the hall, but Kon's hand landed on the door over Peter, stopping it from opening.

Peter's gaze slowly rose to him as Kon stood beside him, expression flat as he cocked his head to the side with a scoff. "You've had that . . . the *whole* time?"

"I—not with me! Para gave it to me for . . . emergencies," he defended, clutching the card. "I usually keep it in my room."

"You never once thought to mention that?" Kon rolled his eyes and released the door, glaring at him as the others shifted.

"It's emergencies only!" Peter fidgeted. "That's the rule. I didn't know you needed it!"

Kon only met him with a stare of disbelief.

"So, will that get us into the fourth floor?" Stormy asked, eyeing the card.

"It should," Peter mumbled as Kon headed down the next flight of stairs. "We could just use—" Peter watched the group rush down the stairs away from him. "The elevator." He sighed and followed.

The fourth-floor door was heavier with thick metal hinges around it and a scanner on the side. The sign next to it read, "No unauthorized personnel." Wired glass windows sat high on the door as Kon checked the hall on the other side. Dim lights hardly illuminated the path; a long ramp led down.

"You think anyone's down here?" Icelyn asked, looking about the dusty staircase.

"I've never seen anyone guarding the tunnels; no reason to." Stormy shrugged.

"It's just an exit," Peter breathed as he took the last few steps. "No one should be down here." He caught his breath for a moment as Kon waited by the door with a frown.

"You know which tunnel to take, right?" Jasamie asked as Stormy adjusted her backpack.

"Southeast, tunnel five." She nodded, her usual demeanor starting to dissipate in the nerves of their trip.

Peter looked at Kon before he scanned the card. It buffered for a long moment before the scanner flashed green, and the door clicked. Kon took a deep breath and opened it. The immediate smell of dust and rock hit them as they peered in. The ramp opened to a large room in the distance.

The floors were no longer tile. Instead, they were hard, cold concrete, walls the same. The group stayed silent as they approached the turn ahead. It revealed a balcony overlooking a massive concrete room, with giant reinforced beams down the middle. There were only a few supply boxes in the otherwise empty dimly lit area as they made their way down the ramp to the floor level.

"I didn't know this was down here," Icelyn started, looking up at the towering ceilings. "What is this for again?" Her words echoed slightly.

"Emergency exits. All these big bases have them," Peter explained. "We use them for discreet supply drops too, so no one's tracking hovercraft drops to the main base."

"We only get supply drops once a month, though," Jasamie added. "We just got one last week, so we're in the clear."

Kon scanned the room, reading each tunnel entrance until he found 'five' ahead of them to the left. The tunnels were large archways, dark inside. There was a stark contrast from the rest of the base. Down there, it felt odd. Unsettling.

As they approached the looming tunnel entrance, its darkness engulfed them. Pausing outside of it, they checked its label one last time. Tunnel 5.

"Cool, huh?" Jyune asked as they looked down the pitch-black tunnel, her voice echoing through it.

Kon let out a tiny sigh. It was that or face the EME.

"That's one word for it." Icelyn shivered.

"I didn't bring my flashlight." Peter began digging in his backpack.

"No need!" Jyune called, sparking a glow of light around her hand as she held it over Stormy's head. It was rare to see Jyune use her powers at all.

"Oh, right."

The ceilings of the tunnel were tall, not as high as the towering room, but despite the height, the tunnel felt suffocating as they entered. There was a rail track down the middle of the floor for supply carts.

"Well, this is . . . creepy," Icelyn said, holding her hands at her chest.

Stormy nodded. "I never liked coming down here."

"I see why." Icelyn sighed.

"It beats the woods," Peter said.

Kon disagreed but stayed quiet. He could've easily navigated to Darnar and the AIP facility alone. A group of people, however, made things more difficult. They always did. There was still a sting of helplessness that he even needed a group—or maybe it was guilt. Did he only accept their help because of his own fear of the new threat? Maybe he was putting them in danger for nothing. He could've been halfway to the Core Sector if he had left the night before—or already in the hands of the EME.

Icelyn spoke as the tunnel stretched ahead and behind them. "So . . . do we have a backup plan if something in this plan goes south?"

"South how?" Peter asked.

"I don't know. EME or something."

"I've been itching to give them a piece of my mind." Jyune grinned, the light in her hands flickering.

"No." Kon looked over his shoulder at her. "If anything happens, leave it to me. You guys get far away from it and hide, okay?"

"You can't even leave *one* for us?" Jyune joked.

His glare said otherwise. "Promise me you'll all listen if I tell you to do something." He scanned the faces of the group. A few gave silent nods.

"We will," Icelyn promised.

"But that's not going to happen," Jasamie said quickly, slicing the building tension. "And if something *does* go wrong, last resort, I brought a radio. We call the base."

Kon liked that idea far less, but it could prove useful for them in the events they did have to split up.

Jyune's elemental light only illuminated a small circle around them. He could use his, if needed, as the tunnel supposedly went on for several miles. It would be a long, dark walk.

Kon kept himself busy watching the dusty floor. His head was heavy in thoughts. It had been ever since the attack. The pressing tunnel wasn't helping. His entire life, while dangerous, Kon had always known he at least had the advantage of power on his side. The EME had only managed to overpower him once. They brought hoverforms and armed forces until he had nowhere left to go. He swore to himself he wouldn't let them corner him again—but everything was new.

Unknown.

While it was new, there was a sickly familiarity to it—the same as before. Rather, it was his mind making connections in the name of fear, or if it was right, he couldn't deny the influx of memories. It happened every year. He hated the tiny things that would set it off; Terrance's accusations his first day there, the files he found in the database, the way students looked at him . . . An old wound had been reopening since he got there. Maybe it knew the whole time how it would go.

Whether he believed in himself or not, the group did. Icelyn was sticking to herself. Her gaze was already on him, however. Careful, soft. She believed in him.

Peter and Stormy had started comparing maps in the back as they bickered over the logistics of the drawn paths. They had been walking for a while. It was hard to tell if time was moving faster or slower underground. The entire tunnel was at a steady incline as it neared the surface. The ceiling was creeping closer the deeper they got.

Icelyn moved in beside Kon, who had stayed at the front of the group, watching the ground. "Are you okay?" Her tone was quiet, the arguing behind them masking her voice.

His chin lifted a bit as his head turned to her. "Yeah?" The events of the early morning felt like forever ago. He had almost forgotten what he told her in the hazy empty halls.

"You just seem kinda quiet," she said. "More so than usual." There was a small grin as she looked back at the others.

He shook his head. "I'm fine."

Her hands toyed at her chest as though she planned to say more, but as her eyes lifted, her expression shifted. "Is that it?"

Kon followed her stare down the tunnel to a faint light.

Their pace slowed as the others caught on.

"That's the end." Stormy sighed in relief.

The light came from a single bulb at the dead end of the path. As they approached, it illuminated the exit, a hatch on the roof. The top of the tunnel was closed, adding to the pressured feeling of the tunnel as they rushed for the hatch. Hopefully, they were far enough away from the EME collecting around the base.

"Are we ready?" Peter asked as they gathered under the exit.

Everyone nodded.

Kon held his breath and reached up for the handle.

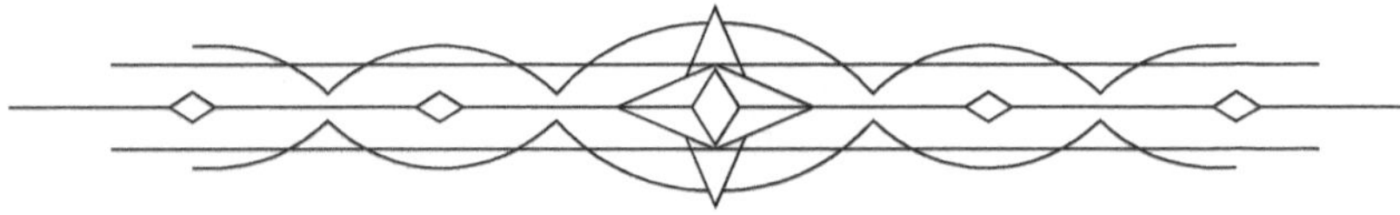

CHAPTER

28

NIGHTMARE

EARLY NOVEMBER 2654

Sixteen years since Avari left.

Just a dip through town. That's all he needed. Find the map, get out. Kon didn't even know what town it was as he looked upon the tiny settlement nestled in the glen of the mountain. There hadn't been time in the previous week to stop for more than a few hours. EME activity had exploded in the days that followed the cottage fire. They knew he was there. Somewhere.

His hope that the tall mountains in winter would deter them had quickly been dashed as hoverforms started sweeping every ridge and valley for him. The woods were full of squads of EME. He had spent days running or hiding, moving so erratically that he had lost every sense of direction.

The town was hardly even a town. It was just a few old buildings along a dirty stone path. Houses scattered the woods around it. Maybe with its small population, the EME would overlook it. He didn't have time for the careful maneuvering that he often did with towns; plotting where he needed to go.

As he hurried along the outskirts of the town, he kept an eye open for a map of the area. Dark clouds festered in the sky. Way down toward the archway into town sat the large sign with the map. There were hardly any people passing in and out of town as he approached. It could be a blessing or a curse. His breath was shallow as he stopped at the sign, taking it in. Town of Mcardta. Northern Dante Mountains. If he headed west, he could get back toward the waterways. The EME would expect that. North? North would land him farther along the mountain range. Maybe he could lose them in the winter weather.

Someone cleared their throat. He locked eyes with a man standing under the outcrop of the low roof of what appeared to be a post office. There was nothing particularly odd about the man—older and stout. Still, he stared at Kon, unwavering. Without hesitation, Kon started toward the archway. He had stayed long enough.

The air in his chest wasn't finding its way. Everyone looked suspicious—the woman packing her cart too slowly, the man lighting a cigar, the taller Rilinquin walking a large white dog. Any of them could be EME—maybe none of them. From his frantic attention to details around him, he saw it; the gruff man from the sign was following behind him. Kon steadied himself. *Almost to the archway. Just another few steps.* A man ahead of him dropped his newspaper at the sight of Kon, holding a hand up with a smile.

"Excuse me, can you help me? This darn map." The taller, older man stepped in front of Kon, cutting him off. He held his map out like he was preparing a question, though words didn't come. What did come was the subtle quiet *click* of something being pulled from a holster behind him.

Kon bolted. He didn't turn or look. It didn't matter. His fears were confirmed the second he took off.

"He's running!" someone shouted.

"Call it!" another yelled.

Of course, it was a trap. He glanced back only once, catching a glimpse of the man with the large wolfish dog, unclipping the leash and pointing straight at Kon.

His stomach dropped. As the barking started behind him, he was already back in the trees, veering off the path. The murky foliage of dead leaves stirred as he rushed through the woods, followed close by the path of the dog. It would be on him soon. At the very least, it gave away where he was, its deep barks closing in with every passing flash of trees. When the gnashing of teeth sounded as though it could reach out and bite him, he finally ignited fire up his arms and ducked to the side. The dog skidded past him, growling and snarling as it turned on its haunches.

Kon waved the fire between them. The dog hesitated in its stance, looking for a way to him. Fire caught on the dead leaves around him, poisoning the cool air with the smell of burnt foliage. After another flash of fire, the dog started to retreat from the flames. It paced before him a moment longer before its tail dipped and it headed back. Maybe someone had called it back. He heard distant shouting behind him and the deep thundering roar of a hoverform.

This time was different. Each time he thought he could slow, the sounds of more EME would set in. It had to be a group of them every mile. He tried to push away the thought that he was entirely surrounded, but in every direction, hoverforms roared. *Keep running.* It wasn't something he was fighting his way out of. Adrenaline drowned out the majority of the toiled twisting emotions in him. He needed a chance, a break in the wall.

Maybe they didn't know where he was. The hoverforms could be a trick, a way to send him into a panic. Part of him wanted to attempt to hide again, but they would search, and those dogs would surely find him soon enough. His only option was to flee.

He could've been running for hours; he didn't know. Part of him wondered if the roaring was stuck in his ears or if they really stayed nearby. Sometimes, he'd see glimpses of lights—EME spotlights in the dipping sun, or were they more swings of his frenzied imagination?

He finally stopped over a creek next to a large old tree. Light rainfall was starting, with the threat of snow if it got much colder. Desperation was the only thing left in him. Not even his own breath stayed as he threw his bag down, then his jacket. Joel's jacket. Panicked hands stuffed them into the deep crevice of the tree as he had before with more supplies. He could circle back and retrieve it later, but he needed a lighter load. Perhaps he could go farther that way. It could be a mistake to leave all his supplies and belongings behind, but if he kept them with him, he would surely have to stop soon.

He pushed himself back up, just as the roaring started to rise again. There was no time to feel the ache in his legs or his lungs begging for air. His nose burned as he checked it. Blood. It was acting up again. Nothing that mattered, though. He was off. Much faster with nothing on him. Maybe he could actually get away.

He couldn't have run more than a few miles when the roaring started to his side. He paused, only to gauge its direction, but it was all around him. Two? Three? checking the woods, he tried to find the source. Forget his burning chest. *Focus.* Through the trees, he saw spotlights. Not just one group but several. How many ships had they sent? It sounded as if the entire arsenal of EME was nearby, surrounding him. Looking for him.

"Up ahead!" one called.

He turned, ready to run as another group started to materialize in the brush ahead of him. They were all around him. Panic crawled up his spine as he spun again, running the only clear path he could think of. He couldn't fight this many, couldn't scare them off with flashes of fire. They knew what they were dealing with, and they had finally collected the proper team to run him down.

As they pushed him into the small field, he realized he couldn't run any farther. The roar of the hoverforms finally began to appear. One directly in front of him emerged over the trees, with a long metal tail twisting to turn the spotlight on him. Its large, dark hull shadowed the field below as it let off its horn; a bone-chilling deep siren that drew out long and low.

He tried to duck back into the woods, but the groups were closer. Far *too* close. Close enough that the individual soldiers spread in a wall. There had to be fifteen or more of them as they backed him into the field, rainfall quickly soaking his shirt. Treading each of his steps with their own, they crept after him, herding him into the center of the field.

Kon cursed his lungs to take in air—to *work*. He would have to fight. Between the hovering shadow above and the newly emerging EME soldiers from every place in the trees, he was surrounded. Fire pooled up his arms, pathetically small in comparison to his usual flames. Whatever fuel his body needed to conjure a fight, it didn't have it in his sheer exhaustion. He raised the trickles of fire, regardless, trying to make space between him and the approaching EME. Rain blurred his vision and fizzled his fire. Their steps hadn't stopped. They were moving closer.

"Put that out," one finally warned, "or we will."

That was when Kon felt it, that nauseating burn of energy. Vinralin. Joel had warned him of it. He circled, looking for the source. It was strongest emanating from the side as he watched one of the men pull the pouch out and hold it up. The flames at his arms struggled to stay lit as the power around him pushed away from the Vinralin into his own body. It burned in his bones as he instinctively backed away from it. He couldn't even feel a panic at the second and third hoverform lurking above. One was starting to lower into the field to pick him up. His lungs had screamed for more air for too long, and he wasn't getting it. Things were going dark as he tried to keep himself alert.

Keep them away, he thought as he circled, making sure no one was getting too close. He had to keep them away—to show he was more alert than he was. A shot from the crowd hit his shoulder, almost throwing him to the ground. Stun rounds. He stumbled, terrashock forming in front of him far too late to block the blow. There was no way out.

Joel had told him to fight, though. No matter what. He remembered the words. *"If you have even an ounce of energy left in you, you use that to stand up and fight them."* He stayed standing as his shoulder started to go numb. A burst of terrashock shot out in the direction of the gunfire, pushing a few uniforms back, but more took their place. The Vinralin was getting closer. The man kept his steady approach. As fire lashed out, it simply dissipated into the air around the Vinralin.

Calls all around him warned him to get down. To stop fighting. He couldn't. He couldn't go with them. He wouldn't.

Another shot hit his side from behind as he flashed out more fire. The burning in his head only increased. Every face was the same, that dark, angular mask staring at him from all directions. It was surely a nightmare he'd woken up from many times, but finally, nothing would wake him from the bad dream. It was real.

Spotlights above blinded him as the Vinralin reached too close to him, and the energy around him shrunk to nothing. He stood, facing the lurking soldiers, ready to fight. He didn't need his powers; he would still fight them—a hard hit struck him in the back of the head. Then there was a call to move in as he collapsed.

The real nightmare was just beginning.

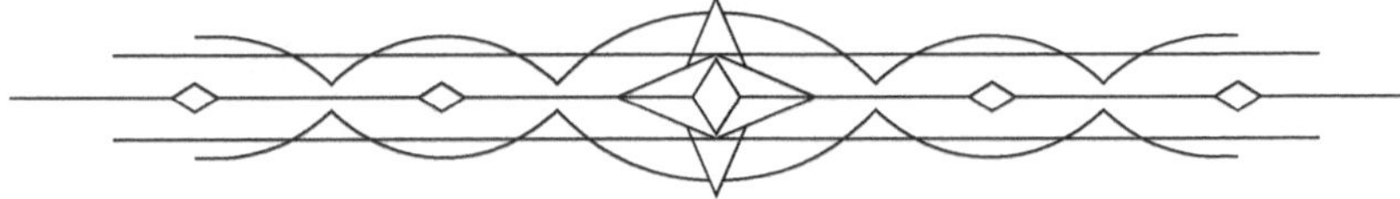

Town of Da

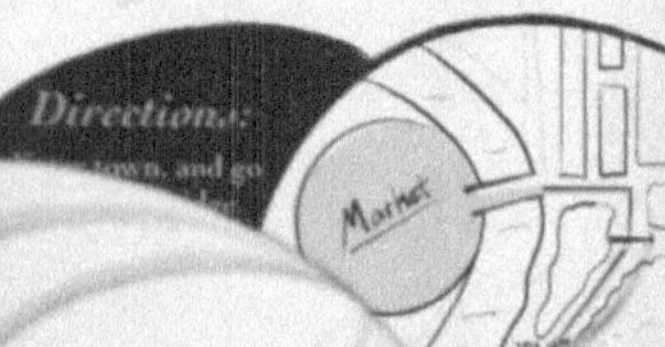

Darnar Farmers Market!
ell, trade and shop fresh local farmed goods
Directions:
town, and go
Market

Tannen Farms
Reecyps, risps, pickleds
£10 Per Pound
WARNING!
ELEMENTAL
EME
EME
Age: 19
Species: Mix
Last seen: West Sector
Hair color: Black
Description: Tall, tattoos, traveling on foot.
Extreme caution. Do not approach. Contact EME immediately.
Hostile. Do not engage, or attempt confrontation. Dangerous, and WILL resist. Report sightings immediately and stay indoors.
Report sightings or leads to EME comm. #3443.0

MISSI

sh Aryps
harvested p
ps, an
jelly, jam,
Juice!
er Fenn Farr
ted South si
rmers Ma

EME

ING
Mayella Lae Yetena
Age: 25
Hair color: black
Eye color: Green
Last seen: Keylon
Any information
TAL
TICE
h EME protocol, please
L Elemental sightings
Failure to so could
result in harm.
all comm. # 34

CHAPTER 29
STORMS WARNING

Present Day

Rain dripped in as the hatch cracked open, staining the concrete floor below. Light poured in with it from the pale sky.

"It's raining?" Peter whined as Kon pushed it open fully.

Relief flooded over him knowing he was about to leave the suffocating tunnel. Wiping his hands, Kon looked back at the group. "Stay here." He started to climb out. The door was covered by thick ferns as he nudged them aside. Rain sprinkled across the woods. Kon gathered himself in the bright light. The sounds of the forest were comforting while he scanned the trees around him. No sign of EME. Just the drizzle of rain on the foliage. "Okay, come on," he called down.

Peter was first to scramble up the wide ladder, struggling with his backpack over the wet railing. After a painfully long time wiggling up the ladder, Kon reluctantly offered a hand, pulling him out, an eye on the woods. "I can't believe I forgot to check the weather," Peter said.

Icelyn appeared next, carefully maneuvering out. Kon helped her with the last few steps. She gave a grin as she leveled herself. "Thanks."

He stayed put to help the rest. Stormy and Jyune climbed up as Jyune peeked out of Stormy's bag at the surroundings. Jasamie exited behind

them as Stormy oriented herself. "Okay. Darnar should be . . . that way."
She pointed down the hill.

Kon took a last glance at the hatch—their only safe way back. It gave
a hard *clang* as it closed and latched.

"It says there's a path around here somewhere." Peter squinted at his
map, wiping the raindrops from his glasses.

"We aren't using the paths," Kon said as he started down the hill.

"Aren't we going straight to Darnar?" Stormy called as they all followed behind through the wet foliage.

"Too many intersections. We can follow the river past it." Kon
assumed they were following by the rushed steps behind him. The river
would be close. It would be their safest bet to town. The drizzle of rain
only increased as they headed down the decline. Dark clouds threatened
a bigger storm in the distance as the terrain started to turn rocky with the
nearing water. Its roar grew louder over the rain as he followed its hums.
Their pace was much slower than Kon would have liked, regularly having
to slow down as they carefully traversed the hill behind him.

Rushing water took up a large part of the bank as Kon stepped onto
the rocky beach. He could hear the commotion of Peter slipping behind
him as Icelyn and Stormy tried to steady him. The river was high from
the rain, muddy brown water tumbling by. Across the water, large rocks
formed a sizeable cliff wall, teeming with moss and overgrowth. A long
roll of thunder let out overhead. The bank opened up a ways down from
them, jutting tall rocks forming overhangs by the water. Cluttered steps
behind him made him turn, just in time to see Peter dusting himself off.

"I'm okay." Peter puffed his hood back up and looked out at the water
with awe.

"Is this it?" Icelyn asked as she adjusted her own furry hood.

Kon nodded, ready to move along the beach, but there was a sound
coming over the churning water. It had to be close to hear it over the
waves: a hoverform. "Wait." He turned as the others were stepping onto
the rocks. "Back." Ushering them into the tree line, they finally heard it
as well. It was roaring as they all watched the sky. The hazy shadow came
first; large and dark overtaking them. Then, with a crack of thunder in

the clouds, the underside of the massive craft appeared. The only break in its large flat body was the four circular holes on each corner of it where its antigravity system kept it hovering above the trees. Its pointed nose kept straight as the long, linked tail swayed behind it, clicking as it bent back and forth, boosting only slightly from the base of the tail.

Kon always thought hoverforms looked like a creature of some kind, with their lanky metal tails built to turn the giant craft. Like a towering metal stingray in shape, poised to attack. Always on the hunt. They never stopped scaring him.

It lurched over the river, the familiar lights lining the bottom of its dark metal exterior. "EME." Stormy grimaced over the sounds of the four propellers. Jyune hid her head in Stormy's backpack.

"Yeah." Kon narrowed his eyes. It wasn't searching. The spotlight up front was off. It was heading somewhere. Its roar faded as it disappeared over the cliff on the other side.

"It's going toward the base," Peter said in a small voice.

They didn't have much time.

"Let's go." Kon grumbled, shaking the uneasy feeling from himself.

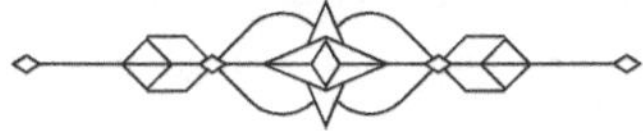

It was only another few miles from town following the river. With the rain lessening, the trek was much easier. When they reached the bend in the river, they turned off, headed straight for Darnar. It wasn't long before signs of town started to appear, paths and posters pointing to town. Darnar was a bit bigger than Calirue and much busier, though it was hard to tell if that would harm or hurt the group as they approached. A larger sign with a map stuck out ahead on the trail.

"Let's check the board. Sometimes, it mentions stuff going on in town," Stormy said.

As much as Kon didn't want to be on a trail at all, being that close to town was hard to avoid. The board had a section for the map of town, a section for fliers, a mix of local farm offers, town events—his heart sank.

"Is that Kon?" Jyune leaned over Stormy's shoulder to look at the poster, overlapping several others; clearly placed in the center, on top of the others, for all to see.

Kon loosely read the info attached next to his picture:

WARNING!
ELEMENTAL
Extreme caution. Do not approach.
Contact EME immediately.

"You look scared," Icelyn whispered as she peered at the photo with creased brows, hand extending to touch it.

He forgot how young he had been. How his face was still round in youth. That young innocence in his face was gone. It had been for a while. He stared at it a moment longer, his expression stiff before his eyes snapped away from it. "It's an old picture."

"The EME must have been through here putting them up. The poster looks new," Peter said.

Icelyn promptly grabbed the paper, ripping it from the wall before she crumpled it up and stuffed it in her bag with a scowl. Her eyes scanned the wall for more. There were several missing posters—a few more Elementals—and then . . .

"Hey, Icelyn is here too!" Jyune pointed.

"What?" Icelyn squinted at the small flier. A missing person poster, sure enough, with a small, old picture of her. "Here?" she said, tearing it down as well.

"You think it's your dad?" Jasamie asked. "It didn't mention that you're an Elemental."

"Probably," Icelyn scoffed.

"Okay, well," Jasamie put her hands on her hips, "Kon can't go in until we know where this guy is. Icelyn shouldn't either. Is anyone else here *wanted* or *missing*?"

Kon and Icelyn slowly looked at Peter, who met them with pursed lips.

He kicked at the dirt path. "I—fine. Yeah, I am. I don't think anyone would recognize me, but I'll stay."

"Right. So, Stormy, Jyune, and I will go in, get information on Tally, and meet you guys back here."

Kon had been watching up the trails for signs of people as he turned back to them. "By the rock," he said, gesturing to one of the large rocks through the trees. "We can't stay on the trail here."

"Okay." Jasamie and Stormy nodded.

"You're sure it's safe for you guys to go in there?" Peter clutched his bag.

"We're regulars. And it's busy enough they won't even notice us," Stormy explained with a confident grin.

"Be careful," Kon said, turning for the rock in the distance.

"You guys too." Jasamie waved before the three turned down the path, and the other three headed into the trees.

They weaved behind the tall boulder away from the path, where Peter plopped down against the rock with a huff. "I don't usually do this much walking," he breathed, clearing his throat.

Kon crossed his arms and leaned against the rock, still put off by the poster. It wasn't like he hadn't seen them before. Maybe it was how close it was to the base or that the paper looked new. That it was recently placed. Icelyn appeared bothered as well, arms folded around her torso, looking at the ground.

"You think there's EME in there?" Peter looked up from his seat as he rubbed his knee.

"I don't know." Icelyn sighed.

Kon's gaze lifted to Icelyn. Her eyes were laced with a silent concern as she found her own rock to sit on, taking the crinkled papers out of her pocket. She unfolded them, searching for any clues.

She shook her head. "Hostile, do not engage," she read. "That's ridiculous."

"It says that?" Peter asked. "I mean, Kon can get a little moody . . . but?"

Kon hit him with a glare as Icelyn read on, "Hostile and dangerous. Why do they lie about this stuff?" She slapped the paper down on her lap as she looked at Kon, who was watching her with a blank expression. "You're like the calmest person I know."

"Really?" he asked in a low voice, almost amused.

"Yeah. They make you sound—scary. I don't think you've ever been scary since I met you."

He gave her something of a sideways grin. "I try not to be."

"You're not." She smiled back, pushing the paper behind the other as she looked at her own poster.

"Can I see it?" Peter asked, sitting up as he recovered. Icelyn handed it to him as she read over her own poster, frowning again at its contents. That time, she stayed silent.

Peter's expression churned to worry. "When did they take this picture?"

Kon kicked at the ground. "Few years ago."

"What happened?" Peter asked. "How did you . . . get away? Where was this?"

"It doesn't matter, Peter," Kon muttered. The dark clouds in the distance left blue skies over them as another hovercraft buzzed in the sky somewhere.

"I didn't know about this." Peter clutched the paper, clearly bothered as he held his questions.

The buzzing grew closer as the hoverform approached. It passed over as the other had and in the same direction. There was silence as it lurched overhead.

"What do we do about the EME?" Peter finally asked in a small voice.

"What do you mean?" Kon asked.

"How do we win this?" he breathed. "There's so many of them."

There was a pang of guilt as Kon watched the dark craft. "This is my fault."

"Why?" Peter asked, a twist of emotion in his expression.

Kon turned away from the craft. "You don't see why?"

"I—no. I don't," Peter responded.

There was a scoff as Kon tilted his head. "Really? The hoverforms aren't enough?"

Peter stood, a poof in his chest. "Yes, really." His voice was hushed but harsh. "Coming to the base was the best thing you could have done. I'm tired of you saying that stuff!"

His quick turn of emotions even surprised Kon, but he stayed steady. "Every person in that base is in danger now," Kon snapped. "Because *I* was there."

Icelyn looked between them, eyes wide as Peter stood his ground.

"*You? You* were in danger!" Peter's voice strained as he held the wrinkled paper out to Kon, who averted his gaze from the image. "You need us. We need you. Whatever happened with the EME—whatever it is you're afraid of—you need us. I mean, what's your plan? Run until you can't anymore? Disappear like all the other Avari? Like you never existed? I don't want that to happen to you!"

Kon's voice lowered, "At least no one else gets hurt."

"No! That's not true. Because whether it's months or years from now, they'll get us too. You aren't protecting anyone, Kon." Peter shook his head. "Where were you even heading before you came to us? What was your plan?"

Kon hesitated as silence followed, his annoyance turning to shame. "The coast. I thought I had time to stop. I should've kept moving." In his avoidant gaze, he found Icelyn again. Her face was twisted in slight pain at the comment, lips pursed. Immediate regret punched him in the stomach at his own comment.

"And it was EME after you. They never sent this Avari?"

"No."

"Don't you see?" Peter held his hands out. "They brought him out because you being with us is a *threat*."

Kon narrowed his eyes at the thought.

Peter pressed on. "Do you think they would risk having him out, looking for you, if it wasn't their last-ditch effort? They're desperate!"

Icelyn stood too, toying with her paper. "I shouldn't know this, but . . ." The two looked at her as she took a breath. "The day before I left, my dad came home, furious. He said things were getting worse. That the EME 'needed to prepare.' He didn't say for what." She dropped her arms to her side in guilt. "Maybe they already knew you were close to the base. But . . . whatever they knew, it scared them." Her gaze was soft on the ground. "You being with us *scares* them."

Jasamie stuck close to Stormy as they entered town. "This is a bad idea."

"It's all about confidence, Jasamie," Stormy explained as she held her head high. "Act like you're supposed to be here and no one will bat an eye."

Jyune mimicked Stormy's straight stance from her shoulder as Jasamie attempted feigned confidence as well.

"You're sure you know where we're going?" Jasamie asked.

"Up ahead. The bakery." Jyune grinned. People on the stone street passed by. Calirue never got that busy in the main part of town. Carts of goods were set up on the streets, selling spices and crafted baskets from distant farmers coming into town. The storefronts were well kept, each one a different style of color and design and with hanging plants on the streetlamps that draped from their baskets. A salon, a thrift store, a pharmacy, then the bakery—a beige brick section of the long stretch of stores, with neatly decorated window displays of bread and pastries.

The bell above the door rang as a girl behind the counter waved to them. Wooden floors under them creaked in the old building, but it was about the only sign of age. The walls were painted a soft salmon color, with fancy chandeliers hanging above them. Several people sat at the glass tables against the wall as they moved to the counter.

"What can I do for you?" the girl behind the counter asked, a lingering distant accent in her tone.

Stormy smiled with a swish of her tail. "Is Beems in?"

"Yeah, he's in the back. I can grab him for you?"

"That'd be great, and—are you restocked on your semi-sweet chocolate morsels?"

"I believe we just got a shipment in. I'll check on that as well." The girl headed into the back room as Jyune browsed the pastries.

"Really?" Jasamie whispered. "Is now the time for shopping?"

"It'll look weird if we don't buy anything. We *only* come here for them," Stormy hissed back.

A moment later an older man swung the back door open, a wide grin across his mustache. He was tall and plump, with a large apron on as he pulled off an oven mitt. "Ah, Stormy and Jyune." He had the same accent as the girl but stronger. "It's been long since you came."

"Oh, you bet!" Jyune laughed.

"We got caught up in baking. You know how it goes," Stormy said with a smile, leaning on the counter.

Jasamie had to give it to her: Stormy had a charm to her.

"It's been going well?"

"Best cookies in town back home!" Jyune declared, disappearing into Stormy's backpack to grab a wrap of cookies. She pulled them out and tossed them to him.

"Yeah, we figured we'd bring some over and pick up some more chocolate chips too." Stormy browsed the breads with wandering eyes. The girl in the back emerged again with a hefty bag of chocolate, plopping it on the counter. "And throw in some of that Tryth bread too, will ya'? We've got some stops to make today." Stormy fluffed her hair, unbothered, glancing back to Jasamie, who was watching her with confusion and a slight impatience.

"Why, of course." The man chuckled as he began wrapping the order up, ringing it into the register.

Stormy squinted at Jasamie with a tiny nod, twirling her burgundy hair before she spoke again. "Anyway, my friend here's trying to find a family friend in town. Garik—uh, Tally. Know him?"

"Tally? He runs electronic store, down by Brookwyn Books, you know?"

"The bookstore, yeah. Next to that?"

"Yes, he has been here many years." The man nodded as he handed the bag over to them with a curl of his lips. "Take care. I will enjoy the cookies."

"You better!" Jyune said.

"Thanks, Beems." Stormy cast a wave over her shoulder. He called something in another language as Jasamie trailed after her. They all sighed in relief as they entered back onto the streets.

"Electronic store, by the bookstore . . ." Jasamie repeated.

"It's toward the end of the street," Stormy said as they began walking. "Might be a little risky bringing Kon, but if we can just slip in, maybe no one will notice us."

"Then we head straight back to the woods. We barely have to enter town."

"See any EME?" Jasamie whispered, glancing all around them at the crowd.

"Nothing yet." Stormy searched the passing faces, looking for any sign of uniforms.

"The pub." Jyune hunkered down in the backpack as they spotted the dark uniforms hovering by the bar. Only two of them, angular masks off as they conversed. It was still worrying, nonetheless.

"If they stay there, they won't spot us." Stormy averted her gaze away.

Jasamie watched a second longer. "*If.*"

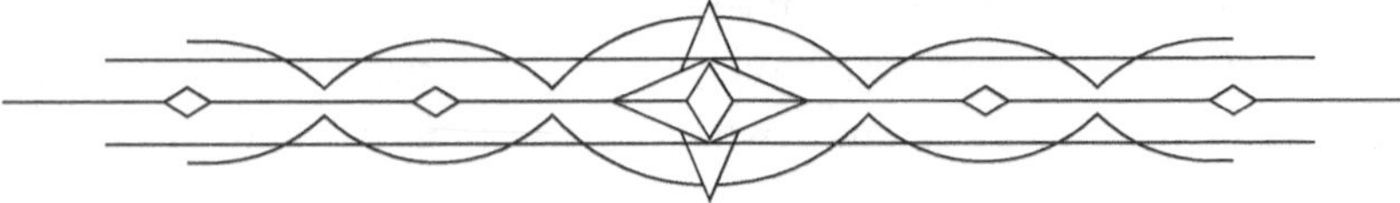

TALLY'S
Electronics and par
TALLY'S

CHAPTER 30
THE SCIENTIST

"On the main street of town?" Kon crossed his arms. "*And* with EME around."

"It sounds worse than it is," Stormy explained with a sigh.

"I think it's doable," Jasamie stated. "It's the third shop. We barely even have to enter the street. We just slip in, slip out. The EME were up the road at the pub. There were only two."

"That you saw," Kon said.

"We have to try." Peter secured his backpack.

Kon gave him an unconvinced glare as he tossed his bag over his shoulder. "Fine. Lead the way." No matter how confident they were, he was going to prepare for the worst.

"We got some bread for the trip." Jyune clutched the large sourdough tucked in Stormy's backpack as they started walking.

"You guys did some shopping?" Icelyn asked with a playful scrunch of her nose.

"We got information. The bread was just part of it," Stormy explained. "Plus, I'm hungry. Can we please stop after this and eat?"

The previous rain had chased most people off the paths to town, puddles dotting the route. Trees stayed thick around them until they had nearly reached town. Kon threw up his hood as passersby appeared. Most were carrying baskets or carts of crops and supplies.

"It's one of their final markets before winter. Everyone's trying to stock up," Stormy explained as she led the way.

It did little to comfort the anxious group. Kon rarely had to enter towns anymore. If he did, it was never midday in a busy trading town. As they crossed under the archway labeled "Darnar" and went left toward the street of buildings, the risk was sinking in. In a way, the mass of people helped. Farm families and traders were bustling along the stone walkway between buildings. There was a good mix of people; humans, Felinians, and some taller Rilinquin, all dressed in raincoats and hoods from the rain. If luck was on their side, there was enough to mask Kon from most suspicion.

"There!" Jyune pointed over Stormy's shoulder to the bookstore ahead on the other end of the street. Next to it, third in the row, "Tally's Electronics and parts."

The group quickened their pace. Weaving through the crowds, Kon kept an eye out over the crowd. EME were usually easy to spot with their dark uniforms. He only took a glance before he looked back down, careful to hide his markings in his hood.

"Alinth was never this busy." Icelyn muttered beside him as they neared the store. Stormy held the door for them as they quickly filed in, sighing in relief. There hadn't been much of a plan for once they got inside, however. They took careful looks at each other before moving farther into the store in a casual attempt to browse. The shop was dim inside, with strips of lights along the walls and shelves. It was a small store, lined with racks of old and new electronics. Bins of wires and parts sat on dusty shelves. The front counter had newer items; communicators and cameras. They paused in one of the back aisles.

"Now what?" Stormy whispered.

"We ask for Tally." Icelyn looked at the desk, where a younger man typed into a digipad. "I'll go. Everyone lay low for now."

Kon nodded, gesturing for her to join as they moved to the front.

Icelyn took the lead as he lingered, careful to not blow his identity.

The man behind the counter met them with a slight grin. "Anything I can do for you?"

Icelyn took a breath. "Is Garik Tally here?"

Kon glanced back at the others, who casually browsed the shelves nearby, listening intently.

"Yeah, what do you need?" The man's expression moved to Kon, where his smile faded only slightly.

"We just need to ask him a few questions," Icelyn said.

"Okay, hold on." The man's demeanor had shifted to something of . . . worry? He disappeared behind the cloth hanging over the doorway. Icelyn turned to Kon with confusion as he gave her a shrug back. He knew something.

After a few nerve-wracking moments, in which the store was silent, someone approached the door and the cloth parted. "This better not be EME. I'm not having this discussion again." An older man in a wheelchair entered, frowning until he saw the two waiting for him. There was a questioning look at Icelyn until his gaze fell behind her, to Kon, where it then faded. "Oh."

"Mr. Tally?" Icelyn asked.

"Yes." He was still set on Kon, a look of disbelief.

"We need to ask you a few questions. About a job you used to work at," she explained as she looked back at Kon as well. He pulled off his hood, given the act seemed over. He knew.

The man looked across the shop at the group, who had all turned to watch. "Come on. Back here." The counter entrance opened as he beckoned them in. "Hurry. Darnar isn't safe."

The group hesitated only for a moment before they joined him.

"James, watch the door." His tone was hushed as he directed them to the back.

Kon ducked slightly under the frame, scanning the storage. Whether the man intended to help or not, he was once with the EME. Kon would keep his wits about him. The back room was small, with boxes lining the walls. There was another hall to the left, leading down a ramp.

Tally entered, pausing to push back his gray hair. "Did anyone see you? EME?" He looked mainly to Kon, who shook his head.

"There were some at the pub earlier, but I didn't see any coming in," Jasamie explained.

"Good. Darnar is too busy to be safe. I didn't know if you were . . . after all these years . . ." He shook his head as he looked over Kon. "Why *are* you here?"

"Mr. Tally," Icelyn began, "you contacted the Elemental Protection System years ago, claiming there was a second Avari."

"Yeah?" Tally breathed, still frowning in guilt.

Kon crossed his arms. "I just met him. Who is he?"

The man's expression folded for a moment as he looked down at the ground, shaking his head in something of disappointment. "Come on." He pushed his wheelchair down the next hall, flipping the light on. The group shared glances before Kon followed first. The ceiling was low as they followed him into a dated kitchen of sorts, wooden cabinets and an old blue table and fridge. To the right was a door, locked with a code. Tally typed the code in, glancing back at them. "I wasn't supposed to take any of this when the program shut down." He pushed the door open into a dark room, revealing another storage area. There was a screen pulled down from the ceiling, with boxes of records and tapes nearby. "I figured I'd try and keep it all safe."

"You have recordings from the Avari Integration Program?" Peter breathed as Tally started up the projector.

"Some. I tried to take as many as I could. Some from early on, some from later." He began weeding through the boxes as Kon shifted, watching the door. Pulling out one of the thin tapes, Tally inserted it into the back of the projector. It flashed for a moment before it started rolling, illuminating a bit more of the room with it. Video from a handheld camera ran. The halls of the AIP facility. Some Avari stood next to doors talking with mentors while others gave the camera a grin. "I figured they'd destroy these if I didn't. Andren Day asked me to try and get 'em out," Tally said.

"Andren Day? You knew him?" Peter inquired, still looking up and down the shelves of boxes.

"Of course, we worked there together. Shame he . . . disappeared like he did." He shrugged. "They pushed all the mentors out first. I knew they'd want this stuff saved too. EME kept us scientists around for . . ." He stopped, shaking his head. They watched the footage play. The camera recording had reached the end of a hall, where a group of three Avari stood, two mentors discussing with them. They turned to the camera before Tally paused the video. "That's Jarauk and Padlin—"

Peter gasped in disbelief, looking at Kon, who stared at the still frame. His parents.

"They look like you," Icelyn said quietly.

Kon set on the two before he saw the third Avari, lingering behind his father like a shadow. Something twisted deep in his stomach.

"That's him." He stared at the violet-blue eyes of the Avari on screen. "The Avari." He was younger in the picture, looking Kon's age. Between his supposed parents and the Avari that had just attacked him, he didn't know which was harder to look at.

"Kyros." Tally said quietly. "He's Jarauk's brother."

There was silence over the room as the news sunk in.

"He's Kon's uncle?" Icelyn asked.

"Why is he here?" Kon asked, though there was a part of him that didn't want to know. Wasn't ready to know.

Tally sighed. "He got everyone out. You included."

"What do you mean?" Kon looked at him, dread rising in his chest.

"I don't know the whole story . . . but when they came in, they wanted everyone. Specifically, Padlin, who had just had you. The only reason they didn't get to you—to everyone—was Kyro. The rest didn't want to fight, but he did. Put up a hell of a fight on his own while the rest started up the teleporter. By the end, you were gone and the teleporter was shut down. He was stuck here." He let out a sigh. "We didn't know where you had gone. We thought you hadn't gone through the teleporter. The EME suspected a mentor fled with you."

Kon looked back at the frozen video. Kyro's expression was less curious than his parents, something more of caution at the camera. Maybe that's why he seemed angry at Kon back in Calirue. Kon was the reason he was stuck here.

"So, what happened?" Peter asked.

Tally pushed his gray hair back, face scrunched. "I shouldn't have stayed. The EME wanted me to come on to continue research, with just him . . . but it was different." He struggled with his words, shame across his face. "The other scientists, we thought maybe if we stayed, we could get them to be—gentler with him. Help him in *some* way. We didn't. I just had to walk away. I couldn't . . . stay there."

Kon was stuck, everything in him wanting to run away, but there were more answers to get. "What do they want with him?" He knew he was asking what they wanted with himself as well. Something he never truly understood.

Tally shrugged. "Back then, it was weapons to fight Koron off planet. Controlled power. That's why they wanted everyone. All these years . . . I kind of just hoped he was—" He shook his head. "If he's out now, they're probably test-running things. You said you saw him?"

"He attacked me," Kon stated.

"They've always wanted you. It was a matter of time before they used him to get to you."

"Why me?" What use would they have for a newborn? None of it made sense.

"They wanted the whole program, but toward the end, they became more focused on Padlin. I don't know why. It was after some other Avari visited. From the Council. Something switched." He clicked the tape back on, letting it play again. Padlin and Jarauk were saying something to the man behind the camera, smiling. Kyro kept his gaze wary. Tally watched the video before looking back at Kon. "I figure, Kyro was the test run. You're the finale."

The words sent a chill down him. Kon's fear was right. Kyro's fate was his own.

The door to the room swung open, the man from the counter bursting in. "Dad, EME," he breathed.

Tally clicked the projector off and ushered them out. "Quickly."

"It's just one. He's asking for you."

Kon looked up the hall back to the store, ready for a fight. The rest filed out with him, Peter being the last to leave as glanced into the room of tapes for a final time, fiddling with his bag.

Tally latched the door closed. "There's a back door, that way." He pointed across the kitchen. "I'm sorry. I wish I could help more . . . but it's not safe here. Go."

Kon watched him disappear into the hall again, part of him still ready to confront the EME, but he backed down. He imagined Tally had far more information to give, but it wasn't worth alerting the EME. There had been enough said, regardless. "Come on," he glanced back at the group, who were wide-eyed as they watched him.

"What if there's more?" Jasamie asked, clutching her bag.

"The sooner we're gone, the better." Kon pulled the blinds to the window on the door back before opening it. He tried to muffle the buzzing of questions and information in his head as they entered the quieter street. There were a few vendors across the river, bordering the back of the stores but with far less traffic. He headed left, back toward the road they had come, stopping at the corner of the building to check the path.

"Wait, he said there was one EME, right?" Stormy asked as she checked over her shoulder.

"Yeah?" Peter asked, zipping his jacket up.

"We saw two . . ."

Kon peeked around the corner of the building to the main road where people still bustled into the street. One inside surely meant more outside. The path right led across the river and to a long wooden bridge. There was a continuation of stands from the market across the water as people wheeled carts and baskets toward it. The facility was south from there, in the other direction. They needed to get back into the woods where they came.

"Stay close." Kon rounded the turn, heading along the stone wall dividing the street from the woods. The best option was back through the busy entrance. Sticking close, the group neared the archway until Kon promptly stopped, causing Icelyn to bump into him.

"What's wrong?" she asked, steadying herself.

Kon watched over the crowd by the entrance. An EME uniform stood, watching faces pass. Panic washed over him as they stood at the divide between the main road and the entrance. "EME. This way." He headed into the streets, watching the crowd for any more of them.

Stormy jogged beside him. "Blocking the entrance?"

"Yes." He scanned for a way out as they headed toward the center of town.

"There's a side street ahead. Come on." Stormy whispered, taking the lead as Jyune stood on her shoulders, scanning for EME as well.

Kon checked behind him for the other three following closely. Stormy quickly diverted them down the gap in buildings. It was labeled "Docks." Most bigger towns had several docking stations for hovercrafts. She paused short of the turn, skidding to a stop as Kon paused behind her.

Ahead, a small dark hovercraft was parked. Kon immediately recognized the colors of it as it unloaded several EME. They didn't seem alert, casual in their movements as they opened the hatches on the side of the craft. Whatever their reason was for being here, it wasn't the group. Yet.

They backed out of the alleyway as Kon counted the arrivals. At least six.

Stormy pushed on down the street. "Okay. New plan." Her voice rose in nerves.

"Where's the next exit?" Kon asked, keeping his cool.

"We might be able to break away in the town square."

Icelyn stuck next to Kon. "There's more? Why are they here?"

"We'd know if it was us," he said as he looked ahead at the opening into the square. The cobblestone street was busy with people still.

Jasamie moved up beside them, worry laced across her face. "I think we're being followed. Black shirt."

Kon checked behind them. Surely enough, there was a man in a long-sleeved, dark shirt walking behind them, watching closely. Undercover EME wasn't uncommon. There was nothing they could do in the busy streets, though. Maybe it was coincidence.

As they reached the round center of town, the brick town hall sat straight ahead. A large tree decorated the circular town center. Another string of buildings lined the stone path, but there was a gap between them; a short alleyway. Kon turned for it, checking again that everyone was in place. The man was still tailing them at a distance, blurred in the crowd. Through the back of the buildings, they could still see the docking station, but it was between a patch of trees. Maybe it was paranoia, but the group of docking EME were gone.

Kon headed straight down the path toward the final trail before woods. They just needed to get into the woods.

"Are we safe?" Peter asked.

"No." Kon checked over his shoulder again, realization sinking in that a fight was coming as the man stayed. "Go straight into the woods. Wait for me."

"What?" Icelyn whispered.

"I have to get them off us." It wouldn't be long before he alerted the others—if he hadn't already. He slowed down, moving himself to the back of the group.

"Are you sure?" Stormy asked, just as a voice cut off her words.

"Stop." The stranger spoke finally. They were just entering the woods as they all faced him. A siren was starting up somewhere in the center of town.

They were out of town. The best place he could've led the assailant. The man wasn't far behind them, hand revealing a pistol from the back of his belt.

"Get down. No one gets hurt," he warned, his messy, light hair brushed over his creased brow. There was a communicator in his other hand. He looked young. One of the newer EME. They were always jumpier.

Kon didn't budge, waiting for his next move as he stared. Normally, the fight would've been over by then, but with the anxious group behind him, Kon was thinking up any way he could avoid what was sure to come next.

The man raised his communicator to his mouth. "I've got them by—" The device crunched as terrashock shattered it, causing the man to drop it. There was far less confidence in his movements as his gaze set back at

Kon, swaying as he held his position. "I said get on the ground," he said with a gulp.

Kon watched him for another moment, the weapon trembling in the man's hand. They already knew. Behind him, the sirens were amping up, louder. They had only moments before the team of EME would find them. He squinted at the man. "Walk." He gestured to the bustling town center behind them. A chance for the EME man to take his life and flee. The energy was already in place, nearly invisible warps of terrashock at the ready before he turned to the others. "Go."

They looked at him in shock. Peter glanced back at the man while Stormy and Jyune shared horror across their faces. Jasamie and Icelyn watched Kon. Icelyn took a careful breath as she locked eyes with him, lips pursed as she trusted his word and started walking. The rest joined her. Frozen by nerves, the man stayed put.

They had only walked a few feet when the shot rang out.

A *thud* sounded on the dirt path. The group spun to face the *bang*, all except for Kon, scowling, before he too turned with a sigh. The man was on the ground, unmoving. It was always the same. He rarely gave them that chance. After years of it, they didn't surprise Kon anymore. He had hoped the group didn't have to witness it.

"W—what happened?" Stormy breathed, clutching her chest.

Kon shrugged as he headed for the woods again. Shooting terrashock never went well. It always ended in the burst energy, the ricochet of the bullet. Somehow, newer EME always forgot that detail. A fitting punishment for the trigger-happy soldier. "We need to go. He already alerted them."

"Did you—kill him?" Peter whimpered, pulling at his collar.

Kon narrowed his eyes as he passed. "*He* pulled the trigger."

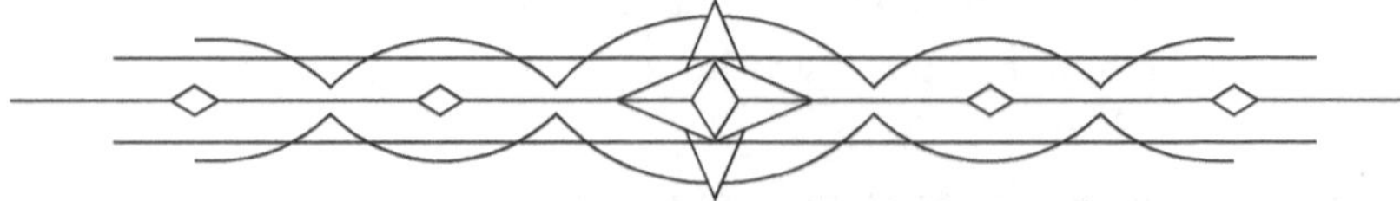

CHAPTER
31
SLOW AND STEADY

"They definitely knew we were there," Jasamie said as they traversed the thick woods. "Do you think they know it was you?"

"Nothing we can do about it now," Kon murmured.

"Maybe we should call Para—"

"No," he glanced back at her. "Having them come get us in a hover-form isn't what we need right now."

"Do you think they know where we're going?" Icelyn stepped carefully around the ferns.

"They'd need a big sweep to find us. We'd hear it coming." Kon shrugged as Peter let out another cough beside him. He hadn't taken the dispute well, bothered ever since they left Darnar.

"That was crazy," Stormy exhaled. "I thought for sure he had gotten one of us. I mean, what was that trick?"

"You can't shoot through terrashock. He should've known that." Kon sighed. He, at least, thought the man had been trained enough to know. The communicator was a warning. There was a feeling of guilt, not that the man had given him a choice. He really had tried not to shake up the group with a fight. If they hadn't been with him, the man wouldn't have even gotten that far. It took years for him to be unfazed by the majority of EME interactions. He didn't blame the group for their shake-up. Icelyn hadn't said much more than a word since.

"Guys," Peter said, "can we uh . . . maybe stop?" He began coughing again as Kon looked him over, confused.

Jasamie's eyes went wide with realization. "Are you okay?"

Peter leaned against a tree and tossed his bag down, clutching his chest as he nodded. Kon watched him with a lowered brow, trying to work out the problem.

Jasamie approached. "Do you have your medicine? Sit down."

Icelyn inched closer, running a hand over her braid.

"Medicine?" Kon checked between them as Jasamie coaxed him down.

"It's in my bag." He wheezed as he fell to a sit.

Kon crouched down to grab the bag. "Where?"

"Front pocket."

Kon unzipped the inner pocket. There were a few snacks, a map, and an inhaler. He pulled it out. "This?"

Jasamie nodded and reached for it, shaking it as she quickly handed it over to him. "Sit up straight."

Peter took a puff from the inhaler and waited, breathing out after a few seconds.

Silence befell the woods as Jasamie met the gaze of the rest of the group. "We should stop here for a while. Eat. Rest."

Stormy and Jyune didn't argue, settling down on the ground, away from them to give space. They immediately started pulling out the food. "Is he going to be okay?" Jyune asked, staying distant as she crouched on a twisted tree root.

"I think I just got kinda worked up back there . . . and all the walking. Allergies," Peter croaked, face flushing.

"I tried to get you guys away from it." Kon moved Peter's bag next to him as he watched.

"It's not your fault. I just got freaked out." Peter took another breath from the inhaler.

Jasamie kept a hand on his shoulder, watching his breathing before she met Kon's gaze, a bit more urgency in her hushed voice. "We really should consider calling Para."

Kon looked almost convinced.

"No," Peter coughed. "It's not that bad. I just let it . . . build up," he cleared his throat. "I just need a few minutes."

"Peter," Jasamie said, "if you're not feeling better, we might not have a choice."

"I'm feeling better already," Peter joked with an unconvincing grin.

Kon dropped his own bag and stood up, surveying their surroundings. They were likely in the middle of the woods. Trees stretched across the flat terrain. If nothing had surfaced from the interaction yet, they had likely successfully avoided the EME. One benefit to the EME being focused on Calirue—there was little attention elsewhere. "This isn't a good place to stop for long." He tried to gather where they were. "There might be a better spot up ahead."

"We'll see if we can head out in a few, but we shouldn't go far." Jasamie moved in to sit next to Peter.

"Anyone want some of this bread?" Stormy asked, trying to lighten the mood. "Fresh from the bakery!"

"Can I make you a plate of some snacks?" Icelyn asked Peter as he focused on his breathing. He nodded as she stood to move over with Stormy and Jyune.

Stormy unwrapped the bread, grinning with excitement, while Jyune pulled out a pile of napkins. "We got chocolate chips too. I bet he'd like those."

"I have some fruit in my bag." Icelyn pulled her bag around and set it in front of her.

Kon watched them a moment longer before he knelt back down by Peter. "Do these usually clear, or . . .?"

"Yeah. I don't have it super bad. Everyone at the base just gets all . . . worked up over it," he said casually as Jasamie handed him his water.

"I'm a medic, Peter. It's my job to get worked up over you."

The sun was no longer directly above them, drifting down as Kon surveyed the sky. The facility was still a hefty walk away. Jasamie would never clear him to walk that distance in the remaining part of the day. He stood again, keeping an eye on the woods around them.

As Peter started to pack his inhaler back into his bag, Icelyn approached with a napkin of assorted foods. "Alright, we have some freshly baked bread, blluru berries, pepron seeds, and some chocolate chips." Peter was pleased with the assortment as Icelyn stood again, glancing over at Kon.

He stood with his back to them, unfolding his map to assess it. There was little acknowledgment of her nearing steps until she spoke. "What are you thinking?" she asked. "Any ideas?"

The woods were drying from the previous rain, the air still chilled in the fall weather. His eyes traced over the map for another moment. "We aren't far from the mountains. Might be a better spot to set up there." He kept his voice low. Of course, not far for him was likely decently far for them as he tried to calculate their version of an easy trek.

"You don't think we'll get to the facility?"

"Not today. It's that or go back to the base." Kon peeked over his shoulder at Peter. "He's not going to want to go back."

Icelyn toyed with her hair. "You think we have enough supplies for that?"

"That's probably the least of our worries."

"What about back at Darnar? You think they're looking for us?"

"They're always looking for me," he joked, giving her a tilt of the head. "I think we're fine, for now." While the events at Darnar surely startled the rest of the group, EME movements were erratic, which meant they likely didn't have a focus that far south. If they *had* spotted him in Darnar, it would only confuse them on where to collect, as most were heading toward Calirue.

Jasamie had moved over to Stormy and Jyune, gathering her own snack as she kept a careful watch on Peter from a distance. He was standing, testing himself as he did some light stretches.

"I think I'm good," Peter stated, voice still a bit hoarse.

"Are you sure?" Kon said as they began to pack up.

"Yeah, I could climb a mountain!"

"Well, that's what we're doing." Kon folded his map away. "The facility is somewhere up on Benova. We'll see how far we can get."

"What if we don't make it by dark?" Stormy asked as she wrapped the bread back into her bag.

Kon shrugged. "We stop somewhere for the night."

With supplies packed, they set out again. Travel was much slower as they kept a gentle pace. Getting up the mountain to the base would be a problem with energy levels already low. As they raced the sun across the sky, they had only begun their trek up the mountains when the clouds started to shift warm in hue.

Kon looked back at the woods below them as they traversed the rocky path up the ridge. Green moss stuck all across the rocky wall to their left and down the cliff to their right. Ahead of them, the mist from a waterfall cast out from the sheer drop to the river below. The golden light caressed the high ridges.

"It's beautiful up here." Icelyn's smile beamed with the sunset as she took in the mountains in the distance.

"We're stopping soon, right?" Jasamie asked from behind, keeping an eye over her shoulder at Peter.

Trees picked back up at the top of the cliff. It would be a safe place to pause for the night. "Yes." Kon scanned the trail to the top, a windy ramp back and forth up the mountain. It looked scarcely traveled, which was good for them. The mountain was too far from towns and too harsh for farms. No one would be up that far into the mountains. It was a good place for a secret facility.

"Jyune, you get really heavy after an entire day carrying you," Stormy said.

"Fine," Jyune declared, climbing from the bag onto Stormy's shoulder as she prepared a leap to Icelyn in front of her. Icelyn eyed her with con-fusion as she got into position and made the last leap to Kon's backpack. "I don't think I've ever been this high!" She scanned the landscape. Kon ignored her as they navigated up the final stretch of winding ramps.

"Did I ever mention my fear of heights?" Peter called from the back as he rounded the turn on the increasingly narrow path. Jasamie reached for his hand, leading him up the last few rocky steps.

The top of the ridge opened to a flat stretch of thick woods. Large, jutting rocks across the ground left fair shelter as Kon scanned for a suitable spot. The waterfall along the ridge could be seen from eye level, the water spilling off the rocky ledge as it tumbled down the sizable cliff to the thin river below.

"You can see for miles." Jasamie gasped, looking out at the mountains in the distance as Kon led them across the edge and toward the woods.

"Is that Palyra Mountain?" Icelyn pointed at the two high ridges in the distance.

Jyune leaped back to Icelyn's shoulder. "Yeah, the base!" Jyune grinned. "Did we really go that far?"

"It feels like it," Peter mumbled.

Kon turned his back to the view, surveying the rocks as they argued over whether anyone could actually see the base from atop the ridge. Jyune was swearing with all her might that she could. There was a decent clearing amongst some overhanging rocks protected by the trees just inside the woods. The cliff's edge was still nearby as the rest lingered on it. "We can stop here," he stated.

As Icelyn joined him to look, Jyune dove from her backpack to a rock as she assessed the area. "Yeah. Yeah, this will work."

The rest settled in, Jasamie still watching Peter as he plopped his bag down on a rock. Icelyn ran her hands over themselves, watching her breath dissipate into the air. "Should we start a fire?" she asked. "Is that safe?" The temperatures had been steadily declining as light faded in the sky.

"Should be fine," Kon said. "Hoverforms usually go around mountains, not over them." Usually. As long as they had no reason to believe anyone of importance was there.

"Sit down," Jasamie gestured to Peter, placing her bag on the ground.

"I told you, I'm fine," Peter protested.

"I'll go look for firewood." Jyune hopped down behind the rock, scuffling the forest floor for sticks as Stormy joined her.

"Are we close?" Peter asked as he dusted off a comfortable spot to sit.

"A few miles," Kon guessed, setting his backpack down as well as he watched Icelyn attempt to chase off the cold. Her pale braid fell over her shoulder in twists of hair that almost glowed in the darkening surroundings. He kicked at the ground in the center of the clearing, pushing dead leaves and rocks away with his boot until the ground below was exposed. There was still decent light in the sky as he started placing rocks around the spot. Icelyn was quick to walk over to help, grabbing a few rocks on her way.

Footsteps behind them indicated Stormy and Jyune had returned, Jyune carrying an armful of sticks while Stormy held a few bigger branches, setting them down nearby. "Will these work?" Stormy asked.

Kon looked over the selection, pulling out the most suitable ones. "For now." Icelyn watched intently at the fire building, soaking in his every step. Once there was a decent pile, he took a bundle of the smaller sticks in his hand. Fire ignited around his fist, instantly catching on the sticks as he placed them within the larger branches.

The others began positioning themselves around the fire as it grew. There was silence over the group until Peter finally spoke in a guilty tone. "Do you think Para knows we're gone?"

"She has to, by now." Jasamie shook her head. "I just hope they trust us."

"We already have good evidence." Peter became confident in his words. "They just have to hold on until we get back."

It was hard to tell what could be happening at the base. Kon hoped their attempts to lay low were enough. In the quiet of the mountains, he could remember how crushing it felt for the EME to be surrounding him. He only hoped the others wouldn't feel that dread. Of course, the dread was warranted. He still felt it every day. Waxing and waning, with every EME encounter.

"What happens if the EME finds us?" Jyune whispered, peering out at the cliff from the comfort of Stormy's bag.

Silence.

"Let's not . . . think like that," Icelyn eventually said, softly.

It might've felt even worse once Kon knew the fate waiting for him if the EME did get that close again. Before, nothing would have prepared him for what came after the EME caught up to him. Finally, he knew what was at risk.

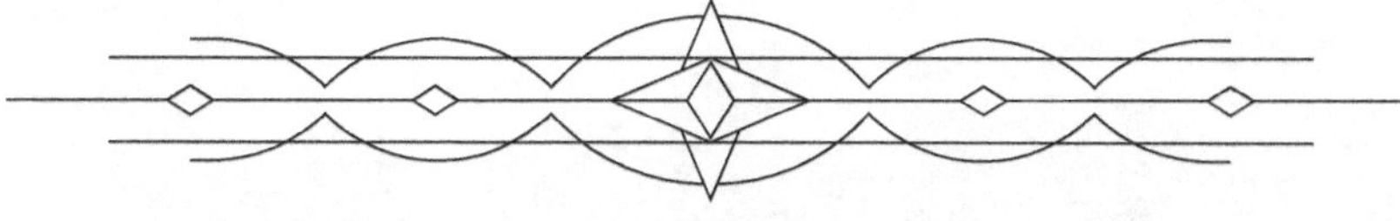

CHAPTER 32

REMNANTS

DECEMBER 2654

Seventeen years since Avari left.

Fire lurched through the long steel hallway. It stuck to the walls, the floor, and the ceiling, pulsing with every step Kon took. Panels of the wall peeled back as terrashock bent and warped the surroundings. He was almost there. The exit was straight ahead while carnage lay behind. The only thing he could keep focus on was the red glow of the exit sign as the lights above him shattered.

From the bend in the hall ahead of him, another group of EME appeared, cautiously setting themselves in his way. They shouted something in his direction, guns raised. Their voices could hardly be heard over the blaring alarm in the halls. Fire pulsed again as Kon stumbled, making terrashock erupt around him. They must have taken it for an attack as shots fired off. It hit the energy with bounces of fire and color as he faltered and fell to the ground once again. His powers were out of his control. *Isn't this what they wanted?*

Commotion from the men ahead was muffled as his head spun. The familiar cold floor stared back at him. He needed to get up.

With another labored breath, he was back on his feet. The men before him were on the ground like the rest, dispatched by an energy that he couldn't control. His legs barely felt like his own. It was a wonder he even made it to the door. He couldn't bring himself to look back to see if he was being followed. Nothing in him wanted to look back down that hallway, not one more time.

As the door cracked open, cold wet air flooded in, clearing his mind to some degree. *Fresh air.* He sucked it in and gave the door a final shove, falling again as he collapsed outside. *Outside.* That time, he landed in a puddle. Rain fell from darkened skies, night closing in. Blotches of water covered the concrete exterior as rainfall worked through the shaky energy around him. At that moment, it was the best thing he had ever felt. Cold, heavy raindrops quickly drenched him. Part of him wanted to stop there, to lie in the rain. But there was yelling somewhere. He wasn't safe yet. With a cough, he pushed himself to his feet again, where in the distance, woods lay. The empty docking station he crossed held no signs of EME. It was strange, the lack of EME. Maybe they finally got the message, or maybe there was something worse inside with the mess he had left.

Energy tore at the barbed fence at the edge of the woods before he even realized it was there. Terrashock had bent and torn it open for him. The fire trying to accompany the energy kept sizzling and reigniting around him in the rain, refusing to settle.

Into the woods, his pace quickened. He didn't know how his body had the strength to keep moving or even keep awake as trees blurred past him. Hoverforms hummed to life behind him. They'd be looking. None of that mattered. He was out.

There was no telling how far he ran. Far enough that he couldn't hear the hovercrafts anymore—only the pattering of rain on the soft under-brush of the forest. Finally, he had to stop, catching himself on a tree so he wouldn't hit the ground again. The outburst of energy around him had barely settled. There were little signs it was still present as he fought to catch his breath. His stomach twisted and ached as he clenched it. Where was he? How far had they moved him?

He coughed again as the ache worsened. Only then did he taste the blood and realize the wet clothes over his stomach were . . . warm. It wasn't rain. His hand pulled back from it to reveal the coat of shining blood. It had drenched the shirt, mixing with the rain.

Kon leaned against the tree in the blur of confusion. A shaky hand pulled up the shirt. He was hit. Somewhere in the crossfire of escaping, in their effort to stop him at all costs, a single shot had connected straight with his stomach. Hazy from adrenaline, the ache of it had only just become apparent. It wasn't a stun round. They had planned to take him down however they could. *If they couldn't have him, no one could.*

He sunk down the tree, his legs finally refusing to carry him another step. *So, that was it?*

A buzzing far in the distance had returned. They'd keep looking. Maybe they'd find him too late.

He couldn't tell if he felt anger or sorrow. If it was tears welling in his eyes or rain. At least he was in the woods. At least he was safe there. Even if it was at the end. He was out. At least he'd never have to go back. If that's what death granted him, he could accept it. The rain around him faded, the light of sunset dimmed. Everything was vanishing, fast.

It was never his world anyway.

What came next might've been a dream. A haze of something surrounded him as he slipped away. He could've sworn he was in someone's arms, lifeless. A warmth radiated from them as they held him close. They were walking, voices of strange unfamiliar dialects. The face of who held him couldn't be made out. It was a glimpse, a blurry one, but he could almost see dark, inky markings across their skin—

Kon gasped awake, jolting up in the patch of soft grass. Woods surrounded him. No more rain. It was . . . early morning? Birds sang somewhere in the trees as the sky stained a gentle orange. He quickly took in his surroundings. It wasn't where he was before. He was lying in a clearing in the middle of the shady willow trees. No sound of hoverforms or yelling or a distant alarm. Just the quiet breeze and song of mourning doves. Maybe it was some form of afterlife—or a dream.

His next instinct was to grab his stomach, where only the dry shirt remained. Faded blood stained it as if the rain had almost washed it away. As he lifted the shirt, there was nothing but a small pink mark, a fresh scar. His eyes drifted to the jagged markings on his side until he covered them again with the shirt. The short-sleeved shirt did little to hide the darkened markings on his arm as he sorely examined the bruises across his skin, down to the steel lock still fastened around his wrists. Although, as his eyes trailed over himself, still taking in the reality, they found the heap of fabric lying beside him. His backpack. Next to it, his . . . *jacket?* It no longer mattered if it was a dream as he grabbed for the jacket, pulling it close. For a long while, he simply sat, hugging Joel's heavy old jacket. The jacket he had convinced himself was gone, along with himself.

He might've stayed there for hours, processing, if it wasn't for the snap in the brush behind him. The crunch of the twig made him spin around to face the threat. In an instant, terrashock erupted at the bush, crushing twigs and foliage in its path. The burst of energy startled even him; all for a deer to bound off away from the commotion. A deer. Not the EME.

Regardless, he stood, shaking, still clutching the jacket in his arms. Maybe it was finally setting in that it wasn't some peaceful dream of an afterlife.

He was there. *He was back.*

The thought only brought fear. He was *back.*

Kon turned to his bag, looking over the drab gray outfit in which they had dressed him. His stomach churned. Without much hesitation, he opened the backpack, relieved with the change of clothes still in it, and quickly disposed of every piece from the facility that he could. The only thing he couldn't rid himself of was the metal bands on his wrists, despite a few tries to slip them off. He kept the worn bandage under them as well. It didn't matter; he needed to get moving.

It didn't take long to realize travel wasn't his best idea. His body wasn't prepared for it anymore. One of the many things he lost in that place. Every twig and rustle pulled erratic fear and energy from him until he found himself nestled in the vines of a large tree, too scared even to move.

He didn't know where he was, where *they* were. Whatever diligent traveling he was usually good at was gone, replaced by one constant, looming fear: *EME*. Nothing would convince him to approach a town, find a map, or ground himself. Not even the rumbling in his stomach. He was stuck, preferring the prospect of starving in the safety of the woods over facing whatever—whoever—was searching to bring him back again.

That feeling lasted through night and day. Most days, he couldn't bring himself to travel, fearful it could lead him straight back to that base. Instead, he slept, letting his body take what it wanted, but sleep never brought relief.

He stopped at a creek. More so, his body stopped him at the creek. Sitting at the rocky edge of it, his eyes lost themselves in the moving water. There was a part of him that wondered why he wasn't okay. Why had he even come back? What reason did he have to be there? Nothing made sense. How he escaped, how he woke up. Nothing felt real, and there was nothing he wanted more than to sleep. To go back to those short moments of emptiness. Peace. That's the only place he could find it.

He might've dosed off until a gasp let out across the water.

Kon shook himself awake—or to the most awakened state he could muster—to face the threat. A girl. Loose strands of honey-blonde hair shaped around her surprised face as she looked him over in silence. She was in several layers of thick clothing, coated over a worn dress, with a basket of berries and greens clutched in her arms. "Are you alright?"

She barely got the raspy words out before Kon was standing, backing away as his breath stopped finding its way. He had seen so many masked faces recently that his brain hardly knew what to do with the girl's innocent expression. Any faces he *had* seen in that base were cold and angry with him. He couldn't tell if she had the same expression or if his brain was warping it into that as he stumbled back.

The sudden force to stand upright made his head spin as the one girl standing before him blurred into two. She took a careful step forward. "Do you need help . . .?"

The world spun with him as everything started to fade, the birds in the trees vanishing into nothing but rushing blood through his ears before he collapsed altogether.

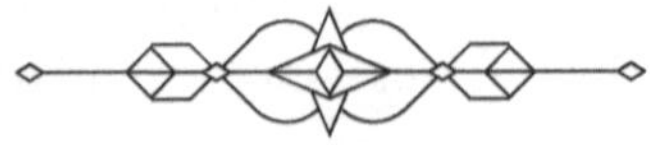

It was warm. Something smelled like food. It was comforting, but he woke with the same fear he always did, jolting up in the—*bed?* Woven sheets covered him. The warm browns and oranges of them matched the rest of the dated, small room. The only dim light came from across the room where a carved wooden dresser sat, decorated with boxes of jewelry and an intricate lamp emitting a warm glow.

Panic washed over him as he quickly focused on the open door. The hall outside was quiet. His backpack sat next to him on the floor as he reached for it. Maybe he could just leave. Run away before—

The girl appeared at the door. Her hands knitted together as her mouth opened in surprise. "You're awake," she spoke, lowering her hands to swipe them over her apron. Her outdoor layers had been removed, showing her thick dress and shirt, tattered and worn like the sheets he kicked off. He pushed himself back on the bed until he hit the corner of the wall behind him. "It's okay, you're safe here." She stayed at the doorway, slightly startled by his frenzy. "Do you remember what happened?"

Kon had frozen, the size of the room feeling as though it was actively shrinking in on him. No words came.

"You—" her freckled face contorted in worry. "You passed out . . . I couldn't leave you there. You looked . . . famished."

He couldn't control the shake in his hands as he stayed curled in the corner. With his quickening breath, the light across the room started to flicker. She joined him in looking at it, though her face lacked any sort of concern.

"I thought you might be an Elemental. I saw the things on your—" she gestured to her own empty wrist. Thankfully, there was no mention of his markings. "Did you escape those EME people?" She took a step inside, hugging the side of the door in an effort to make him feel less trapped. "I see it on the news sometimes. It's horrible, but you're safe here. What's your name?"

No response. In fact, he couldn't remember the last time he had spoken—or been allowed to speak. The flickering of the lights overhead slowed as he silently coaxed his erratic energy down.

"It's just me and my dad here. He's gone on a work trip. No one's going to see you. It's only me." Her face was round with youth, looking no older than he was, but her cheeks held a glow of life that was missing from his own. "I have stew. I've been preparing it all day. Can I bring some? I can't stand the thought of when you last ate. Please."

Even if he wanted to talk, he wasn't sure if he could.

She took his still silence and backed into the hall again. "I'll be right back."

He might've bolted at that moment, but something told him if he stood, he'd end up back in the bed again. Even if he made it back into the woods, he couldn't survive like that much longer. If he wanted to live, he was stuck here for the time being, whether she knew it or not. He questioned if he wanted that at all, but something deep in him did want to survive, for a reason he didn't understand. The hope grew stronger as she returned with the food, its smell filling the room.

She beamed with pride as she brought it over. A tray of soup, a slice of thick, fresh bread, and freshly picked blluru berries. Her raspy voice stayed soft. "My mother used to make this when I was sick. It always made me feel better." She slowed as he started to instinctively shrink the closer that she got. There was a hesitation before she set it on the nightstand next to the bed, moving away again. Her worn dress floated over her boots with every step she took back as she looked over him with sympathy. "I hope it'll make you feel better too."

Kon felt guilty in his fear, but it didn't matter. Everyone was scary, and he wasn't moving.

The girl paused at the door. "I'm Dany, by the way." She thought over her next offer. "If . . . you're feeling better later, I think I can get those things off." She gestured to her hand again. "If you want." The flow of her dress trailed behind her as she disappeared back into the hall. He could hear the steps of her moving about the kitchen while she cleaned dishes and hummed.

It took his body an extra few minutes to unlock itself and a whole lot of self-convincing that he hardly had the energy to muster. The smell of the creamy stew did the other half of the convincing. The last time he had real food, it was the small safe house in the mountains. It felt like a lifetime ago. He couldn't even guess how long ago it was. *Weeks? Months?* All he knew was sometime in those mess of events, he had turned seventeen.

Dany stayed away for a while, allowing him to process his surroundings and come to somewhat of a conclusion that he might be safe here. Nothing might completely rid him of the damage done, but it was a step toward fixing himself, or that's what he told his anxious mind. She might also be able to give him valuable information he was lacking on where exactly he was.

She appeared to retrieve the plate, and the next time she returned, it was already getting dark outside—from what he could tell out the small window. She brought him another offering of snacks before she wished him a good night.

He only got up once, when he hadn't heard noise for a while. Bag in hand, he stepped toward the door. The house creaked with each step. Something stopped him before he reached the hall. The urge to stay, hide. He could leave, grab his bag, and run, but he might never find where he was, might never find help. After several minutes of standing at the door, bag clenched hard enough in his hand to stain his knuckles white, something finally gave way. Laying the bag where it had been, he slipped back to the safety of the bed. It felt better than the forest floor, after all.

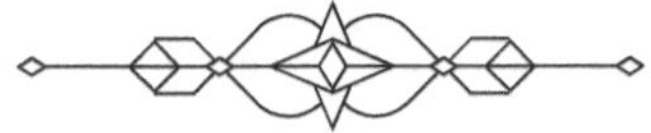

The sharp smell of coffee woke him. For an instant, he was back in the green house, Joel making his usual early morning coffee, but as his eyes adjusted to the unfamiliar brown room, reality returned. Nonetheless, it was the first time in a long time he had woken peacefully, not gasping in the panic of waking up in those cold rooms again. His body felt stronger. As he came to, he could feel the unfamiliarity of the room; the old knitted blankets, the sag of the soft mattress. Despite it all, his urge to bolt had held off.

Finally, without his bag or thoughts of escaping unseen, it was easier to enter the hallway and follow the drift of fresh coffee. His mind still lingered on the hope that Joel would be there, sitting at the counter. He wondered if there were any way to make it back to them. His hand swept over his face in fatigue. Even if he had the strength to explore, it didn't mean his body wouldn't fight him on it. As the room stretched closer, old ceramic tiles echoed the quiet footsteps of someone.

Ahead, the slightest of humming came from the kitchen, a gentle harmonizing with the rustle of the wind through the open window. It reminded him of Seelia, for a reason he couldn't be sure. Maybe it was the exhaustion, still trying to drift him away to sleep, where he could dream that he instead walked to greet the mother he had lost so many years ago. It was a tire that didn't shake with sleep. One that set deep into his bones.

The only thing that shook him from the walking dream was the sight of someone other than Seelia. A small round table in the center of the room held a fresh cup of coffee, wisps of steam floating into the warm kitchen. Dany stood at the counter, peeling aryps over a woven bowl. The creak in the floor alerted her to his presence. Sweet fruit still in hand, she turned to him. Her thin lips parted in surprise, but maybe only for the fact he was standing. Her shock held for a moment before she smiled. "You're tall." She laid the aryp down as she wiped her hands. "Are you feeling better?"

Kon had been fighting with the words the whole way down the hall when his brain would focus long enough, trying to muster the courage to speak. The tiles on the floor brought more comfort to look at than her warm grin. He didn't know why he was still afraid of her. "Where are we?" His voice was coarse and small, but the words were out.

Dany stayed put, a glimpse of sympathy. "By the coast. The closest town is Velkost, south of here."

It sounded familiar. A town he probably avoided in the last few months. He was still in the north. It was no longer the comfort it used to be. It was just a threat, but for the first time since being back in the woods, his brain was finally starting to route a plan, a direction he could travel.

Dany hesitated slightly, gesturing to his hand. "Can I . . . try to get those off? If you're ready." She paced forward, using her cup of coffee to draw closer as she reached for it.

He didn't move, just hovered in his stare at the floor. His body was trying to go to sleep again, something that didn't mix well with the caution he felt. When his eyes did lift, it was only to scan the counter and shelves for any sign of danger.

"I think I can," she promised. There wasn't the strength to argue as she turned to a cabinet on the far end of the counter, pulling out a strange tool. "My dad works on Anaiess Advancement Technology. You know, the high-tech stuff we don't have here. I think one of these might work." She gestured back to the table with a smile. "Sit."

He could feel his brain trying to turn off; shut down and follow instructions, fall into the routine he had been on for who knows how long. Maybe in that instant, it would help. Slow and careful he sat, as a breeze accompanied the sun in through the window, casting through the room.

She sat across from him, holding the tool so he could see it. "He uses these to unlock faulty droid systems—it scrambles their locking system or something. Like a digital lock pick. It looked like it might work on those too." She held out her open hand. "Can I see?"

He tentatively offered one arm, jaw clenched in his wary state. Along with coffee, the sweet smell of aryps still filled the air.

She was right to pick up on his caution. The tool only resembled something he didn't trust. His fear hadn't gone unnoticed as she moved slowly. "It won't hurt." Her hand carefully found his, turning it over as she peeled his jacket back to look at the cuff. After a moment of inspection, she nodded. "Yeah. It should work. Looks like a digital function." Silver tool in hand, she carefully hovered it over the underside of the band. The dish on the end of the tool blinked green rapidly as it read the system it was presented with.

His gaze had gone hazy as he tried to will himself to stay put. Nothing in him was okay with her touch, but he forced himself to bear it. She only wanted to help. He needed to stay still, even if his lungs felt too deep to pull air in. Even if the room was closing in on him. After a few long, painful seconds in which he may have forgotten to breathe entirely, the device on his wrist blinked green and clicked. Even the familiar *click* of it sent him in a blur of dissociation. Fear in the smallest of familiar sounds. He had to force himself to refocus his eyes, to watch that she was, in fact, removing it.

Meanwhile, Dany was grinning ear-to-ear as the band opened, and she plopped it on the table. "See? Easy." His expression didn't falter. There was hardly anything he felt for the freedom she had granted him. Though, she didn't seem bothered by his lack of excitement. "The other?"

He pulled his hand back, replacing it with the other one. The shift in weight was unfamiliar as his hand fell into his lap, still bandaged. The wraps were worn by then. He hadn't had the resolve to change them out from under the metal devices. He had a sinking feeling. Even as she removed the second one with ease, she couldn't remove the scars forming under the bandages. The permanent band. A permanent reminder. Maybe he'd leave the wraps on, hide the reality of it a bit longer.

She pulled the metal remnants back with her, away from him. "All gone."

But it wasn't gone. Nothing from that place felt *gone*.

His hands slipped from the table, back into hiding. The wraps covered the markings on his hand still, and he was glad he couldn't see them. They only bothered him to see, as always.

Across the table, Dany's smile had faded back to sympathy. She pulled her hands over the devices in an attempt to hide them from view. Her tone was soft. "Give yourself time. Loss is never easy."

Loss? Maybe he had lost something.

Kon realized he'd never looked her in the eyes. He wasn't even entirely sure what she looked like as his gaze stayed locked on the grooves of the wooden table. He couldn't even guess what color eyes were staring back at him.

She stood, collecting the remnants of that facility like junk as she disposed of them in the trash. Her dress twirled as she turned to him. "You'll find yourself again. They didn't win. They won't win."

He left that night. It was cruel to put Dany in danger. That's what he told himself, at least. He was grateful for her. She had surely saved his life. That would have to be enough of a reward for her. There was nothing else he could offer, besides a swift exit like he had never been there. It was for the best that he left and stayed by himself. He had enough of himself left to know where he was and what he wanted.

Peace. Safety.

Perhaps it didn't only exist in the haze of sleep. In the distant mountains, within the quiet woods . . . maybe he could find it out there.

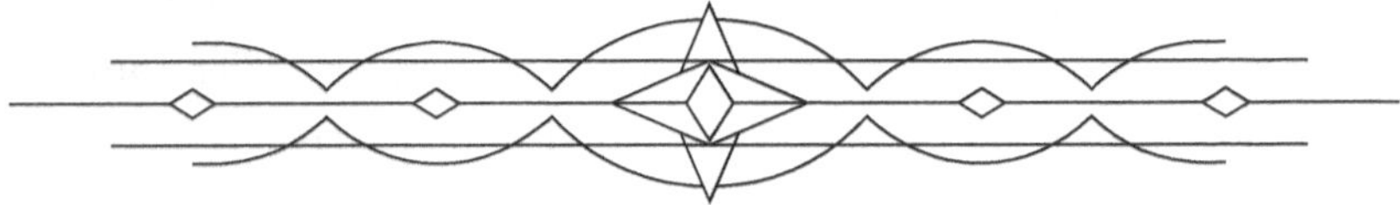

CHAPTER
33
GONE

Present Day

Para, Terrance, and Deyin stared at the screen in the Radio Room, the camera pointing to the staircase replaying the group's exit. "They left right before the meeting," Deyin said. "I got the alert that the tunnels opened. I figured it was maintenance."

Para stayed locked on the video. "Why would they all leave? If Kon wanted to slip out, he wouldn't take five students with him."

"Maybe they got a bad idea from that database," Ashdyn joked, leaning against the far desk. She dusted a fleck off her shirt. "Did you ever bring that up to him?"

"No." Para frowned at the screens.

"The doors were locked, right?" Terrance asked, still glaring at the monitor as he leaned over the desk.

Deyin replayed the footage from the main tunnel once more. "How'd they get in?"

"The kid probably has more tricks up his sleeves." Ashdyn's tone was, in the least, entertained. "Honestly we should just be impressed."

"Access key, it looks like." Deyin squinted at the footage.

"Where'd they get that?" Terrance muttered.

Para let out a gasp, cupping her hands over her eyes in realization. "Peter . . ." her hands pulled up to her head as she massaged her temples. "He must've used his."

"I mean, we only give them to students we trust." Ashdyn crossed her arms. "You really think he'd abuse it like that?"

Para shook her head, still trying to rub away a headache. "For Kon? Probably."

"Well, I'm taking *that* key back," Terrance growled. "Which tunnel did they take?"

"Five. Heading southeast."

"There's nothing down there." He straightened, putting his hands on his hips.

Deyin turned in his chair, watching their scowls with slight worry. "Maybe they had this planned. Jasamie never mentioned anything to Ryv?"

"No, it's not like her to hide stuff from us . . ." Para crossed her arms in thought. "Kon just seemed tired last night. I figured he'd go to bed. I was worried he'd . . . leave. Not like this, though."

Ashdyn scrunched her nose, pulling at her fitted shirt. "Darren was bugging him last night."

"Bugging Kon?" Para sat up from the table, an edge of annoyance in her tone. "What did he do?"

"I don't know. Said some pretty harsh stuff. I thought we got through to him."

Terrance scoffed. "I swore if I had to pull him into my office again—"

Para's expression was folded in something of guilt. "I didn't think the students were bugging him."

Ashdyn shrugged. "He didn't really seem much different. Maybe it was nothing."

"Maybe, but if we let stuff like that happen, he's not going to feel safe here." Para watched the cameras as Deyin shuffled through the various footage.

"I'll talk to him, *again*," Terrance glanced back at the monitor, only to harden his scowl.

"He wasn't trying to hide this time." Deyin rubbed his stubble, pausing the screen on the image of Kon's defiant glare at the camera. "What changed?"

"Maybe he's more comfortable." Para tugged at her braid, eyeing the image with a mixed expression.

Terrance stepped back from the table. "Is that a good thing? He's abusing our cameras and access keys now."

"Yes." Para's tone was confident as she held his gaze. "It means he's starting to trust us."

"He can't just do whatever he wants," Terrance said.

"I don't think they broke into our tunnel system to goof off. This kid is smart," Ashdyn argued. "You can't deny that, Terrance. He's been skirting the EME for years."

"Yeah, and—?"

"And I think he has a plan. We just need to figure out what it is, so we can help."

"Where does that tunnel let out?" Para folded her arms, looking back at the digital map.

"By Darnar." Deyin expanded the view of the surroundings. "There's just mountains after that."

Para stared at the map as her eyes drifted around Darnar. The large span of woods, the winding river . . . Benova Mountains. "The base," she breathed.

"What?" Terrance narrowed his eyes on the map.

"Could they be going to the Avari facility?" She leaned in, pointing to the mountains just south of Darnar. "It's up in Benova, isn't it? That wouldn't show on a map."

Terrance leaned his head back with a sigh. "You've got to be kidding me."

"Watch the radios by Darnar. See if anything comes in." Para grabbed her radio from the table, tucking it in her belt. She headed for the door. "Let me know."

"Where are you going?" Ashdyn asked.

"To pack."

"What should we do?" Ashdyn looked between them.

Para took in a breath, pulling the door open as light flooded into the dark room. "Prepare for the worst."

Terrance straightened out as Deyin hovered the screen over the mountain range. "Warm up the hoverform."

Kon dropped extra wood by fire that had sizzled to a small, warm glow. Stars twinkled above while they slept below the two moons rising into the sky. Next to the crackling fire, there was an empty spot between slumbering heaps—someone was missing.

His eyes quickly found who. On the cliff, illuminated by the moonlight, was the soft pale glow of Icelyn's hair. She sat near the edge, staring off toward the waterfall. Even as he approached, she didn't break her stare until he sat down beside her, resting his arms on his knees.

Her gaze fell on him for a moment as she scooted closer before looking back out to the stretch of mountains. "It's so peaceful out here."

"Couldn't sleep either?"

"No." Her jacket lay over her shoulders, almost brushing his. Her hand held a crinkled paper.

Kon recalled Icelyn's fear, early on, at the prospect of being in the woods by the base. "Are you still scared, being out here?"

"Not when you're here."

There was a pang of guilt as he toyed with his sleeve. "You're okay after Darnar?"

"I mean, I should've been scared—but you weren't. So, I wasn't."

"Who said I wasn't scared?" he joked.

"Well, you hide it well then." Her grin seemed bothered. It faded slightly as she looked down at the rocky cliff.

"You've been working on your shield?" He gestured to her jacket partially off. The air was chilled, ready for snow.

"Yeah. I think it's been working more. I feel like I should be cold." She chuckled as she reached into the air, trying to gauge the temperature.

"Yeah." He rubbed his hands together in the frozen air. Icelyn was quiet, turmoil clear in her eyes. Part of him didn't want to ask. "What's wrong?"

Her words came softly as she unwrapped the paper in her hand. "He's looking for me." She looked over the missing person poster, a mix of anger on her face.

"Your dad?"

She nodded.

"Maybe he's worried."

"He had my entire life to be worried. I was always in danger there." She took another glance, then flipped the paper away.

Kon extended a hand. "Can I see?"

Icelyn let out a huff and scrunched her nose as she handed it over. "It's embarrassing."

The paper was crinkled and worn, having been balled up several times over by the looks of it. He glanced over the information. "Icelyn Jane?"

"Yeah." She grinned, watching him carefully.

Icelyn Jane McCathy. The picture was of her posing in a group, wearing nurse scrubs as she smiled at the camera. "When was this?"

Her hands wove into each other, squinting at the photo. "It was a nursing class I took last summer. I guess he couldn't find a better photo."

A corner of his mouth curled in a grin at the innocent picture, one she definitely noticed as he handed it back to her. "You looked happy. Maybe he misses you."

It was hard to tell in the moonlight, but the slightest rosy pink had sparked across her cheeks. Icelyn took a last look at the poster before she started to fold it. Her words came slowly as she tucked it away. "Do you think all of this will end one day . . . or will it always be like this?"

"It's all I've ever known." He shrugged. "I don't know what an end means."

"I guess I'm just trying to figure out what goals to set for the future," she said as a gentle breeze blew past them. "What do *you* look for out here? What do you want in life?" She turned to him.

The moon was bright, casting upon the waterfall as he watched it in the distance. He never set many goals for his life. It always felt pointless—but there was something his heart ached for sometimes. Something he could find in rare moments in the woods or on a cliffside with the moons shining bright above. "Peace."

Her eyes softened as she watched the mountains again. "That's a good place to start. I guess I've always wanted practical things. To go into medicine, to have a garden."

"A house by the ocean?"

"Yeah." She rubbed her sleeve. "Boring things."

"It's not boring." He looked over the furrow in her brow. "It sounds peaceful."

The galaxy above them was clear and bright with the lack of towns for miles. Kon watched it for a moment before he looked back at the stretch of mountains. It *was* peaceful there. That's what he liked about the wilderness. He could forget about the troubles of a society he had been rejected from. Though peace also brought memories. The stars above him reminded him that his parents, his species, were existing out there. Without him. The stretch of mountains reminded him that every dip and town he crossed presented a danger.

It was never true peace.

"Are you . . . ever angry they left you here?" Icelyn watched the inky sky.

The question hung in the air. *Angry.* That was one word for it. More often, he simply found himself confused. Had it all been an accident? Happenstance? Or was it a very deliberate, known decision? "Sometimes."

Her knees folded to her chest as she wrapped her arms around them. "Would you go back to your planet? If you could?"

"I don't know." He could scarcely imagine it. "Would you go to Makova, if you could?"

Her breath let out in a sigh as she turned to him. "At one point, it's all I wanted." She shook her head. "But would I fit in any better there? I can't even speak Makovan basic—I wouldn't even know how to be that version of me if I ended up there." Stars above twinkled, mocking their tether to the planet.

Her words reflected his own. His whole life, he yearned to be in a world he'd never been to, but if he woke up tomorrow, back with his own people, would anything change? "I guess I can't go back either. I'd be an outcast there too." He'd never be one of them, truly. Just as he'd never fit where he was. "I don't think I have a home anywhere."

Her expression lifted in sympathy. "Maybe we have to build our homes."

"How do you figure?"

Icelyn pressed her cheek into her hand. "I don't know."

The fire popped in the distance, its warm glow even reaching them at the cliff as it mixed with moonlight to illuminate the grass below. For a while, it was silent. Only the distant sound of rushing water and crackling fire. It had been a few years since he enjoyed the company of someone else. It was a scary thought; enjoying someone's company meant caring for them. Having people to protect would always put him at risk in the face of the EME. Had they had anyone to hold over him, they would. Just like his parents. Just like Joel and Mallia. The EME had pushed him from every sense of family. They would destroy any avenue of peace he had. Kon kept telling himself he wasn't in too deep. It was still early. He could still leave when he needed to. Though it might hurt, he could do it.

He could walk away from Para's steadfast pride in him.

He could walk away from Peter's persistent hope that he was the key.

He could walk away from the base, to keep the others safe.

He could walk away from—

Icelyn spoke, as she stared out at the mountains. "I'm glad you let us come with you." Her head tilted slightly, tracing her icy eyes to his face. "You're the only person who makes me feel . . . safe."

He could walk away.

He scrunched his nose slightly. "You don't feel safe at the base?"

"Safe—in myself. Safe to be me. You're my favorite person there."

He could . . . The thought diminished. "Why?"

"I don't know. It gets chaotic there. But when you show up, I always know you'll be this—stable, calm. It's comforting."

"You're my favorite person there too." He didn't know why the smile was hard to form, or if one was even there at all.

Icelyn, returning a smile, told him it was, and then trouble creeped over her expression once again. "That picture . . . from Darnar," she hesitated. "What happened?"

Usually, he would avoid those thoughts, but he found the words coming easier. A rare time he could loosely let them in. "They cornered me up north. A few years ago. I think I blocked a lot of it out. It's just bits and pieces."

"How did you . . . get out?"

"It all gets fuzzy toward the end," he said, watching the ground as he kept a careful barrier between him and the memories. "Something they did backfired, I don't know." It only got hazy when he disconnected himself from it. Too far into thought, too familiar of a sound, or place, and the memories became painfully, painfully clear. Like a tide, forever shifting its capacity of waves. Sometimes, the waves of memory could scarcely brush him. Other times, they could flatten him, swallowing him whole. It was better to convince himself that the waves didn't reach him anymore. That he had walked far enough to escape even the big ones.

Icelyn pulled her hair over her shoulder. "My dad used to talk about you," she admitted as he turned to watch her, surprised at the comment. "I remember a few years ago. He came home *so* happy. Grinning from ear to ear." There was a look of disgust on her face. "He showed me . . . that picture. I didn't even know you, but it haunted me. For years. The way he talked about it like you weren't just . . . a kid my age."

Kon watched her carefully, emotions mixed at her view. He knew how the EME saw him. A monster, a *threat*. They never saw a person, a scared child, but it still hurt to hear.

"Then, a month or so later, he came home furious. Saying something happened. Something went wrong."

Silence followed as Kon's gaze lingered on her. His eyes traced the grass and rock below them, seeking some comfort before he looked back out at the view. His mind grazed at those memories. What *went wrong*. A wave, small and gentle, washed up to him. "I think a part of me died in that place," Kon finally said, voice quiet, calm. "This is all that's left."

Somewhere behind her fluffy bangs, a sorrow sat, watching him. A combination of pain and anger. Maybe he had gone numb to the reality of it. Slowly, she leaned in, until her temple rested on his shoulder. A cold hand reached to brush his. "It's enough for me. I'm glad I got to know any amount of you."

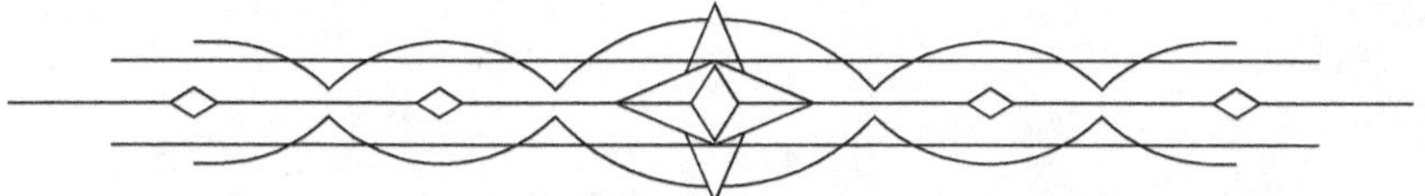

AV RI NTEGR TION
PROG AM

CHAPTER

34

THE FACILITY

"I'm going to feel this for *days*," Peter whined as he stretched. "I thought a few laps around the base was a workout."

"You should've taken those gym classes," Jasamie said, still watching him carefully. They had been walking uphill for most of the day.

"We have to be close." Stormy rattled open her map. The sun was rising into the sky as they took the final trek.

Kon watched through the trees. He had never been around that area. Joel hadn't ever told him where the AIP base was. Had he known, he would've gone back when he still clung to a curiosity of his parents, his origin. Maybe that's why Joel hadn't mentioned it. There was no telling what condition the facility was in. The EME could be comfortably watching it. They might've cleared it out years before, but it was their best lead. He slowed. Ahead of them stood a tall steel fence where the trees thinned. The rest caught up.

"Is this it?" Icelyn asked as they came before the large security fence covered in forest growth. They approached the rusted sign, hardly visible under the growth of vines. The letters were worn, barely readable:

Government Property.
No Entry.

"Yeah," Kon narrowed his eyes at the rusted sign. "This is it." He scanned for a way over or around. The thick metal of the security fence spanned at least ten feet in the air, each metal bar speared at the top. They weren't climbing over.

"You think there's a gate?" Peter asked, looking down the line of fencing.

"There's gotta be. Come on." Kon started down the fence. It was hard to see much past the overgrown undergrowth, but the facility was in there. Somewhere.

Peter was fidgeting again. "You know, I think they got most of their supplies by hovercrafts. What if there isn't a . . . gate?"

"There!" Icelyn pointed to an arch in the fence ahead.

It wasn't much of an entrance at all, the path to the gate being small, barely visible even. Upon getting closer, it didn't seem any more promising. Kon reached for the thick padlock holding the gate closed, along with the reinforced latches running up the solid metal gate. Locked.

"They must've locked it when they left," Peter said, squirming. "How do we get in?"

Kon gave the heavy lock another tug before he stepped back to assess the fence for weak points. He'd have to make a way in.

"Your father didn't leave you a key in that book?" Jasamie raised a brow toward Peter.

"No . . ." He looked about ready to check.

"Stand back." Kon set his bag on the ground as he looked the fence up and down. The others scuffled back to watch. He took in a breath and held a steady stance, focusing his energy on one area of the barred fence. The air started to bend and warp as terrashock congregated around the metal. Keeping the energy in place, he approached, reaching into the warping terrashock. The metal was starting to heat and bend on its own, turning shades of orange as he grabbed one bar and pulled it to the side. It bent with ease under the pressure and heat of the terrashock as he pushed the other bar the opposite way, creating a decent gap in the fence. The energy dissipated as he stood back. It was easier than trying to blast the gate open. "Be careful, it's hot." He grabbed his bag and tossed it across the gap.

One by one, they squeezed through the newly melted gap in the fence.

Peter wiped his hands on his jacket, still fidgety as he crossed past the fence. "I've read about terrashock, you know. How it warps and distorts things? It's like one of the least understood Elemental powers—" His tone was high-strung as he looked around. "Scientists think it could be the same type of energy that creates black holes . . . out in space."

"Peter, are you okay?" Stormy frowned as the rest of them crossed over.

"Yeah, I'm just kinda freaking out." He ran a hand over his hair and fixed his glasses. "I think I ramble when I'm nervous."

"We're not inside yet," Kon mumbled as he headed straight through the fence toward the thick of the woods. Up the hill a bit, there was a clearing, a space between the trees with a concrete floor.

"What is it?" Jyune piped up as they approached.

"A landing pad," Kon said, stopping at the edge of the platform. It was sizable, definitely for hoverforms. Thick roots and creeping vines had started to take it over. The pad was cracked in some spots, worn with age. Their surroundings were heavy in vegetation. An overhang sat away from the landing pad; the short rocky ledge gave a window out of the trees. He scanned past the docking station where the trail led into the thicket. There was the faintest of metal siding peeking out.

The trail was dense and hardly visible. There was at least the comfort that it seemed no one had been there in a while as Kon pushed the brush aside, moving closer to the building. Tall thicket covered its siding. It was barely noticeable that they were on another concrete sidewalk leading to the dip in the siding. The front door. The building was low to the ground, hidden like a bunker. No visible windows from the front. Concrete walls only spanned twenty feet or so, indicating the rest of the facility was underground.

The group settled under the overhang of the door. Icelyn pushed some vines from an old sign next to the door:

Avari Integration Program
Authorized Personnel Only.

"This is really it," Peter breathed.

Kon was less thrilled as he scanned the heavy doors.

"Can you bend this one open too?" Jyune asked as she surveyed the worn building.

"There might be a security system." Kon looked over the card scanner next to the door. Its light was off. He moved closer, listening for the familiar buzz of electronics. Nothing. The rest stood in anticipation as he carefully moved to tap the scanner. Still nothing.

"No power?" Peter asked, inching closer.

"Don't think so. We could still trip something." Kon eyed the door. From the surroundings and the overall condition of the base, he assumed it was properly abandoned, but there was always a threat. He looked over the metal door. It looked as though it had been busted open. A thick chain held it closed. The gap in the broken door wasn't enough to see anything inside besides darkness. Being that it was a bunker, there were no back doors or windows. Maybe there would be emergency exits on the ground, but chances were they were covered by thick overgrowth and locked.

"You think the EME did that?" Icelyn asked, gesturing to the smashed door.

"I guess so." Peter sighed.

Kon took a step back. "Get ready to run if something goes off."

The group stepped back as he took his position in front of the door. Energy started around the chains that were locking the doors together. Terrashock weakened and pulled at the metal. There were sounds of it twisting and bending apart, before he ignited it, pushing inward. The chains gave slightly. Kon frowned at the failure of the first blast before the second blew both doors wide open. Dust clouded the air as silence took over. The group waited, listening for any signs of danger. Kon took a step inside, light filling the dark hazy room. It was a small entrance, with tile floors similar to the base. Something of a front desk to the side with a seating area.

"Oh, my God." Peter coughed through the dust, staring up at the posters on the walls. Old posters about the Avari Integration Program, things that had been removed from the public ever since the program went down. "We're in."

"Be careful. Let the air clear." Jasamie frowned at Peter as she hovered near him.

"No way. I'm fine." Peter swatted the debris out of his face.

"What happened here?" Icelyn asked, looking at the chairs strewn across the room. It was hard to tell in the old room, but she was right. The walls had cracks down them and the lights above were shattered. Age hadn't done that.

"News articles never really said what went down inside." Peter scanned the damage as well. "But a fight sounds about right . . ."

Kon was still surveying for signs of EME, but there was nothing. The only footprints in the old room were their own.

Light came from the open doors as they examined the old entry room. Straight ahead of the doors was a wide staircase. Worn golden letters over the stairs read "Avari Integration Program," though some had fallen off.

"Maybe we can get the power on?" Icelyn suggested. "Where would that room be?"

"Let's go down. Stay close." Kon started down the steps. The divider in the middle of the stairs was partially bent to the side, another sign of a fight. The stairs led to a long, wide hallway. Rooms on both sides had large windows looking in, some partially shattered. One looked like a classroom while the other had science equipment and tables, although it was hard to tell for sure in the dim light. The hall stretched on into darkness. The outside light couldn't reach much farther. The musty smell of dust and age floated around them as Kon scanned for signs of power. Hidden in the dark beside the staircase, he almost missed the panel beside one of the rooms. An electricity symbol marked it.

Peter wiped one of the remaining windows to peer into the rooms as Kon opened the circuit breaker, glancing over the switches and labels. Broken glass crinkled on the floor as some of them moved to look into the rooms. At the bottom of the panel, a larger red switch was turned to

"Off." He stared at it for a moment, taking a deep breath of the musty air before he switched it on.

At first, it was quiet, then the sound of buzzing. The lights overhead that hadn't been shattered started to light one by one, illuminating the stretch. Everyone had stopped to watch the hall until the lights inside the rooms came on next. With lights on, the extent of the damage was clear. Glass windows were shattered all down the path and doors blown off their hinges.

"Is that blood?" Icelyn whispered, looking at the window to the classrooms. Dried liquid ran down the glass. She stepped back as they started to notice dried pools on the ground as well.

"Wait." Peter paused. "Didn't Tally say Kyro was the only one that fought back?"

"He did *all* of this?" Icelyn scanned the crumbled ceiling.

Kon's focus was down the hall where the lights flickered with their aged wiring. For a moment, he almost remembered this base. Or something like it. A memory. The EME. Himself walking from another base as the walls around him shattered. It was a similar destruction. Desperation.

"In here—Look!" Peter called, coughing again in the static air. He pushed the door to the lab room as the hinges crunched open.

Kon took another breath and turned from the stretch. It wasn't the time for old memories. Peter was walking in the room by the time Kon reached the door. It was much taller than most doors—one where he didn't have to duck to enter. Icelyn was more cautious, looking at the microscopes and strange devices on the tables. Stormy, Jyune, and Jasamie were entering the room across the hall slowly.

"This must be one of their labs," Peter gasped, a giant grin of excitement across his face. "They had like fifty scientists working at this base. Doing studies and tests." He started opening drawers and cabinets. The room had a high ceiling, the same as outside. White cabinets stuck around most of the walls, matched with long spans of counters. There was a table in the middle full of various equipment.

"What kind of . . . tests?" Icelyn asked, glancing at Kon with a furrowed brow.

"They did the same thing with all species that came in." Peter opened a cabinet of vials, reading them before he moved on to another drawer. "Medical examinations, bloodwork. Really trying to understand the species for medical purposes and stuff."

"And the Avari? They were okay with all these tests?" Icelyn walked down the line of machines in the center of the room, examining them in confusion.

"Yeah, I mean, until the EME tried to take over. They were apparently fascinated with the science Anaiess scientists were doing. It was all to integrate them into society. Then the EME wanted to use them for war or something." Peter pulled a notebook from one of the cabinets, flipping it open. "But Avari didn't come here to be weapons. So, they left." He went quiet as he started reading.

Icelyn examined the equipment as Kon stood idly by the door.

"There are so many good notes in this!" Peter flipped through the notebook. "I can't imagine what's in the deeper labs."

"Deeper?" Kon asked with a frown, looking back up the stairs with a careful eye.

Peter shut the notebook and tucked it under an arm as he finished checking cabinets. "Well, this lab is probably the show lab. You know, with the windows." He pointed at the broken windows. "They had a lot of Anaiess higher-ups and news stuff come to visit the program, so this whole main hall was kinda for the tours. There's stuff deeper they didn't see."

"Where? We shouldn't stay long." Kon stepped back into the corridor, still watching for signs of danger as the situation sunk in.

"There's nothing much in here." Jasamie glanced back into the other room as she joined them.

Peter was stuffing the journal in his bag as he started down the hall. "It should be this way. I've only seen pictures, but maybe I can find it."

The path led into a wide round room. Kon could see it before they even entered. Straight in the back center of the room: the teleporter.

"No way! It's still here?" Peter quickened his pace into the room toward the large machine. "I heard they destroyed it . . ."

Kon was slower to approach. It was a circular ring, made of thick white metal, standing on a platform. It made a sort of archway, empty in the center. Control panels to the side of it were strewn open, wires torn and destroyed. The rest of the room was equally as messy. Debris littered the ground, and windows on the curved walls were shattered as well, revealing the control center behind them. The entire room appeared to be the epicenter of the remnants of a fight. Though the only thing that was untouched was the towering teleporter.

Peter had stopped short of the platform, staring up at it in awe. "This is how Avari came over . . . and how they left."

"How does it work?" Icelyn asked, examining the torn control panel.

"Well, it takes energy from both sides to congregate it here specifically. Before this, the portal could open anywhere." Peter turned and pointed to the windows. "The main control rooms back here would watch the radiation levels and adjust the speed to help someone cross over—" Peter rushed over to look in, still talking, but Kon didn't hear the rest of it as he stepped onto the platform and examined the ring of metal and wires of the teleporter. It stood nearly ten feet high, towering over him. Looming. The last place his parents stood—without him. He reached out to wipe the dust from the cold plate on the side.

ARC
Albara Rift Control

But it was just an old dusty ring. His hand dropped from the cold metal as the conversation behind him drew closer again.

"There's no way to start it back up?" Icelyn dusted off the panel.

"Not without the Avari. It's useless until they want to come back." Peter shook his head.

But they never did come back. Kon already knew that much. They didn't want to come back. Not for him or Kyro. Kon stepped off the platform. "Where's the room you were looking for?" he said, glancing down the two adjacent halls they hadn't explored.

"Wait, wait, I brought my camera!" Peter remembered as he pulled his bag open and dug through it.

Kon ignored his excitement as he approached one of the corridors. The sign above it marked 'B.' The one across from it read 'A.' There was a list of rooms: Laboratory, Medical, Mentor Offices, and several others. That was it. He turned to the others, just as the flash of Peter's camera went off, aiming at the ARC. Stormy and Jyune peeked over his shoulder as the picture printed from the front of the small silver camera.

"Para's not going to believe this." Peter grinned as he stared at the photo.

Kon lingered, the nerves of their situation wearing off for everyone but him.

"Maybe we should split up?" Jasamie suggested as she looked down the 'A' hall. "Might cover more ground. Give us more time to find evidence."

"We could meet back here," Icelyn agreed.

"Does everyone know what to look for?" Peter stuffed the photo in his backpack as he fixed his camera strap over his shoulder. "Anything pertaining to Kon, his parents, or my dad."

They all nodded.

"Someone should watch the door," Kon added from the side. "Find exits if you can."

Stormy plopped her bag down. "Me and Jyune can stay in this area and watch the door."

Peter nodded and moved toward Kon. "Kon and I will check the 'B' hall for B21."

Jasamie and Icelyn shrugged at each other. "We'll check the 'A' hall," Icelyn said.

"Okay," Stormy put her hands on her hips. "If someone *does* show up, we'll split off to come get you guys."

"Let's hope no one shows up." Icelyn gave a grimace as she turned to face the 'A' hall.

Kon hesitated, unconvinced with the plan, but turned nonetheless. "Be careful."

Peter was quick to run after him while the others went in their own direction. He let out another cough as the dust kicked up. "Okay. B21," he grinned.

"Are you going to need that medicine again?" Kon asked, noticing Peter's rising cough in the poor air.

"Maybe . . . but it's not slowing me down yet. I've waited my whole life to get in here!"

"Just take it easy." Kon watched the first door pass. B1; a room full of equipment. B2 seemed to be an office or database of sorts.

"Did you ever think you'd get in here?" Peter made careful measures to check each door they passed.

"No. Figured they cleaned it out or something."

"I mean, if Tally got stuff out, I'm sure others did. I just hope it's preserved well." The space down that way didn't appear affected by the fight but remained as aged as the rest. The lights above flickered as they followed the path down. "Anyway . . ." Peter started, his tone shifting. "I'm sorry about back at Darnar."

"What do you mean?" Kon said, shoving his hands in his pockets.

"I mean, finding out that it's Kyro—and he's related to you. It sucks, is all."

Kon let out a tiny sigh. "Yeah."

"But I still think we can help him." Peter's tone grew more confident. "Now that we know they have him, Para and Terrance can try to pull some of the EME's deep files on him."

"I thought you guys already pulled EME files?" Kon asked as he scanned the passing doors.

"Some, yeah, but to my knowledge, none of them ever mentioned Kyro. Only you. It's weird. They must've really been trying to hide him being here."

"Not anymore," Kon said.

As they rounded the turn, Peter let out a tiny gasp. "Library!" They were in the teens as he rushed toward the B15 door. It let out a similar crack as the others when he thrust it open, dust kicking up again. He disappeared inside as Kon glanced down the hall before following. The lights inside were dimmer, several of them out completely as Peter scanned through the bookcases. It was a smaller library than the one at the base. Shelves lined the walls and center of the room, filled to the brim with books.

"You think any of these are actually about Avari?" Kon asked, reading over the nearest ones. Anaiess fauna and flora books, history of the nation . . . most pertained to Anaiess.

"Probably not, since they were trying to get Avari familiar with this planet," Peter said. "But there's got to be a few . . ." He moved up near the desk to the left, scanning the books around and on it.

Kon stayed put, looking down at the dusty carpet. The room gave a much warmer vibe than the rest of the base. There were wooden shelves and bookcases and labels on each shelf in large letters. The air was even harder to breathe in there with the stale scent of carpet and old books. He watched Peter carefully, not convinced of his optimism.

"Aha!" Peter finally called, pulling a small book from the pile on the desk. "Translations!" He coughed as he scanned for anything else of use before heading for the door.

"Avari translations?" Kon asked.

"Yeah. There's not a lot. They didn't share a ton about their language." Peter flipped through the pages. "But this is something I've been trying to get my hands on for a while." His grin stayed plastered on his face as he reached to stuff the book in his backpack, which was quickly filling to the brim.

The next part of the hall was marked 'Mentor Offices' as they approached.

"B21," Peter breathed, pointing ahead to the door. "It's a mentor's office?"

Kon scanned the first mentor door: B20. He paused to read the name on it. "Rose Deeitro." His gaze lingered on it for a moment. "Wait."

Peter stopped from his beeline to the door. "B20? What about it?"

Kon opened the door, light filling into the dark office. The lights flickered on as he flipped the light switch. The desk was centered with the door and two shelves on the back wall on either side. It was decorated in soft grays with a colorful rug in front of the desk. Picture frames lined the desk, some having fallen over. Most items on the shelves had been pushed onto the floor.

"Rose Deeitro? Do you know her?" Peter asked, appearing at the door.

Kon picked up one of the picture frames. It was two women. Rose and the familiar Avari he knew to be his mother. "I think she's the one who got me out," he said.

Peter joined him to examine the photo. "Really? She *was* Padlin's mentor. Makes sense." He moved around to the front of the desk, peering in the already open drawers. "Looks like they already ransacked this room. Probably took everything looking for signs of you." He read over a few loose papers.

Kon put the picture down with a sigh. Did they know Rose had taken him? "What if they raided B21 too?"

Peter's face flashed concern as they moved back into the hall, staring toward the door. "My dad thought whatever it was, is still in there. And so do I." He approached the door with confidence. "Only one way to find out."

Kon stopped, realization setting in that he might've been closer to the answers all along as he saw the name on the door: Joel Gavins.

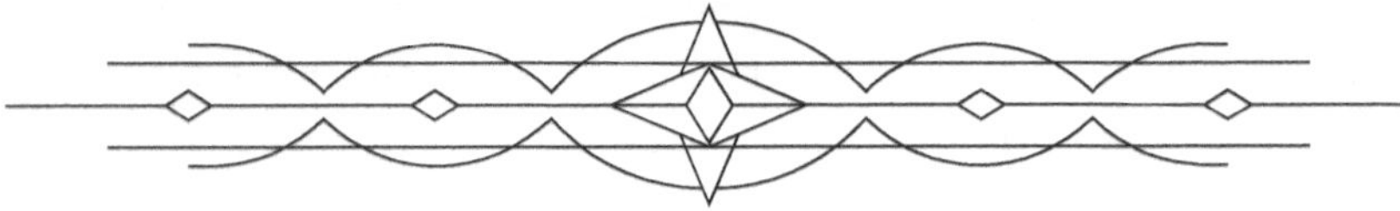

6 mo. ♡

CHAPTER

35

FAULT

Icelyn stepped over loose paper as they made their way down the hall, checking each door's label. "This place reminds me of the base." She checked another door. Faded purple lights inside revealed rows of planters with empty soil, void of gardens.

Jasamie adjusted her bag as she peeked into some sort of cafeteria. "There's a lot of these bases on Brynden Ka. They probably picked a decommissioned one like we did."

"Kinda feels like they were trying to hide it, doesn't it?"

"Yeah." The flicker of light above drew Jasamie's attention. "Maybe the government always planned to take over the Avari Program."

"You think they did?" Icelyn was met with a shrug from her as their footsteps disrupted the years of dust underfoot. Something in her heart ached at the thought. Maybe it was because the plan to use the Avari meant that Kon would never find the peace he was seeking. Surely, somewhere along the line, Anaiess had wanted to give Avari a place there.

"Wasn't the last Anaiess integration for Makovan people?" Jasamie glanced back at her.

"Yeah. It's how my grandma came over." There was guilt in her words—that her people's integration had worked, and that one hadn't, though Makova had a long-standing alliance with Anaiess. Turning on their people would've meant war. Regardless, that was its own war in a way. The backlash of Avari leaving had turned EME harsher on Elementals.

"Looks like we're into the dorms," Jasamie said as they passed through the shift of windowed rooms and offices to a hallway of doors labeled with unfamiliar names, each decorated in its own way. Some were plain, others had posters and pictures around the name, showcasing personality.

Toward the end of the hall, they found a familiar name. "Padlin," Icelyn read, the door decorated with intricate drawings of strange flowers and a few photographs of Anaiess flora as well.

"Jarauk," Jasamie said next, facing the door across from Padlin's. "This is them?" His door was much less decorated, a few pictures taken with mentors. A majority of them were strewn on the floor, ripped from the door.

"Yeah." Icelyn breathed. Creaking only slightly, Icelyn pushed Padlin's door open into the dark room. With the click of the light, the room unfolded before them. It was a decent-sized room. The bed to the left of the door and a bookcase and desk on the other side of the room filled with books. There was a bathroom to the right, past the dresser, and pictures decorating the wall near the bed. Woven intricate decorations hung around the ceiling like nothing she had seen before. Something from Padlin's home planet, perhaps. There were several objects that looked to be of Avari origin.

Maybe the most harrowing thing about the room was the wooden bassinet next to the bed. Icelyn couldn't draw her eyes from it as she approached. A small basket and cabinet to the side of it held an assortment of newborn items: diapers, bottles, and toys. The image hurt, maybe from the realization that they had planned and prepared for him. Her gaze finally drifted to the wall full of pictures taken at the facility. Padlin with mentors—other Avari—outside, holding native flowers in the empty garden they had passed, full of vegetation. There were several of her and Jarauk. Icelyn reached for one in particular; the two of them standing close, outside her door, with wide grins from both of them, her pregnancy showing clearly under her shirt as they held an ultrasound photo.

"Didn't Peter say nothing in the media mentions her being pregnant?" Icelyn turned to Jasamie, who was reading something from the desk.

She glanced up from it with a shake of the head. "Yeah, something like that."

"It doesn't seem like they were hiding it." Icelyn looked from the picture to the crib.

"Maybe someone else was." Jasamie skimmed the writing again.

Icelyn tucked the picture into her pocket, taking a last glance at the crib before she assessed the remainder of the room. The soft pink rug underfoot sat on dusty tiles matching the rest of the facility.

Jasamie turned with papers in her hand. "It says here they were meeting with Andren Day concerning the child. So, Peter's dad *did* know something?"

"Concerning what, though?"

"It doesn't say." Her eyes hovered over the paper for another few moments before she plopped it down.

"What would be the problem with having a baby? Wasn't the point to start a life here?" Icelyn checked the shelf. It was mainly books on plants and a few old novels.

"Tally said they wanted Avari for war. Maybe a child got in the way of that." Jasamie scrunched her nose at the papers, folding them up to stuff in her bag.

"Their plan was threatened by a child?" Icelyn shook her head.

Jasamie's next words sent a shiver down her spine. "Or maybe a child was the perfect clean slate to make a weapon."

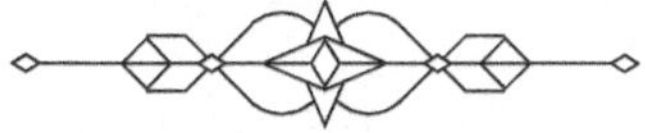

Peter pushed the door open carefully, clearing his throat. Kon lingered in the hall. He couldn't place why his body didn't want to enter the room. Peter was already scanning the shelves by the time Kon stepped in. The office wasn't nearly as lively as the other. It shared the same desk and shelves but was less decorated. There were picture frames on the desk as well. It wasn't as destroyed as Rose's office, though books and files were strewn over the desk.

"Do you see a . . . a safe or anything?" Peter started pulling books off the shelf, checking each one for a secret compartment.

"Are you sure it's a code for a safe?" Kon watched him, his movement frantic with each book as he dropped them on the floor.

"I don't know. It's just got to be in *here*." He pulled the last books out and stopped, coughing again in defeat as he stepped back, reaching for his backpack.

Kon took a more cautious approach, moving around the other side of the desk as he examined the folders. They were stacked on the desk—but something was off. The layer of dust around them had been moved. Pushed aside. A much newer layer of dust lay over it. "Someone was in here."

"What?" Peter whipped around, inhaler in hand as he tried to calm himself.

"These have been moved." He nudged the files to the side in the same pattern as the dust.

"Like recently?"

Kon's gaze lifted to check on him. "More recent than twenty years ago."

"Could it have been my dad? It had to be—" Peter was interrupted by another cough as he finally used his inhaler.

Kon watched him for a moment before looking back at the folders. The one on top was labeled 'Meeting logs.' "Maybe he left these here for a reason." Kon flipped the top one open.

Peter grabbed the paper from his pocket, moving in closer to look at the evidence. "Logs? Seems like something the EME would want. Why didn't they take these?"

"They were put here recently." Kon shrugged, reading the first page:

01-10-34-25-70.
January 10th, 2634 Ko 25 Nyx 70.

The day the Avari integration program started.

Peter held out his note, squinting at the long series of numbers as he struggled with his breath. "It's a date."

Kon read over the text; mentions of starting up the teleporter, the successful first members of the AIP. He flipped the page. There were mentor logs from the same day. His eyes fell onto Joel's name again. Logging the first meeting with Jarauk had gone well.

Peter's shifting increased as he read. "All this time, he wanted me to find these logs? I thought it might be a date, but it never led to anything . . . Let me see, what's this date?" Kon stepped to the side as Peter stood before the folder, looking over the note labeled '1010371071.' "October 10th, 2637 . . . What gyn is that? A month before the program closed—El?" He started searching through the pile of folders, moving them aside until he got to the last one. It was much thinner than the others. He flipped each page, looking for the series of numbers until they were almost at the end, and the date appeared. There was only one log that day:

10-10-37-10-71

Feilar Council members arrived to speak with Padlin Syron concerning recent onset of heightened Elemental symptoms. Suspicions point toward complication in pregnancy. No Anaiess personnel were permitted to join. Findings of the child's condition remained vague. Council members declined comments.

Diagnosis of child from parental comment: Airay Xieryn
Proceed with caution.

They both stared at the page, dust settling in the air before anyone spoke. "Diagnosis?" Peter finally whispered, reflecting Kon's own thoughts. "Proceed with caution? They mean you?"

Kon shook his head, eyes locked on the faintly familiar word. *Airay.* "Do you know that diagnosis?"

Peter stared. "It looks like the Feilar Avari—wait." He began digging in his backpack, pulling the old translation book from it. "Maybe we can look them up. I don't recognize . . . X—Xieryn?"

Kon read the log over a few more times, soaking in every detail. Council? Complication? It was around the time the EME started moving in. Was it because of this?

Peter skimmed the translations. "Hmm. Xieryn isn't recorded here . . ."

"Okay, the other word?" Kon asked, rising discomfort building in him as the words stared back at him.

Peter searched for another moment before he set the notebook down over the folder, opening to the right page. "Okay," he breathed. "*Airay.* Different. Apart from normal—" He didn't read the last word as he looked at Kon.

Kon stared at the final word, his diagnosis. "Flawed."

There was silence as Peter drew back from the notebook. The room felt as still as the dust that hung in the air. Peter cut through the silence with a feigned casual tone. "So, they thought something was wrong. I mean, maybe it wasn't true? Why would that push the EME to take over?" His attempts to play it off didn't get far as the silence from Kon remained. "We don't even know what the context of that is—I mean, you're not flawed?"

Kon thought back to all the moments his powers stuttered, glitched. The faint murmurs of the word from EME scientists, always when his powers were being tested. It all made sense. "They left me here." He hardly realized the words had been said out loud as the gears in his head turned. It was a choice. A conscious, deliberate choice.

"We don't know why, though," Peter tried to soften the blow of it all. "I mean, I believe the theory that maybe babies can't go through the teleporter, and it was all just . . . bad timing."

Kon merely watched him with a flat expression. The toil on his face had only lasted a moment before he wiped his expression clear. "It doesn't matter. We should go." His gaze lingered on the picture frames on the desk. Most were of Joel and Avari, but the one on the end, closest to the desk, caught his eye. It was Joel holding Mallia, a newborn at the time.

They were born only a few months apart after all.

Peter's arms hung as he looked about the room.

"What?" Kon asked.

"I just . . . thought there'd be something here about where my dad went." He checked the bookcases again halfheartedly. "I thought he wanted me to find him."

"Maybe there's something in there." Kon gestured to the folders.

"I mean, this looks like almost every log from the program. My dad probably snuck them out when the EME came in. We *should* take them regardless." Peter stuffed as many as he could into his backpack before piling the rest up in his arms.

"Are you good?" Kon asked as eyed to the inhaler on the table.

"For now," Peter nodded, pushing it in his pocket, disappointment in his composure. The hall was cooler again, the lights brighter and flickering still. Peter lingered in the hall, head down. "Kon."

Kon turned to him with a dry tilt of the head.

Peter shuffled the folders in his arms, looking for words. "Kyro fought them so you could get out. You were worth it to him. I just don't want you to—"

"I'm fine, Peter." He shook his head, looking down the rest of the hallway. "It doesn't change anything."

Peter nodded, kicking at the dust on the tiles. "Maybe the others found something useful." When Kon didn't move, Peter gave a nervous fidget, speaking up again. "It's okay to be mad . . . Just, talk to—"

Kon shushed him, still turned away, peering down the hall. "Look." Heading from the office, down farther into the base, were faint, subtle footprints.

Peter moved closer, watching how they trailed into the office and then back out in the same direction. "He *did* come here."

Kon didn't want to confirm Peter's suspicions, but he too felt that the prints in the dust had to of been Andren Day. "He never went through the main entrance," Kon accessed, stepping along the prints now as they walked farther *into* the base.

"Fire escape?"

"Has to be."

Following carefully, Kon stopped, staring back the way they came. "Wait." He held a hand out as he watched down the long hallway. There were footsteps approaching. Running.

Stormy turned the corner, glancing back before she ran for them. Worry coated her expression. "We're out of time. We need to leave," she breathed upon reaching them. "Jyune went to get Icelyn and Jasamie—"

"Are they outside?" Kon asked, walking to her.

"He's already inside. We need to go!"

Kon stopped dead in his tracks. "He?"

Stormy's expression told him everything as his heart sank. Kyro.

"We have to get the others."

"Kyro?" Peter stuttered. "Why is he here?"

Kon was already headed for the entrance. There was no time to question it as they rushed down the hall. Upon nearing the last turn, they slowed, carefully approaching the ARC room. Kon gestured for Stormy and Peter to stay as they pressed against the wall, clutching their belongings. Air from outside had drifted down into the halls as the smell of rain and trees lingered in the air. Kon took a deep breath and glanced around the corner. The room was empty, only the mess of shoeprints on the dusty floor. The 'A' hall was empty too as Kon scanned for the others. The left control room was dark through the windows, but he could see Jyune peeking out.

She perked up upon seeing him, and a moment later, Icelyn also peered around the edge of the window. She frantically scanned for him before locking eyes, shaking her head at him as she raised a finger to her lips.

He frowned in confusion, just as they both ducked out of view. The tall figure appeared from the center hall. It *was* Kyro. Kon ducked back around the corner. His chest tightened at the realization, originally hoping that Stormy had been mistaken—that it was just some EME, as crazy as that sounded, *hoping* for it to be the EME who showed up. But there was something scarier than them, and it was finally here.

Kyro scanned the footsteps in the dust before he looked up at the ARC. He seemed frozen in memories. A pang of empathy formed in Kon, but it cut short as Kyro's head turned to him. He jerked back, flattening himself on the wall. Fear instantly overrode the rest of his emotions as he held his breath. A fight was coming much sooner than he was prepared for. He didn't dare look again as footsteps started toward them slowly.

That was EME's plan: to scare him. He had to focus. Get to Icelyn and the others. Get out.

Peter and Stormy stepped back, startled as fire ignited in Kon's hands. He was ready to swing out, launch the first blow . . . until an alarm went off somewhere in the center room. A blaring red light filled the hall. Kon held back his attack and checked again. Kyro was staring up at the ARC as the large light on top flashed, matching the lights above the control rooms.

Back behind the panel, Kon found Icelyn, her hand on the table of buttons as she looked from Kyro to Kon. A distraction. She and the others ran for the door to the center hall, opening it as the alarm muted most of its sound. They rushed across the hall into the next room toward Kon. All they had to do was escape through the control room door into the 'B' hall, but Kyro was no longer looking at the teleporter or at Kon. He stared straight at the escaping group. In an instant, terrashock shattered what little windows were left in the room as someone inside screamed. Kon couldn't see the damage from his position as he stepped into the hall, ready to attack. A moment later, the door to the hall opened. The three were between Kyro and Kon, and Kyro had spotted his target. His focus set straight through the others onto Kon.

"Go," Kon ordered them as fire ignited around him, terrashock forming to stop the next attack.

The three barely made it behind him as another blast erupted. Fire mixed with Kon's terrashock in a bright wall of twisting energy and flames. He always noticed his fire leaked into his other abilities more when he was afraid like it was some symptom of fear. But as he blocked the blow and backed off, he could see how much fire was around him. Lights above them were shot, shattered in the energy. Kon watched Kyro through the hazy warping terrashock. He was watching right back, with the same emotionless dead expression as the last time.

Something in Kon churned. He turned to the group, holding a hand up to prolong the barrier as if it would somehow protect him from the threat. "Are you okay?" He checked over the three, backed against the far wall. Icelyn looked shaken while Jasamie clutched Jyune with wide eyes. He received a few quick nods, all of them coated in debris. Their expressions on him folded as warm liquid pooled at his nose.

Not now. Not while facing Kyro. He wiped it away with a sleeve, staring at it before he looked back to Jasamie, radio in her hand. "Call Para." Whether he was running from fear or logic, he couldn't say. But that wasn't the place to put up a fight. Especially if what he thought was happening, was. If the trickle of blood meant anything like it did years before, they needed to run.

Fear flashed across their faces, maybe from the realization that Kon would never have called Para unless he, too, was scared. No one argued the plan as the group nodded in agreement. Jasamie pulled out her radio and began dialing. Kon took a last look at Kyro, who hadn't moved. That was almost more unsettling as if he knew he had them cornered. He didn't need to attack. Kon hoped he was wrong as he disappeared around the corner with the rest.

"Th—There's an exit at the end of the hall. There has to be," Peter said, half bewildered. "Do you think he'll follow us?"

Kon checked behind them again as they rounded the second turn. Nothing.

The lights above flickered more the deeper they ran. Before they knew it, they were back at B21.

"We follow his footsteps. It should lead us out!" Peter called.

As if triggered by Peter's cry, the lights shut off. The halls plunged into darkness at the sound of the base losing power. Everyone skidded to a stop. The slight hum of energy in the walls was gone, leaving the group in still, dark silence. Only the sounds of panicked breaths were let out before anyone spoke.

"He must've flipped the breaker," Jasamie whispered, lowering the radio.

Fire sparked around Kon's hand as he held it up, lightly illuminating the surroundings. "Hurry."

Jyune stuck out a hand from Jasamie's arms, giving a bit more light, but it was faint as they continued to follow the footprints, the years-old trail of Andren Day, hopefully leading them to safety.

"Do you think EME are waiting outside?" Icelyn asked as they navigated the dark hall.

Kon shook his head. He didn't want to think about it. They'd be stupid if they didn't take advantage of the moment. Surely, there was something awaiting them. "Just stay close."

"We're almost out," Jasamie explained to the radio. "They might be waiting outside."

"We can still get out of this." Kon hardly believed himself. Odds were mounting against them every extra second they stayed in the base. The exit sign had gone dark too as light finally shone where the footprints led out. Flames reflected off its red door as Kon pushed it open. It went to a damp concrete staircase leading up to a hatch. "Stay quiet," he said as he followed the steps to the hatch, ducking through the low ceiling. It must have been overgrown he figured when the first push didn't work. It took several more before the door budged, and the sound of undergrowth snapping came with light flooding into the staircase. A final shove knocked it open as he pushed roots and weeds out of the way.

The rest of the group hung back as he stepped out, scanning every direction as the smell of dense forest filled the air. There was another smell, a familiar one. Hovercraft exhaust. Though faint, it was there. And coming from somewhere in the sky, he could hear the low roaring. There was no telling if they had dropped Kyro off like in Calirue or if they were waiting nearby guarding the exits.

"Okay, hurry." Kon called to the rest, keeping his head on a swivel as they joined him. They were against a steep hill with the flat terrain leading back to the entrance.

"Which way?" Icelyn questioned, trying to familiarize herself.

Kon attempted to orient his position. "We can try to circle back to the gap in the fence." Nerves wracked inside him as he worked to push away the confrontation. He should've known Kyro would show up. Frowning to himself, he shook out an arm, preparing for a bigger fight.

As he glanced back at the group, the reality hit him. They needed him to be strong. Each one looked at him to get them out. Afraid of the EME, afraid of that Avari, he was the only thing that stood between them. With a shift of his shoulders, he straightened.

Their speed kept brisk as they maneuvered through the trees. Kon was careful to listen for the *buzz* in the air. Somewhere in the sky, it circled. Maybe more than one, drawing ever nearer. Through the swaying of the trees, EME were out there.

"D—do you think he followed us?" Peter stammered from the back, looking behind him as he clutched the folders tight in his grasp.

They were nearing the end of the flat stretch. The cliff downward was beginning again. Gaps in the trees showed how high they were, casting out to the mountains in the distance. If Kyro had flipped the breaker, it meant he was heading back to the entrance. He would be out before them and in the blur of trees, he could be anywhere. Somewhere within the steel fence surrounding them, he was lurking.

"No," Kon started, as he froze dead in his tracks. Ahead, in the silent forest, the gentle soft colors caught his eye from the brush. Roses. Memories danced, but only for a moment until his vision drifted past them.

Staring back was Kyro.

Once by one, the rest of the group spotted him until they all had stopped. Kyro wasn't moving. He stood still as a predator, hunting its prey.

"What do we do here?" Jasamie asked. No one dared to make sudden movements.

Kyro started toward them. Slowly, silently, through the trees.

Kon let out a tiny breath.

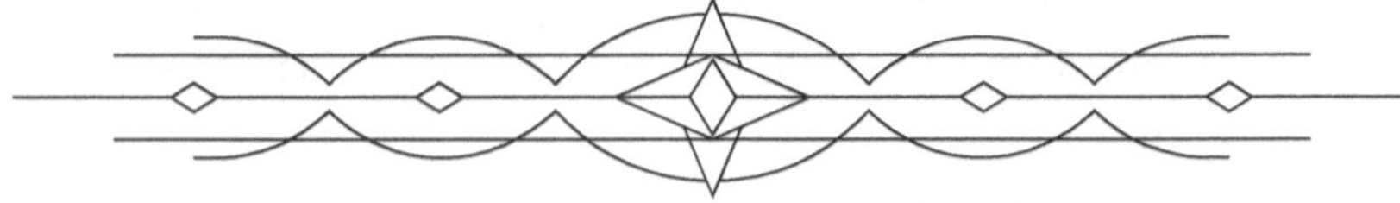

36

FIRE

"Get out of here." Kon glanced back at the group as he dropped his bag behind him. Kyro had stopped a short distance from them, eyes set on Kon, unwavering in the still woods. He was frozen again. Kon took the opportunity to scan for any details he could. He was still wearing the collar, earpieces wrapped around both ears, likely being given orders at that very moment—there had to be a camera somewhere too.

The EME would be there soon.

There wasn't time for any more analyzing as fire started slowly up Kyro's arms.

Against his instructions, the group behind him hadn't budged. Jasamie held her radio in her hand, afraid to make a sound.

Kon looked back at him. "Kyro," he started, raising a hand gently. No fire yet. Perhaps the most emotion he had seen from him, Kyro's head tilted slightly at the name, eyes narrowing.

"Kyro, we can help you," Peter spoke up in a shaky tone, stepping forward next to Kon. "We can get you away from—"

Fire erupted around the Avari's arms as his body twisted, launching the blast of channeled terrashock at them.

Kon pushed Peter back, catching the blow as his own energy ignited. It exploded in another wall of fire and warping colors as he glanced over his shoulder. Icelyn had pulled Kon's bag into her arms as the others helped Peter off the ground, eyes wide. "Go. Now," Kon hissed.

The fight was on. The group rushed for cover as Kon let the energy around him activate. Somewhere behind him, Jasamie was frantically explaining the situation as they ducked behind trees. It was time to zone in, focus, just as another wave hit him.

The heat of the fire brushed Icelyn's cheeks as she ducked behind the tree. She peeked around, watching the second blast erupt between them. On the ground beside her, Peter couldn't take his eyes from the fight, stunned in awe, watching the colors of terrashock ignite in the air.

"Are you okay?" She knelt next to him.

He shook his head, eyes still locked on the fight.

"Yes, outside the AIP facility," Jasamie spoke frantically, with the radio pressed to her ear as she covered the other from the sounds of energy sundering. "Yes, he's here. Kon's holding him off." She glanced back at the fire. "I don't know how long we have." Jyune hid in her coat, head barely poking out to watch the commotion.

Stormy stood rigid, staring at the fire. Icelyn checked over a shoulder in time to see Kon fold away from another hard wave of energy. Her heart lurched, scanning the foliage around her as if she'd find something of use. Maybe that was how the first fight went. But something felt wrong. Kon's power wasn't moving like Kyro's. It was sparking, twisting, igniting in odd pops of energy; fire, terrashock—and light. "We have to help him." She met eyes with Stormy, who was nodding slightly.

"Yeah." Her voice was small as her tail flicked with anxious energy. "What can we do?"

"I don't know, maybe . . . distract him so Kon can get an attack in." She grabbed a rock, standing up.

Jasamie unplugged her ears, staring at the two gathering themselves.

"What are you guys doing?"

"I can—I have fire," Stormy stuttered. "It's not much but . . . maybe,"

"What? No," Jasamie argued, lowering the radio. "He said stay out of it."

"We have to try *something*," Icelyn urged. "Para won't be here in time."

Jasamie gave them a frown, folding her brows as she put the radio to her ear again. "Where are you guys?"

Shaking off the nerves, Icelyn prepared herself, dropping Kon's bag next to Peter. "Take this."

Peter was snapping out of his stunned phase as he reached for Kon's bag, then looked up at Icelyn. "What are you doing?"

Icelyn winced at the tall, colorful flames before them. "Helping."

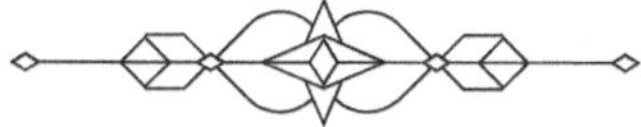

It was Calirue again. Kyro's blasts of energy outnumbered his own. There was hardly time to launch an attack with each manifest of power being used to stop the oncoming attacks. Kon needed a plan. The shield of terrashock around him wouldn't last much longer as he curled away from the flames.

His powers were acting up, the same as before, pops of terrashock and jittery energy. It wasn't listening to him. Maybe that was the *Airay* in his system. Would it be his undoing once again? He tried to pull at the energy where it wanted to push, making a viable shield even harder against the attacks.

Between the slams of energy from Kyro and the growing shine of light within the terrashock, he didn't see a way through. The first time his powers acted up, when he was thirteen, it had been enough to dispatch every EME soldier around him. The second time, he only remembered the aftermath; burning cracks in the walls, shattered energy erupting any-thing around it, the muffled screams through ringing in his ears.

He had always wondered why it faltered.

Maybe a falter was what he needed.

The grip he held on his energy loosened, bringing forth the pressure in his head as his nose burned with another rush of blood. The next blast from Kyro sent sparks of light and electricity sparking around the terra-shock shield. They sundered out as Kon stood, facing Kyro again. Kyro was slowing, watching the pops of unstable energy with something of confusion—curiosity.

Kon's head spun as he wiped his nose. Kyro had paused altogether. With the question on his face, it confirmed one thing, something Kon always knew, that kind of energy wasn't normal.

By then, it was a struggle not to hold it back. Each ripple and thrash of enraged colorful power in front of him pulled more energy out of him that he wasn't giving willingly. His next idea couldn't be a good one; he took a deep breath and pulled his body into position. Kyro was backing away, the first retreat. An arm raised in a shield of terrashock to block the blinding lights.

Kon had never freely tried to control the episodes. They always came when he had the least amount of control. But as he swung the energy aimed at Kyro, he had no idea what to expect. He didn't expect the flash of light, a power he always had trouble conjuring. Nor did he expect Kyro to fold back as hard as he did, crouching for cover as the radiant energy slammed trees. He could've sworn some of the thick evergreens bent. Or maybe it was him falling to the ground, as half his consciousness went out with the blast.

The next thing he saw was the twisted roots of the trees under him. A mix of rough roots and soft moss cooled his burning hands. *Why was he so hot?* He barely caught himself in a kneel, vision blurred. Drops of red stained the mossy roots he stared at. *Get up.* He couldn't black out—not when, in the distance, Kyro was standing up, far more cautious as he started to move. The fire etching around his arms dissipated. Relief that he was stopping lasted only a moment as he raised his hand at Kon. Whatever he sent was invisible—until he felt it.

An icy chill ran over Kon. The air was cold enough to see his breath as he realized the source. Kyro had switched from fire to—ice? There was another wave of cold that hit him before he realized *why*. Everything around him, including himself, was in flames. At least his shield energy was stable, protecting him from the fiery energy that was still twisting and popping in erratic motions around him. He could only hope the group was far enough away as the roaring of a hoverform came nearer.

The cold air dissipated the burning brush but only agitated the powers around him. He needed to send another attack, whether he could handle it or not. Glancing behind him, there was no sign of the group. *They got away. Called Para. Made it to safety.* It was relieving. At least they might make it out. He turned back to face the tall figure before him. And then a rock hit Kyro. From somewhere in the brush—it came whizzing through the air with force, bouncing off his shoulder just as a second one launched from the same direction. Kyro pulled his head back, dodging the second one. Through the twisting purples and blues of his terrashock, Kon could see where they had come from, and his heart dropped.

Icelyn stood, far too close, rock in hand. Fire licked around her as she stood steady. Her powers must have been working just enough to allow her to stand within the flames, ready to attack. Kyro watched her with a blank face. He might've ignored her completely and turned back on Kon if it wasn't for the ball of fire that came from the opposite direction. It connected straight at Kyro's head, engulfing the top half of him in fire. He didn't react to it. As it dissipated from his face, he held the same expression as he turned to the assailant.

Stormy. Her eyes widened as she lowered her arm.

There was no time for a second attack before terrashock detonated square in her chest, throwing her backward. She landed against a tree with a *thud.*

"Stormy!" Jyune shrieked as she charged from somewhere in the trees to between Kyro and Stormy, letting off a large flash of light, just enough to blind him.

Recoiling from the light, Kyro turned toward Kon, who was back up. Electricity ran through the breaking strings of terrashock around him. Light was emanating from the heaviest patches of it as Kon faced him. But Kyro didn't have time to react. Unmoving, the energy in front of him detonated straight at his core. It knocked Kyro back as fire overtook the surroundings again. Branches from trees snapped in the energy. Several from the group were yelling, maybe calling for Stormy as Jyune ran for her. Or calling for cover, as Icelyn ducked away from the energy. The ringing in his ears muted it all. Pressure in his head screamed for him to stop, but he sent another.

Energy from Kyro was dissipating as he remained on the ground. Kon could hear bits of commotion over Stormy. He kept his glare on Kyro. Only then did he try to settle the frayed energy, push it back down before it consumed him completely and leveled the forest. "What do they want with me?" Kon demanded, steadying his tone as he fought his own conscience. He could taste something metallic as he hovered in place. Light seeped from the energy around him as it started to dispel, piece by piece, retreating back into his body.

Kyro was frozen on the ground, eyes hazed as he listened to whatever EME orders were being barked through the earpieces. He showed no signs of hearing Kon as he finally met his gaze. There was no energy around him besides Kon's, which was starting to fizzle. His next move was done slowly, almost holding back. Kyro reached for his belt, pulling a thin vial of green liquid from it, capped with a needle. It only took a second for Kon to realize: he was too close.

There was a flash of regret on his face, but only for a moment. With the needle clenched in his fist, Kyro sprang into action, charging through the remaining glitchy energy, and shoving Kon to the ground. No more power—it was pure force. Face to face, he had almost forgotten the strength Kyro had over him. Panic flooded over him as they fell. The energy around him went off in spurts, but it was once again working against him. The blast aimed to push him ignited next to him, dissipating into thin air.

Kon fought through the ringing in his ears as Kyro held him down. If he landed it, it was over. Kyro uncapped the needle as he bent away from the frantic reaction of failed energy. Memories of similar needles flooded his mind. Panic. He couldn't rely on his powers in this condition. Not anymore.

Kon caught the hand containing the needle, holding it at bay as he tried to move Kyro's heavy weight off him. His other hand frantically reached for the knife in his pocket, aiming it at the closest target—his side. Kyro recoiled from the blow as Kon slashed the next blow at his arm, sending the needle flying into the mix of moss and roots.

"They're coming!" Peter called from somewhere in the trees.

Kon hadn't even noticed the growing roar of a hoverform as Kyro pinned the weapon. "I'm not going back," Kon stuttered, trying to yank his hand from the grip.

Kyro was unreadable as his loose hand checked his side, holding a hand up to assess the blood. It only slowed him a moment as Kon tried to break his grasp with his free hand.

"Get off of him!" Icelyn yelled from somewhere, but no one dared to try an attack again. Kyro ignored them the same way he ignored everything else.

Kon watched his own sizzling energy refuse to cooperate as Kyro pinned him, digging in his bag again while he held the knife to the ground. Hand coated in his own blood, he began to pull out a shiny ring of metal cuffs. The EME would be here soon.

Kon couldn't let him. He couldn't end up there again. Kyro pressed against his neck with an arm as he pried the knife from his hands. Head throbbing, Kon reached around him with his free hand for anything hidden among the twist of roots and thick ferns; a rock, a weapon, anything—

A needle.

It wasn't until the injector was in Kyro's side that he realized what Kon had done. He finally shoved away from him, standing frantically to pull the needle out as Kon tried to catch his breath in his panicked lungs. He got himself into a sitting position as his heart pulsed in his head. As Kyro held the near-empty needle in a shaky hand, there was only shock— anger?—across his face.

"Stop," Kon tried, holding out a hand, desperate to break the fight. If the injection was what he thought it was, he wouldn't be up much longer.

Kyro didn't seem to care as fire flashed up his arms again.

Relief flooded through him, regardless of the anger, that the needle wasn't in himself. With a glance over at the group, he could see they were huddled around Stormy. Jasamie dug in her bag, still holding her radio as she handed Icelyn a flare gun. "They need to know where we are. Go." Icelyn jumped up, checking on Kon again before she ran for the gap in the trees.

A wave of fire brought Kon back to Kyro, whose movements were already starting to slow. Kon could hardly stand as he held a hand to block the fire. It wasn't calculated, targeted blows. It was just waves of angry fire as Kyro approached. He seemed nearly done as he pushed another wave of fire out while the flare lit the sky red above them.

Kyro stumbled, falling to a kneel as Kon stood, hands still out. "Stop," he pleaded to no avail as Kyro took one last lunge at Kon.

Back on the ground, Kon guarded himself with an arm, waiting out the short time before he surely dropped. It was obvious Kyro wasn't seeing clearly anymore as he wavered over him. The sky stained a bright red behind him as the flare dissipated into shades of pink. Kyro drew a trembling fist back until his eyes softened slightly. With a shake of the head, he focused his gaze, looking over Kon with confusion as his body swayed. "Jarauk?" Kyro's voice was rough, quiet.

The first words Kon had heard from him. A name he knew. Kon only had time to look at him in question before something on Kyro's steel collar began beeping. The green ring flashed red, followed by a quick series of beeps as Kyro's expression turned to pure horror. With a jerk, he fell backward, away from Kon. The sound of electric shocks started up.

Rising slightly, Kon stared. He had done, or *said,* something the EME didn't like. His fear of Kyro twisted into guilt as he watched the man curled up on the ground, waiting out the timer. Even after it had stopped, he didn't move. Kon carefully sat up fully, his body aching. Fear in his chest kept him from moving further as the threat before him melted. A thick fog in his head clouded him as he looked Kyro over. The buzzing in the sky was nearly over them. Another series of shocks started up again as Kyro folded in on himself. It was as if Kon could feel the sting of it himself, staring in silence.

Wariness was starting to wear into sympathy as Kon inched closer, kneeling over him. "What do I do?" he asked frantically, seeing only himself in the lone, broken Avari before him. "How do I help you?"

The second attack stopped as Kyro took a breath in, losing energy. It was the first time Kon felt Kyro was *truly* looking at him. Not the EME—Kyro. He fought to form words. Only two came. "Kill me."

Kon froze, staring at him as the ringing in his ears increased. At first, he thought it was his own ears until he realized it was coming from the earpieces secured around Kyro's. A piercing ring Kyro could do nothing about, drowning out anything else Kon could attempt to say and defusing any conversation to be had. Another wave of electricity started in the collar. The EME had blocked Kon from the only Avari left. The only family he had. He only had those two words. A plea.

Maybe he would've done it—but something in him took over. A deep-seated horror in what he watched before him. He could do nothing but stumble back, falling onto the roots behind him. The image of Kyro, the memories of the EME, he could hardly find air in his own lungs. It might as well have been him on the ground. Him in the clutches of the EME.

Him wanting to die.

It was hitting again, that feeling deep in his chest, that wave coming to crash into him, proving he hadn't gotten far enough away.

He couldn't help Kyro.

Icelyn appeared beside him, careful to kneel, as her pale braid flopped over a shoulder. "Kon? We need to go," she urged, glancing over Kyro with caution. "They're coming."

He didn't budge. Something in him didn't want to leave. He saw himself in Kyro. How could he just walk away? Abandon him, again? But with the rising *buzz* in the air and memories fresh, all he could do was force himself to his feet and back away until he bumped the tree behind him. He turned from the scene, hiding behind the tree with what little barrier he could put between him as his panic turned quickly to the urge to flee.

"Kon?" Icelyn had followed after him, looking over his expression for an answer. "We have to go."

Kon breathed, chest tight in the mounting realization. The hoverform was there, a low roar in the sky. The sun disappeared as Kon finally broke his distant gaze to look through the trees. The hoverform was above them, a dark shadow in the sky.

"It's them!" Jasamie called over the buzzing.

Icelyn recoiled, watching through the trees, where the large craft stopped above them. It wasn't the dark gray color of the EME. Its crimson-red hull shone in the sky.

The Base. They were here.

The others were helping Stormy up, supporting her as she clutched her ribs. Stationed above them, the hoverform let out a blaring warning as it started to drift back, spotlights lifting to the sky where the second hoverform lingered. That one *was* EME.

A horn let off, deep and piercing. The fight wasn't over as the gray EME hoverform lurched to a stop in front of them. Its horn blared back as they faced off one another.

"Guys, come on!" Jasamie called over the deep roaring as the large red craft started to lower to meet the cliff side near them where Icelyn had let off the flare. Its bottom ramp opened, lowering to make a bridge onto the craft. She turned back to Kon who was still staring into nothing, his breathing shaky as something of fear sat in his eyes. Blood from his nose smeared his cheek as more ran red.

"Kon," Icelyn said, reaching for his hand as she moved closer. It was rough and hot, nearly too hot to touch as she pulled it to her chest. "It's okay. Let's get on the ship."

His gaze moved to the hoverform again, where the rest were helping Stormy get in. He wavered like he might collapse altogether as tiny trickles of terrashock still floated around him. They had no power to them, occasionally drifting close enough to brush her. A feeling of something thick—a break in the seamless air.

"It's the Base, see? Come on." Icelyn pulled at his hand gently, leading him toward the ramp. She didn't know what was wrong. They just needed to get to the craft.

Terrance, Ashdyn, and a few others were outside the ship, rifles at the ready, aiming behind Icelyn and Kon. She carefully peered behind him where Kyro still lay. EME soldiers surrounded him. guarding him, while the Base guarded Kon at a standstill. Rifles drawn from both sides, they stood their ground. Neither was leaving with what they wanted.

Kon seemed to be coming to, the fogginess in his eyes starting to lift as he focused on the familiar faces around him. He turned, pausing just short of the ramp.

"Get on," Terrance ordered, aiming down the sights of his rifle.

"We can't leave him—" Kon protested, fire sparking up his free arm as Icelyn clung to his other. It was far from functional, in tiny glitchy flames across his sleeve. He couldn't last another fight. Maybe he didn't notice his sway, but Icelyn did as she held his arm, still pulling to keep him steady.

"Nothing we can do this time. They're not going to let us take him." Terrance held his position, as did the EME. Guarding Kyro with guns drawn, but not pushing to go for Kon. Both were willing to split fairly. Likely the only and last time they ever would.

Icelyn held onto Kon, hoping the fire around him wouldn't reach her. "Kon, we have to go. We'll find another way."

"If we fight them now, people are going to die," Terrance said, slowly backing up the ramp.

Kon finally gave in. The fear and haze in his eyes had been replaced with deep anger as he headed up the ramp.

The craft latched shut as the hoverform started to move. Dark metal floors filled the decent room within the ship. There was seating down the sides as pipes and metal frames lined the low ceilings. The rest of the group was at the far end of the room, still gathered around Stormy as a medic assessed her. Peter was attempting to catch his breath as he paced the room, dropping Kon's bag and his armful of folders.

Para tried to slow him down with a hand. "Do you have your medicine? Let the medic look—"

"I'm okay, I'm okay," Peter panted, hand tight on his chest.

"Who wants to start explaining?" Terrance tossed his rifle over his shoulder, looking at Kon too.

"We needed answers," Icelyn began. She still felt a sense of protection over Kon as she watched his eyes set on Terrance with a defiant glare. Terrance's expression lingered down at her with something of confusion. Only then did she realize she was still clutching Kon's hand. Her hands trembled, stuck in their grasp on his sleeve and palm, and then she noticed he was holding onto her as well. Icelyn released her stiff hold, composing herself. "We figured there would be something at the facility to help us. The plan was to come right back."

"Mhm," Terrance scoffed. "And who masterminded this plan?" He held a glare with Kon.

"What do you want from me?" Kon snapped, only making it a step toward him before Icelyn blocked his path.

She could still *feel* the energy around him as she held her hands at his torso. If no one else could see he was having trouble settling it, she wouldn't be the one to bring attention to it. She kept her gaze on Terrance over her shoulder. "It's not his fault." She frowned. "Leave him alone."

"I'm just saying, I don't think he came along for the ride."

"It was my idea!" Peter coughed, still taking deep breaths. "I talked him into it—"

"Okay, all of you, stop," Para's voice rose above the others. "Just, stop. We'll discuss it later. Terrance, go see if we're being followed." She watched between them with arms tucked at her chest. "Peter, focus on your medicine. Are you two okay?"

Terrance let out a sigh as he exited the room through the large sliding door.

"I think so." Icelyn nodded, taking the time to look over Kon. "Are you okay?" Besides the cut on his cheek from the previous fight, she couldn't see any noticeable injuries, though she hadn't seen him like that before. It was more evident back in the woods.

But he pretended it wasn't happening. That his breathing wasn't off, that there wasn't a flicker of nerves showing in his eyes or the beginning stages of invisible terrashock trying to form around him. "I'm fine." His fluffy dark hair was dusted over his narrowed eyes, stuck on the ground.

She glanced over to Stormy, where Jyune was curled beside her. "Is Stormy okay?"

Para watched over her shoulder for a moment. "Might be a broken rib. Hopefully nothing worse." Her tone was flatter than usual as she kept her arms crossed, disappointment stuck on her face.

"We thought the EME would stay around Calirue," Icelyn said.

Para gave a shrug. "So did we. Then the radios reported Kon in Darnar."

Terrance appeared back at the door. "They turned around. Headed back the way they came." There was no relief on his face. "We're safe . . . for now."

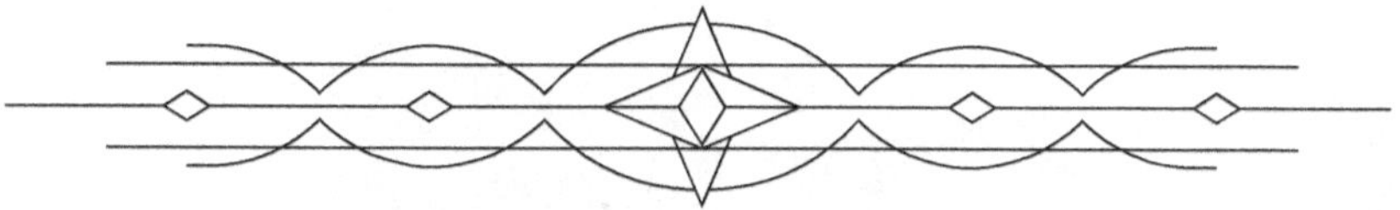

CHAPTER 37
SAFE

It didn't help that Kon had only been in a hoverform once, and it was the same bad memory he was always fighting off. He stood rigid in the ship, numb to the soothing from Icelyn and Para until the ship was docking back onto the large platform in which it usually sat, it only ever rising above ground for launch. Kon had never known it was right there under the field the entire time.

"Get them inside. We'll power it down," Terrance called as the ramp opened.

Fresh air mixed with fuel wafted into the ship as the grass field appeared before them. Para led the group off the concrete base as the hoverform's engine quieted. Jasamie and Para supported Stormy as they headed for the hatch on the ground. Spirits were higher as they approached the safety of the base. Even Stormy was talking again, stifling laughter as she clutched her chest. Kon glanced back at the hoverform, a slight shiver going down him as it started to sink into the ground to join the rest of the base. Its crimson hull shined in the lowering sun.

The fresh air was calming. There was the slightest comfort in him to get back into the base. It was an unsettling feeling when his usual wishes were to be in the woods, safe from others. A small part of him was eager to get back into the safety of the bunker now. The thought only made him angry with himself.

"Careful," Para warned as they took the steps down the hatch, Alaura greeting them at the door. "We'll take you to the Defensive Wing med bay. Ryv will want to monitor you for a bit."

"You'll be all fixed up soon," Jyune said from Jasamie's shoulder, her hand firmly on Stormy's arm. Stormy gave a willing chuckle, her face still scrunched in pain.

Alaura watched Stormy in silence before she found Kon the moment he appeared at the door. It was as if he had spoken, said something to surprise her. At first, he ignored the stare, until the realization hit him. Whatever silent powers he was still fighting to condense around him— Alaura could see them, and for once, since knowing her, she looked . . . surprised. To his relief, she didn't speak a word of it. Her eyes narrowed in the slightest before she turned back to follow Para down the hall. Their voices hummed as the groups started to break.

Peter's weak cough cued Para as she glanced over her shoulder. He made attempts to hide near Kon.

"Peter, come on. I want you checked out too." Para nodded for him to join as he hesitated. She didn't wait for his protest before turning back to Stormy. "Now, what happened again?"

Kon stopped in the center of the mural room as Icelyn lingered nearby. Something in him wanted to distance himself from the whole thing. If he had just been faster, better, no one would've gotten hurt. *What if Kyro had done more?* What if he had shoved just a bit harder? The terrashock that sent Stormy back was hardly anything compared to what he had sent at Kon, like flicking away a bug. Part of him was grateful that Kyro at the least seemed less violent toward others. That his focus was only on Kon. Whether it was direction from the EME or Kyro's own preference, it was the only thing that kept Stormy from a far worse injury. Her fate shouldn't have been up to them, though. If he had just—

"Kon?" Icelyn interrupted his thoughts, carefully maneuvering in front of him, stepping as though the sound of her shoes on the tile could spook him. "Are you okay?"

His gaze set on her easier that time, the fog of the fight passing slowly. "Yeah." He found his eyes drifting over her to the group down the hall. "I should've stopped him."

"You did. I mean, you won this time, didn't you?"

The words stung. There was no winning. It hadn't been a fair fight. From the group intervening how they could to the EME deciding Kyro had failed and stepping in. Nothing had been fair to Kyro. He would've won had it not been for the advantages Kon had.

All of that, just for Kon to reject the single grace Kyro had asked of him. He felt sick to his stomach. He had failed the one strand of family he had on the planet.

Icelyn's shuffling brought him back again as she dug into her pocket, pulling out a slightly wrinkled photo. "I found this," she said. "It was in Padlin's room."

He took the photo, another pang in his chest. It didn't make sense. The joy in their faces. The excitement in their eyes as they held the ultrasound photo of their unborn child. Yet, here he was, alone.

"I just thought you should have it. I don't know." She pulled her hands to her chest with a tiny grin.

"Thanks." He examined the photo a moment longer before pushing it into a pocket with a sigh. Some questions answered, but there were also a million new ones.

There was a strange stillness to the base. Even while heading to their rooms, there were scarce signs of students. Those that did meander the halls did so somberly. It must have been a collective realization that things were going wrong. That the hoverform had been sent out, that it had to do with the EME and Kon. The students who had been cautious of his arrival were right—including Darren and his icy words the other night. They had reason to be mad. As Kon pulled the photo from his pocket in the safety of his room, he had a right to be mad as well.

He forced himself to examine it closer, away from the judgment of others, where he could feel his brows creasing the longer that he looked. The others acted like he should be overjoyed at the images of his parents, but it just brought a stiff ache somewhere deep in his chest. Jarauk did look like him. Padlin's eyes were the same large golden ones as his, just as Joel had said. Their markings were dark and jagged. Padlin had the same series of markings across her cheek as he did. The small stray mark under her eyes, the tiny dot below it, just like his, nearly connecting to the long stripe that disappeared above the ear into her hair.

He tossed the picture on the shelf by the door, tossing the tangle of questions and thoughts with it. Maybe Peter found more answers in their trek. Something he would surely piece together as soon as he escaped from the med bay. After all, he knew more about the events that took place twenty years before. The logistics of the Avari Integration Program, the meaning behind those logs, Garik Tally's words. Kon never got too close to the information. Half the facts Peter would spew at random about Avari were stuff he hardly knew about himself. It was better to pretend he wasn't something different. The thought made him feel better.

Nothing ever made him feel like an Avari. What did that feel like, after all? From what he could gather, he was never normal. Whatever came after his diagnosis—his Airay—was bad enough to end the program and cause his parents to abandon him.

He dropped his bag, a sharp sting of anger still piercing his chest. Whatever set him apart from Avari or his parents, he was born with it. There was never a point that he stood a chance of belonging. All that time, looking for his place in the world—it never existed.

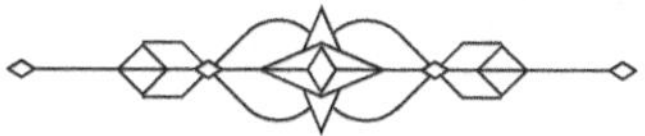

"Mmm, doesn't appear to be any internal bleeding." Ryv examined the screen next to the bed. "We'll keep an eye on it."

Icelyn leaned in with Jasamie to watch the screen as he flipped through the X-ray scans. She had found herself in the med bay after a failed attempt to settle in her room. Even grabbing a bite in the cafeteria proved useless. Everything felt different. Kon had disappeared into his room or outside. She wasn't sure. There was no use worrying over it anyway. He'd want to be alone. The urge to be surrounded by others had pushed her into the Defensive Wing, seeking the group.

"See the cracks?" Ryv said as he glanced up from the notes on his clipboard, watching the two of them converse over the image.

"I think so." Icelyn nodded as Jasamie pointed to the slight discrepancy in the X-ray.

"So, she's okay?" Jyune asked, having stayed stationed next to Stormy at every moment possible.

"Yes, but given the situation, she got lucky," Ryv said, spinning in his seat. "You all got lucky." He cast a disapproving look at Jasamie specifically.

"I said I was sorry," she fussed, pulling from the monitor with a sigh.

"Sorrys never heal anyone," he explained as he stood, turning his back to them. "Let's see if the swelling is going down."

Icelyn moved aside as Stormy removed the icepack from her ribs. Jasamie had her head thrown back looking at the ceiling before tilting it toward her. "I think we're grounded," she whispered, rolling her eyes.

Icelyn nodded, smirking slightly as she glanced at Peter, who had a solid scowl as he sat across the room by the door, arms crossed in retaliation from Alaura's refusal to let him leave without a checkup. His armful of folders sat in the seat beside him.

Para entered, as she scanned Stormy. "How is everyone else?"

Terrance had tailed behind her, stopping at the door. His expression spelled only trouble for them.

"No other injuries from what I can tell." Ryv shrugged, drying his hands.

"Good. Peter?"

"Still waiting," Peter grumbled.

Para nodded, folding her arms in as her brows furrowed. "What about Kon? I figure he's going to be hard to catch for an assessment."

"I think he's okay." Icelyn rubbed her hands together, dispelling the cold from her. "I'll try and find out next time I see him."

"Well," Para sighed. "I'm glad everyone's okay. But I have to stress how dangerous this could've gotten—*did get*. I know you don't want to hear it, but you're all lucky to be here."

Alaura slipped around Terrance into the room. "I'm particularly disappointed in our two young medics who supported this." Her gaze tracked Icelyn and Jasamie, though it was hard to tell how she felt in her stone-faced expression.

"We didn't have a choice," Jasamie stated as Icelyn started to fold into herself with the eyes of the heads of the base watching them all.

"How's that?" Terrance asked from the door. He'd had a clench in his jaw since earlier.

Jasamie glanced at the others. With looks of caution and no words coming, she took the reins again. "A trip was going to be made, regardless." She worded her sentence carefully, glancing at Icelyn. "I figured it was best to make the trip with the best plan." She was clearly trying not to fault any specific member of the group. The explanation only brought harder frowns.

"What do you mean?" Terrance asked.

Peter stood from his chair with vigor. "Kon was going to go anyway. Don't act like that surprises you." There was a sting in his words—one that shocked Icelyn and the others—telling by the wide eyes of Stormy and Jyune. Even Terrance seemed, at the very least, confused. Peter carried on. "If we had let him go alone, we never would've seen him again. You know that. He wanted us to stay. We all decided to go—" His sentence ended in a cough.

"Sit," Alaura warned.

Para's expression was clear. Peter was right. "Why the AIP facility?" she asked, masking any comment on the right or wrong of the trip.

"I—it's a lot to explain." Peter murmured.

"Well, I want to hear it," Terrance said.

"Not now, he needs to rest." Alaura flashed a glance at Terrance, holding a paper bag out to Peter. "Medicine. Twice a day. I want to see you tomorrow too."

"Fine," Peter growled. "Can I leave now?"

Para ushered them out of the room, leaving Stormy time to recover. With the clear of Alaura, Peter quickly retreated to his room as the rest exited back into the hall of the larger med bay lined with doors to individual rooms.

More serious medical matters were handled down there, Icelyn had learned. It held the bigger machines, even a room prepped for surgery. Run by the older base staff, Icelyn hadn't yet gotten down there. Her excitement in the bigger medical section was blurred by the situation at hand, as Terrance turned to face Icelyn and Jasamie. "Alright. I want to hear everyone's story. Who's going first?" He kept his arms crossed.

Icelyn and Jasamie paused, turning slowly back to Terrance as they exchanged careful glances.

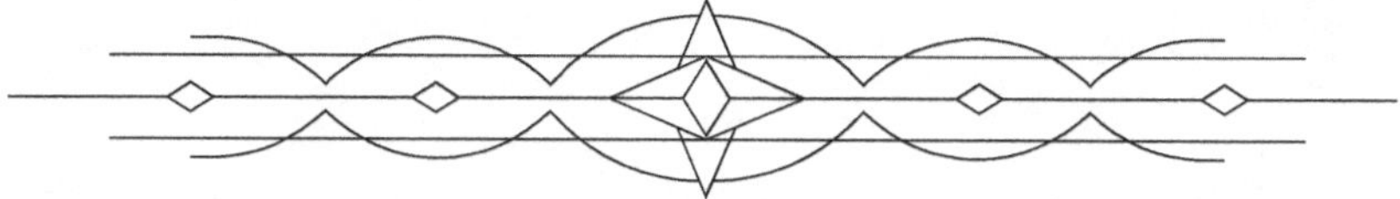

Canned Aryp
Reecyp Chedd Soup
Hi, hope you're OKAY :) -M
you
areful

CHAPTER 38

HIRAETH

JANUARY 2654

Seventeen years since Avari left.

Snow lay thick in the sparse woods, a white blanket across the frozen trees. Kon's eyes scanned every disturbance of snow for tracks. Any sign of another person. It was nothing but him that early in the morning.

It had taken Kon weeks to trek to that point. His method of navigation and moving was completely different ever since he escaped Kain Kodan. He had figured out the name of the EME base when he stumbled across an Elemental care package. There had been a few he ran into in the past; small boxes hidden in the woods with food and maps and vague information on where to go—and where not to go. Never anything damning in case EME were the ones to come across the packages.

At the sight of it, he almost ignored it completely. Those always meant there was a safe house nearby. Therefore, there was nothing safe about the area. But he was lost again, somewhere in his slower careful travel, he had lost precise direction, and towns were out of the question. Inside the box, he left the supplies but plucked a map from a selection of several, all wrinkled and folded in age.

The map was Brynden Ka. A small green mark circled his current location. It wasn't far from where he *thought* he was, almost back into the core sector, but it was straying cautiously close to a small town. He just had to get around the large lake in his way. What drew his attention next was the large red 'Xs' marked. Four of them. The farthest south one, labeled "Kas Kiza," sat right below the core sector, a bit into the south. On the east side of the Core sector, another labeled "Keel Kydu." Off the West Coast, on a small Island, "Kai Keda." That one, he had heard of. Every Elemental knew of Kai Keda. It was the largest base. The mothership of EME movements and where many powerful Elementals ended up—those who had exceptional control over their abilities or a large emit of energy. Or Avari. Even with his distance to Elementals, he had heard the rumors, theories, of the experiments they did there.

In large red letters across the map, it marked:

STAY AWAY.
EME BASES HERE.

The last one, north, just above the town of Velkost, Kain Kodan. From the hard twist in his stomach, he knew that's where he had been.

He wanted to tear up the map, purely to get the name of that base out of his head, but it could prove helpful if he ever strayed too close to another one. That might've been his mistake. He couldn't have been far from Kain Kodan when they found him. They must've been pushing him there all along.

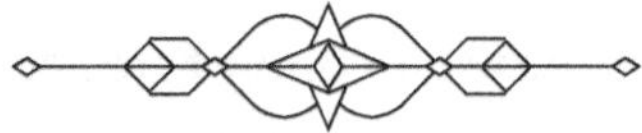

Almost two weeks later, the map still sat at the bottom of his bag, untouched. He walked across the snowy, dead field, void of the flowers that once lay there. The blanket of snow was undisturbed. No one had been there. That was probably for the best as he approached the old cabin.

The door creaked open, looking even more weathered than it had when he and Joel arrived. Years ago, he would have been eager to get to the cabin, excited hands shoving the door open, bag over his shoulder as they arrived for the weekend. It was always his favorite place. Now, his hand took the doorknob quietly, wrapped in thick cloth in the icy temperatures. The clothes he wore were far worn, tattered, and aged. His movement was careful like a cautious animal scavenging for solace. The last time he entered, he hadn't needed to duck. But the frame had finally nearly grazed his head as he stepped inside. His breath still pooled into the open air, as he examined the familiar kitchen. Cold light illuminated the dark, dead house. It looked like the power had stopped working.

On the table across from the kitchen, a box of supplies sat; cans of food speckled the table, along with blankets, radios, and notes. All of it lay untouched. All that time, they still left supplies. They still came in hopes he'd one day be there. He stepped closer, reading over the carefully written notes stuck to blankets, cans of food, and radios. It seemed Joel had brought a crafted note at every supply run. Some were more aged than others in their spread across the table. He moved closer, reading some of them. *Hi, hope you're OKAY*—finished with a smiley face and signed *-M.* Her next ones read, *I miss you. Be careful,* and, *We hope you're safe.*

His eyes traced over them. Something numb burned inside him, but that was the only emotion. The only feeling he could muster. He wondered if he would even be happy to see them. If Mallia stood in the room, there might be no emotion at all. He didn't know if he was capable of it. It was strange feeling nothing at the sight of their love for him. How wide had his disconnect grown? Although, he still wore Joel's jacket, and Mallia's bracelet was nestled somewhere in the inner pockets.

It might've been pointless to come here. Something deep in him hoped that the visit might spark something, bring a piece of him to life. Though he hated to admit it, a part of him hoped Joel would be there. He wouldn't dare go to the green house. It would leave a trail straight to them, but he could go to the cabin. For a moment. Maybe seeing Joel would have sparked something if that hadn't. Joel always had words of wisdom. Some of them might've gotten through to him. Nothing he said to himself ever did.

Kon stared at the supplies, contemplating. He should leave them a sign. Something to tell them some shred of him still existed in the world. Something they would know. He took some of the canned food. In their place, gently on a crème-colored blanket, he laid Mallia's bracelet, with its soft purple flowers and silver accents. They'd at least know he'd been there. That he was alive. That's all they needed to know. The tug of anxiety was already present, pulling him back toward the safety of the woods. He couldn't stay long.

If he couldn't find peace, maybe they could.

In the quiet morning, he followed the rocky incline up the snowy hill. If there was one benefit to having his powers, it had to be the ability to keep himself warm. And being able to do this in the frigid Brynden Ka winters gave him an upper hand in travel. No one else would be traversing the dangerously low temperatures. It was probably the safest he felt in a year. Though food was proving hard to find, he made do with what hunting and foraging skills Joel had taught him. His findings at the cabin helped.

There had been hardly any signs of EME since he passed through the core sector back into the Eastern region, a relief, but it brought little comfort. Nothing did anymore. That's probably why he found himself climbing the ridge, an ache in his heart. He was seeking something. Maybe a glimmer of peace.

His warm breath fogged the air as he ducked the last few branches out into the clearing. The ridge lay ahead, dropping off into the winding mountains below. He slowly stepped up to the familiar view. Sunrise peeked over the distant mountains, casting a soft light across the frozen morning. His eyes followed the dips in the mountains to the small town below. Calka.

He had climbed the ridge before, leaving the Gavins. Thinking back, he remembered the beauty of the land. The hope that had filled him. He took it all in. Hopefully, Joel and Mallia were down there, safe, content. Maybe Mallia had started that flower shop of hers.

His gaze stayed, searching every corner of the land for that peace. For that hope. He couldn't even call the view beautiful. Had the EME taken that too? Every view he took in was him searching for danger, an escape route. Still standing on that ledge, he wavered, looking for anything. Any sign of joy in his heart.

Nothing. There was one thing festering where that hope and wonder once lay inside him.

Fear.

His gaze hardened as warm tears started to form, blurring his warped vision of the world. Standing in bitter defeat, his bag dropped from his shoulder into the snow. Finally, after weeks of broken lack of emotion, it was there. Tears came faster, running down his cold bitten cheeks as his breathing caught in his throat. What little air came out was cast into the air in wisps.

With a staggered breath, he sucked the frigid air in, sinking to the ground with a weep. Perhaps there was nothing left of him to find. From his seat in the snow, curled in on himself, wishing he had never reawakened in that quiet field, anger began to fester in him. It coaxed him, almost sweetly, drawing his tears away as it took the place of grief. Gently, slowly. Who knew anger could be so gentle, building the walls of safety around the wound inside him? Walls of anger, protecting the last remaining drop of the gentle being inside.

It had to be that way. The choice had been made for him by the cold clutches of a world that rejected him. By the hard hands of the EME who grasped for him.

Maybe his only solace on that cold, snowy cliff was anger. The only warmth to find him was the burning fire lit inside. A fire built by grief, ignited by anger.

He would let the fire burn.

He might even let it consume him whole, as long as it caught fire to every EME who dared to reach for him again.

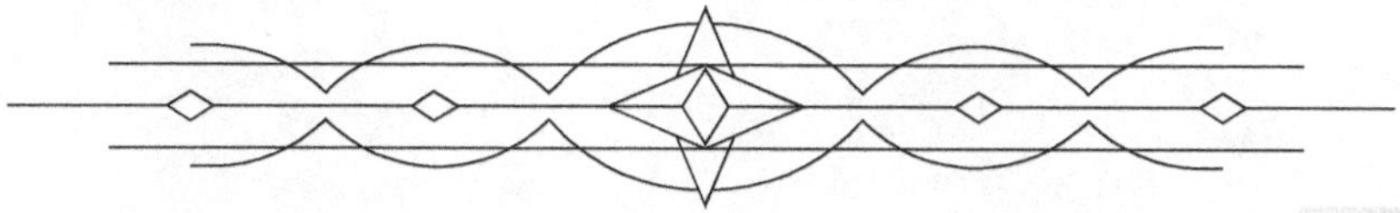

CHAPTER 39
THE TRUTH

Present Day

"Go on." Terrance gave a nod of his head, hands on the keyboard to his digiscreen.

Para sat in the other chair as Icelyn pursed her lips in thought, tugging at her sweater sleeve. There was no telling what the others would say. Were there right and wrong answers? From the frown on Terrance's face, it felt like it. "About what?" Icelyn asked.

"Everything." He sat back slightly, waiting.

After another long follow of silence, Icelyn's lips still sealed, Para tried, "How did this idea come about?"

Icelyn's eyes darted to the desk in front of her, memories of the last conversation she had in Terrance's office, the one concerning her father. Somehow, it felt even harder to discuss. "I . . . don't want to get anyone in trouble."

"No one's in trouble." Para tilted her head. "We just want to know what happened."

Icelyn hesitated for another moment, still searching her mind for the best answer. "We wanted answers . . . about the Avari. We thought maybe if we knew who he was, we might have something to fight the EME."

"Well? Who is he?" Terrance prompted. There was sarcasm in his tone as if he didn't believe they had achieved their mission.

Her mouth parted for a moment before she closed it, thinking through her answer. Maybe if she could answer most of their questions, less would be thrown at the others. "His name is Kyro. He was in the Avari Integration Program. He's . . . he's Kon's uncle."

"His uncle?" Para repeated, her expression twisting as she whispered her next words. "God . . ."

Icelyn continued. "He stayed behind so the others could leave, so they could get Kon out when he was a baby." Her words came slowly. "The EME has had him ever since."

Terrance was typing, a sign that she was giving the right answers . . . she hoped. The hardened edge in his voice was ever so slightly being replaced with curiosity with the next sling of questions about Darnar, Garik Tally, everything. Terrance seemed pleased with his notes as he looked back to her. "So, you ran into EME in Darnar. We heard the radios. What happened?"

"One of them followed us to the edge of the woods. Kon . . . stopped him." She replayed the moment back. How Kon looked at her, hoping the man would simply back off. But he didn't. He took the shot while their backs were turned. A last cowardly attempt but something Kon anticipated. The thought of it saddened her—that he knew them well enough to know how it would end. How to defuse it with such ease. How many encounters it took to be that *calm* about it.

"They didn't follow you? To the facility?"

"I—no. We lost them in the woods." She looked down at her wrinkled pale sleeve, worried her fidgeting might pull it apart at the seams.

Para shifted in her chair as she spoke. "Did anyone mention any other plans? Icelyn, it's important that you all tell us. We can help."

Terrance was more straightforward with what they were asking. "Is Kon planning to go anywhere else?"

Icelyn swallowed. "No." In truth, she didn't know. Would he tell anyone if he were? She even worried about where he was right then. It was clear he liked his space. Was there enough to keep him here? It was her hope that he had found something of happiness here. She had noticed the growing amusement at the base life. How his expression over the days seemed softer, less bothered. He was different inside than his exterior portrayed. But away from that, when he wasn't fighting the EME, when things were safe, everything about him radiated—gentle. Icelyn wondered if he knew that.

Terrance brought her back to reality with more questions about the facility. Icelyn made mention of the files, the photos, everything left behind. Half of it was untouched. "If they didn't clear it out then, they probably will now." Terrance shook his head, adding to his digital notetaking.

Clear it out? Icelyn silently cursed herself for not taking more. For not pulling each photo off the wall in Padlin's room purely to keep it away from the EME. Pull the notebooks from the shelf maybe. Preserve what she could.

After more tapping from Terrance and a long fit of stiff silence, Para spoke again, her tone much more forgiving. "What was the Avari— Kyro—doing this time? It looked like Kon won the fight. We couldn't tell from the craft."

Flashes of the memory flourished. The fire from the fight. She'd never seen so much energy. So many colors of flame and warping terrashock. "He did, but he wanted to help Kyro . . . we just ran out of time." She could feel her face scrunching with the revisiting thoughts. The look of fear and horror on Kon's face as he looked upon Kyro. But not fear of him, fear *for* him. Then the shutdown, him retreating in defeat from the scene. She didn't know what he had seen. What Kyro had said to scare him so badly.

"Help him?" Terrance raised a brow.

"Get him away from them." She pulled at the strands of hair around her face, becoming too aware of their placement. "I mean, we should try, right?"

"We're looking into it." Terrance's tone seemed repetitive, as though he had rehearsed this answer many times in the last day. "We still know nothing about where they're keeping him or if we even have the resources to contain him."

"Contain?" Icelyn squinted. "Why would we . . . need to?"

The expression on his face made her feel small like she should've known the answer, but he answered anyway. "I don't think he's going to welcome a rescue with open arms. He'll see us the same way he sees them." He pushed back from the digiscreen, casual in his explanation. But the next part sent a shiver down Icelyn's spine. "I'm guessing, the second he gets a chance at freedom, from us or them, he's going to go off. They've made a ticking time bomb."

Freedom. Was that even possible for him there? For Kon? They were both trapped. Which one would erupt first?

It was as hard as they anticipated getting Kon back into that office. He sat with arms crossed and eyes narrow as he watched Terrance. His was the last story they needed to gather. He knew they were looking for him the next day as one by one the others mentioned getting whisked away for questions, making mention of Terrance's bad mood ever since it all started. Sure enough, Para had finally managed to talk him into the office.

"Tell us what happened," Terrance started off, brows already furrowed, the stress from the recent events in the permanent crease of his brow.

"With what?" Kon asked, an ice to his tone.

"Everything."

"You didn't get enough from the others?"

"I want *your* version of events."

"Why?"

Terrance ignored the question. "How'd you guys get this . . . idea?" It was clear he held back more descriptive words, remaining curt with his phrasing.

Kon gave a shrug, keeping his gaze on him. Para sat nearby again, looking between them with thin lips.

The silence bothered Terrance, as he let out a breath. "We made it clear to everyone here that it wasn't safe to leave."

"Is that why you locked the doors?" Kon lifted his chin.

Para butted in quickly. "We lock the doors to remind students it's not safe to hang around outside the base right now, but anyone can leave at any time. Just tell staff, and we'll open them." She straightened in her chair. "But out there . . . we can't protect people. We just want everyone to think it over before they leave and risk that."

Terrance pulled back from his keyboard, accepting he wasn't getting any notes out of Kon. His hand ran through his dark hair. "You can leave whenever you want. I draw the line when you start sneaking around and take five other students on a field trip."

"Field trip?" Kon retorted.

Terrance leaned back in his chair. "It's not the first time you've gone on an adventure where you weren't supposed to be."

Kon figured they might've known about the database. "Are you accusing me of something?" His head tilted as he egged him on.

Terrance's voice lowered, finally matching Kon's tone. "You know exactly what I'm talking about. Don't play that game."

Kon leaned back slightly, lowering his chin as he kept his eyes locked on Terrance. "What? Am I being too—combative?" His eyes narrowed as he recalled Terrance's own words on his entry form. "Standoffish?"

What came next surprised him. Terrance stared a moment longer in realization at the words before he let out a breath of a smirk, shaking his head as a grin started to cross his face. The grin of someone who was about to take the bait. His mouth opened—

"Okay, stop," Para blurted before she rubbed her face with an exhaustive sigh. "I knew this wouldn't work. Terrance, just let me—"

Terrance stood before she could finish, seeing himself out as silence took over the room.

Kon's gaze was set on the floor as he felt Para's eyes on him. There was the slightest feeling of guilt, but not toward Terrance. He could push all he wanted. Kon would push back.

Para scooted her chair in slightly, resting an elbow on the desk as she watched him. When her words came, they were soft. "What happened?"

He didn't know what she wanted out of all of it, either of them. Maybe it was "mandatory" in the base's rules to take stories when something happened. Maybe they just wanted to know how to help. But it didn't feel like it. Their questions always came to him as intrusive. Something in him wanting to hide away from it. As the irritation in him started to melt, there was one answer that begged to be given. The thing that had bothered him since it happened. He hadn't told anyone else, but the words burned in his chest. "He asked me to kill him." His voice came out dry, quiet. It was the only thing he felt important enough to tell.

Para's posture softened as she leaned in to face him more. "Kyro?"

Kon nodded, clenching his jaw as he fought for his expression to remain blank. "I couldn't do it." His gaze stayed in his lap as his hands rubbed over the markings on his hand.

"There was nothing we could've done back there. Don't blame yourself for that."

"I should've just done it." He shook his head, his expression starting to falter to something of anger. "I froze."

"No, Kon. That's not his only option, okay? We know they have him now. We know who he is. We can work toward a plan. We'll get him out." She shifted as though the next words hurt to say. "What's most important right now is keeping *you* away from them. If we want to rescue Kyro, we need you. Okay?"

"What if I'm not enough?" Maybe he meant to say the phrase in his head, but it had slipped out. That word drifted in his head next; *flawed.* Did the EME know what "Airay" meant? Maybe they didn't. Maybe that's why things went so wrong in their experiments. It might even be funny, the thought of them wasting almost twenty years of searching to discover he wasn't good enough for their plans. Did Kyro know? The only Avari left there. The one that fought hardest to protect him. He let him down. Kon never even knew Kyro existed, that someone who fought to save him was still paying for it all those years later.

Did the Base know?

Para's tone stayed steady. "You already are. You've done enough to make them bring him out. We never would've known he existed otherwise. You're already helping him."

He asked another question no one had ever answered for him. "Why do they want me?" He wiped at the markings on his hand, once again trying to rub them away. "If they have him . . . why do they need me?"

"I—" Para sighed. "People always want control of what they can't understand."

How could *a world like this understand him?* He didn't belong there. He was nothing to the world beyond a danger and a power to harness. Maybe that was always the plan for Avari.

Para took his silence in strides, collecting herself. "I know they want you to feel alone in this, but you're not." She tilted her head. "Elementals? We're *with* you. I promise we're in this together."

Kon finally lifted his gaze to meet hers. Despite everything the EME taught him, that time, he believed her.

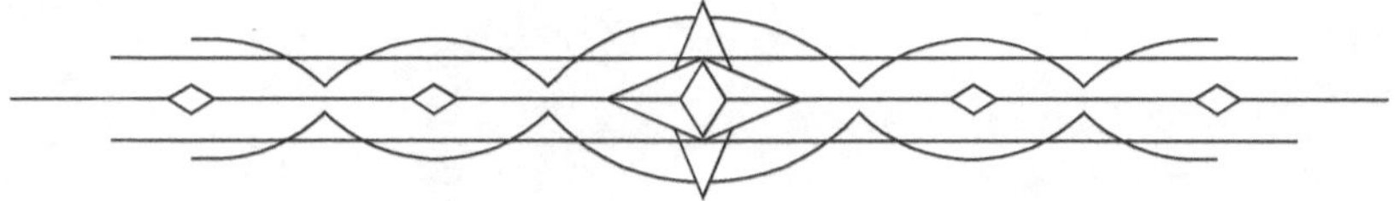

ART
CLUB
SALE
AME
NIGHT

CHAPTER 40
SENSE OF SECURITY

"How close are they?" Kon asked, afraid to hear her answer.

"Surprisingly distant." Para assessed, seated at her desk as she glanced over papers. "Some went toward Alinth, a good bit went back toward Darnar and the coast. I think they're confused. We put out some fog too."

"Fog?"

"Distractions," Para stated, stacking papers dismissively. "We have a grid system set up to confuse them. Planned reports of Elementals or attacks near a hot area to draw away EME. We sent them toward the coast with a few 'sightings' that might sound like you. So far, they're buying it."

"Sound like me?" He crossed his arms, partially amused. "How's that?"

"Reporting a lot of fire and terrashock." Para shrugged. "I don't know. We've never faked an Avari. Hopefully, they buy it and think you left us."

"You don't think them sending Kyro to Calirue was weird?"

"Of course, it's weird. They know we're in the area. That's nothing new. I'm guessing the bait was to draw you out." Her tone stayed mild. "This has been building for a while. We just need them to think the events at the facility scared you enough to head off from us again." Para navigated her digipad screen while Kon leaned on the door to her office. "Do you remember the EME from the Help Key?"

Kon narrowed his eyes, his long sleeves pulled over the markings on his hand. "Core Sector."

Para nodded. "I was looking into it after it happened, trying to piece together why they'd be this far west."

"Probably trailing me," he guessed. "I thought I lost them past Venburg."

"Well, that's what I thought too, but it's not the first time Core Sector has crossed through here." She frowned at the screen, adjusting it. "They wash through every few months."

"What does that mean?" Kon shifted his weight, stepping inside a bit more.

"We think it might be some plan to drive Elementals to the coast. I don't know what's there waiting for them. Nothing good."

Kon frowned in thought. He had been heading toward the coast. Maybe they had started pushing him toward a trap again. Coming across Para in the woods might've saved him. The thought didn't cross his mind at the time—that they could be herding him somewhere specific again. "Have any Elementals come from there?"

Para shook her head, her expression twisting to concern. "No. It's a red area. We have Elementals find us from every other direction. Not there. I'm worried it has to do with Kai Keda."

Kon held back a wince at the name. He had thankfully only ever been near the smaller, northern base, and it was bad enough. He didn't want to imagine what Kai Keda looked like. "You think that's where Kyro's been?" He didn't want to think about it. It would be the base he would end up at, for sure, if they found him again—a place he couldn't escape, an island with no way out.

"Has to be."

The high voice of a child snapped him out of his thoughts as he glanced back into the hall. Icelyn had returned from her trek to retrieve Jasamie and the kids, relieving her from babysitting. Kon had stuck behind to wait for her. Icelyn held Ency's hand while Jasamie continued her conversation with Kydah.

"We're back!" Icelyn said with a feigned excitement for the child in hand. Ency's usual pout on his face turned to a beam at Para as he ran for her. Toy in hand, he greeted her with a clinging hug.

Kydah was more casual when strolling in, holding her coloring book. "Do you still have that book on frogs?" she asked Jasamie, who was dusting off herself.

"I think somewhere."

"I need it for my research," Kydah stated.

"Oh, okay."

Para pulled Ency onto her lap. "Thank you. I'm sure Jasamie wouldn't mind the help from time to time."

Jasamie nodded to them quickly as Kydah explained her elaborate drawing of frogs.

"I don't mind babysitting." Icelyn grinned. "I used to babysit my cousins before they moved."

Kon started to dip from the room, moving out into the hallway again as they talked. He had never adjusted to the casual conversations within the base. Attempting to move past the events the days before was proving difficult. He had spent most of the previous day hiding from the heads of the base who either wanted a medical evaluation on him or pushed for details of their excursion. The others settled back in almost immediately. Perhaps Kon never settled in to begin with. At least the base didn't feel *as* suffocating. It had the slightest feeling of security.

With a final thanks from Para, the two emerged back into the hallway as the three started off for the entrance. Students were busy with posters again, but their attitudes were different ever since Calirue. They stood rather somber, their posters no longer focused on clubs or events. Kon had noticed it in the mounting tension. More signs advertising self-defense and survival classes, Elemental training. He didn't know if warnings from Terrance and Para had prompted it or if the general consensus of the base was to prepare for the worst.

There was a sinking guilt any time he'd catch the eye of a student putting up a poster. So much so that he kept his gaze on the tiles below as they walked.

Jasamie looked over at Kon with surprise. "I don't think I've ever seen you without your jacket."

Icelyn turned over her shoulder as Jasamie planted herself at the med bay. "We were going to go see Stormy. You?"

Jasamie stayed at the door. "I'll go see her later," she said with a huff.

"Still avoiding your dad?" Icelyn poked.

Jasamie gave a little smirk. "You two have fun." She dipped into the med bay.

In her flurry of excitement, Icelyn had mentioned it to him—the Defensive Wing med bay and how she wanted to be upgraded to working there. Kon avoided it the same as the other.

Approaching the door, Icelyn peeked her head in as Kon scanned the unfamiliar narrow hallway. "We came to check on you." Icelyn smiled as she crept into the room first.

"Oh, hey." Stormy lowered her book as Jyune rubbed a tired eye. "Ryv said I could go back to my room soon. Maybe tomorrow."

"Well, that's good, right?" Icelyn pulled at her fingerless gloves that ran up her arms.

Jyune gave a sly smirk at the mention of it. When she wasn't in the med bay with Stormy, she was eagerly preparing Stormy's room for a welcome party, gathering friends and gifts for the occasion. She had pressed Icelyn and Kon to join. While Icelyn agreed to come, Kon had been rather blank over it. It was odd seeing Jyune by herself, scurrying about the halls in preparation. The busy work of preparing a surprise seemed to distract her from her missing partner. Jasamie and Icelyn had offered her a shoulder to ride on, but she refused.

"Yeah. It's too boring in here," Stormy groaned.

"There's been lots of visitors," Jyune said. "Even Jackson came by. They brought her a flower." The comment made Stormy scrunch her nose in a lopsided grin.

"News spreads fast. You're the talk of the base—fighting an Avari." Icelyn commended.

Stormy's cheeks blushed shades of pinkish purple across her lilac skin. "Oh, come on. It was hardly a fight." Her eyes panned down to the bruise on her chest.

"The fire was pretty impressive," Kon said, crossing his arms in the mounting discomfort of the medical room. He had never seen Stormy use her power, let alone mention it.

There was a glint of pride as Stormy's face lit up. "Thanks."

"I mean, who else in this base would've squared up with an Avari besides Kon?" Jyune boasted.

"It was Icelyn's idea." Stormy chuckled. "I couldn't let her go in alone."

Kon was slow to glance at her with narrowed eyes. She noticed but avoided his gaze.

"Have you guys seen Peter?" Jyune asked as she stroked her tagune.

Icelyn pursed her lips in thought before looking at Kon. "No? Not today . . ."

Kon shook his head with her. Peter's absence *was* strange. He hadn't seen him since they returned.

"He never stopped by to get his medicine," Stormy added. "Alaura had to take it to him."

"Is he okay?"

They shrugged as Ryv appeared in the doorway, clipboard in hand. Kon had successfully avoided both med bays since he got back—and both medics. He wasn't going to fail his avoidance then. Alaura and Ryv had hardly caught a glimpse of him, despite Para's recommendation for him to get checked. She had continued fretting over his lingering symptoms—ones he didn't understand how a medic would be able to treat. They were caused by his own powers. No medic could fix that.

"Ah, I wasn't sure you'd come by," Ryv commented to Kon as he entered. "Did Para send you for a check?"

Kon was already moving for the door in an attempt to flee the appointment. "No." Alaura was no doubt also searching for him.

Icelyn stumbled after him in confusion. "Well, we'll come see you in your room tomorrow?" She waved over her shoulder as Kon dipped back into the hall.

"Yeah, sure," Stormy called. "Stop by. Jyune will have cookies."

"Yeah, *cookies*." Jyune hinted.

Back in the hall, Kon was already making his way out as the padding of Icelyn's boots treaded behind him to catch up.

"What was that about?" she asked, peering over her shoulder as they exited.

He gave a shrug. "They've all been trying to check on me."

The corner of her mouth pulled back in amusement. "They're just worried about you. I mean," she hesitated, "what *was* all that—back in the woods? With your power."

First, Para had brought it up, questioning his symptoms. It dashed his hopes that no one would bring it up. For all they knew, maybe it was normal for an Avari. But as Icelyn kept her eyes on him, he couldn't say for certain her mindset.

"I don't know. It's always done that."

"Your powers? They didn't do it the day we met—did they?" A question that showed she saw through his casual brush-off.

He shook his head reluctantly. "It just hits in waves."

"Maybe you *should* let them look? Has the nosebleed stopped?"

"Yeah." A lie, as he had stopped another bout of it that morning. It wasn't often that it flared up; an unlucky circumstance of using his powers as much as he had been since arriving there, picking fights with EME and then Kyro. It was no wonder it was getting temperamental again. He usually avoided fights. The less he used his power, the more stable it became. He just needed to let it heal—or rejuvenate. Whatever it needed to do. However, the worst flare he ever faced years before took weeks to mend. In fact, it was never truly the same after that. He simply learned to adjust to it. He changed the subject before she could question further. "Your idea, huh?"

Her face flushed slightly. "Oh, that." She shrugged. "I just wanted to help. It felt wrong to stand by."

"It was dangerous," he murmured, tone lingering in a gray area.

"I knew that. We both knew." Her smile faded a bit as she thought on it. "I just wish he had come at me instead of her. It was my idea."

The thought hurt to think about. "I'm sure she doesn't want you thinking that. Neither do I."

She gave him a coy look.

They entered back past the mural; it was strange to see no one working on it. Most days, at least one student was painting a tiny corner, adding their mark to the vast collection of colors and designs. But this day, it sat alone.

Icelyn pulled her hair over a shoulder, still wavy from the braid it had been in. "We should check on Peter."

"He's probably just busy—reading or something," Kon said.

"Maybe, but it's not like him to hide like this." They passed the several students taping posters. "It couldn't hurt to check."

Peter pulling them in for a twenty-minute lecture on Avari could definitely hurt, but Kon stayed quiet. He had those folders anyway, maybe he had found something. However, it *was* unlikely that he would make a sizable discovery and not bolt to find Kon.

Just past Para's office, a fret of commotion from inside made them both turn. "I'm not changing my mind. I've seen enough," a girl spat as she exited Para's office. Her dark straight hair fell around the large hiking bag on her back. Joining her in the hall, a Felinian boy had a similar setup: a large bag and a thick jacket.

"It's not safe out there, please," Para pressed, joining them in the hall. By then, every student nearby had turned toward the arguing.

"It's not safe in *here*," the girl bit back—words that made Para flinch as her brows creased.

Kon felt Icelyn's hand grip his sleeve ever so lightly.

"The sooner we leave, the better," the Felinian boy said, tail hanging low as he brushed his pale hair aside.

Despite the pain in Para's expression, she pushed on. "If you just give us a few days, we can relocate you somewhere safely."

"I don't think we have a few days, Para." Without another word, the girl turned for the door, followed reluctantly by the boy.

Para wavered as her head finally turned to meet the eyes of the stunned students around her. Her gaze stopped on Kon. There was a dread on her freckled face as she pursed her lips. Their eye contact lasted only a moment before she turned to follow the fleeing Elementals. Kon hadn't seen regret like that from her.

"She can't stop them all," a nearby Rilinquin said, handing another poster to their partner, who was still staring down the hall in shock. "She should stop trying to go after them."

How many students had left in the time they were gone? Kon finally turned to Icelyn, who was still holding his sleeve. Her gaze remained on the empty hall for a moment longer before she met him. Her voice came in a whisper. "Not safe here?" Her brows furrowed in worry as her hand numbly dropped to her side.

"I don't know." Kon shook his head, turning away as eyes were starting to stray from Para to him. She seemed confident in their position when he talked to her. Perhaps some students had less belief in her.

Silence stuck in the hall until they entered the dorms. Only then did Icelyn's nervous fidgeting expel words. "Nem said a few students had left. I didn't know it was this many."

"For the same reason?" Kon kept his eyes on the tiles. A reason they wouldn't say outright, no doubt. Though, he was almost surprised the girl hadn't turned to him and denounced her reason with a point. It was clear what she meant.

"I don't know." Icelyn's hands hadn't stopped stroking her wavy hair even as they approached room one hundred.

Kon hoped there would be some sign of life from the outside, but the door held no clues. Beside him, Icelyn gave the door a frown. He sucked in his pride and knocked. Nothing. Icelyn knocked next, pressing her head to the door.

"I'm busy," A muffled Peter called from within.

"Peter? It's us." She pulled back to give Kon a shrug.

The door shot open as Peter looked straight past her to Kon. He still had checkered pajama pants on, his hair fluffed in every direction. "Get in." The only words he mustered before rushing them in.

"Where have you—" Icelyn stopped short at the sight of his room, "been?"

Books, newspapers, and loose papers were organized over the floor, coating almost every inch of the dark gray faux wood underfoot. He stepped around them and placed himself back down on the pillow at the epicenter of the pile.

"Staying busy?" she asked with a twist of her brows.

Kon scanned the rest of the dimly lit room. A few club posters lined his walls. The shelves held various trophies and medals from the base's club events, while the rest of the room lay thick with books and research. The collection of papers hanging behind Peter caught his eye. It was an elaborate string of theories.

"I've got to get through all these." Peter grabbed a folder from the pile again.

"The data entries?" Kon scrunched his nose. "All of them?" He looked over the shorter pile as Peter added the current page to it, moving on to the next. All of them.

"Did you know your parents were the first Avari signed up for the program?"

"No . . ." Kon shared a glance with Icelyn.

"And the Feilar tribe—your tribe—was at war or something with another. I think that's why they wanted to come here, but they wouldn't talk about it anymore. At least not yet." His eyes stayed glued to the papers.

"And your dad?" Kon stood in the small circle of clearance around the door, looking over the wall.

"Nothing yet." Peter's replies were curt as he skimmed each page.

"Maybe you should give it a rest; eat something?" Icelyn tried.

Peter looked up from the paper, clueless. "Why?"

"Maybe some air would help. Go for a walk around the base?" Icelyn eyed the empty bags of chips.

"There's no time for that." Peter returned to reading. "The EME is probably at our doorstep."

"Para said they lost us," Kon attempted, though he hardly believed the words himself.

"Can we at least help?" Icelyn asked.

Peter had stopped reading, telling by the hard stare locked on the paper. It took a long draw of silence before he placed a worn bookmark in the folder and shut it. "I do have something else I could use some help on."

"Name it," Icelyn prompted.

Guilt flashed across Peter's face for a moment before he stood to grab his backpack. It was strewn over his bed, most contents out already. As he dug in the bottom of it, he looked over his shoulder at them. "I couldn't help it." He pulled a single tape from its hiding spot deep within his bag.

"Is that one of the tapes from Tally's?" Icelyn gasped.

"Yes."

"You stole that?" Kon was impressed more than anything, maybe even amused.

"Yes." Peter hung his head. "I saw it sitting there—away from the others. All by itself. I just . . . What if we never get that footage? I had to take *something!*"

"Why that one?" Kon eyed the tape, clutched in Peter's guilty hands.

"Because." He held it up, showing the label. "I didn't know what it meant at the time—but I think it might be important." The tape read, in heavy red ink, *Airay.*

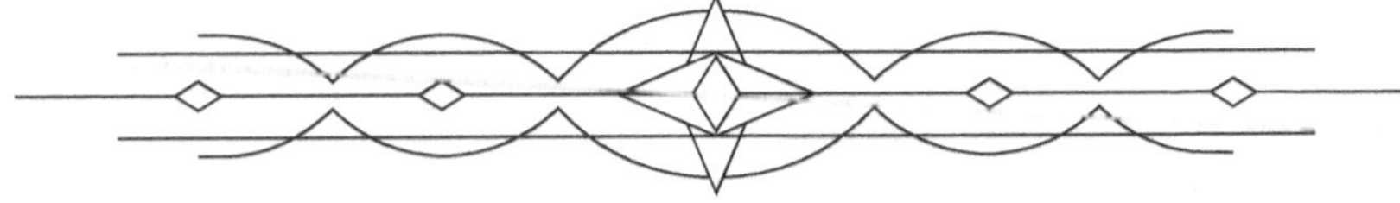

BATTLE
BR
AIRAY
TRANSLATIONS
AVARI
ARCTIC

CHAPTER

41

THE TAPE

"You stole it?" Para gasped, looking over the tape in Peter's hand.

Peter hung his head again, still hugging the tape as they stood in Para's office. "I had to," he sniffled. "I know it was wrong, but I just—"

Kon watched Para warily. She panned over the papers on her desk. "Okay." Her shoulders still held a stiff disposition, looking as though the upset from the fleeing students hadn't completely left her mind. "What do you think is on it?" The kids played on the carpet as she tried to straighten the mess across her desk. She met Peter again as he squirmed.

"Maybe something important. We need to watch it," he pushed. "Don't we have a player somewhere?"

Para massaged her temples, lacking her usual enthusiasm. "Yeah, down in the Defensive Wing." She pulled off her jacket as she stood. "Come on." She ushered the kids out of the room, plucking Ency into her arms as she walked. "We were planning to reach out to Tally about the tapes. See if he'd be willing to part with them."

"We need to. They're not safe there," Peter said, excitement back in his system as they headed down the hall.

"Well, sounds like he's had them there all this time. Hopefully, they can last a few more days."

Kon and Icelyn stayed quiet as they followed. Peter was out of his room at least.

Para stopped at Terrance's office, peeking her head in while the others waited distantly. "Can you watch them?"

Terrance looked up from his paper, his expression soft before it lingered past her to Kon where it hardened. "What's going on now?" He stood, meeting her at the door as he looked over the sight before him. Peter looked worse for the wear while Kon and Icelyn stared back at him in contempt.

"We just need to use the V player." She huffed, handing the toddler over as Kydah zipped about the halls.

Terrance tapped her arm. "You okay?"

"It's just been a long day." Para sighed, giving a tired grin as she started down the halls again. He nodded and backed off, his usual curt demeanor seeming to vanish in the presence of his children. He called Kydah over to him with a smile, watching them leave. It was a side of him Kon had rarely seen.

He had also never seen the Defensive Wing that deep in as they traveled past the med bay and down the staircase. The second floor wasn't much different, with smaller hallways leading to offices and storage mostly.

Para counted out the doors as though she wasn't confident in her direction. "Should be this one," she said, pushing it open. Inside, the room was dark and dusty, suggesting hardly anyone came down there. As she flicked on the lights, it looked to be some small closet of sorts. In the center of the room sat an old, outdated video player attached to a projector, aimed at the blank wall. Cabinets lined the rest of the walls, full of other tapes and electronics.

As Peter clutched the tape, he circled the projector. "Does it work?"

"Hopefully." Para looked over the triangular player, tapping it to life.

Peter's eyes stayed glued on the device, unsettled as he waited impatiently. Kon checked the hall one last time before closing the door.

"What do you think it is?" Icelyn asked.

Peter was too distracted dusting off the projector lens to bother with theories.

Kon could only guess what the tape contained. Its title was telling, but what more could it possibly tell?

"Okay, let's see if it works," Para muttered, shutting the lights off as the projector lit the wall with a blank square of light.

Peter carefully fumbled the tape into the V player, nearly shaking with excitement. The screen turned a dark shade as the quiet sound of the outdated player spun the tape inside. Everyone waited. Even to Kon, it felt like a painfully long few seconds before the screen flashed and the tape began. It was an office, the camera shaky as someone fidgeted it into place. They let out a sigh as it finally straightened out and they moved to the chair, plopping into frame. The only sound was Peter sucking in a gasp of realization. "Dad." The man brushed his messy blond hair aside, straightening his glasses. Andren Day.

"I'm afraid I don't have much time," Day began, voice coated in thick defeat as he spoke to the camera. "I'm sorry to bring you into this. I have to split up my evidence. It won't be long before they try to wipe away everything I've unearthed. So, this next piece is going to you. I entrusted you to keep other tapes safe. I hope you'll protect this one as well."

Despite the shock from Peter, Kon had entirely frozen. He had never seen Andren Day in Peter's passing mention of him, only the blurred photos from the database. But *that* man . . . he had *seen* that man. A deep, forgotten fear crept up his spine.

No one spoke as Day continued. "I hope you'll forgive me for this decision. I hope *everyone* will forgive me." He shook his head, pinching the bridge of his nose. "It's currently November thirteenth, year 2654. The child is in the custody of the EME."

Hit with the immediate sinking pit in his stomach, Kon could only stare. His mind started to search for the familiar face in the dark, suppressed memories. It wasn't a tape from the AIP facility.

"They contacted me requesting again to help them—further their exploration. I rejected their games with Kyros over fifteen years ago. But . . . I've accepted their offer this time to oversee the progress of this boy. It's my only way to save him. I don't know if I can forgive myself for what it's going to take to get him out. It's my only chance. I'll try to update."

Kon could feel Icelyn's and Para's eyes on him as they both realized the words being said. It didn't matter, though; Kon's gaze was set on the man. He knew that man. The pit in his stomach knew that man. In an instant, the memories swept over him: Andren Day approached him in the tiny room in that base. He was accompanied by several masked EME. Plenty of officers and scientists funneled in and out. He might not have remembered him if it wasn't for his comment. *"It's nice to meet you, Konali."* No one else knew his name, let alone his full name. He convinced himself at the time they had gotten it from his parents, who scarcely used it. *"I hope we'll be able to help each other in this,"* Day had said, giving him a curt smile. At the time, it was nothing too strange. He hadn't had the energy to think of it as weird. He had already been told plenty of backhanded promises of better treatment in trade for complying. It was never true.

The next memory crawled itself into his head as his thoughts hunted deep for the face. Day stood over him, next to the EME soldiers, watching him with pity. *"It won't work with him in this condition,"* Day said to the men. *"You can't keep Vinralin radiation going this long. Are you trying to kill him?"*

Another swirl of memories faded in and out. Day approached him again in a cold room he had spent too much time in. He looked over him with a scrunch in his face, examining his condition like countless others had. There was only disappointment in his expression. He was one of the few faces that wasn't covered. *"We can try a test. See if he's ready."* Without much interest, he was gone again. The test hurt.

Kon was back in the dusty projector room where the camera cut for a moment. Everything had closed in on him. His breathing, the room. He hardly even noticed Icelyn's hand brush his. Her focus had dropped from the video to looking him over in silent worry.

When Day appeared again before the camera, he was wearing a uniform. A sickly familiar one. An EME scientist. The lab coat and gray patterned undercoat were burned into his brain. Kon knew it instantly. It always meant something bad was about to happen. Day's eyes were dark circles, as his previous energy was gone. He sat before the camera somberly.

"It's December eighteenth," he breathed. "I made progress. I convinced them of the tests we needed to run. They're tomorrow. This is my only chance to free him. If I do this right, he'll free himself." His eyes were hazy, tired. "When this works, if I make it out, I'll have to run. Either way, I'll be gone. Don't look for me. Look for him. Contact the EPS, maybe. I can't. They're watching me—but we have to get help for him and Kyros. I'll never forgive myself for this. I don't expect him to forgive me either. The test will need to be harder than I hoped." Day faltered for a moment, squeezing his eyes shut as if the thought burned his brain. "They don't know what I know. That's my only advantage. They won't be prepared when I set it off. I know he can do it."

One final memory flashed, one that was blurred and distorted. All he usually remembered was the pain of it. But the familiar face appeared again, crouched to his level. His face held something of worry, maybe panic. *"Come on. We're going to try it one more time. Give it your all."* Kon's only response was feebly shaking his head as he sat on the floor, blood from his nose forming a puddle in front of him. *"One more."* His voice was urgent. *"Give it everything, Konali. Please."* The last word came in a whisper. Day and the EME personnel retreated behind the heavy glass again.

One more time.

The words echoed in his head. *What I know about him.* It all started to make sense. Andren Day knew. Maybe he was the one who diagnosed him as Airay, to begin with—but he knew. Had the test been to trigger his flaw? His one shot at escaping?

The video cut to black as the player hummed with no tape left to wind. Silence hit the room. Stunned, wordless silence.

Andren Day.

Kon needed to get away from the reality of it. Peter's father was responsible. The man who knew the most of Avari, who had fought hardest on their side. He was *there*. For his own good or not, he took part in nearly killing him. Or killing everything that made him a person.

Kon didn't even notice Peter was staring at him until Para spoke. "Kon . . .?" Her mouth stayed parted in shock.

Next to her, Peter was watching him, a similar sorrow on his face, but at that moment, all he saw was Andren Day. Energy was seeping out, still anxious and unstable, as it festered around him, looking for something to condense. Looking for the threat that felt so very real in that room.

The V player crunched, whirling as the tape hissed to a stop in the crushed machine. With the *crunch*, they all recoiled, Kon included, who fumbled for the door. There wasn't enough air in that closet. His power was still on the defense. It wasn't safe in that room, for anyone.

Icelyn had reached for his hand in an attempt to slow him down. "Kon, wait," she said, but he pulled his hand from her grasp, escaping into the hall as the wave of memories swallowed him whole.

Icelyn stood, her empty hand still reaching for nothing as light from the hallway illuminated the dark room.

"I didn't know . . ." Peter breathed, his eyes welling with tears as he stared at the door. "I didn't know," he stuttered again, backing into the cabinet behind him.

"Okay—okay. Just," Para looked between him and the door. "Let's just, calm down for a minute." Her eyes latched onto Icelyn as she found her way over to Peter, who was starting to audibly weep.

Icelyn's stun wore off quickly, only a single thought. *Go after him.* She didn't waste a second breaking into the hallway, her mind spinning with the confession she had just witnessed. What had happened to Kon? What had Peter's father done? Surely, something evil—but to free him? It didn't matter. Kon was already gone from the hall. *Outside.* He would want to get outside. Were the doors still locked? Worry setting in deeper, she ran for the stairs, yanking the heavy door open as another door closed above her. "Kon?" She raced up the stairs, nearly tripping as she tried to keep pace. Back in the main hallway, there was only base staff in the halls. Her pace kept steady as she ran for the doors. There was one pressing thought; she had to reach him before he hit the woods or she'd never find him.

Ahead, Terrance was exiting his office, confusion across his face as an alarm rang out. "What's going on?" he asked, turning toward the door, but Icelyn dodged him, heading into the mural room. That's when she saw it—the cause for the alarm. The front door had been ripped open, bent in warps of terrashock, nearly torn from its hinges. "Icelyn?" Terrance called again.

She only looked back once as she kept for the door. Daylight peeked through the open hatch as cold air swept into the hall.

"Icelyn?" Jasamie echoed from the direction of the med bay, but Icelyn didn't dare stop.

Up the stairs and into the field, she could finally see Kon moving across the rocky field toward the woods. "Kon!" she shouted again. Tall grass flung aside as she ran for him. "Stop!" What was her plan? Maybe there was a fault in her judgment as she approached, but it didn't matter. She had to try.

Pops of terrashock disturbed the grass around him as she made the last stride to him, just short of the woods. In her better mind, she might've tried a slower approach. But in the chilled air of the field, there was only one thing she could think to do. She pushed straight through the energy around him, grabbing for his hand. That time, she didn't let it slip away. "Stop." As he turned to face her, she didn't hesitate, wrapping her arms around him. A beg for him not to run.

He didn't.

"I'm sorry," she said, the only words she could find. "I'm sorry. It's okay." Her face was buried into his shirt. Cool air breezed past them as they stood under the old oak tree, alone in the field. He was unmoving for a long while as she kept her hold. Then gently, slowly, she felt his arms wrap around her in return. Gradually, his grip tightened, until it matched her own, and she could feel his chin rest on the top of her head.

Birds whistled in the nearby forest. Her head stayed at his chest, listening to the sound of his heartbeat, his slowing breaths. The panic in her own chest started to melt as his warmth drifted over her. Words weren't needed. She hoped he felt the same relief she did in their embrace. A hug that felt right, overdue. Time could stop there for a while, in the peace of it all. As soon as they broke, the world would start moving again.

Questions would be asked; answers would be needed. They both knew that. So, for that long still moment, they stayed.

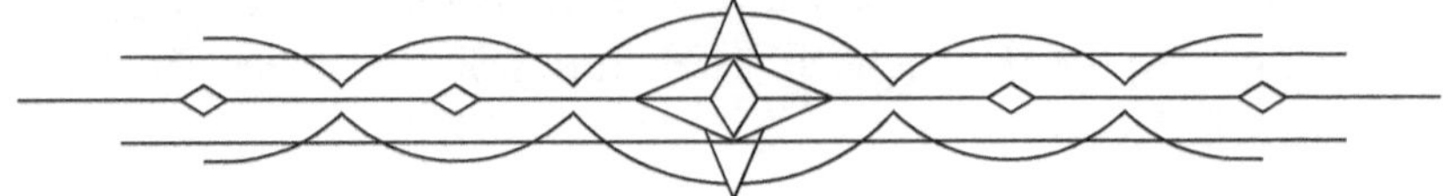

CHAPTER 42
METAMORPHOSIS

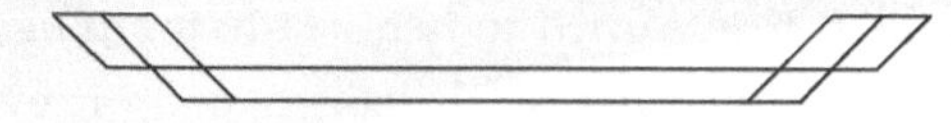

NOVEMBER 17TH, 2647

Ten years since Avari left.

"Can I do it?"

"Just this once."

Fire ignited in the eager hand. One by one, it lit the candles.

"Okay, okay, not too much," Seelia said, grinning at him. "Now, blow them out."

Kon smiled upon his successfully burning birthday candles, settling the licks of flames at his hand as he took a breath to blow them out.

"Alright. Here's to ten big ones, yeah?" Jack leaned on the table, taking a snag of frosting from the hefty vanilla cake covered in chocolate frosting. "Now, give me some of this. I almost snuck down here to eat it last night."

"I'd say this is a new best cake of mine," Seelia stated as she pulled out the plates. Her warm brown eyes watched Kon. "Did you wish for something?"

He scrunched his face for a moment. "Yeah." His lips pursed, content on keeping his wish to himself.

"You know what I wish for?" Jack hummed, still eyeing the cake as Seelia cut slices. "Another trip to Venderwal for Light Day."

Kon's face lit up. "Are we going back?" He slid his plate closer as she laid the cream-colored cake before him, decorated in thick chocolate icing.

"Mmm, we'll see," Seelia grinned. "Eat up, we don't want to miss the bus."

They ate through their cake swiftly, and Kon was off, rushing to the door to grab his jacket. His excitement could hardly wait as Seelia and Jack readied themselves.

After a painfully long several minutes, they finally met him at the door. He reached for the handle as a soft hand plucked at his hair. "Let me see," Seelia said as Kon turned to her, nearly jumping to get out the door. Her hand fluffed the sides of his hair, swiping it over his pointed ears before she nipped at his nose. "Okay."

The door shot open as Kon raced down the steps past the frozen winter flowers.

Calin was along one of Brynden Ka's few lower airway systems. It allowed fast travel on their part as they took the short walk through the neighborhood toward the station. Jack always caught the bus in the morning to work, but Kon rode it far less often. Seelia was adamant about keeping him away from such a busy place, save for special occasions.

As they stood in line to board, Seelia fidgeted in her dress and shawl. Her hand traced over his hair a few more times before she pulled up his hood entirely. The wide track of the airway levitated the hoverbus as they boarded, humming in its familiar noisy rumble. Seelia was quick to pick a seat away from others in the far corner of the bus, seating Kon on the last seat as she and Jack blocked the rest of the occupants view of him. By then, he was used to her fussing. It was normal, constant.

Kon didn't know why she was so defensive of him, avoiding onlookers and conversation any time they were in public, lifting up his hood when his hair failed to cover his ears, and ensuring no one looked too closely at him. He knew plenty of Rilinquin kids with pointed ears, so he didn't know why it mattered. The seats filled around them until most were full, and the bus started off down the track, lifting in elevation slowly as it joined the rest of the floating traffic above. He always enjoyed the window, turning his back to the crowd to watch the trees below them grow more and more distant.

They had promised to take him to the Brynden Ka Nature Museum. Months before, his school has planned the trip for his class. When Seelia and Jack heard of it, they refused. Seelia removed him from school that day, not willing to let him go that far alone. She tried to explain it to him lightly that it wasn't his fault, and she would make it up to him. She never told him why he couldn't go, though.

Kon turned back in his seat, grinning ear to ear as he sat in the safety of his hidden seat. Looking about the strange steel metal interior, Kon peeked around Seelia to peer at the rest of the bus. The patterned blue rug trailed down the center walkway, lined with bags and seated people. Turbulence had smoothed as they levitated on the lower airstream. He could feel Seelia's hand graze his hood, fixing it into place once more as he sat back.

The man across from him adjusted his newspaper, holding it up to read. Kon knew he should avoid looking at people to prevent showing his eyes. It was always a rule of theirs, but the paper across from him drew his attention. The title of the newspaper stuck out to him, a familiar word in bold letters:

Brynden Ka News Today:
10 Years Since Avari Left.

The image below was of a group of people. Several of them towered over the humans, inky markings across their skin. He had heard of them before, Avari, but not often. Only in passing magazines and newspapers that Seelia and Jack read. He had noticed her getting more anxious lately, specifically with him going to school or leaving the house. Several times a week, she had been checking his arms and cheeks with a look of something—worry, but he never saw anything to concern her.

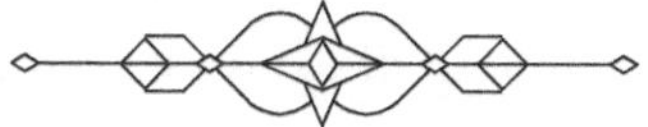

It was dark by the time they got back. Seelia pulled the soft sheets across his chest, drawing her hand gently over his messy hair. There had been a sadness over her most of the day. A muted one he hardly noticed, but as she brushed his curly hair, her face was twisted in a pained smile. "Happy birthday," she said with a pursed grin.

"Goodnight." Kon grinned back, afraid to ask why her eyes didn't match her smile.

She headed for the door, dodging the few toys across the carpet. There was a whispered *goodnight* as the door shut quietly.

Kon wondered why they couldn't always go on trips like that. Even a trip to the market was usually off-limits unless he pleaded with Seelia the majority of the week. He understood they couldn't afford many trips, but even simple ones out into town were usually turned away to the cautious shoulder of them both. Maybe there were things about the world he didn't understand yet.

Drifting off to sleep, a raised voice shook him from his daze. It was strange enough for him to sit up completely. His parents rarely fought as he listened to the muffled response. Curiosity drew him from the bed, moving to pull the door open silently. He crept into the narrow hall, crawling to peek down the stairs. They were in the kitchen, their voices a bit clearer, just out of sight.

"Shhh, we don't need to wake him over this," Jack said. "We don't even know that they'll come in."

"Seven to ten, Jack. That's what we've been reading." Seelia's voice was strained in a hush. "What if this is his last *normal* birthday?"

"Okay, well we shouldn't think like that—"

"We have to!"

There was an audible sigh from Jack, followed by a long silence. "Nothing has come in yet. Maybe him being here just—made them not come? A deficiency or something?"

Seelia was silent in her upset before her words came slowly. "And what if they *do* come in?"

"Then, we've been planning this since he was a day old, Seelia. We know what to do. We'll check his arms before school, try and catch it before it sneaks up on us."

No more words came as the house fell into silence again.

Kon drew back from the step, stumped. He found himself looking over his arms in confusion, looking for whatever scary marks they worried over. What were they anticipating appearing? His mind drifted back to the train and the newspaper article that stared him in the face. The Avari and their strange, long jagged markings.

Her words stuck in his head. *Last normal birthday?*

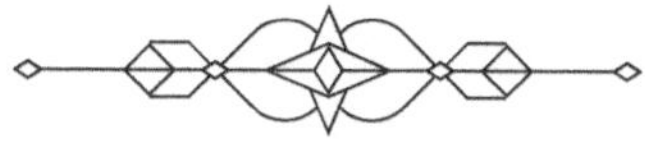

NOVEMBER 17TH, 2655

Eighteen years since Avari left.

Kon took a quick glance over the dark markings that strayed onto the top of his hand before fixing his sleeve over them. There was another moment collecting himself as he pulled his bag off its perch on the knarled tree roots. The trees here were giant. Tall reddish trunks scaled high into the sky, where their dark evergreen branches blocked the majority of the high sun. He couldn't stay on the path long, merely following it until its supposed bank up ahead. Heading straight from there would lead him back into the south. It would mark the third time he'd strayed down that way.

Circling Core Sector in small and wide circles seemed to be his best tactic. If EME got too heavy, he would switch direction and move inland or out. Each rotation around the sector would take him several months. None of his rotations ever left him free of EME encounters, but they were becoming a regular occurrence.

A tiny murmur in the brush brought his attention from muddling in his pockets, where an orange cat emerged onto the trail, letting out a trill of greeting—maybe the only face he welcomed anymore—as it quickly brushed itself against his boots. He crouched to welcome it. *There must be a house nearby. All the more reason to keep moving.* After a good minute of petting the ginger cat, he departed.

Walking straight past the bend on the trail, it took the rest of the day to cross into the south. He figured he was getting close as the mountains in the distance seemed to be leveling out. Turning from the cliff, he dipped back into the darkness of the woods. There had been the *hum* of a hoverform somewhere in the sky for a good portion of the day. It was too distant to worry about, but he did know EME could be anywhere, especially where he passed through. He had come to learn it was a popular place for Elementals to pass as well, all trying to avoid the busier fuss of Core Sector.

Avoiding towns had been the more important change in his routine. Becoming fully self-sufficient left the EME little trails for his location. The only information they got on him anymore was scout party calls or responding to "maydays." Arriving at the distress signals usually only revealed a heap of EME, the ground charred around them. Not many Elementals were that bold; it was likely obvious who left the damage.

As the sky was darkening, Kon's rather peaceful travel was interrupted by the hurried shove of brush in the thicket. Pausing, he stood in the clearing to listen. The running was fast approaching, but it wasn't EME. That much he knew. Moments later, a group of three teens burst out of the brush, backpacks heavy on each of them. They all gasped as they came to face him, nearly falling over each other—two teen girls and a boy. In the pastel sky, the only thing he could make of them was the tattered clothes and clear stress on their flushed faces. Elementals.

The group must've quickly gathered he wasn't the threat they were avoiding as they straightened out. The girl in front took in a deep breath. "EME are coming," she stuttered, a warning to him. "They're following us." It must've been easy to guess he was at the least another Elemental to them. Her blonde hair stuck to her face as she pulled at her backpack, the other two clinging behind her.

Kon didn't often seek out Elementals. In truth, he avoided them the same amount he avoided the EME, figuring them together was a potent mix for danger. But that girl reminded him of someone. Another Elemental he had met, long ago, fighting to get to safety. Her hair was similar, honey blonde, over her face, though this girl had plenty of life still in her. He looked past them, where the lights were coming into sight. Without much thought, he nodded to the less traveled trail he had roughly been following. "Go."

Without any protest, the group rushed past him and back into the woods. The blonde girl flashed him a look of worry mixed with relief before she was gone.

Kon stayed put, waiting for the group of EME to follow. The scouting party wouldn't find the Elementals they sought.

Four of them pushed out of the thicket, the same as the others had. If their masks could've shown shock, every one of them would've had it as they came face to face with the tall figure before them. They held obvious confusion, first raising their guns before they dropped, then raising them again. "Where did they go?" one spat as the others slowly came to the realization.

Kon tilted his head at them in disappointment. It usually didn't take them that long to realize.

"Call it in—it's another one," one growled, just as the air around them ignited in fire and terrashock. The four men flew back in the blast, their thick vests crunching with the force.

Kon still hadn't moved much, unwavering. He might've even looked bored as he sent another bump of terrashock at one attempting to get up. They didn't move after that.

To his left, the last moving form sat up, yanking off his dented mask as he fought for breath. The unmasked man finally met Kon's gaze. "Stop, please," the EME soldier coughed, raising his hands as a trickle of blood ran down his temple, staining his dark hair. "I'll leave. I won't call them. Just—just let me—"

The air crunched again, and the man went silent, falling back to the forest floor.

Kon had stopped hesitating long before.

He lingered for a moment longer as the forest fell quiet again before he turned to head back into the woods, shoving his hands in his pockets.

CHAPTER

43

WHAT WAS LOST

Present Day

Entering back into the base proved difficult. Icelyn's gentle nudges hadn't worked, but she didn't push Kon on it. Instead, they sat in the setting sun with the company of the several stray cats that had come to know Kon and his similar nature. They quickly found the two and sat in the grass, making themselves at home with the company.

Kon wouldn't say anything more about what Andren Day had discussed. It was clear enough something bad happened. Icelyn didn't ask. Pulling at the long grass instead, she talked. About anything that came to mind. About her thriving plant she had saved, about Stormy's surprise party. The outfits she had snagged at The Closet, and how she had witnessed two girls fighting over a shirt. Anything to bump the bad thoughts from his mind.

Hidden in the shade of one of the lone trees and the grass around them, Kon simply sat, folding tall wisps of grass into each other. He and Mallia had done that often, making tiny woven bracelets from the long blades.

Icelyn was pleased with the finding. "My mom taught me to make them too." She grinned, braiding her own grass as she sat across from him.

There wasn't much commotion from the Base. At one point, they had noticed what looked to be Para peek out at them through the open hatch, but she merely dipped back down upon confirming they hadn't strayed far. Kon imagined Terrance wouldn't be pleased with the door being destroyed. If he had an ounce of thought at the moment, he might've simply demanded they unlock it. Para had promised they would if he asked. He believed her to a degree. But it was an unfortunate barrier that got in his way at the wrong time.

He'd apologize later.

Words weren't finding him, and the only person who wouldn't demand conversation was Icelyn—his one current tether to the Base. While her best attempts wouldn't save him from the damage done years before, it helped. Maybe no one could cure the waves that washed over him, but she had at least interrupted it. That's all he could really ask for and more than he expected. They were both new to that base, and in the fresh confusion of base life, they had found each other; A comforting outlier to everyone else's fast-paced life in the safe house. Maybe it's why they took to each other so well.

As his mind started to clear out the fog of memories, it uncovered what he hadn't noticed at the time in that dusty room. The look on Peter's face. Pure guilt. It wasn't his fault. Peter couldn't have known anything that had gone down. His steadfast urge to get to the bottom of the mystery had been successful, but it was a painful success. Then there was Para's face. Sorrowful, but knowing. He didn't want to know how much the base knew. Maybe he avoided safe houses for that reason. It brought too many things to the surface. Things he had spent years outrunning, mentally and physically. As tasking as his nomadic life had been, it was easier to run away from it all. That's all he had been doing his whole life. Running. Hiding.

Kon was born into fleeing, after all. He might've even been the cause of it. If he was the reason the Avari left, maybe he was running from himself, and no amount of distance would escape that.

Rays of the sun were dipping beneath the distant mountains, staining the sky purple in the last drops of daylight. Icelyn tied the loose ends on her bracelet, looking it over in pride. Between conversation and visits from cats, she had successfully woven her straw bracelet. "And . . . done." She held it up, a grin of satisfaction with her work.

Kon looked over his own. It had been a while since he made one.

"Here," she said. "It's for you." She had been stealing glances while making it, estimating the right size. Her hand extended for his, taking it gingerly as she fastened the braided grass bracelet on his wrist. Her hands weren't as cold as usual, careful not to disturb his sleeve as she adjusted her creation. It was intertwined with a few tiny white fall flowers. One of the only things budding in the cold field.

His eyes grazed over it to her, giving her the smallest grin. "Trade?" He held his out to her.

"Yeah," she smiled, presenting her own hand for him. Her hand was soft as he pulled the ends of the bracelet secure. The smile stuck on her face as she examined it. "I love it."

Night would be setting in soon. The field had already grown dewy and chilled, and the singing of nightlife critters was already beginning; a few lonesome crickets, a distant owl. A cool breeze brought only the lingering smell of the forest. He was starting to feel safe. Was it the woods, or the Base making him feel that way? Maybe it was Icelyn.

Her next words came slow as her gaze flickered from her new gift to him. "Are you ready to go back in?"

As decently comfortable as he had gotten with the base, it still didn't beat the peace he felt out there. But all the reasons she would tell him and that he told himself were right. There were still answers to find. Safety to seek. The base provided those. He let out a small sigh. "Yeah."

"Come on." She stood, unwrapping herself from the few cats that lay around her. Dusting herself off, her hand extended with a grin. Her pale hair was nearly glowing in the soft twilight. He hesitated before accepting her offer. She pulled his hand in, holding it close with both hands. "We match again," she cooed, comparing their bracelets side by side as she led him back to the hatch.

They had parted by the time they reached the door, preparing for time to start moving again. Down the stairs, cats had let themselves in through the bent door as more followed behind Kon and Icelyn. The mural room had become a hub for the social cats.

Deyin was attempting to unscrew the bent bolts of the hinge while Terrance stood nearby with Para. His disposition was one more of concern as he rubbed Para's arm in comfort. Their children and several students were welcoming the few cats by petting them. The Stray Cats Club had no plans of missing their chance of cats infiltrating the base once again. Most looked up to watch the two's reappearance.

Terrance said nothing as Kon approached Para again, reluctantly. His gaze held on the floor, turning back to glance at the door. "Sorry."

To his utter surprise, there was no retort from Terrance—hardly any flash of anger at all in his tone as his hand held gently on Para's arm. "We'll get it fixed."

"Do you want to talk . . . in my office?" Para asked, her hands cautiously at her stomach. Her eyes shone even darker bags than earlier. When he gave a shrug, she beckoned him to follow, pulling him from the cold air still wafting through the door. Past the med bay, Jasamie lingered at the door, watching them in confusion. Upon reaching the office, Para paused, glancing back to Icelyn. "Can you give us a few?"

Icelyn stayed put in the hall, giving a pursed grin. "Yeah." She retreated slightly as Jasamie approached. Kon gave her a last look. She nodded to him, maybe a silent confirmation that he *should* talk to Para before he closed the door behind him.

The room was still messy with paperwork. At a glance, he could see the papers on her desk were something of exit forms for the students that had departed. There were more of them than he thought. Para let out a tired sigh as her chair swiveled to face her digiscreen.

"Where's Peter?" Kon asked, lingering closer.

"I don't know. I calmed him down a bit. I think he went to his room." She pushed the loose hair from her braid aside, giving her head a disappointed shake. "He just needs to process it, like you."

Peter had gotten part of the answer he wanted. He knew the reason, but it still didn't answer what happened after. When the flare hit, Kon knew the damage it caused. He saw the destruction, the lifeless heaps on the floor. Had Peter's father even made it out? He grimaced at the thought. Maybe he had. He would have to be in hiding anyway. The EME would be furious about his betrayal.

When no response came, Para started again, resting her elbows on the desk. "I know you don't want to discuss what happened with the EME," she bit her lip, "but does this have to do with what's been happening to your power?"

He sighed, crossing his arms over his torso. In all honestly, he was surprised she hadn't pushed him on it more until then. There had been an obvious attempt to give him space. He could appreciate that. "You really want to know?"

"I wouldn't ask if I didn't think it was important." Her stare stayed steady, but there was clear hope in her eyes. Hope that he could at least trust her to some degree, enough to tell her.

With a deep breath, he finally sat down across from her.

He told her everything.

About the first time his powers acted up. The event in Calka, the unfortunate EME that met his first flare. How, ever since, they built in instability over time, bringing bouts of nosebleeds as the first sign. He told her it got worse after the EME incident, taking weeks to stabilize enough to viably use it without it blowing up in fits of explosive energy. How each one seemed to chip away at something, leaving his power different and in need of relearning. Even then, he was suppressing the change in it. He'd have to face it soon enough and learn the new normal of his unstable energy. Then he told her about Peter and his discovery in that base. His "diagnosis," according to the Avari. The flaw in his system. He had never told someone so much.

Para stayed silent through most of it, asking the occasional small question, only when he would pause. At the end, she sat rather somberly, in thought of it all. "Do you think he . . . damaged something?" speaking of Andren Day.

Kon had always wanted to blame EME for "breaking" his powers, but in reality, the instability had always been there. They, or specifically, Peter's father, had merely activated the flaw. Kon wondered how he even knew to trigger it like that, in a way that nearly caved in the solid, thick facility. *He* couldn't even use his powers like that. Yet somehow, Andren Day knew how. Maybe there was something deeper to it. "I don't know. It's always acted up. It just got worse after that." He tried to keep the fresh memories at bay. "Sounded like he knew what he was doing." For better or worse, Peter's dad knew all along.

Para twisted her braid in her hand, deep in thought. To his surprise, she hadn't written or typed anything down the entire time. She merely listened to his every word, soaking it in. "And you think they knew about this before you were born?"

"Seems like it," he shrugged. "I guess that's why they left me here."

With a twist in her expression, she tilted her head at him. With her voice just above a whisper, she spoke carefully. "You don't know that."

"You think it was something else?" His question was genuine, but he didn't see any better theories. Perhaps new eyes on the information could bring more answers. Something he hadn't thought of before.

Her hand ran over her braid in thought. "Sometimes, people do stupid things to protect people they love." There was a flicker of memory in her gaze on her desk as she contemplated saying more. "My father fled off planet with me to Koron to 'save me' from the EME. It was the worst thing he ever could've done for me, but he didn't know that."

His hands fidgeted with each other in his lap as he shrugged, eyeing the woven grass bracelet. "They couldn't have thought I was safe here."

"I know. But I think you're more than you think you are." Her words hung in the air as he watched her. Her eyes stayed set on his. "You're not flawed." Behind those misty, storm-colored eyes, she meant it. She believed.

No response came. His stare only faltered, falling to the floor in thought.

Para continued. "I won't pretend to know what's going to help you. That kind of trauma isn't . . . an easy fix. You know that. But I'll do what I can to keep you away from resurfacing it." The cards and drawings painted a mural behind her. "What I do know is that you being with us has effectively pushed the EME into an erratic state. That might not sound good—or look good—but it is. It means we're doing something right. I can't convince everyone of that, but I hope you feel it too. We're close."

Kon's gaze on the floor lingered. Years before, he thought he had learned EME movements. They always got "erratic" when closing in on him, but not like that. Not to the level of sending an Avari after him. Peter had said something similar, that their frenzied state was a good sign, even with its present danger. It meant that they had no control over the situation and they were grasping for a hold. Regardless, EME being so close was enough to trigger fear in the students and even himself. "Why are students leaving?"

Her head shook in defeat as it took a long moment for her to form the words. "They're scared. We knew this would get worse before it got better. It's going to keep being scary. And I can't tell them it won't be. I can't stop them if they feel like they're in danger. We are." It was clear the words stung as her nose scrunched in the unfortunate reality of it. "But we've always been in danger, and to fight this, we have to turn and face them."

Them. It wasn't just the EME they had to face. It was the entire nation. A whole planet. As it was, the nation was currently behind the EME. Not that they knew everything they did. The EME was always smart about their image. Their lies of "wanting what's best and safest for Elementals and the nation." It was a clever, evil con. Para had mentioned the Elemental Protection System had the goal of shifting the media's image. Turning the nation on the EME was likely the only true way out.

The next words she spoke came gentler. "We really did try to find you after—you got out."

Maybe if he had let himself be helped those years before, he'd be more ready to face his looming future. He ran his fingers over the shaky dark markings extending onto the tops of his hands as if trying to wipe them away. "I didn't want to be found." The EME had successfully cut him off from any help he should've taken. Any love that tried to protect him. He cut it all off, thinking it was for the better. Was it?

"Then you found me instead." Para grinned. "Why did you . . . help me?"

Recalling the scene he had watched unfold, the truth came easier. "You reminded me of someone. Felt wrong to walk away."

She held her gaze. "Does it still feel wrong to walk away?"

It was a hard question. A double-edged sword. Abandoning the base, leaving them to fend for themselves or staying there as the EME closed in on him. Either way, he was putting himself and others at risk. But when he thought about it—the mounting tiny ties that had attached him to this base—the answer slipped out. "Yeah." He finally met her eyes. "I don't want to regret that." Getting involved like he was meant facing parts of his life he prayed he could forget. Maybe Joel was right. Running wouldn't always save him. Eventually, he would have to face it—in the form of picking apart his past, the past of the Avari, to find the key. Maybe to save himself. Or face the reality of the EME catching up to him again.

Andren Day wouldn't be there to save him next time—if he could even bring himself to call that *saving* him. The EME surely wouldn't make the same mistake again either. Even if he wanted to leave the base, he couldn't face Kyro alone. That much he knew.

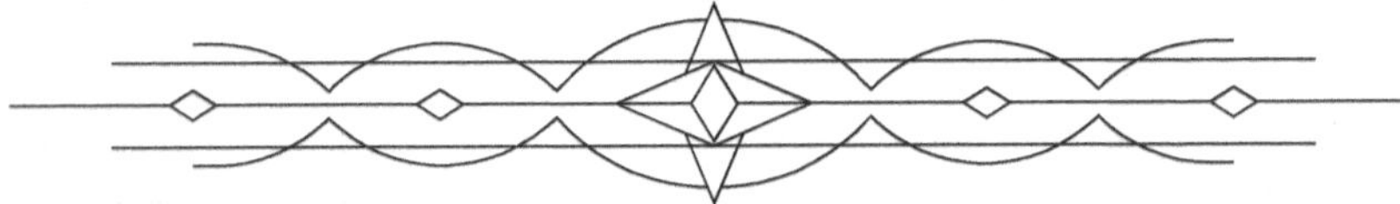

Icelyn watched the children bounce around the rug in the small living room, flying their toys over invisible obstacles. Her eyes trailed the warm interior of the apartment. "I didn't even know they had apartments like this."

Jasamie stirred the pot on the stove, glancing over her shoulder to Icelyn, who leaned on the table in her large sweater. "Yeah, they're mostly for staff and families that come through."

Located on the Defensive Wing's second floor, Icelyn had only come down that far to retrieve Jasamie and the kids for Para. They both sat in the apartment, sharing the task of babysitting. It was becoming a comfort being there, helping the base. It was possibly the first time she had stopped running from everything. She was so used to shying away from confrontation, trying to hide away as possibly the only Elemental in Alinth. Finally standing up to defend something felt—good.

"So, is Kon okay? After the—" Jasamie flipped the macaroni back into the cheese, thinking of the right word as she pulled at her yellow scarf. "The door?"

Icelyn pursed her lips, looking over the children's drawings stuck onto the brown fridge. "Yeah, I think he's okay." The guilt of it all still struck her hard. She didn't know *why* she felt guilty, but she did. Maybe it wasn't guilt she was feeling that twisted in her stomach at the thought of Kon's expression on that tape. After what he told her on the cliff, maybe nothing could make her heart stop aching at the thought of it all.

Jasamie was quiet, but as she sat back to wait on the pot, there was a grin across her face. "You two have gotten pretty close, huh?"

"Me and Kon? I mean, maybe." Her words came fast from her mouth as her eyes darted to the wooden cabinets. "We're both new and got here at the same time—I've made a lot of friends, I think. I guess . . . he's been one of them, yeah?" she winced at her own words.

If Icelyn's embarrassing spill didn't spring a haze of blush over her cheeks, Jasamie's laugh definitely did. "Relax," she said. "It's cute."

"What do you mean?" Icelyn asked, unhinging her hand from the wood of the chair she hadn't noticed she grabbed.

"I mean, he's pretty—aloof, you know? It's nice to see him trust someone."

"He's coming around." Icelyn sunk into the chair next to her, distracting herself by diverting her gaze to the children, closely discussing their share of toys. Ency made his way over to her, clutching the old stuffed cat plush. No words came as he watched her with doleful eyes. His shaggy black hair reminded Icelyn of Kon's, curly and messy around his face.

Jasamie took to the pot again, giving Icelyn another sly smirk as she started mixing. "Yeah. Maybe." She chuckled, glancing back as Ency placed his hand on Icelyn's knee. She tested the consistency of the macaroni and cheese before clicking off the oven. Placing the bowls at the table, Jasamie called over Kydah before she plopped down in the extra chair, giving Icelyn a tilt of the head. "I'm glad you've warmed up well here. It's not always the easiest."

"It helped to make friends." Icelyn twirled a strand of her pale hair. "I feel like I belong here more than I ever did back in Alinth."

"I forgot how lonely I was here sometimes before you came along."

Icelyn had almost forgotten what friends gave. Closing herself off from everyone to her father's warnings that she was only "dangerous company" to them—an Elemental hidden under the guarded arms of EME. It felt good to find trust in people. People who understood her and her dreams.

They shared smiles in the silence of the apartment. Moments later, the front door creaked open as Para shuffled in with Terrance.

"There she is!" Jasamie called to Ency, whose expression immediately rose at the sight of her while Kydah spun out of her chair to get her pile of drawings.

"Hey, just in time for snacks." Para let out a sigh.

"Yeah, they just sat down," Jasamie confirmed as Icelyn stood.

Para laid her coat on the rack, placing a folder down on the table as she ran her fingers through Ency's tousled hair. "Well, thank you. Both of you."

Terrance was quieter about it, flashing a curt smile as Kydah pulled him toward the living room to see her spread-out collection of drawings.

The door clicked behind them as Icelyn let out a breath in the cool halls. "Do you think they're still mad?"

Jasamie gave a casual shake of the head. "If you're getting babysitting duty, they trust you. So, no, I don't think they're mad." She stifled a laugh.

"Well, I'm glad our trip didn't ruin their trust in me."

"I think they're proud of us, in a way." Jasamie shrugged. "Are you going to Stormy's party?"

"Yeah." Icelyn picked at her sweater as they exited down the familiar gray halls.

"Has anyone checked on Peter? Since—?"

"I don't know." Icelyn hummed. "I think Kon was going to."

Jasamie grinned. "That might help him."

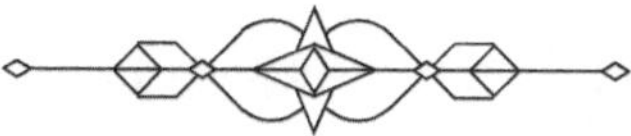

Sun was setting as far as the base lights showed, already shifting slightly orange. Kon swept a hand over his face, staring at the missing door to the base. Para said they had another somewhere to fix it. For the time being, the hatch above would have to be enough; the hatch, which was already open as the sun shone down the steps. There was someone outside. Para had told him as she left for the night that Peter had finally left his room and asked to go outside.

As Kon entered the field, the sun was glowing a much more exquisite orange than the base lights did. It cast golden light across the trees and soft grass as he scanned. Perched on a rock, Peter was curled up, knees pulled to his chin. As Kon approached, Peter didn't move from his stare over the trees. There was no book clutched in his arms or close beside him. It was just Peter that time. The only indication that he gave to acknowledge Kon was a tiny turn of the head, though he avoided looking.

Kon sighed. "You know none of that had to do with you, right?"

Peter didn't respond at first, scrunching his face in disagreement before he finally croaked out the words. "He told me he was helping people." There was a sniffle as Peter hugged himself tighter. "The morning he left . . . he told me he was going to fix everything. I thought he was helping. But he was working with the EME. I trusted him."

Kon had put an equal amount of thought into the confession. Maybe for him, the grief of it all had happened years before. For Peter, it was fresh. "Maybe that was the only way."

The comment made Peter look at him, tears glistened on his cheeks.

Kon kept going. "Maybe I'm mad at how it had to happen—but," the words were hard for him to say out loud, "if that's all he could do to save me, I get it."

Peter uncurled himself slightly, wiping a cheek. "I just . . . I thought he was doing good. I thought this whole time, he was doing what was best."

"Maybe he did do what was best, even if it wasn't a good thing." He absently rubbed his wrist, taking in the golden sky.

"He hurt you, though—he—" Peter frowned, facing Kon with an anger that hadn't settled yet. His sweatshirt bunched over the rest of his disheveled outfit as he sat on the rock.

"If he didn't, I wouldn't be here." Kon knew it was true. Andren Day was the only reason he could stand here at all. "I'd still be there." Despite it all, he had done more for him than his parents had. He protected Kon when the Avari failed him.

Peter looked regretful with his next words. They came cautiously. "What happened . . . after? Do you think he—?"

"I don't know." Kon had wracked his brain as much as it could bear that day to find any memory of that face for the sake of closure. But everything that came after the test was a blur. It was impossible to know what became of Peter's father. Maybe he did make it out in the chaos of it all, just like Kon did. For Peter's sake, he hoped he was out there, somewhere.

Peter hesitated. "Do you think you'll . . . stay?"

Kon kicked at the weeds below him, giving a shrug. "There are things left to figure out. Maybe it's best for now." A thought he'd still need to convince himself of fully.

Peter's mood improved ever so slightly at the proposition. "Good. You're important in all this."

Kon wavered as Peter was uncurling himself from his seat. "You think so?"

"I know it. My dad knew you were Airay. Whatever that means. It was worth everything to him. *You* were worth everything." Even with the crease in Peter's brow, his tone stayed steady. "I'm going to figure it out. For all of us."

Maybe he was right. Maybe there was more to it all. More to *Kon*.

With a heavy breath, Kon watched the tops of the fading trees blur into the sunset. "I'm sorry that he's gone."

Peter slumped, his hair messy as he pulled at his glasses. "I don't know if I can forgive him. For that—for leaving—for everything."

For Kon, it felt easier to forgive someone like Andren Day over his own parents. Someone who had tried to do good for him. He had risked everything for him. Kon might never know *why* he gave up all he did, knowing the danger he was in. Why he was worth it to someone he saw as a stranger. Maybe he truly did believe in him—something he and Peter had in common. Kon met his gaze. "I'm willing to try if you are."

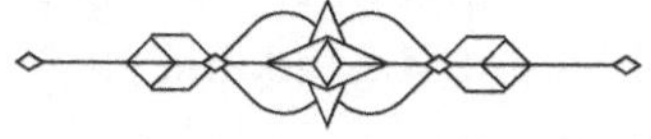

Reluctantly, Kon found himself in Stormy's colorful tapestried room. Icelyn had pulled him down there in the last minutes before Stormy arrived. Her excitement over it had been in the least, entertaining, taking his hand and pulling him toward the decent collection of students. Even Peter had gathered himself from his funk enough to show up.

Jyune had given specific instructions as the students stuffed into Stormy's room, prepared for the surprise. Kon tried hard to stay away from the crowded students awaiting her arrival. Icelyn was squished beside him as they stood in the back corner, thoroughly entertained with the proposition. She and Jasamie had attempted cupcakes earlier while Jyune had amassed a large sum of cookies, and a few others brought brownies.

The idea of a party was uplifting to many of the students who had been running on low hope for days in fear of the looming EME threat. Things were clearing, however, to Kon's surprise. It was no wonder they were as confident as they were when he met Para. He thought her confidence was the usual safe house morale. But it was different. They were living up to everything they had promised and more.

One of the students ducked back into the room, shushing everyone as they flipped off the lights. When everyone fell silent, there was only the sound of footsteps and Jyune's misleading casual tone as she approached with Stormy. The dozen or so students in her room made no delay in surprising Stormy as she came to face the parade of celebration with the flip of the lights. Someone had thrown confetti while the rest eagerly welcomed her in. Stormy clutched her ribs in shock, a gasp across her face as Jyune climbed onto a nearby shoulder. Ryv had told her she would need to avoid using Stormy as a taxi for the next few weeks to be safe. She was taking it in strides.

While the group showered Stormy with balloons and treats, Icelyn lingered close to Kon. He could tell she was surveying him for signs of slipping out. He couldn't even deny he was watching the door. It was some deep-seated habit. The prospect of any amount of crowd still unnerved him, but he could at least try to be present. He could take in the enjoyment of the others maybe and find joy.

Jyune presented Stormy with the array of cupcakes, brownies, and cookies lying on the table they had brought in and the shower of gifts from students—mainly new cooking supplies. Jackson had shown up as well, to Stormy's delight, presenting her with another more thought-out bouquet of flowers and heart cookies. The beige and ginger Felinian *was* tall, as Peter has described, though not close to Kon's height.

Peter watched them, still missing his book. "You think Jackson's going to hang out with us more?" he questioned. "Now that they're . . ."

"I hope." Jasamie shrugged as they all watched Stormy's enamor with the Felinian. "She seems cool."

"Stormy has a lot of friends." Icelyn assessed. Her shoulder brushed against Kon as she watched the crowd. Even Nem and a few other Luneduine had shown up, dawning thick shades to protect against the bright lights of the daytime room. They stood clustered together, holding a gift bag of jelly pastries, having gotten up early to attend the late afternoon party.

"I think the Base needed this." Jasamie let out a relieved sigh. "Things have been bleak."

"Yeah," Icelyn said, enjoying the banter they watched from afar. "It's nice." She looked up to catch Kon's gaze, giving a satisfied grin. He was less enthusiastic but entertained it.

They waited their own turn to welcome Stormy back in the chaos of the party. There was a wash of relief over her face that the whole group had shown up, even Kon.

By the time Kon could validate slipping out the door, Jyune had turned on music and dimmed the lights to a glow of pink, many still lingering in the colorful room. To his displeasure, the party had spread to the halls too, with students filling the strip of dorms. Some from Stormy's room had even walked their plates of snacks down the hall to share. It seemed most of the base had shown up to partake in some form, even just for the sake of being social. Down by his room, a rowdy collection of students sat on the floor. Kon made for the best escape he could, out of the dorms.

As he stood in the silent, dim-lit sunroom, waiting out the buzz of the dorm hall's party, he hardly noticed Icelyn at the door.

"I thought I might find you here."

He gave her a half grin, lingering closer.

Her hair sat over a shoulder, pinned back with a tiny, sparkling clip. "I'm glad you came. I think it meant a lot to Stormy."

"Wasn't so bad."

Her hands fell in front of her, running over each other slowly. Something seemed to fluster through her like a cold breeze had bunched her shoulders. "You know, you can always come to me if you need to get away."

As he approached, meeting her in the center, his eyes fell over her easier. From the soft whisps in her hair to the pale pink growing in her cheeks. How her dimples folded in her smile. "I know."

She held out a hand for his, taking it carefully to inspect the healed scrapes on his palm. "These look better."

"You're cold." He ran his other hand across hers in an attempt to spread warmth to her.

She met his eyes, far above her own in their closeness. The crease in her cheeks remained as his gaze drifted from her pink lips to her eyes; the same calm they always were. His hand rose to graze her cheek, brushing a lock of pale hair back, ever so gently. It was as soft as it looked. Folding it behind her ear, she leaned into his palm.

"You're warm," she smiled.

With that she drew closer until her head rested on his chest. The embrace came easier, wrapping his arms over her shoulders where his chin nestled into her soft hair. Maybe the company was better than being alone. He wasn't sure the last time he felt that.

"Are you sure you're okay?" she whispered. Her arms folded around him as she brushed his back.

In the dim room, with gentle orange lights casting in from the hall, he felt safe. Maybe for the first time in years, he felt *okay.* "Yeah." That time, he meant it.

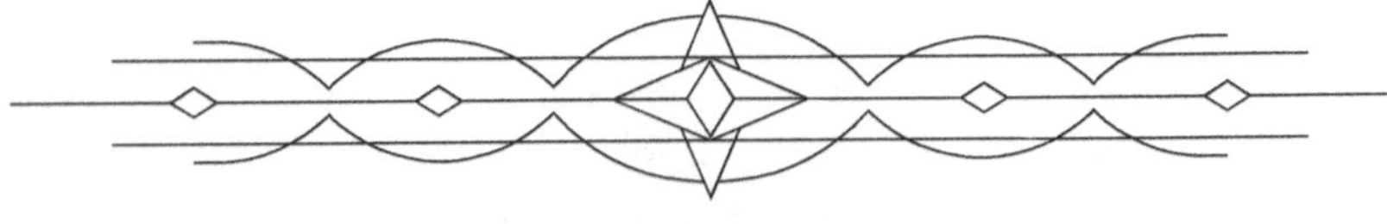

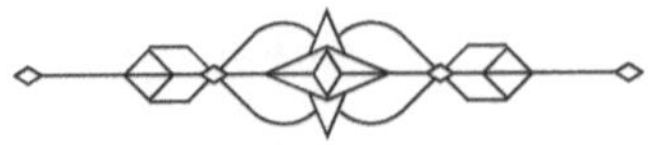

"How soon until he's ready again?" the bearded man asked in his coarse voice, pulling at the collar of his suit as he leaned on the desk. They watched through the glass where the EME uniforms sat with Kyros.

"We're running the tests now. He's stable, but I would wait. We can't afford to lose him to them."

The man nodded stiffly, his jaw tense. "Have we narrowed down the location?"

"We're working on it." The officer at the panel shifted, rubbing his deep red hair in the low light of the room. "It should be soon, although—" The man stopped, pursing his lips.

"Say it." The man turned to the Rilinquin officer.

The Rilinquin wavered with a flick of his pointed tail, picking up a few papers lying out. Each one contained a picture of either Kyros or Kon. He sighed. "With all due respect, Mr. Kernan, the levels between them, I'm not certain Kyro can do this."

"We can pull the Vinralin back more, stabilize his numbers. If they aren't reaching, we can amplify."

"Sir, that could prove . . . dangerous. It could overload and backfire on him."

Kernan straightened, meeting the eyes of the nervous officer. "If it gets us our *asset*, I don't see why it matters. This was never about *him*." As the officer dropped his head in respect, Kernan looked back to the files before him: the image of Kon in the corner, followed by the report documents. "The boy's getting erratic again. We don't have much time."

"Yes, sir."

"If this gets out, if he ends up out of our hands . . . off planet, even . . . We could lose everything. This has to be controlled before it catches Galactic attention."

"Of course, sir."

Kernan slapped a hand onto the desk before him, to the wince of the officer. "Imagine the consequences of Koron obtaining this . . . instability." He gave a shove to Kon's file. "If we don't contain it, we'll have much bigger problems in this war." Kernan shook his head, looking back at the white medical room where Kyro sat motionless as medics assessed the healing wound on his side, red and agitated across the countless faded scars.

"Shouldn't be long," the officer said softly.

Kernan stepped back with a sigh of disinterest. "I've grown bored of this. Make sure he's ready. Send everything else with him this time.

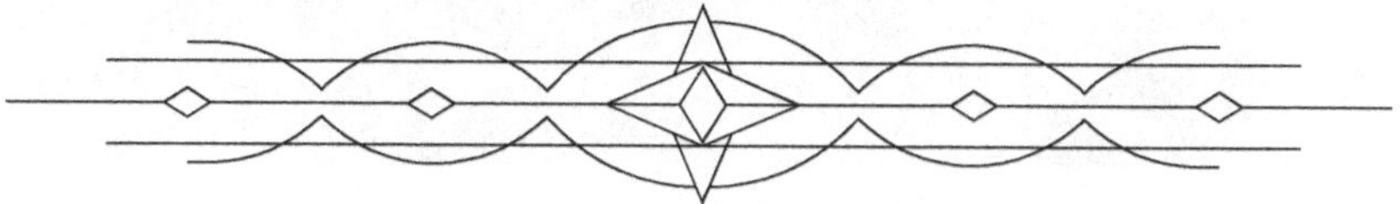

CONCEPT ART

THE BASE

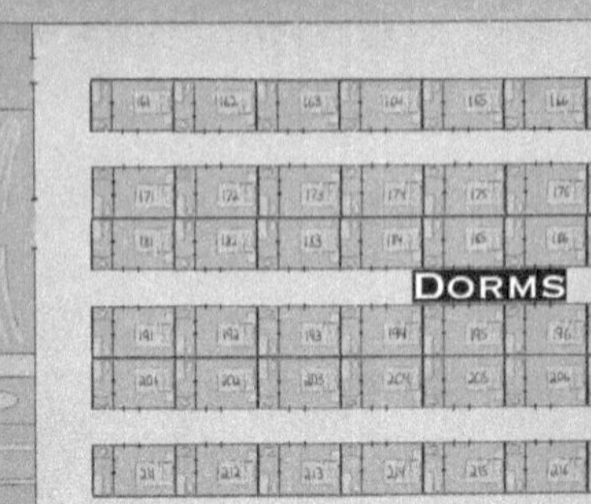

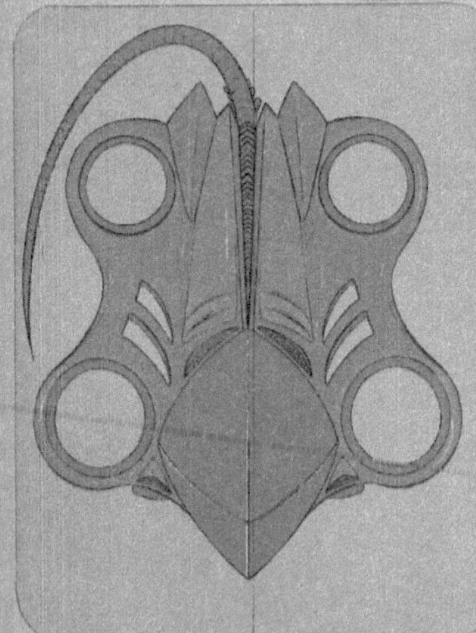

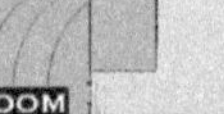

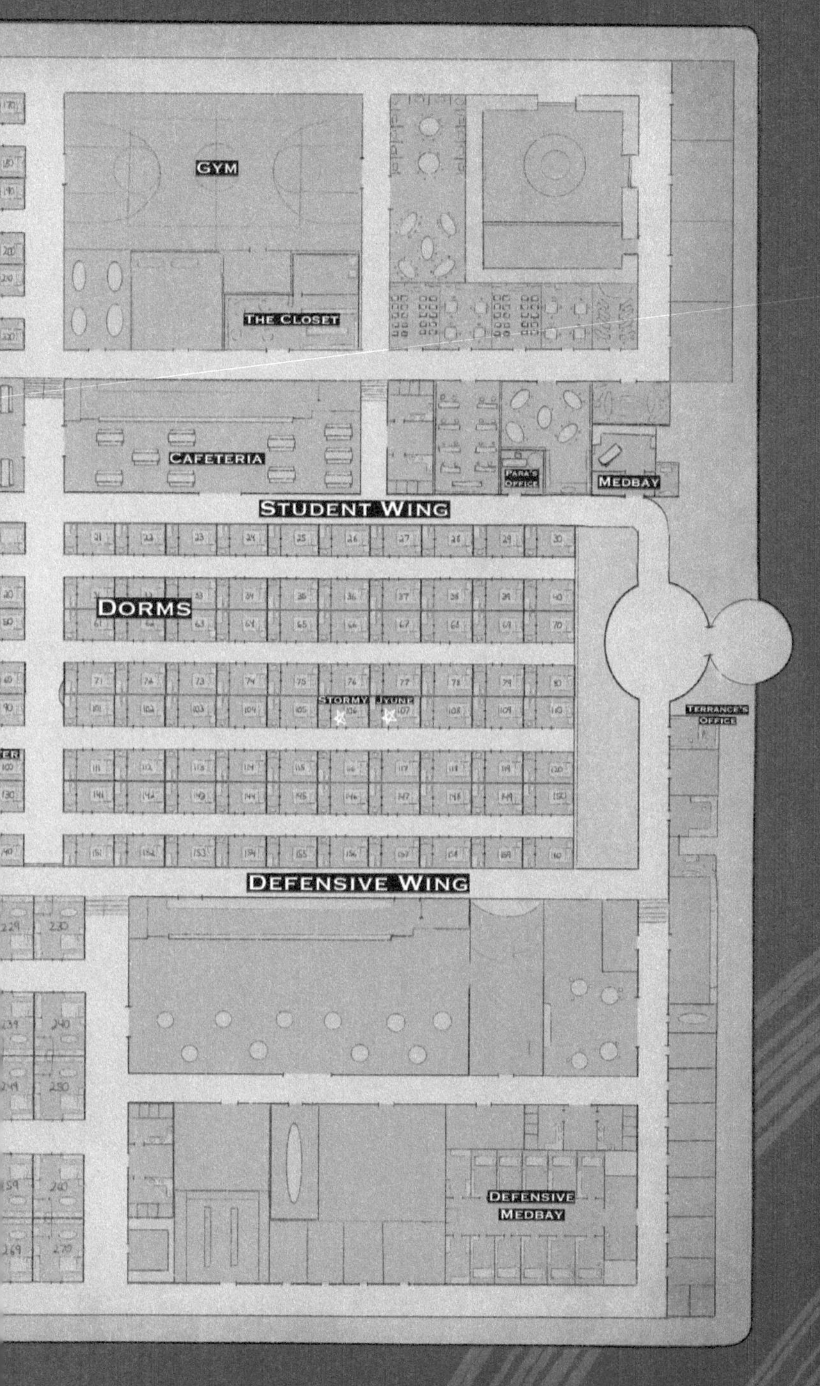
GYM
THE CLOSET
CAFETERIA
PARA'S OFFICE
MEDBAY
STUDENT WING
DORMS
STORMY JYUNE
TERRANCE'S OFFICE
DEFENSIVE WING
DEFENSIVE MEDBAY

EME
ANAIESS FLAG
Safe
Caution
Danger
INRALINITE
ACTIVATED
NOTICE
In compliance with EME protocol, please report any and ALL Elemental sightings and indivuals. Failure to do so could result in harm.
Call comm. # 3443.0
EME
Reporting Elemental findings not only protects you, but your town and neighbors. Elementals are a danger to themselves and others. If you know an Elemental, we urge you to call comm. # 3443.0, in their best interest, and yours.
WARNING!
ELEMENTAL
Age: 19
Species: Mix
Last seen: West Sector
Extreme caution. Do not approach. Contact EME immediately.
Hair color: Black
Description: Tall, tattoos, travelling on foot.
Hostile. Do not engage, or attempt confrontation. Dangerous, and WILL resist. Report sightings immediately and stay indoors.
Report sightings or leads to EME comm. # 3443.0

Thank you.

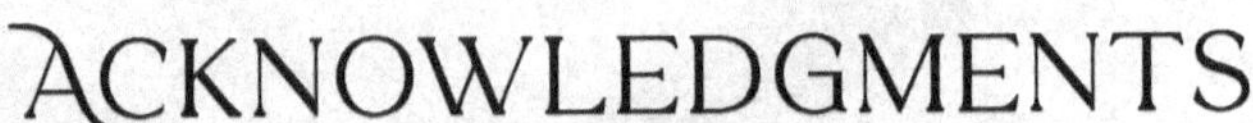

ACKNOWLEDGMENTS

This book started as a dream. The dream of a 14 year old with few friends. I wanted to get away from the world, and make a better one. Little did I know, I could. Ten years later I hold that same story in my hands, and I'm grateful for every person that crossed paths in its making. There were people in my life that believe in me when I continuously lacked the belief in myself. They saw my worth, and built me up.

Firstly, to the very first fans of this book, Maranda and Austin. Both of you found me when I had no one. I was just a girl drawing away in her notebook in Health class, and you saw me. My deepest thanks to Maranda for seeing through my art to the story within it, and pushing me to sit down and write it. I'm not sure I ever would've without you. A thanks to Austin, who supported me along the way, and took such an interest in my characters from the beginning. Both of you were so eager to read the beginning stages of this story, and were a deep driving force in me finishing the first drafts in high school. You were my biggest fans, and I don't know how I ever deserved you. Though we may not talk much anymore, I hope you know how deeply I appreciate you.

Next, a thanks to my family, because I hardly say it enough. You never frowned upon this dream I had, or my career in art. You kindled it with kindness and love and let me know it was okay to dream. To my mother specifically, who continuously stepped up to help me through every new turn in my life. From my art career, to my writing. You were my first editor, and helped me fill in the blanks when my brain fizzled out from the sheer confusion of publishing a book for the first time.

To my father, whom I may never fully understand. I think we're alike in more ways than we admit. We share a love of sci-fi and fantasy, and a deep love of creativity . You always pushed me to be better, to grow and evolve, and never settle for what I see before me, but instead strive to improve it. From late night computer problems, to driving hours to watch me table at my first convention, you showed up.

To my sister, who has always been a stable, perfect version of me. I never stopped looking up to you. We're very similar in our perfectionism, and you're often the only person who truly understands the struggles I face. We are both people who have been set back by our health, but have never let it slow us down. We fought through everything we faced, and we came out the other side.

To my few close friends, I've never had many, but the friends I've had these last few years have been the truest of them. People who support me through every turn and doubt I face. You pushed me forward without doubt, and loved me at my worst. To Logan, my longest friend, who waited eagerly for me to gather the courage to bring this book to light, and has been honest and genuine through some of the roughest points in my life. To Braxton, who has been one of the kindest, encouraging and empathetic people I've ever met. You always had hope in me, time and time again when I couldn't find it in myself. And to Clara, a star in my life, and an incredible friend.

As well as the people whom I met in finalizing this book. To my editors, Tricia, Erin, for providing honestly and depth for me, and assuring me my dream wasn't crazy. To Travis, for making a truly stunning map for my universe, one that went far beyond my expectations. You helped me hone in the graphic design of my book, and gave me valuable information and grace in all my chaotic questions and ideas. And to my proofreaders, Mozella and my mother, who worked with my schedule and took care in the final sweep. All of you provided me with such amazing information in the self-publishing world, and treated my book with such respect and care.

And lastly, to every person who's followed my journey, new or old. Rather you came from Instagram, Tiktok, or just happened to find yourself here, I appreciate you so much. My audience following my art was the final push I needed to get this book out there. You all helped me believe in myself, and realize this dream didn't have to stay in my head forever. I've met so many amazing artists and authors online, who have given me so much support and love. Some of you are just starting out, some of you are far past me. Please know that I'm always rooting for you. I've been touched so deeply by the messages I've receive. I never knew I could inspire people the way I've been told. If you're here reading this, know I can never thank you enough for being here.

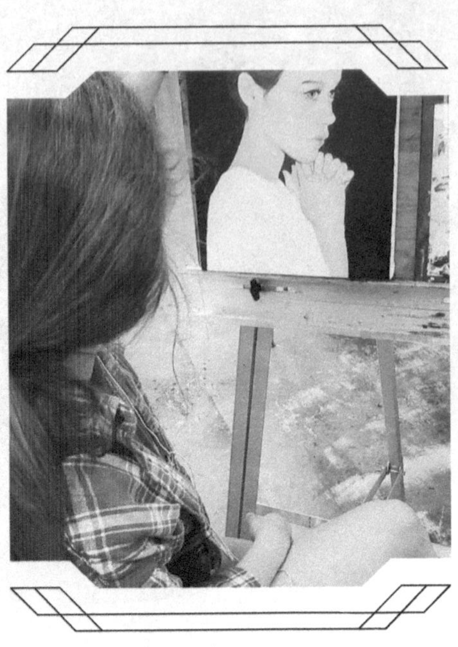

Alora Cosner, Coz K. A., is the author and illustrator of the fantasy world of Airay. She has garnered international interest with her art and visual storytelling around Airay. Branching out from success in illustrating, she plans to bring countless stories from the Airay universe in the future, always hoping to mix art and writing for a truly immersive experience. She is from a small town in West Virginia, where her appreciation of nature and life grows within her work.